STRADDLING
BLACK
AND
WHITE

a novel
by

KIM SALZMAN

FROM THE TINY ACORN...
GROWS THE MIGHTY OAK

www.AcornPublishingLLC.com

For information, address:
Acorn Publishing, LLC
3943 Irvine Blvd. Ste. 218
Irvine, CA 92602

ISBN-13: 978-1-952112-96-6 (hardcover)
ISBN-13: 978-1-952112-95-9 (paperback)
Library of Congress Control Number: 2021921490

Dedication

To my husband, Oren, for his unremitting love and support.

To my children, Gal, Maayan, and Ella, for being my light.

And to the more than 4000 Ethiopian Jews who died on their way to Israel. This novel is my humble but earnest attempt to pay homage to their tremendous sacrifices to make *aliyah*.

Tigest—1991

In the land of Ethiopia, children were raised to obey their parents and follow in their footsteps. Obedient boys grew up to be like their fathers, and docile girls grew up to be like their mothers. That was the way of the land, from time eternal. Tigest had learned the laws of the land when she was a young girl, and, while she often resisted them and even loathed them, with the passing of time she had resigned herself to accept them as her fate. There really was no other choice. But Tigest's fate, and that of her family's, was forever to be changed on two different days—decades apart from one another but equally momentous and life-changing—when she left home.

On the first of those two days, Tigest was an innocent thirteen-year-old girl who unknowingly walked out of her home towards a new life forced upon her.

And now on the second of those two days, Tigest turned her head and looked at the place she had called home for the past two decades and then towed her frail body and her five children behind her. She felt her eyes well with tears, but quickly wiped them away lest her children see. There was much to be excited about, of course—a new life awaited her in the bustling capital city of Addis Ababa where she would wait to immigrate to Israel, or make *aliyah*. The prospects of living in the Holy Land and reuniting with her eldest daughter seemed more real than ever now. But, despite her best efforts, Tigest's hands wouldn't stop trembling. She was, after all, leaving behind all that she had ever known. Village life may have meant suffering from the incessant village gossip she so despised and toiling from dusk to dawn to feed and clothe her hungry children, but at least it was a life with which she was familiar. And she had spent enough time in the nearby city, Gondar, over the years to know that city life simply didn't suit her—the filth, the rampant diseases, and the maimed beggars on the streets made her feel deeply uncomfortable and left her longing to return to the simple yet tranquil village life to which she was accustomed. And while living in the Land of Milk and Honey had always been her dream, she was afraid that she was too old to start a new chapter; too old to learn the language and the culture, too terrified of the unknown, and too scared of failing.

Though not yet forty, Tigest was already feeling the signs of aging, her posture slightly hunched and her looks no longer the envy of all the other women in the village. Life had been hard on her, and she was beginning to feel that years of longing for what could have been on top of years of backbreaking labor were finally taking its toll. She wasn't sure she was up to it—both the journey and the destination terrified her, even though she had been singularly focused on leaving for years now, especially ever since she had made the impossible decision to send her first born to Israel without her. But her devoted children's words of encouragement and elation that their day had finally come gave her the strength she needed to walk out of her home for the very last time.

How ironic, Tigest thought to herself. After all these years, her bony, calloused feet were now following in her eldest daughter's footsteps, and not the other way around. The laws of the land were slowly but surely becoming obsolete.

Chapter One

Azmera—December 1984

Azmera sat on the ground kneading the *injera* dough for the week ahead. It would take a full five days of fermenting, and multiple steps along the way, before it would finally be ready to eat. Its familiar pungent smell wafted through the air, soothing Azmera's senses all at once. She pushed down with her right hand while she held up her left, shielding her eyes from the blazing Ethiopian sun. Azmera's biceps burned from the kneading required to prepare enough dough—and what would later turn into batter—for the six hungry souls she called family. With each movement around the large plastic bucket, she willed her body to grow a third hand. She could use one, after all. Her father, Kebede, had left Ethiopia for Israel months before, leaving behind her mother, her four younger siblings and an increasingly unrelenting list of household chores.

The fourteen-year-old-girl paused her kneading to remember her father, the father who had taught her to read under the light of the moon, and the father who had tickled her behind her knees until, in between bursts of laughter, she gasped for air and begged him to stop. Azmera felt a strong breeze creep under her robe and her body shivered from head to toe. She looked up at the sky and saw an angry rain cloud quickly replacing the sun, poised to unleash its wrath on everything below it. Knowing Mother Nature's volatility better than she knew herself, Azmera hurriedly gathered her things and hustled into her family's *gojo*. Their family's hut was remarkably robust and served its purpose as shelter from the sudden rainstorms typical of the Simien Mountains; this despite the fact that mere eucalyptus tree branches served as its skeleton and reeds and mud as its insulating meat. Azmera nearly tripped over her bony feet as she hugged the bucket close to her chest. The skies opened on the earth below seconds after she made it safely inside her one-room home.

Azmera dusted off the dirt she had collected outside and sat herself down to continue the task at hand. The monotonous task of kneading allowed her mind to slowly drift away into a river flowing with memories and thoughts. Her cheeks burned when she recalled the boy in the neighboring village—the one with whom she had exchanged many coy glances but far fewer words. Her stomach lightened when she fantasized fleeing from her mother's infinite demands on her, the eldest child in the family. Her chest ached with longing when she recalled her father telling her stories about her people, the *Beta Israel*, and its longing for Jerusalem and Zion. Her eyes filled with tears when she imagined how brilliant his life must be now in Israel— the Jewish homeland—that foreign land she and her family, and her ancestors, had prayed towards since, well, forever.

"Meri!" shouted Tigest, Azmera's youthful-looking mother, "Stop your daydreaming for once and come and light the oil lamps before it gets too dark, or we won't be able to see anything but the whites of our eyes!"

Azmera snapped back to reality and did as she was told, illuminating the *gojo* one lamp at a time. Her eyes were drawn to the dancing flame in front of her, so strong and vibrant that it was hard to believe that its glory was finite. Tigest, often mistaken for Azmera's sister, looked behind her to confirm that her younger children were sufficiently preoccupied drawing images in the dirt ground. Their floor was covered by a round knitted rug Tigest had knitted when she first got married. It warmed their feet in the rainy season, and on days like this one when the rain caught them all unprepared.

To Tigest's initial chagrin, the rug she had spent hours meticulously knitting did not extend to the walls of the *gojo*, leaving the dirt ground on the sides exposed; for years, she had considered knitting another rug which would fully cover the ground of her home. When her children discovered that the exposed ground served as a drawing board—providing Tigest with hours of quiet she so desperately needed—she learned to appreciate the rug's unintended flaw. Tigest confirmed that her younger children were still engrossed with drawing images of trees, baboons, and cows, and then turned towards her oldest. Her eyes were downcast, but Azmera could tell they were full of tears.

Tigest laid one hand on her growing pregnant belly while gently placing the other on her daughter's shoulder.

"You need to leave for Sudan tonight," Tigest whispered, trying her best to mask the tremble in her voice. Azmera lost her grip on the lamp and watched as it fell to the ground, the knitted rug absorbing the shock of the fall. Azmera felt her heart stop.

"What do you mean, *tonight*? You told me that the plan was for us to leave together once the baby was born!" protested Azmera.

"Your Uncle Solomon just got word from *Kes* Yonas that the mission is coming to an end sooner than planned," Tigest explained quietly, her voice barely audible. Azmera usually took pride in the fact that her paternal grandfather, *Kes* Rahamim, had served as the village *Kes* or Jewish spiritual leader before he passed away; her entire life, Azmera had observed her father's great reverence for his father and his standing in the community and, as a result, her family's. It meant that her family was oftentimes the first to hear of anything consequential for their village and its people, even after he was no longer alive. Now she resented the special treatment.

"Once the mission is over, there's no guarantee if or when there will be another. I'm in no position to be making the journey to Sudan now—let alone any time soon. I refuse to let you sit around waiting for me. If you don't

5

leave now, you may not ever be able to leave. I can't let that happen." Tigest turned her face away from Azmera and stared blankly at her younger children. Their sweet naïveté meant that they had no idea what was transpiring just a few feet away from them, and so they happily continued to draw images with their fingers on the dirt floor. "Your future belongs in the Holy Land, where your father is waiting for you—not here. Go and pack your things. Your Uncle Solomon is waiting for you to join him."

Azmera stood up, wanting to protest. Her mouth gaped open as she stared vacantly back at her mother.

"You need to get moving. There's no time," Tigest commanded, her whisper growing more insistent.

"You know I've been waiting to go to *Yerusalem* like everyone else. But why tonight? Why not tomorrow? Or the next day? And most importantly, why not with you?" asked Azmera, unable to comprehend the sudden urgency.

It was true that she and her family had dreamt of Jerusalem ever since she could remember. Azmera knew she should feel excited that her moment had come, but she couldn't help but feel deceived as she listened to her mother explain to her that for weeks already—ever since her father's first sign of life from Israel—she had been planning to send her eldest daughter to Israel together with her brother-in-law, Solomon, while she would stay behind with her remaining children. Her four young children and the fifth on the way anchored Tigest heavily to the land, at least for the time being. Azmera, her eldest, however, was strong and old enough to survive the journey alone, especially with Solomon's help. Better to have one child safe in Israel than none, Tigest reasoned. Tigest also knew that Kebede shared a special bond with Azmera, his first born, so he would care for her upon arrival in Israel. At least she hoped he would. Besides, Azmera was old enough to care for herself.

What Tigest didn't share with her daughter, though, was that she wasn't confident that Kebede even wanted her—his wife of fifteen years—to join him in Israel. He had left so abruptly, with so little care for her well-being or that of his own flesh and blood, that avoidance altogether—especially when reuniting with him would have meant risking her pregnancy and her young children's lives on the journey—seemed the most appropriate response.

Azmera's lips curled downwards into a pout that was more fitting for a four-year-old than a teenager. And while she nearly always did as her mother told her, she couldn't help but put up a fight this time. She felt deeply offended and horribly betrayed. Her mother was treating her like a child by callously determining her life's fate without first feeling the need to consult with her. The more she listened to Tigest relay the turn of events leading to the decision, however, it dawned on her that no matter how much it made her blood boil in the past, her mother wouldn't be around for much longer to tell her what to do. With the pout still firmly planted on her face, Azmera began to listen to her mother.

Earlier that day, Solomon and Meskie, his perpetually sullen wife, had been tending to their herd of goats as they grazed on the brittle grass that was growing sparser by the day. Solomon and Meskie paused when they saw the village *Kes*, Yonas, hurriedly approach them with a concerned look on his face. *Kes* Yonas had been trained for years by *Kes* Rahamim, Solomon and Kebede's father, and he attributed all his knowledge and understanding of the *Orit*, the Torah used by the *Beta Israel*, to the esteemed man. Even though *Kes* Rahamim was no longer alive, *Kes* Yonas treated *Kes* Rahamim's family, especially his two sons, Solomon and Kebede, as if they still had a special status when it came to communal matters. No one was nearby, but *Kes* Yonas nonetheless signaled to Solomon to come closer. He whispered to him that several Jewish newspapers in distant America had reported on the covert operation airlifting Ethiopian Jews from Sudanese refugee camps to Israel, thus putting the continuation of the operation at immediate risk.

Meskie kept her distance as she watched her husband and *Kes* Yonas talk in whispers. She knew not to intervene; after all, she was just a woman, and communal matters were left to the men. But she knew something was wrong when she saw Solomon's face turn forlorn, his eyes cast downwards and his robust frame slightly hunched over. His eyes filled with tears as he approached his beloved wife. Meskie knew without Solomon saying a word.

Minutes after learning of the upsetting news, the plans Solomon had made months before—and in turn, the plans Tigest had made for her daughter—began unraveling like fine cotton. Suddenly, every day and every hour had become crucial if they were to make it to Sudan before the airlifts came to an end. The journey ahead of them was arduous and long. There was no more waiting.

Azmera bemoaned all that was happening to her and collapsed to the ground. She clung to her mother's right leg like a needy toddler, regressing into the little girl she once was. If she held on tight enough, she would never have to let go. The wetness from the tears in her eyes and the mucus in her nose dampened her mother's robe, but Tigest didn't seem to mind.

"I can't leave you. I *won't* leave you. *Please* don't make me leave you!" pleaded Azmera to her mother whose eyes were glistening with tears she struggled to keep locked inside. Tigest took a deep breath and tried to push her daughter away from her, but Azmera's toned muscles would not budge.

"Meri, don't make me say it again. You *will* do as I tell you to do," commanded Tigest in her sternest voice, the voice she summoned whenever one of her children dared to try on obstinacy for size.

Still clinging to her mother's leg, Azmera began to trace her hand over her mother's body. Her arms were still wrapped around her mother, but she already felt herself forgetting her. Azmera desperately attempted to commit to memory every feature she, until now, had taken for granted—every line, every mole, every muscle, and every scar. She knew she had no choice but to do as her mother told her—not to do so would be considered *balage*, defiant behavior prohibited in Azmera's world. As Azmera let go of her mother's thighs, she moved her hands upwards to Tigest's belly. She would not only be parting from her mother and her younger brothers and sister, but also from the baby growing inside her mother's womb.

"Solomon will be here soon, Meri. Enough crying. I need you to be strong," demanded Tigest.

But Azmera could not muster the fortitude her mother demanded of her. In one perfectly ordinary moment on an otherwise perfectly ordinary evening, her life had come crashing down into tiny pieces. And despite her mother's reassurances to the contrary, the young girl feared it would be impossible to put them all back together. Still, Azmera composed herself as best she could and collected a few belongings, including a warm shawl and scarf that Tigest had woven for her in celebration of her twelfth birthday over two years before.

Azmera was like a second mother for her younger siblings, far more than just an older sister. They were still, in fact, children—her brothers, Daniel ten, Desta eight, and Amara six, plus her sweet little sister Gabra who had just turned four. Azmera had first become a big sister when she was a toddler just learning to walk; but after two months of living, Azmera's baby sister stopped breathing. Like other traumas Tigest had endured before, she never spoke of her loss again. The children that followed several years later were raised by their mother and father, and their doting older sister, Azmera. And just as her mother was strong for her, Azmera knew she needed to be strong for them—or at the very least to give the illusion of strength. She bent down to the ground where the children were now waiting patiently for their daily ration of *injera* with orange *shiro* (chickpea stew). She gave each a gentle, slow kiss on the forehead. As she looked into Gabra's almond-shaped brown eyes, she remembered how her baby sister had rolled with laughter every time she tickled her on the side of her belly. Sadly, Azmera knew that this memory and so many others like it would be forever fleeting, quickly forgotten, and soon replaced by new ones.

✡

Azmera's Uncle Solomon burst into the *gojo*, his feet thick with mud and his back towing a full jerrycan inside a brown knapsack. An imposingly tall man, Solomon gently shook Tigest's hand while nodding his oval-shaped head. He plopped himself down by the fire, avoiding any eye contact with his soon-to-be travel partner. Solomon began rubbing his hands together briskly to warm his chilled body.

"It's really coming down outside," Solomon announced to no one in particular. "Make me some hot *bunnah* so I will have energy for the night, Azmera. By the time I finish my coffee, the rain will have passed, and we can go on our way."

More than twenty years of living in the Simien Mountains had taught Solomon that storms like this one would not last long. The clock was ticking, but their journey would have to wait until the downpour came to an end.

Azmera began the coffee ceremony, which she knew better than the palm of her hand. She roasted the coffee beans on a flat iron pan over their charcoal stove. It was the same stove her father had proudly managed to bring back to the family after one of his many journeys to the city of Gondar, the heart of northern Ethiopia. When the coffee beans turned a shimmering green, Azmera began to roughly grind them with a pestle and a long-handled mortar made of heavy stone. The repetitive crushing and pressing of the beans was almost musical, its rhythm energizing and meditative at the same time. Its earthy and intoxicating smell permeated the air, awakening Azmera's senses. As she continued to crush the beans into a fine powder, she wondered to herself how she would ever find her father in Israel, assuming she were to make it there alive.

Azmera recalled the day, not long ago, when her mother received the first news from her father. After she and the other children were supposed to be fast asleep, she watched from underneath her quilted blanket as her mother sat on the knitted rug, her hands trembling as she read Kebede's words. Azmera didn't understand why her mother hadn't told the children that she had received a letter from their father, but her mother's stealthy ways with this letter and the others that followed made it clear to her that it was better not to ask. Instead, her mother briefly informed them the next morning that she had received word that Kebede had arrived in Israel and was studying Hebrew, but she failed to provide any more details, including how he got to Israel and where in the country her father was living. The only city Azmera knew in the Holy Land was Jerusalem. It appeared in all the prayers her father had taught her, but there was no telling whether her father was in fact living there. Azmera had always felt frustrated by the lack of communication between herself and her parents; they shared very little with her, and held deep disdain for her natural curiosity. She felt all the more frustrated, then, by the tense secrecy in the air surrounding the departures of her father and others like him. Everyone in her village of course knew that they had walked to Sudan where they had waited for an airlift to Israel, but no one wanted to talk about it for fear of getting caught—and possibly even tortured—by the authorities. She continued grinding the coffee beans, her mind a haze of clouded thoughts.

Snapping her back to reality, Solomon impatiently shouted at her, "Wake up, girl! Don't you see there's nothing left to grind?"

Azmera was used to her Uncle Solomon's sour demeanor, which she usually attributed to the crops that weren't coming in as he had expected, or to Meskie, his despondent wife who, on the rare occasion Azmera spotted her venturing outdoors, always appeared sedated. This time, however, Azmera was both the target and the cause of his anger, and the unfairness of it all lit a fire inside her. She slowly stirred the ground beans into the black clay pot and poured Solomon his first cup of *bunnah*—with two more to follow to complete the ritual coffee ceremony they were accustomed to. Before serving his coffee, Azmera turned her back as if to add a spoon of sugar. It was her way of getting back at this evil man—albeit her father's brother—who was cold-heartedly taking her away from her beloved mother *Enati*, her brothers and sister, and her whole world. He was taking her away from all that was most precious to her, so she naturally wanted to reciprocate the deed. For now, though, letting loose a thick wad of spit into his cup of coffee would have to suffice.

As Solomon reveled in his coffee, Azmera smugly turned to Tigest who was finishing kneading the *injera* dough, getting rid of any of the remaining lumps Azmera had left behind. She kneaded the dough with such grace, thought Azmera, as she watched her mother's lean arm muscles hard at work.

"*Enati*, will I ever see you again?" Azmera asked, her eyes raised towards her mother's like a wounded ibex staring at his predator.

Tigest continued to knead the dough even though it was more than ready to be put aside for fermenting.

"Yes, baby. I will find you, no matter where you are," Tigest asserted, her voice choking back tears. Her eyes left Azmera's, falling downcast into the bucket sitting in front of her.

In truth, Tigest was a pragmatist. She knew that the airlifts were coming to an end, and she didn't know if they would ever resume. An entire lifetime's worth of backbreaking labor would amount to only a fraction of the cost of a flight to Israel for her and her children; besides, everyone knew it was impossible for *Beta Israel* to get a passport to travel to Israel.

Tigest often withheld the truth from her daughter, but she never had a penchant for lying. Now, however, she found herself making a promise she knew she could not keep. Her daughter needed to have the inner strength to survive the journey ahead of her. Tigest knew the truth, but her daughter could not. She was very likely parting from her eldest daughter—her beloved little girl who had saved her life the day she was born—for good.

Tigest insisted that Azmera eat a hearty meal of *injera* and *shiro* before beginning the journey. Azmera had no appetite, but Tigest forced her to finish every last bite even as she choked up with tears. Solomon slurped down the last drop of his third cup of coffee and decisively turned to his niece. Without even looking outside, his body felt that the storm had passed. It was time to go, he urged. He and Azmera had a long journey ahead of them and little time to complete it. They needed to get moving.

Azmera tried to stand up, but a gagging reflex sent her crashing back down to the floor. She waited a moment for the urge to vomit to subside. After she mustered enough strength to stand, she placed her things inside the knapsack Tigest had prepared. Azmera's hands fumbled around in the knapsack to make room for her scarf and sweater, when she discovered a thick wad of *Birrs*, more Ethiopian currency than she had ever seen, two large, neatly folded pieces of *injera*, and two large bags of *kolo*, or non-perishable roasted grains—perhaps more food than her entire family's weekly consumption. The generous rations of money and food brought tears to her eyes. Her mother's gesture of love for her made it even more difficult to understand how she could so willingly let her go.

There was no more procrastinating. Azmera hugged Tigest one last time. Her body was numb.

"*Salaam*," Azmera whispered goodbye reluctantly as she walked out of the *gojo* into the moonlit sky.

Chapter Two

Tigest—December 1984

Tigest turned away from her younger children while her eldest walked out of their *gojo* for the last time. The sound of her children's soft whimpers grew louder, none of them understanding why their sister had just abandoned them. Tigest couldn't bear to look at their eyes as they patiently waited for their mother to serve dinner. Her insides twisted and churned, but she remained calm on the outside. She didn't want to upset the children any more than they already were. More than anything, she wanted to chase after Azmera and tell her that the entire plan had been a huge mistake—a joke, even—but she knew that wasn't an option. Instead, she forced herself as much as possible to focus on feeding the four hungry souls sitting in front of her, all the while ignoring her rumbling stomach and the baby kicking her inside. She had demanded that Azmera remain strong. Now it was her turn.

As she rationed the portions of *injera* and *shiro* onto a rusty tin platter, Tigest caught a glimpse of her children's eyes. They were filled with sadness and hunger, and most of all, disappointment. She knew they were famished; after all, they spent the entire day outdoors in the sun tending to their chicken and goats, collecting water from the stream and washing clothes, with little food to sustain them. It pained her to look at their ribs, which had become more prominent with each passing day. Their desperate gazes, Tigest knew, would haunt her for years to come.

The same fields she and Kebede had tilled day and night to provide food for their family now stood parched and brittle, having lost nearly all hope in Mother Nature for sustained nourishment from the sky. The past year's disappointing rainy season had long-lasting implications for the year to come, with the market price for teff increasing threefold as a result. Tigest had given Azmera the bulk of their remaining *Birrs*, and with her husband no longer around to shoulder the burden, the little money she and Kebede had managed to save in their fifteen years together was quickly dissipating. She knew that the ten kilograms remaining of teff flour would not last forever, but if she was stingy with her babies' rations, she could do her best to make it last as long as possible. Even more so if she was stingy with her own.

"*Enat,*" Daniel cried, his voice resembling the village dog, a tick-infested mutt who would whimper on a nightly basis as he surveyed the village—often to no avail—for anything edible to consume, "My belly hurts and I can't fall asleep."

Daniel lay in his bed with his two younger brothers and sister, all of whom had already fallen into a deep sleep. He had been suffering from stomach aches and diarrhea for quite some time now, but Tigest was numb to her oldest son's pain. At the ripe age of ten, he was now the man of the house. Tigest could not afford for him to be sick, and while by now Daniel understood his role in the family, at times the little bit of boy still left in him took over. Tigest sat herself down on the rug, cold from the rainstorm outside. She stroked Daniel's stomach while humming softly, hoping her voice would distract him from the pain.

As Daniel's eyes slowly began to shut, Tigest felt her eyes well with tears. Maybe my children would be better off, she thought to herself, if they were no longer trapped in this infertile and cruel world. At least then she could let loose all the pain she had pent up inside for so many years and scream at the top of her lungs. Even better, maybe everyone would be better off if *she* were no longer in this world. At least then she wouldn't have to bear the pain of losing Azmera. At least then she wouldn't have to bear watching her children suffer.

Her life would be so much easier if she didn't have to live it anymore.

Tigest—1964

The first time Tigest spotted a group of white men, she was eight years old and had recently begun making trips to the stream to collect water. In her first year of collecting water, Tigest did so with great pride—after all, only "big girls" were sent to collect water from the stream, and now she finally got to join them. Growing up, she had watched the older girls from her village perform this daily ritual with envy, wishing she too could discover what lay outside the confines of her small world. On her first trips, Tigest relished singing songs with the older girls as they walked side by side, each carrying a yellow jerrycan tied onto their back that would weigh heavily on their spines on the way home. Their stories had prepared her to expect sightings of other villagers collecting water or setting out for a journey to the nearby town of Debark or even to the distant city of Gondar. She was also prepared for the occasional run-in with a Christian staring back at her with dread, foolishly petrified that, as anti-Semitic legend dictated, the Jewish girls standing before them would turn into werewolves and eat their Christian children. Other expected sightings were the families of baboons playing with one another, much like she played with her sisters. On those auspicious trips, Tigest and the other girls would stare at the baboons in awe far too long, even if Tigest knew it meant having to sprint back to the village lest she face her mother, who would surely be livid from her abnormally long absence. And while Tigest had heard of other village girls' exciting accounts of their run-ins with strange men wearing strange clothes covering their pasty skin, she could not fathom the day would come when she would finally see them face to face.

As a young girl in her first year of making trips to the stream, Tigest's body had yet to develop enough stamina to endure her daily trip without significant hardship. While she liked to think of herself as one of the "big girls", she was in fact the youngest of her walking partners. She often found herself lagging behind the older girls as they effortlessly made their way up steep inclines marked by trampled-on grass and goat droppings. Tigest didn't mind being left behind, though. Her only concern was taking the next step and the one after that, as she gasped for air and felt her muscles burn.

On a particularly hot day in the middle of the dry season, Tigest set out with the other village girls to perform their daily ritual of walking to the stream. The salty drops of sweat trickling into Tigest's eyes and down into her mouth were a slight annoyance, but a tolerable one. The steep terrain and her resulting hyperventilation, on the other hand, proved to be quite a challenge. With every excruciating step she climbed up the mountain, Tigest felt her muscles burn and her lungs burst. The blue skies, crisp mountain air and protruding cliff looming above her—a visual marvel to wonder at when making the descent on the way home—were now invisible to her. All she could focus on was on her feet moving one step at a time.

Tigest's body collapsed out of sheer exhaustion and relief when she made it to the highest point of elevation for the day. The hardest part was now behind her, leaving her only a few hundred meters—all of them downhill—from the stream. The fact that she would have to climb the same incline on the way back home with the full jerrycan weighing her down didn't matter to her now. Instead, she basked in the glowing sun and took a much-deserved break before continuing her way to the stream.

As her heavy breathing began to subside, Tigest heard muffled sounds approaching from a distance. She was all alone—the other girls were far ahead of her and had likely already arrived at the stream by now. She quickly pulled herself off the ground. She knew her mother would strongly disapprove of any stranger seeing her as she was, alone and sprawled out on the ground with her legs spread open. She curiously peaked up her head and arched her toes to see who and what was coming her way. As their voices grew closer, Tigest timidly crouched alongside a rock and stared in awe at several white-skinned men climbing her way, making sounds she couldn't decipher. Tigest felt a tingling sensation of nervous excitement going up and down her spine. She contemplated hiding, but the high elevation and open expanse left little to hide behind. She remembered that the older girls didn't seem to be afraid of the white men when they told of their encounters—so she hoped that she had no reason to be afraid either. She decided to stare unabashedly at the freckled, pasty men, her eyes barely pausing for a blink. Her face reddened when the men awkwardly flashed goofy smiles in her direction.

"*Salaam*," several of them hollered with a friendly nod of the head towards the young girl.

Surprised to hear these men speaking to her in her language, Tigest replied with a "*salaam*" of her own, and then inquired into their mysterious skin color in her mother tongue. The men's blank looks on their faces revealed that they did not know a word of Amharic but for the one greeting they had managed to memorize from their guidebook. As they continued to speak to one another in an indecipherable combination of sounds, Tigest approached one of the men and pointed to the skin on his arm, and then to the skin on her arm. She then raised both of her hands into the air, conveying the innocent curiosity that the mysterious color of the men's pale skin had aroused in her.

The men, amused by the little Ethiopian girl's wonder at their skin color, chuckled to themselves while doing their very best to communicate to Tigest that they had come in peace via seemingly rehearsed body language. They repeated *"salaam"* followed by "hello," prompting Tigest to repeat after them. Her curiosity for more was piqued. She asked the men to repeat the bizarre word several times before she knew it was ingrained deep in her head. *Hello,* she repeated to herself, is like *salaam,* only spoken by the men with the pale, freckly skin.

From that moment on, Tigest looked forward with anticipation to her daily trip to the stream to collect water, eager to have yet another encounter with these odd but friendly men or others like them. With any luck, she would collect not only water, but also a few more words in English with which she could impress her little sisters. After all, she was a big girl now.

Tigest—1969

"But I already went to the stream earlier this morning, *Enati,* and I was about to go to afternoon lessons in school! Why do I need to go again?" Tigest protested like the thirteen-year-old teenager that she was, not wanting to miss another day at school due to her mother's demands yet again.

Tigest had been attending school irregularly for several years now courtesy of her father's brother—he was a teacher in the nearby school and managed to convince her parents that there was some value in their daughter attending school, even if it took her away from her other chores and responsibilities. Tigest took pride in knowing that she was one of the few literate girls in her village, having learned how to read at the age of eleven. Now not only would she have to miss another precious day at school, but she would have to make the grueling trip to the stream during the hottest time of the day after having already been there earlier that morning. Tigest's sense of obedience, while fierce, only went so far. So did her agreeable nature, particularly ever since she had begun menstruating—just a few months prior.

"Tigest, don't make me say it again. You will do as I tell you," Abaynesh sternly snapped at her daughter, averting any possible eye contact by focusing on the newborn son in her arms.

Tigest knew very well from the tone of her mother's voice that it would be futile to try to pick a fight with her, especially these days. Her mother had become noticeably distant from her several months ago, right around the time she had begun menstruating. Tigest attributed it to the fact that her mother had just given birth to yet another hungry mouth and to the failing harvest season that was proving woefully insufficient to feed the entire family.

"You'll have to go by yourself. All the other girls are busy with their chores," her mother explained as she tended to her now nursing baby.

Tigest was puzzled by her mother's sudden willingness to let her walk to the stream alone—after all, she had always insisted that Tigest walk with other girls from the village as a form of group protection warding off any danger. Little did her mother know, however, that Tigest often began the walk with the others but quickly strayed behind, at first due to her young legs which failed to keep up and later due to the many distractions along the way. It wasn't the walking alone that now bothered Tigest—it was being forced to walk in the first place. Tigest discretely rolled her eyes, careful her mother wouldn't catch a glimpse of it, and then grabbed the jerrycan and set off. She didn't know it at the time, but this would be the first of the two times where the simple act of leaving home would prove to be momentous and life-changing.

Over the years, Tigest had learned to appreciate her trips to the stream as not just a burden but also a privilege—while physically taxing, they were also an escape from the other mundane tasks of housekeeping which her mother demanded of her, especially on the days when her mother didn't allow her to attend school. Washing and mending clothes, kneading the dough for *injera*, sweeping the rug, and taking care of her little brother and sisters often kept her occupied from dawn until dusk, so the daily trip to the stream was a welcome change from the otherwise humdrum of her young life. More than anything, though, for Tigest these trips provided an opportunity to catch a brief glimpse of the outside world—or at least as "outside" as she ever hoped to see. If she were lucky, she would encounter the rare group of white tourists hiking in her backyard, a fascinating sight that had intrigued her ever since she was a little girl.

But collecting water for the second time that day—all alone, and on what should have been a school day—just didn't make any sense.

As a seasoned thirteen-year-old, Tigest had collected water from the stream hundreds of times. But its typical appeal did not outweigh the annoyance of having to miss yet another day of school, where they had just begun reading newspaper articles. Her teacher would give his students old copies he had purchased in Gondar months earlier, and Tigest looked forward to reading a new edition every time she went to school, and learning about what was happening in her country—or at least what happened several months prior. The pages were often torn, and the ink smeared, but it didn't bother Tigest in the slightest. She could read, and that was all that mattered. She hated her mother for taking her away from school, and her beloved newspaper. Tigest set out on the trip, kicking her foot at the ground as she watched the dust rise, dissipating speck by speck into the air. The kicking helped quell her anger—the anger she felt towards her mother for always telling her what to do and the anger she felt at herself for always listening.

Tigest arrived at her normal resting spot and took in the sights around her. From a distance, she could see a beige ibex staring suspiciously in her direction. It was as if it was contemplating whether she was someone to be trusted or someone who might turn on him and the herd. Tigest deliberately extended her right knee and slowly bent it to the ground, a gesture of peace to the proud ibex. Ordinarily it would have put the animal at ease. The ibex would then continue to carry out his business as usual, patiently grazing every blade of grass within reach. This time, however, Tigest noticed that the ibex's anxious gaze remained in place, its eyes still inexplicably affixed in her direction. Tigest stared back at him, wishing she knew what he was thinking. It quickly became clear to Tigest that the proud animal was not staring at her, but rather at something—or someone—directly behind her.

As Tigest turned her head, she felt a hand, bony and rough from years of plowing the fields, gently but confidently grab hers. Her face grew pale with fright, certain she was being attacked by Christian bandits who she was told would sadistically take pleasure in persecuting their Jewish neighbors. Tigest tried to scream for help, but no words came out of her mouth. She pulled away but the strange hand pulled back harder. When the bony, rough hand finally lost its grip, Tigest fell headfirst to the ground, her head landing forcefully on the edge of a jagged rock.

Tigest woke up in a strange *gojo* with a strange young man standing by her side. Her head pounded and her throat felt sore and parched. She nodded her head in thanks for the cup of water the man served to her. She struggled to remember how she had ended up in this *gojo*—much larger than her family's—and with this young man, but her memory failed her until she reached for the back of her head and felt a bulging lump that was now throbbing with pain. The young man forced an awkward smile in her direction and even went so far as to offer his hand for shaking, a suspiciously kind welcome to what Tigest assumed was his place of dwelling. He seemed pleasant, but not enough to distract her from worrying about how angry her mother would be with her for returning after dark, and even angrier for returning home empty-handed.

As Tigest grasped the young man's hand, the rough layer of skin rubbed against hers, making her heart pound with fear. She pulled her hand free of his and tried to run past him out of the hut, but he was too quick for her. He grabbed her arm and pulled her back to the dirt ground.

"Don't go, Tigest," the young man said.

Tigest's eyes widened with surprise. The young man standing before her somehow knew her name.

The young man's voice trembled as he continued, "My father and I came to meet you on your way to the stream to tell you the news, but then you fell and hit your head, so I brought you back to my home. You've been unconscious for hours now, and we've been waiting for you to wake up."

Tigest felt her eyes well up with tears as she whispered, "What news?"

The young man standing before him took a deep breath and replied, "It has been decided that you will be my wife. This will be your new home."

Tigest's body froze. She pulled her eyes up from the ground to look at him. The yellowish tint in his eyeballs was vaguely familiar to her, reminding her of childhood trips to the neighboring village where her mother would purchase kerosene and the occasional roll of fabric. Tigest wiped the tears away from her cheeks and focused her attention on the distinct feline tint, trying her best to jog her cloudy memory of her childhood past. He wasn't the grouchy man who would grunt as he poured a gallon of kerosene for her mother, she knew. And he clearly wasn't the woman with the warm smile who would help her mother pick out a roll of fabric to outwear the entire family. Maybe he was the grouchy man's son, the one who used to lay his eyes on Tigest so long it would make Tigest blush. Tigest eliminated that possibility in her head, confirming to herself that that was the boy who died from cholera during last year's dry season.

Tigest knew she knew the young man standing before her, but his identity was stuck on the tip of her tongue.

"Who are you?" she asked, her voice at a near whisper and her head still foggy from the head injury. Her entire body shook.

"My name is Kebede. I know you from your visits to my village. My father Rahamim is the village *Kes* here and, with your parents' consent, he has decided that we are to marry."

Kebede's father had bestowed the name Kebede to his son, the name meaning "heavy" and "strong" in Amharic. From a young age, Rahamim made it clear that he expected Kebede to live up to his name; Rahamim would shout at and humiliate young Kebede any time he cried, insisting he needed to remain strong always and keep any emotions he might have to himself, including when he broke his arm at the age of five. While Kebede did his best to live up to his name and speak to Tigest with the strength and confidence his father had instilled in him, the nervous tremble in his voice couldn't be concealed. At once, Tigest recalled having met Kebede years before in the village market. She recalled her mother conversing with Kebede's as she watched the older boy show off his kicking skills with a new soccer ball he had acquired. She knew him, this future husband of hers. His hands may have roughened over the years, but Tigest was looking at a boy, not much older than she, his smooth facial skin interrupted only by his protruding cheekbones.

The more Tigest looked at Kebede, the more familiar he became, his yellow-tinted eyes uniquely eerie and beautiful all at once. Suddenly she recalled a recent outing to the neighboring village's market where she saw her father converse with what appeared to be the neighboring village's *Kes*, dressed in a white turban and cloak. It was Kebede's father, she now understood. That day wasn't long after her mother first learned that Tigest had found blood between her legs. Tigest made nothing of her father's conversation at the time, though—her father always held great respect for all *Kessim*, no matter what village they came from. As she jogged her memory even more, she recalled an earlier visit to the neighboring village where she had seen the boy with the yellowish eyes staring at her with desire—at the time, though, it had seemed like nothing out of the ordinary.

From a young age, Tigest had grown accustomed to people staring at her strikingly beautiful face. As she grew older, though, she found it to be quite a nuisance, precluding her from enjoying the anonymity she so cherished, especially when leaving the safety of her own village. Until recently, Tigest would avert her eyes the moment she noticed anyone of the opposite sex looking in her direction. Only upon catching a glimpse of the grouchy man's son, did she begin to feel a warm tingling in her stomach, a feeling which had her anxiously waiting for another opportunity to play eye games with the mysterious boy—that was, until he got sick. But being his wife was never a consideration. Nor was being anybody's wife, for that matter. After all, she was only thirteen years old, and most of the girls in her village didn't marry until at least the age of fourteen.

"What do you mean we are to marry?" retorted Tigest, no longer as fearful of the boy she knew standing before her, "You are dreaming. My parents would never agree to such a thing."

At that moment, Kebede's father, *Kes* Rahamim—the same *Kes* with whom she had seen her father whispering weeks before—walked solemnly into the hut. *Kes* Rahamim's white cloak and turban combined with his deep, deliberate voice lent him an intimidating authoritativeness.

"There you are wrong, my daughter," retorted the *Kes*, his voice deep and decisive. "Your parents have agreed to the marriage. They simply can't make ends meet anymore, and they need our help as soon as possible. Unlike them, we can provide for you. The marriage ceremony will take place now."

From a distance, Tigest heard the faint beating of a drum, growing louder with every heartbeat. Kebede's mother, adorned in a vibrantly white cloak, quietly joined her husband in the *gojo*, and nodded her head at Tigest approvingly. She invited the drummer, who had by now arrived at the entrance to the *gojo*, to enter. Tigest spotted her own parents approaching the *gojo* from a distance, sluggishly towing along with them two emaciated cattle. Tigest presumed it must be some sort of dowry. But for Kebede holding on tightly to her hand, Tigest would have collapsed upon spotting them.

Tigest wanted to scream with anger at her parents, unable to grasp their betrayal. She knew her parents had been struggling to provide food for her and her siblings, but to think that her father had arranged for her to be married at thirteen years old and that her mother had deviously sent her to the stream as a sort of marriage trap was too much to bear. Tigest pondered the dozens of curses she wished to shout at them for robbing her of her life. But then she saw her parents close up for what they were—a total wreck, their eyes not even capable of facing their daughter's—the daughter they had deceived; the daughter they were willing to give away. They kept their distance from Tigest, emotionally and physically preparing themselves for what they were about to do to her.

"Give me your hand, dear," commanded Kebede's mother, who began elaborately painting her future daughter-in-law's arm with henna, a brown dye that turned Tigest's body into an extravagant art canvas. Kebede's mother's elongated arms and fingers had a gracefulness to them from afar, but their first touch revealed a roughness from a lifetime of hardship and toil. Despite her own mother's betrayal, the teenage girl felt a deep longing for her mother's touch, rough and soft at the same time.

Tigest knew from her much older cousins that the henna ceremony was the first step to the *chuppah*, the canopy under which the Jewish marriage ceremony would be performed. But they had all married after their fourteenth birthday, and she had only recently turned thirteen—plus, they had met and gotten to know their husbands-to-be, and even celebrated their wedding with the entire village for a full week under the glowing summer sun. Tigest had always remembered the many wedding celebrations in her village fondly; they were filled with joy and plentitude. This, however, was nothing like any of the other weddings she had attended—with two hungry cows, the lone drummer, her parents and Kebede's as the only witnesses to all that was about to transpire.

Long before becoming a *Kes*, Rahamim was known to be a man who commanded respect and instilled fear in anyone near him. Everyone obeyed his every word. When he instructed Tigest to move outside the *gojo* to the *chuppah*, she knew she had no choice but to comply. She stared at her parents dumbfoundedly, her eyes welling up with tears.

"Why are you doing this to me?" asked Tigest, deeply confused by all the events that had transpired and not sure she wanted to know the answer from her parents whom she had always adored.

In truth, her parents had been distant from their daughter for months now—their distance not a result of the newborn baby as Tigest had assumed, but rather the discovery that their newly menstruating daughter was being courted for marriage by a well-off family during a time of great hardship for their own. *Kes* Rahamim had made it clear that Kebede wanted to marry immediately, and he had his eyes set on Tigest. Kebede was the son of a well-respected *Kes*; it would have been a missed opportunity to turn down the offer, Tigest's parents convinced themselves.

Refusing to look his daughter in the eye, Tigest's father, Avraham, replied, "We had no other choice. Kebede comes from a good family, and they can provide for you. We just can't any longer."

The thought of her family giving her away like they would one of their goats smashed her heart to pieces. She looked straight into her parents' eyes, but they refused to look back at her, their oldest daughter. Tigest looked into *Kes* Rahamim's eyes longing for compassion—after all, that's what his name meant in Hebrew—but found none.

The wedding ceremony was mostly a blur to Tigest. She stood to the side in complete silence, her head throbbing with pain. Kebede began to recite the Ten Commandments, after which *Kes* Rahamim began reciting prayers in *Ge'ez*, the liturgical language used by the *Beta Israel*. She was a spectator in her own wedding. When *Kes* Rahamim finished reciting the last prayer of the marriage ceremony, he placed a multicolored cotton headband on top of Kebede's head, nodding encouragingly as he did so. Kebede's mother congratulated her son, and then turned to Tigest and reluctantly kissed her on the cheek. Tigest's parents looked defeated but relieved all at once. The *Kes* turned his back to his son, prompting his wife, Tigest's parents, and the drummer, to join him, leaving Tigest and Kebede alone. Tigest felt tears roll down her cheek as she followed her newlywed husband into his home.

Their first few hours together as a married couple were filled with a painful silence, despite Kebede's efforts to initiate conversation. From time to time, Kebede stared awkwardly at his newlywed wife with desire, eagerly surveying her body as if it were a piece of freshly slaughtered meat on display.

"You know that I've been watching you over the years. You are the most beautiful girl I have ever seen, and I told my father that I had to marry you," explained Kebede, with a gentle but awkward smile forming on his face.

Tigest was silent, taking no comfort in her husband's intended compliment. She had never appreciated her own beauty, finding it to be more of a burden than a gift—and now more than ever she wished she were a plain, homely looking girl.

Tigest tried her best to keep her distance in the small *gojo*, her new home, but she feared for what was to come. As the night progressed, she felt Kebede staring at her more intently. He stood up with a determined look on his face and approached his new wife.

"I don't want to do this. Please don't touch me!" begged Tigest. She wanted to scream like she would on her way to collect water when the valley below would echo her words, but she knew she couldn't. Besides, her head wouldn't stop pounding and she could only muster up muffled words without wincing in pain. Kebede hesitated for a moment to decide what his next move should be. He remembered how, as a child, his father would demand that he live up to the meaning of his name—strong and heavy—a name he was given in memory of his late *Kes* grandfather who was known for his strength, both physical and mental. He pulled his thirteen-year-old wife's body tightly towards his, paying no attention to Tigest's wet tears soaking his face. Kebede clumsily attempted to search his wife's body with his coarse hands as Tigest felt a salty mix of mucus and tears drip slowly into her mouth. Tigest tried to push him off her, but her condition left her weaker than usual, and Kebede managed to anchor her much smaller body heavily to the ground. Kebede lifted her clothes to reveal to him all that was beneath.

As Kebede entered her, Tigest howled like a pack of jackals at sunset, the kind that sends the livestock grazing outside the *gojo* into a state of panic. She felt her entire insides being ripped apart.

"Please, don't. Please, don't," begged Tigest of her husband thrusting inside her. But Kebede continued to drive deep inside Tigest. Her head became dizzy as she struggled to breathe through her mucus-clogged nostrils.

Several thrusts later, Kebede finished. He turned his back to Tigest and wiped away a cocktail of his semen and her blood. Kebede looked at the blood-stained ground. He grinned to himself with satisfaction and checked to make sure that the colorful headband was still neatly placed on his head. That way everyone in the village would know that his new wife was pure before the marriage, and that Kebede had now rightfully staked his claim. As Kebede pulled his robe carefully over his body, Tigest lay on the ground in a pool of her own blood and wished she would die. She had no idea that a seed of life had already been planted inside her.

Chapter Three

Azmera—December 1984

"When I agreed to take you along with me, Azmera, your mother promised me you'd be strong. And what do I get?" admonished Solomon, "A weak little girl."

With each verbal assault from her uncle, Azmera found herself despising him yet wanting to please him all at once. Azmera chose not to respond and instead continued walking the grueling pace her uncle had set as best as she could. Suddenly, the once-challenging two-kilometer trek to the stream now seemed like child's play. Dawn was breaking and Azmera and her uncle hadn't stopped to rest ever since they had left Tigest the evening before, what now seemed like a lifetime ago. Oddly enough, Azmera welcomed her aching legs plaguing her body as a much-need distraction from all that she had left behind.

Solomon amazed Azmera. She had always known him to be stoically industrious, tilling his fields from dawn until dusk every day. Every day, of course, except for the Sabbath, when he would pray together with Azmera's father in the village synagogue. As she witnessed him walk kilometer after kilometer while carrying the heavy knapsack on his back, Azmera gained a new-found appreciation for her father's little brother. With this, however, came the realization that she could never live up to his demands; Solomon's stride was still going strong, while Azmera's was fading with every step she took, this despite the fact that he was carrying virtually all of the burden, both physically and mentally. Her young body needed a rest, but she simply could not bring herself to ask for one. Solomon was in charge, and she would have to keep up. Besides, the thought of losing face in front of him was far more painful to bear than dragging her protesting body all the way to Sudan.

Azmera could not recall the tracks she and Solomon had made thus far; her otherwise keen sense of direction had failed her miserably on this journey thus far. She found it easier to put up with the grueling trek—both physically and emotionally—by affixing her eyes to the ground while methodically counting every step she took.

"*And, Hulet, Sost, Arat, Amist, Sidist, Sebat, Simint, ZeTen, Asir,*" Azmera counted to herself in groups of ten, the repetitive rhythm allowing her body and mind to transcend beyond the exhaustion and pain.

With her gaze focused downward, though, Azmera missed the spectacular view of the dawn sun lighting up the rugged cliff extending beyond the plain in front of her. The cliff was calling out for attention, much like Azmera used to do when she would eagerly raise her hand to answer one of her father's questions about the Song of Psalms, proudly wanting to prove to him that, as always, she was his diligent student. But Azmera paid no attention to it. Nor did she notice the young baboons playfully running around in circles. Only when Solomon uttered the words, "Let's break" did she notice the sun rising in its glory right in front of her eyes. The sound of those two desperately-needed words snapped Azmera out of her hypnotic state. She plopped herself onto the rocky ground, unsure of whether she would ever be able to stand up again.

Solomon carefully removed the heavy knapsack strapped around his shoulders, and took out the jerrycan. They had enough water to last them until they reached the next water spring. In an unexpected gesture, Solomon extended her the water before taking a sip himself. Azmera took several large gulps and then returned the water to Solomon who, without hesitation, put the cap back on the jerrycan without partaking of its contents. Large drops of sweat slowly trickled down Azmera's back as she struggled to catch her breath. This rocky spot in the middle of the Simien Mountains, a spot farther from home than she had ever been, would surely be her final resting place, she thought to herself with self-pity. She had nothing left in her to give and no one she could give it to even if she wanted to. The people she loved most had already abandoned her.

Solomon sat on a boulder ten feet away from his niece, his back resting against the yellow jerrycan. He always made a concerted effort to keep his distance from her, as if she had the measles. They had walked all night long together, this being the first real break they had taken in hours, and thus far Solomon had uttered exactly three sentences to his niece. Yes, Azmera was counting—her uncle spoke to her so little that it was easy to keep track. In fact, these three sentences were more than he had ever uttered to her when he would come visit her father. A subtle nod of his head was the only acknowledgment of her existence he had ever volunteered until now—that was, if she were lucky.

"Here, have some *kolo*," Solomon commanded, thrusting towards Azmera a bag of roasted grains he had taken out of his pocket.

In her constant state of food insecurity, Azmera had long ago learned that food was made to be saved, not eaten, and she had managed to refrain all night long from touching any of the food her mother had given her despite her growling stomach and aching muscles. In fact, she had refrained from opening her knapsack altogether, even though the chilly night wind had her longing for her scarf and her sweater. She knew that a mere glimpse or whiff of her mother's *injera* would awaken not only her appetite for sustenance but also for her mother's embrace. It was easier, then, to keep her bag closed altogether.

The *kolo* Solomon offered her, on the other hand, was free of any provocative sentiments. She swallowed down one handful after another. She knew she should have been more judicious with her ration, but her body needed sustenance. Solomon waited for his niece to finish and immediately thereafter stood up, signaling that their short break had now come to an end. Dawn was breaking, and Solomon hoped they could continue walking for a bit longer before resting until sundown. Azmera was so absorbed in her own suffering that she failed to notice that Solomon had eaten nothing during the break. He anxiously waited for Azmera to gather herself and her belongings before continuing their journey. Her body was weak and on the verge of failing her, but somehow, she managed to gather strength from Solomon's endless reserve of energy and will. She dragged herself off the ground to continue their journey, paving the way to their foreign homeland.

Glaring into the distance, Solomon looked calculatingly at the terrain that lay ahead of them. From the position of the rising sun, he knew they were headed in the right direction to the border with Sudan, but this was still uncharted territory for him. Getting lost was simply not an option. Solomon knew that walking at dawn was dangerous, but he also knew that time was running out. Every extra kilometer they could squeeze in could be the difference between arriving in Sudan in time or getting left behind. It could be the difference between life and death. While he felt burdened by Azmera's presence, he found her company, such as it was, to be somewhat of a comfort with all the uncertainty surrounding them. With his older brother, Kebede, waiting for his daughter's arrival in Israel, he knew he could not let him down. She forced him to remain strong, even when he wasn't.

"Why don't you ever talk to me?" Azmera asked with an air of gall she was trying on for size.

Back in her village, she would never have dared question Solomon, or any elder for that matter, with such effrontery, but now she felt like she had nothing to lose. After all, Solomon couldn't abandon her in the middle of nowhere, could he? Just as the words exited her mouth, she wished with all her might that she could swallow them back whole. But she couldn't. Solomon slowed down his pace for a fraction of a second. It was as if his body had been jolted backwards by his niece's audacity. He quickly regathered himself, though, resuming his brisk pace without uttering a word. Azmera breathed a sigh of relief, thankful that Solomon had chosen to ignore her question rather than respond with a slap across her face the way any right-minded elder, especially a male elder, would have responded. While Kebede's silence thus far was intolerable, Azmera could at the very least appreciate her uncle's heightened sense of self-restraint.

The unlikely pair continued trekking through increasingly sparsely vegetated terrain, with Azmera taking notice of how the grass became shorter and finer with every grueling step she climbed. When Solomon reached the peak, still painfully out of Azmera's reach, he swiftly crouched down to the ground and signaled to Azmera to do the same. Azmera wasn't sure what Solomon had seen, but she knew that whatever it was, it wasn't good. She froze in a crouched position, grimacing to herself in silence as she felt her thighs turn limp and collapse from underneath her.

Solomon crawled his way back down the hill he had just climbed, motioning to his partner to do the same. Azmera's heart sunk to the ground when she realized that the effort she had put into every step uphill was now going to waste. Solomon led her back to where they had come from at an unusually brisk pace. Azmera grunted with utter frustration. Not only would she now have to conquer the ascent twice, but she was certain that Solomon would, in his patronizing way, refuse to share with her whatever he saw that prompted the abrupt turn-around.

Solomon guided Azmera, both moving stealthily like field mice searching for food. Solomon found a resting place for the day—a closed-in area with jagged rocks—and pulled a blanket out of his knapsack and hastily laid it down. Azmera had to restrain herself from plugging her nose when

Solomon removed his shoes, the foul stench awakening her otherwise dulled senses. He rested his head on the blanket, signaling to Azmera to do the same.

Azmera's frustration with her uncle was festering to the surface. She couldn't tolerate being treated like a little girl any longer and was mustering up the nerve to tell Solomon as much when he turned to her in a whisper, "There's a Christian village beyond this hill and I spotted some villagers outside of their huts, despite the early hour. They cannot see us. We'll have to wait here until nightfall before continuing the journey."

While Azmera appreciated the real danger of being reported to the authorities by the Christians, she sensed an overly anxious tone in Solomon's voice. Solomon had made it clear to her from the beginning of their journey that every minute was crucial, but apparently daytime minutes didn't count. There was no choice, then, but to sit and rest—and with any luck, sleep— until the sun made its descent beneath the vast Ethiopian sky.

Chapter Four

Tigest—January 1985

Tigest put her children to sleep in the make-shift bed she and Kebede had made for them years before. She and her husband had always taken great pride in their work despite its simplicity. The bed frame was made from a combination of straw and mud; the blankets from scraps of fabric that Kebede had salvaged from the dumpster on one of his many trips to Gondar. As the children grew bigger, of course, the bed grew increasingly crowded. Still, the children never complained about their nightly sleeping arrangements; instead, the sound of each other's gentle breathing inside the pitch-black *gojo* put them at ease. But now Azmera's absence left them tossing and turning at bedtime, searching for that warm comfort that their big sister had always provided them.

As Tigest watched her children struggle to fall asleep, she wondered how Azmera would handle the solitude that awaited her, both in Sudan and then, God willing, in Israel. While she might be heading to the "Holy Land" and ostensibly a better life, she was doing it all alone, without the embrace of her *Enati* and without the unconditional adoration bestowed upon her by her three brothers and little sister. Sure, Kebede would be there to take care of her, Tigest tried to reassure herself. But she couldn't suppress the feeling that even with Kebede by her side, Azmera would still be all alone.

After watching her children toss and turn for what felt like hours, each of them finally succumbed to a deep slumber. Most nights, Tigest waited for her children to drift off to sleep before she began tidying the hut—sweeping the rug, scrubbing the coffee pot, rinsing the tin cups, and meticulously taking inventory of how much teff, water and beans remained. On this night, however, Tigest did not have the energy to be reminded yet again that the food she had to feed her children was quickly diminishing with no real prospects for replenishment. On this night, her heart needed a break—she had already suffered enough emotional toil since she had made her daughter leave her home for a new one. Never mind that she couldn't afford to take a night off from her daily chores; on this night, Tigest desperately needed some sort of reassurance that her eldest daughter would be okay and that her father would love her and care for her just as she had always done.

In the months since her husband had abandoned his family for Israel, he had unexpectedly proven to be remarkably consistent in his letter-writing. Until now, Tigest relied on her brother-in-law, Solomon, to make the trip to Debark, the closest village from which one could receive and send mail. He traveled there on a regular basis to sell ceramic pottery bowls and plates his wife, Meskie, had made. The extra income was helpful for them over the years, especially when the harvest let them down. Of course, now with Solomon gone, Tigest wasn't sure she would be able to receive any letters from Kebede. Nor from Azmera.

Tigest was so surprised by the delivery of Kebede's first letter that it took her a full week's time—until Solomon delivered the next letter—for her to find the strength to read it. Tigest, after all, had assumed that Kebede's decision to leave his wife and children behind reflected his overwhelming boredom and distaste for her, or at the very least general apathy for all that she represented. In their fifteen years of marriage, Kebede rarely showed affection for his wife, instead treating her as a business partner whom he took to bed whenever his whims took over. He had stubbornly insisted on marrying her and only her—largely due to his initial physical attraction to the beautiful girl Tigest once was—but he had never allowed himself to get truly intimate with her. Strangely, Tigest had slowly fallen in love with the man who had forced her into marriage and into his bed, even if he did slap her across the face from time to time when he lost his patience. She had come to accept her fate; it wasn't that different from the fate of most of the other women she knew, after all. In fact, Tigest felt a sense of security in Kebede's stoicism and fortitude. Her love for Kebede was especially strange, she thought as a tear slowly trickled down her cheek, given that he never had seemed to fall in love with her.

In the hut's darkness, Tigest lifted up the rug and clumsily searched for the tin box she had hidden deep in the dirt ground. She dug with her fingers, struggling to keep quiet so as not to wake the children. As a cold piece of metal surfaced against her hand, it suddenly dawned on Tigest that she no longer had anyone from whom to hide the contents of the tin box. After all, Azmera was the only child of hers who had learned how to read—Kebede had begun teaching her at the age of ten after she stubbornly insisted on joining him in synagogue on Shabbat mornings, and he even allowed her to attend school from time to time—and of course she was now gone. Tigest lifted the tin box from the earth. She carefully wiped the dirt off the surface to protect the few letters she had received from getting soiled. The dirt had begun to sink into the opening of the box making it increasingly difficult for Tigest to open. Her heart began to race furiously as she tried to pry the box open with her thin fingers, using more force this time than she had the previous time. To her relief, the box finally opened and Kebede's letters revealed themselves once again to her reminiscing eyes.

✡

Kebede—December 1984

Tigy—

Last week I arrived in the Holy Land after several miserable weeks in Country X. Israel is nothing like I expected. Everyone moves so fast and there are so many cars and buses that it's easy to forget that this is the place where our forefathers came from. For now, my dream of living in Jerusalem is on hold. Instead, they have placed me in an absorption center in a small town in the middle of nowhere called Dimona. Nothing in Dimona feels holy. The best part of my day is when I go to my Hebrew class. My teacher is Israeli, and she is amazing. She has been so kind and welcoming to us. Hebrew is a difficult language, but I study religiously every afternoon and feel that I'm improving like the younger boys in class. We also have classes teaching us how to get along in Israel, and about how to talk with Israelis. While the daily routine here is different, I am surrounded by other Ethiopians and have met very few sabras, Israelis who were born and raised in Israel. My teacher and the absorption center's manager are the only "real" Israelis I've gotten to know. I left Ethiopia hoping I'd arrive in Israel and feel like a changed person—a stronger person— and, more than anything, like an Israeli. And when I'm studying Hebrew, I do feel like I am slowly getting there. But most of the time, I don't feel like I belong and I don't know if I ever will. I definitely felt that way when they taught us how to clean our asses—one of the most humiliating experiences in my life. I feel it when my teacher tells us about her life on the kibbutz—Kibbutz Revivim— and how they celebrate all the holidays together and how almost everyone serves in elite IDF units. I feel it when I see Israeli families on picnics in the park nearby—and I'm all alone. And I feel it in their stares back at me. They might be excited to have us in Israel, but they still look at me with curiosity and suspicion, like I don't belong. Back home, everyone looked up to me as the son of the village Kes, but here I'm just another primitive Ethiopian. I know it's just the beginning and I need to be patient. I pray I won't always feel this way.

I hope that you and the children are managing without me. Send them my love.

Kebede

Tigest—January 1985

"Send *them* my love," Tigest repeated to herself. It was as if he wanted to make it extra clear that he was not sending his love to her. The picture Kebede painted was bleak, but Tigest felt a twinge of envy, nonetheless. Envy that he had the courage to leave everything in his life behind and follow his dream to Zion. Envy that the unknown to her was now becoming familiar to him. Envy that he was learning how to speak Hebrew. Envy that he was now officially an Israeli citizen. And envy that maybe he, the father of her children and the man that she somehow learned to love over the years, had finally fallen in love—with someone else.

The morning sun's rays lit up their *gojo* and Tigest lay in bed, unable to pry herself out of the comfortable nook the mud bed frame provided. She woke to the sounds of her son, Desta, and her daughter, Gabra, giggling on the ground, amused by the holes and mounds of dirt they had created in the ground that was not covered by the rug. As Tigest's belly grew, she found it increasingly difficult to get the day started, her body craving just a few more elusive minutes in bed. She grumpily scolded Desta and Gabra for blatantly violating the rules of the house and making a mess she knew she would have to clean up later, when she felt a piece of paper slide off her chest and onto the ground, right before the curious eyes of her children. Gabra, proving to be as bright as her sister, picked up the piece of paper—an uncommon sight for her—and inquired as to what it was.

Tigest contemplated whether she should tell Gabra the truth or not—whether she should tell her of the letters from her father, or whether her four-year-old little girl even remembered who her father was.

Instead of complicating matters, Tigest callously stated, "It's kindling for the fire," and threw the letter—which she had poured over time after time ever since Kebede left her—into the fire pit used for cooking and *bunnah* ceremonies. Tigest lit the fire and watched the letter dwindle into tiny, glowing specks of nothingness.

Chapter Five

Azmera—December 1984

Azmera stared in awe at the setting sun, its glorious colors painting the Ethiopian sky in yellow, pink and orange. Like the sun sinking into the earth, so too was she. Her body was draped on the ground like an overweight elder baboon basking in the sun, unable to even lift its head. The exhaustion was overwhelming, and as she nodded off, she secretly found herself thanking God for the fact that her people had such an enemy in the Christians of Ethiopia. How ironic, Azmera thought to herself: they may have spit at us as they called us *Falasha*, stripped us of our land, forcibly baptized us, and attacked our synagogues, but at least because of them we have to take a break from walking during the day! Her mother had taught her to always remain optimistic, even in the worst of times. Despite her father's abandonment and the ever-dwindling bag of teff flour, her mother never pitied herself or her situation, at least not as far as Azmera could discern. And now here was Azmera—banished by her own mother, passed out from sheer exhaustion, and partnered with an uncle who seemingly couldn't stand her. She was so thirsty that her mouth felt like cotton. The Christians up the hill could attack them in an instant. But instead of cursing her luck, she found cause to rejoice.

Solomon sat up, his back resting on a boulder jutting out of the rocky soil. He began sorting through all his belongings, as if he were a shopkeeper taking inventory. Azmera's eyes were growing heavier with each passing minute. She found it strangely meditative to observe Solomon take stock of his knapsack, methodically counting each crumpled piece of paper, each ragged article of clothing and the remaining pieces of *injera* that made Azmera's mouth water. Azmera watched Solomon compulsively count and recount the few possessions remaining to him, as if the number would change from one count to the next, and as if how much *injera* or *kolo* remained made any real difference—they would, after all, only make a small dent in their hunger. Solomon, however, was anxiously waiting for the sun to set so they could continue the journey, and checking and double-checking his belongings helped to pass the otherwise stagnant time.

More than anything, silence was what best characterized Azmera's time thus far with her uncle. He rarely initiated conversation, and Azmera followed his lead. The tense silence from their first day together, however, gradually dissipated into a comfortable silence that allowed Azmera to appreciate the deafening quiet of the barren mountains surrounding them.

Azmera's almond-colored eyes found a brief refuge under her closed eyelids when she was brutally awoken by piercing gusts of wind. The landscape surrounding them was so barren that there were no trees rocking back and forth to hint at an approaching storm, and no trees to slow down the howling wind. The clouds raced overhead, and Azmera and Solomon anxiously stared at the dark and ominous sky emerging above them.

"It's raining again?" cried out Azmera at the sky, angry at Mother Nature for waking her even though she knew that she should be grateful for any amount of precipitation, even if it didn't conform with her expectations. It was nearly January and what should have been the rainy season had ended several months earlier.

Azmera, sluggish from the sudden wake-up call, found herself shivering uncontrollably as the temperature dropped. One by one swollen drops of rain began to pounce off her exposed skin. She debated whether to take her scarf and sweater out of her bag for warmth, knowing that their fate was doomed if she did—they would surely be soaked within minutes. But while the rain might have caught Azmera off-guard, neither Solomon nor Azmera were strangers to the ways of the Simien Mountains. Storms, while tempestuous, rarely lasted long. Azmera decided to brave the cold and rain in her barebones clothes, knowing that the warmth of her scarf and sweater would be patiently waiting for her when the sky and her body dried.

Just as the rain began to intensify, Solomon extended his arm towards Azmera, offering her what seemed to be some sort of plastic sack.

"Thank you," Azmera mumbled to her uncle, who nodded his head in reluctant acknowledgment of his niece's gratitude.

Azmera was bewildered by this strange plastic sheet that crinkled when touched, but even more so by Solomon's concern for her wellbeing and his ability to surprise her. After all, she had watched him count all his belongings only a few minutes before, but somehow this plastic sack, which apparently would now keep her dry, had escaped her attention. Even though it was the dry season, and even though rain was unlikely, Solomon had come prepared. Azmera draped the poncho over her body, shielding her from the sheeting rain. She felt safe for the first time since she had left home.

Solomon

Solomon reveled in his senses as he watched, listened, and felt the weather change all around him. He was captivated by how the blazing wind gusts and the ferocious downpour quickly gave way to a gentle breeze and a patient, light drizzle. His awe for Mother Nature had been instilled in him as a young boy. It started at age five when his father would take him to sow the teff and corn fields, where he saw firsthand how his parents toiled away to feed him *injera* at dinnertime. It continued as an eight-year-old when Kebede, seven years his senior, brought him along to slaughter a goat in celebration of the New Year. There, Solomon was brought to tears as he watched his childhood pet's eyes begging for mercy before its life came abruptly to an end. It culminated at age thirteen, after becoming a bar-mitzvah, when his father asked him to join him on the annual twenty-day journey to Gondar to buy staples for his family. Until then, Kebede had been his father's right-hand man on the journey, but he had a new wife and baby to care for—so Kebede reluctantly surrendered that role to his younger brother, Solomon.

It was on that journey that Solomon learned the hard way how to survive in the outdoors. Though his father was the village *Kes*, he preferred teaching his sons to become men by way of experience instead of fatherly or even spiritual guidance. When both food and water began to run low, he deliberately left his son to his own devices. The thirteen-year-old boy shamefully shed a few tears in front of the man he idolized when he first understood the severity of their predicament. But Solomon was determined to make his father proud.

Family legend told how Solomon's childhood came to an end not after the ritual *bar-mitzvah*, where he led the other villagers in reciting prayers in *Ge'ez* on Shabbat, but several months later, on that storied journey. On that journey, Solomon found himself walking for twenty days straight. On that journey, Solomon found himself with tears in his eyes as he raised a knife against a befuddled chicken who seemed to have lost his way. On that journey, Solomon learned how to create a makeshift tent out of a few twigs and pieces of burlap, shielding him and his father from the bitter mountain cold at night. On that journey, Solomon followed a herd of ibex to a hidden spring of water from where they could refill their water supplies. On that journey, Solomon became a man. And made his father proud.

Azmera—December 1984

Azmera felt herself nodding off as the rain came to a lull. A sweet and earthy post-rain smell awakened Azmera's senses, and she brushed off the drops of rain from the plastic sack wrapped around her shivering body. She squeezed her hair like she would squeeze a dirty rag wet from washing the dishes. Solomon began to gather all their belongings, while signaling to Azmera by way of a stern nod of the head that it was time to get moving. Nighttime was approaching and they did not have a second to waste.

Azmera's body howled with pain when she dragged herself off the ground. Despite the rest, although granted courtesy of the Christian village over the hill, her body now felt betrayed. Just when it thought that the nightmarish journey had come to an end, it had awoken to discover that their journey had only just begun. As Solomon confidently took his first steps up the hill towards the Christian village, Azmera became filled with animosity for the man in front of her who was responsible for causing her such pain and grief. Somewhere deep inside, Azmera knew that her hatred was not rational, especially considering Solomon's unselfish act of sheltering her from the rain at his own expense. Still, hating Solomon served as a much-needed distraction from her aching muscles and aching heart. More than anything, hating Solomon meant that she could not dare show him any more weakness lest she be forced again to accept his help. Azmera determinedly charged after Solomon, who had already gained a considerable lead in front of her. The sun made its final descent into the horizon, leaving only the luminous stars and half-crescent moon to light the way.

Chapter Six

Tigest—1969

Tigest's first few months of marriage were plagued with nausea and an unremitting lethargy that made her feel anything but like herself. While still just a girl, Tigest had a keen understanding of the way the world—or at least the way *her* world—worked. She knew that no man, especially a man as stubborn as Kebede, would tolerate the sluggish girl she had become. She was barely able to get out of bed in the morning, let alone tend to the livestock and till the two acres of teff and corn fields Kebede had inherited after their wedding. Surprisingly, Kebede seemed undisturbed by Tigest's lack of energy. In fact, he kept his distance from her at all costs. To him, Tigest was simply a stranger living in his home whom he now had to tolerate, except of course for when his lustful impulses took over. Kebede still did, in fact, find his wife to be strikingly beautiful, despite Tigest's many grievances against him. He had desperately wanted to love her when he insisted on marrying her, and he had desperately wanted her to love him back; but Tigest's cold demeanor never let him forget what he had done to her. Even so, he did take pleasure in the fact that this stranger acquiesced, albeit unenthusiastically, to him every time he took her to bed. And every time he came inside his wife, for a brief moment he felt like she was no longer a stranger, but rather a part of him.

One evening, as the rain pitter-pattered on their rooftop, Tigest settled into bed. She was desperate for a good night's sleep after an endless day of smacking Kebede's filthy work clothes in the nearby stream until they were clean. Just as her eyes began to drift into a world where she was still a carefree little girl with no responsibilities, she felt Kebede climb on top of her and press his weight tightly against her body. By now, Tigest knew what awaited her. Since marrying Kebede, she had resigned herself to relinquishing the rights to her own body whenever it so pleased him. And while she had once been a feisty little girl with a backbone as strong as iron, Tigest was quickly growing old enough to know that she had no choice but to succumb. And so, she did, night after night. Kebede hastily undressed Tigest out of her cotton frock nightgown, and without wasting any time, entered his wife for the fiftieth time since their marriage three months earlier. Yes, she had counted.

Despite Tigest's initial disinterest in intercourse with her husband, she occasionally surprised herself by enjoying the act for the few minutes Kebede was inside her. This time was different. With each thrust deeper inside her, Tigest felt an excruciating pain unfamiliar to her. She curled her hand into a fist and stuffed it into her mouth to keep from screaming out in agony. It was better to suffer in silence lest she anger her husband before he reached his climax. He was known to lose his temper, after all. Tigest was certain that Kebede was slowly killing her, ripping out her insides. Knowing that Kebede never took more than a few minutes to finish, she began counting to herself to distract herself from the agony her husband was inflicting on her. This exercise of enormous self-restraint was not unfamiliar to Tigest. She was well-trained in defying the physical; she had learned to do so as a young girl when she went to collect water from the river. Tigest knew that all pain—or at least all physical pain—was fleeting. She just had to wait a few more minutes for it all to be over. Until the next time.

Kebede let out a snort as his body trembled into a short but powerful climax. He stood up from bed and performed his ritual, using a piece of cloth to wipe off the stickiness that Tigest so despised. This time, however, not only was he covered in the sticky gel of his own, but also in a brownish blood from Tigest. The blood covering him startled him, so much so that his muscles contracted tightly, negating the pleasure he had experienced just seconds earlier. The sight of blood wasn't unfamiliar to either one of them; after all, it had been only several months since Kebede forced himself on Tigest for the first time, resulting in dark blood stains on her robe. Tigest never managed to remove those stains no matter how much scrubbing and chafing she did. She decided they were there to remind her of that otherwise ordinary day when Kebede stripped her of her childhood. But that day was a lifetime ago, and Tigest had stopped bleeding while having intercourse with Kebede for months now, so the brownish blood caught them both by surprise. More than anything, though, Tigest felt overwhelmed with shame that her body had betrayed her in front of Kebede. She didn't want to appear weak in front of her strong husband. Her body was controlling her, not the other way around—it reminded her of how her little sister must have felt when she would wake up in the middle of the night in a pool of urine.

In fact, Tigest had only just begun menstruating right before Kebede stormed into her life. The year before, she had started to develop small breasts which were conveniently disguised by her long, flowing robes. Tigest was mortified by her changing body and the utter filthiness of all the blood "down there"; she was so mortified, in fact, that for months she managed to hide from her mother the changes to her body, until one day when Tigest bled through her clothes for everyone to see while shopping with her mother at the market.

"Tigest, this blood has brought shame to our family," scolded Abaynesh, as she rushed her daughter out of the bustling marketplace filled with withered onions and tomatoes for sale.

Humiliated, Tigest lowered her head to the ground and bunched up the bloodied part of the back of her robe, grabbing on to it tightly to hide it from the many passers-by.

"Don't you remember what it says in the Torah?" barked Abaynesh, "When you bleed, you are dirty, and when you are dirty, no one wants to be around you! How long have you been hiding this from me?"

Tigest knew her mother wasn't interested in a response. Instead, she was making a last-ditch effort to salvage her reputation lest anyone overhear their conversation. Abaynesh was furious at her daughter for not sharing the news with her, especially when Tigest should have known fully well what it implied.

After this episode of public humiliation, Abaynesh explained to her daughter that she would need to go to the *ye-dam gogo*, a *gojo* located a safe distance from the center of their village, whenever her menstrual cycle arrived, just like all the other women did. There she would need to remain indoors until all signs of bleeding were gone. Inside that modest mud hut, Tigest would need to wipe herself repeatedly with scrap pieces of cloth her mother had once used to sew clothes for the family. It was there that Tigest would bide the time to pass, waiting until her period would ultimately go away, until she could resume her carefree way of living. It was there that Tigest learned to hate her body—to hate what it had made her become.

"I don't know why I'm bleeding like this," Tigest muttered to herself just loud enough so Kebede could hear her.

"You should pay a visit to that Italian doctor next time he visits our village. You know, the fat one with the crooked nose?" suggested Kebede.

Tigest nodded her head in agreement. She was taken aback by how patient and understanding Kebede was. His unexpected concern for her drew Tigest closer to her husband; it was the first time since they married that he had shown any interest in her well-being. His lack of disgust diminished Tigest's feeling of shame, allowing her to focus on the cause of the bleeding. The last time she had her menstrual cycle, she calculated, was over three months ago, right before she married Kebede. It was her fourth menstrual cycle ever, although thus far there had been nothing cyclical about it.

Tigest had watched her mother's belly grow countless times—sadly, three more times than the number of her four younger siblings—and she noticed that every time her mother carried a baby in her womb, she stopped sequestering herself in the *ye-dam gogo* like she ordinarily would. The last time Tigest had bled was months ago. Now she was bleeding again, but it was different than before—far less blood and browner in color. Tigest's strong intuition knew what was happening to her body, but she was afraid to acknowledge it. She would keep it to herself for the time-being, at least until the Italian doctor made his rounds again. Or until her growing belly gave it away.

One month later, Tigest was just beginning to drag herself out of bed when she heard Kebede's voice in the distance.

"Tigest! He's here!" Kebede had left their *gojo* before sunrise to be the first one in line to buy kerosene. He returned to his wife carrying an enormous yellow jug on his back and a smile on his face.

"*In eh-heedt!* Let's go!" shouted Tigest to herself as she sprung out of bed. She knew she better hurry lest she spend an entire day waiting in line to see the doctor, or worse yet, not see him at all.

After two hours of standing in line and anxiously shuffling her feet, the Italian doctor motioned to Tigest to enter his make-shift clinic, a brown pop-up tent with a flap that opened with a nervous excitement and hopefulness and closed all too often with grief and despair. Tigest nervously told the doctor about the bleeding, but didn't volunteer any other information. The doctor, used to treating young girls ashamed of their bodies and what their husbands had done to them, placed a stethoscope on Tigest's belly and listened as Tigest and held her breath. Tigest wasn't sure what it was she wanted to hear from the doctor. In fact, she wasn't even sure she needed to see the doctor in the first place. She hadn't bled since the alarming episode in bed a month prior and, other than feeling a little tired, she felt perfectly fine.

"Tell the girl that she is pregnant, nearly half-way through," the doctor scribbled onto his notepad as he explained indifferently to the interpreter by Tigest's side. "She needs to take good care of herself, eating lots of carrots and leafy green vegetables, even if it means that her husband eats less. Oh, and citrus fruits are important too."

"I will do my best," replied Tigest, desperate to please the doctor and comply with his recommendations, while very much aware that her reality was far different from his. While there had been plenty of rainfall that year, her diet consisted nearly exclusively of corn, *injera*, and *shiro* chickpea paste, not the vegetables and fruit the doctor had recommended. Still, Tigest surprisingly felt lighter when she stood up to leave. She opened the tent flap with a sense of relief and joy, not the grief and despair she had witnessed in so many others before her that she had dreaded feeling herself.

Tigest returned home where she found Kebede tending to the goats. Without saying a word, Tigest approached her husband and hugged him like she had never hugged him before. After many months of being trapped in a place of darkness, the idea that she had a baby growing inside her brought her back to life. How ironic it was to her that Kebede of all people, despite what he did to her on that cursed day months ago, would be responsible for it. For the first time, she felt a strong sense of attachment, if not love, for her husband.

Kebede was caught off guard by this sudden display of affection from his otherwise cold and reserved wife, and didn't reciprocate at first. He had been certain that Tigest despised his existence—her cold demeanor towards him gave him no reason to believe otherwise. While he knew that he had probably been too rough with her the day they married, and perhaps even on the days that followed, he never apologized to Tigest or acknowledged his transgressions. At that moment, however, what had happened months ago seemed to no longer matter.

Kebede slowly gave in to the warm embrace from his wife, indulging in the thought that maybe, just maybe, she would finally become his.

Chapter Seven

Kebede—January 1985

Kebede lay on a thin mattress placed on top of a worn-out box spring and tossed and turned all night long. Insomnia had plagued him ever since arriving in Israel. In those haunting hours between lights-out and the 6:30 am wake-up call for breakfast in the dining hall, Kebede had too much time for idle thoughts. His sleepless musings varied depending on how he felt on any given day, but they almost always went back to one thing—Tigest. Back home in Ethiopia, he rarely had trouble settling into sleep; the long day's work in the fields sufficiently drained both his body and mind clean. Shortly before he left for Israel, however, he found himself inexplicably restless at night. It was on Azmera's thirteenth birthday—when Azmera turned the same age as Tigest the day they married—that Kebede first began to squirm in his own skin. It was on Azmera's thirteenth birthday—when Tigest gave her eldest daughter a beautifully embroidered dress she had worked on for months beforehand—that Kebede turned his back to hide the tears streaming down his cheeks as his daughter proudly tried on her new dress. It was on Azmera's thirteenth birthday, what should have been just another celebratory milestone in his daughter's life, that Kebede looked into his daughter's innocent, sparkling eyes, opening his own to what he had done to Tigest so many years ago. It was on Azmera's thirteenth birthday, amidst the festive singing and dancing, that Kebede knew he needed to leave Tigest to escape the daily reminder of what he had done. Maybe that way he would be able to sleep again at night. But it was not to be. He had climbed the mountains of Ethiopia and trekked through the desert of Sudan, surviving hell along the way, but Kebede quickly learned that no matter the distance between them, his wife could not be escaped. And so Tigest continued to haunt him in his small dormitory room in the middle of the vast desert in the middle of nowhere in Israel. Tigest—his wife who made him feel guilty every time he thought of her almond-shaped eyes. Tigest—the mother of his five children—whom he had abandoned. Tigest—the girl, who at the same age as his eldest daughter, upon whom he forced himself the night of their marriage. Tigest—the woman who had forgiven him time after time whenever he slapped her across the face, leaving a red, swollen mark on her cheek. Tigest—the woman who both loathed and loved him at the same time. Tigest.

Kebede—October 1984

The rainy season had just come to an end when Kebede left his home, even though that year it had never really begun in the first place. Two of Kebede's childhood friends, Zenebe and Mualalem, had already left for Sudan, and Kebede couldn't let himself fall too far behind. After all, even Tigest knew that her husband's own sense of self-worth was measurable only by comparing himself to others. His competitiveness had always driven his every move; even his insistence to marry Tigest was partly in response to his friend, Zenebe, after he first expressed interest in her. So just a few days before he left home, Kebede informed his wife that he had decided to go to Israel, without consulting with her first. As he looked into her disappointed eyes, he reassured her that he would send for the family to join him after he had learned the language and found a job. What he didn't tell Tigest, though, was that he hoped that the time away from her would heal his guilt-ridden wounds now festering at the surface. What he also didn't tell his wife was that he genuinely hoped that acquiring a new citizenship would be like acquiring a blank slate—free of any scratches, bangs, or transgressions.

"You can't let the children know of my plans until after I've left, otherwise they're bound to tell one of their friends and who knows what that could lead to," Kebede whispered even though no one but Tigest was near him, "And if anyone comes looking for me from the police or the army, you must insist that you have no idea where I am. Just say that I simply left one day and never came back. If you want, you can say that I found another woman, whatever you think will convince them."

Tigest nodded, understanding her role in ensuring her husband's safety. While lying would likely work with a soldier patrolling the area, especially with the soldiers just doing their job to feed their families, Tigest, and everyone else in their village, knew the truth. Those who had left were surely en route to Israel via Sudan, or, for the lucky few, had already arrived.

"It's time for me to leave," Kebede announced one night while lying in bed with Tigest, with Gabra snuggling between the two of them. Tigest had anxiously anticipated this moment ever since the day Kebede detected that his friends' once perfectly tilled fields were now sloppily tended to by their eldest sons left behind. Kebede was a lot of things as a man, but more than anything he was competitive—especially with Zenebe and Mualalem, his good friends but even better rivals. Knowing that they were on their way to fulfilling the Zionist dream while he lagged behind was too much for Kebede to bear. Tigest was certain that was the primary factor motivating her husband to leave with such urgency. What Tigest didn't know was how Kebede could no longer bear the sight of her, particularly now that Azmera was looking more like her with each passing day. Both his wife and his daughter had become daily reminders of his past, a past he needed to escape.

Tigest couldn't help but feel insulted by Kebede's declaration of his intention to leave, but she knew that he had made up his mind. There was no point arguing with him. Her relationship with Kebede had always been built on the premise that things were better left unspoken, and she wasn't about to change this dynamic now, even though she knew that her menstrual cycle was suspiciously several weeks late. There was no point in sharing with Kebede this news—news which Tigest herself was still struggling to digest. It was clear that he had made up his mind, and Tigest had her pride to uphold. A husband should stay by his wife's side because he *wanted* to, not because he needed to. And besides, she knew how much pressure Kebede was already feeling to provide for his family. Learning that his family of seven was expanding to eight would not have served his morale before embarking on the treacherous journey to Sudan. With all this in mind, Tigest responded to Kebede's declaration with an indifferent and mumbled "okay". She pretended to be half asleep, despite being wide awake from the stress of contemplating being left alone to care for five children, with one on the way.

Tigest's lack of a response was followed by a long silence from Kebede, but this time the silence felt different than the characteristic silence that had marked their relationship over the years. This silence could be felt in the tense air they breathed, made all the worse as Kebede attempted to create distance from Tigest in their already crowded bed. Tigest was hurt by Kebede's decision to leave, but so too was he by her apparent indifference to him leaving. Their troubled history had hijacked their relationship throughout the years, leaving them emotionally paralyzed, each by the other—and unable to communicate in any meaningful way. Tigest may have forgiven Kebede for what he had done to her when she was just a girl—younger even than Azmera—but neither of them could forget, let alone talk about it.

"Bring your warm jacket with you and take a few extra sheets of *injera* and a big bag of *kolo*," Tigest whispered to Kebede, careful not to wake up Gabra after she had finally fallen asleep, her cheek squished to the side as it rested on Tigest's breast.

Tigest wanted to tell him to be careful, but hesitated. Any sign of affection would unsettle the chilled relationship they had thrived on for the past fourteen years. Kebede had considered leaving in the morning after hugging his children and telling them he was going on another journey to restock up on supplies in Gondar, but Tigest's chilly response made him feel as if he were merely taking up space in a home where he was no longer welcome. Besides, he could make more progress if he began the journey at night. He grabbed his warm jacket and food just as Tigest had insisted. He circled the small *gojo*, giving a kiss on the forehead to each of his five sleeping children. He lingered as he bent over to give Azmera, his daughter of fourteen years, a kiss goodbye. He didn't notice that she had learned from her mother the art of pretending to be fast asleep.

Kebede—November 1984

The crooked branches holding together Kebede's makeshift tent creaked as the wind gusted and the treacherous night approached. Kebede had been in Tawawa refugee camp for two weeks now. While he had managed to leave Tigest and his children behind, the sleepless nights continued, leaving him weak and weary-eyed by the end of each day. Instead of ruminating on his past, however, Kebede spent his nights hard at work. The howling winds of the harsh Sudanese desert kept him alert and on guard. Tempestuous sand storms were a regular occurrence since having arrived at the camp, and he would spend much of the night protecting his tent from flying away while at the same time attempting to shield his eyes from the sand blowing in the air. There were six other men in his tent, yet four of them were too weak to be able to lend their efforts to defend their new home from the storm's havoc. Ordinarily, Kebede would have also been deemed too weak to do much of anything, let alone fight sand storms and winds of fifty miles an hour. His blistered and bloodied feet from the journey to Sudan had yet to heal—leaving him wincing with pain from even the slightest pressure on them. For Kebede, mustering up the mental and physical strength to walk a mere two steps was now nearly as challenging as the trek to Sudan. Kebede had always prided himself on his strength and invincibility, but since arriving at the camp, his body had not been able to heal properly with those cursed sand storms keeping him awake at all hours of the night. Even the still desert nights found him restless; no matter how hard he tried, he couldn't escape the image of his children sleeping soundly as he sneaked out into the night, nor Tigest's indifference towards his leaving.

"Come help me hold on to the tarp, NOW!" shouted Kebede, waking up his two able-bodied tent mates, men who were otherwise strangers to Kebede.

Since arriving at the camp, Kebede found himself so focused on surviving that he could not afford to expend any energy on getting to know the men sharing his dwelling. The two other men, also too weak to function in normal circumstances, grudgingly pulled themselves up from the ground and obeyed his summons to work, grateful to have a leader in command of the situation. They painfully but quickly limped over to Kebede who was struggling to single-handedly return the tent's tarp, flapping violently in the wind. The three men together managed to overcome the tarp from three corners, the fourth corner still flailing as much as the secured three corners allowed it. Kebede abandoned his corner, hopeful that he had fastened it tightly enough to provide him sufficient time to take care of the fourth and final corner. The wind was a close match even for Kebede, but he managed to secure the fourth corner, stabilizing the tent, at least for the time-being.

Satisfied with his work, Kebede heard a noise approaching from the distance, a faint humming barely audible in the howling wind.

"Stand guard!" he shouted, fearful that the refugee camp was about to be attacked yet again by bandits.

In Kebede's few weeks at the camp, he had been fortunate enough to cope only with the elements dealt him by Mother Nature, and not local Sudanese hoping to get their hands on the meager food rations allocated by the camp, but he was well aware that the threat of attack was looming. Kebede and the other two men searched for an object that could pass for a weapon for whatever awaited them. The sand storm was more effective than any weapon, though, and would undoubtedly slow down whomever was approaching—whether ravenous bandits or hyenas. Nonetheless, Kebede grabbed a fist-sized rock he found lying next to the tent.

With dust and sand painting mini tornados in the air, Kebede squinted his eyes to try to get a glimpse of a run-down green bus rolling down the dirt road bordering the camp, its lights dimmed and its engine humming softly. The sun would make its ascent into the sky shortly, but for now the storm painted the sky with low-hanging, ominous clouds darkening with each passing minute. Kebede and his two partners quickly ruled out the threat of bandits—bandits could not afford to buy shoes, let alone a motorized vehicle. With bandits ruled out, Kebede began to fear the arrival of Sudanese soldiers. In Kebede's two weeks at the camp, Sudan's soldiers had curiously turned a blind eye in the direction of the camp, a camp that provided refuge to Ethiopians—Jews, Muslims and Christians alike. Their arrival, however, felt inevitable, leaving everyone on edge at all times, particularly the Jews. After all, Sudan, a country in the thick of a civil war, hated Israel and anyone trying to escape to Israel more than they hated each other. Several minutes of quiet followed, lessening Kebede's fear, enough so that he was ready to try to get a few more hours of sleep. As Kebede turned towards his tent, he saw the shadow of a man slowly approaching him. Kebede's heart fluttered; his fear disappeared entirely when he heard it—the greeting he had been waiting to hear ever since he was a little boy.

"*Shalom, chaver,*" whispered a short and muscular man, "What is your name?"

The man's greeting of "hello, friend" with Hebrew's thick and guttural "cha" was music to Kebede's ears.

"Kebede Rahamim, the son of *Kes* Rahamim, may his memory be a blessing," answered Kebede, trying to conceal the slight quiver in his voice.

The short man sighed with relief when Kebede announced his name, as if he had found a lost treasure. Kebede understood that the man must have been the notorious *Falasha-Finder*, the man tasked with identifying Jews in the camp. Adrenaline rushed through Kebede's veins as he answered a few more questions satisfactorily confirming his identity, sensing that his life was about to change. The *Falasha-Finder* signaled to Kebede to head towards the bus parked in the distance as he continued his search for others.

Having arrived at the camp two weeks prior, Kebede knew that there were others far ahead of him in the imaginary line determining his and their fate. But he nonetheless had held out hope that his day would come sooner than for the others. He was, after all, the son of a *Kes*. Plus, his father's brother, a veteran in Israel who had written to Kebede boasting of his connections with the Mossad, Israel's national intelligence agency, encouraged Kebede to go to Sudan as soon as possible, promising to pull strings to get his nephew on one of the first planes out. It didn't come as a complete surprise, then, when the *Falasha-Finder* tapped him for departure. Kebede hastily gathered his *tehillim* prayer book, *yarmulke* and backpack, his hands trembling with excitement at the thought of what awaited him. Kebede's other Jewish tent-mates understood perfectly well where Kebede was headed, but they couldn't comprehend why Kebede—having arrived long after them—was one of the first to leave. They looked on with envy as they watched their tent-mate and unofficial leader leave with all the others blessed to be picked on that blustery night.

Their envy was quickly displaced by frustration as the winds strengthened. The two remaining able-bodied men were once again forced to fend off the sand and wind from destroying their shelter for the remainder of the night.

All that followed next seemed like a blur of distant memories, too surreal to be real. At his new home in the absorption center located in Dimona, a remote and neglected immigrant town the government used to house immigrants like himself, Kebede found himself surrounded by other newly arrived Ethiopians, so much so that in many ways his new home in Israel eerily resembled his old home in Ethiopia. In fact, ever since arriving in Israel, his only interactions with Israelis had been of a bureaucratic or condescending nature, or both.

"In Israel, we have indoor plumbing, and we relieve ourselves in the bathroom. You will be expected to do the same. This is the toilet paper you use to wipe yourself after defecating," explained Rotem, his cultural instructor, in the first "cultural integration" class provided to Kebede's cohort as he pointed to the roll of toilet paper in the communal bathroom, "and this is how you flush the toilet when you are finished," while pushing down the flush button on the toilet for all to see.

"You also should consider changing your name so you'll fit in better," recommended Rotem, "a modern Israeli name will do each of you much good. I can't force you, of course, but many of the *olim* from other countries changed their names, too, and it helped them to better integrate. Besides, if you don't, no one here will know how to pronounce your funny names."

Rotem abruptly turned to each of the new immigrants and proposed new Hebraicized names which started with the same sound as their original name.

Rotem turned to Kebede, looking him deep in the eye, "Hmmm, how about Kfir instead of Kebede?"

Kebede, whose name was bestowed to him by his *Kes* father in memory of his *Kes* grandfather who had passed away one year before he was born, was reluctant to abandon the name that had accompanied him his entire life, a name whose meaning had in many ways shaped who he was as a person—strong and hard. At the same time, Rotem made it clear that his past identity no longer mattered. Despite Rotem's condescending ways, Kebede had no doubt that he only had Kebede's best interests in mind. After all, he had moved to a new country to start a new life and put behind him his old one. Kfir it was then, or at least when he introduced himself to a white Israeli.

"*Atah, at, hoo, hee, anachnu,*" Kebede practiced his pronouns repeatedly in his Hebrew class at the instruction of his teacher, Shifra.

The small and stuffy *ulpan* classroom where Kebede learned Hebrew daily was his only refuge in the first few months in Israel. Kebede was fascinated with learning to speak the official language of prayer for the Jewish people, having primarily recited prayers in *Ge'ez* back in Ethiopia. He felt more and more Israeli with each new phrase or expression Shifra taught him. She had the unique ability to make Kebede and his other classmates truly feel like they were Israeli in a place where everyone else made sure to remind them how different they were. From the very first day of class, Shifra spoke Hebrew and only Hebrew to them, forcing her students to grasp the language quickly. She made it a point to refrain from mocking or so much as grinning at her students' thick Ethiopian accents and mispronunciations, which often rendered their Hebrew nearly impossible to decipher. For this, Kebede was eternally grateful.

His teacher would, however, lose patience with Kebede on days when the consequences of his insomnia would get the better of him. Shifra would watch as Kebede's eyelids would grow heavy in the middle of an oral reading, prompting her to abruptly wake him to read the next paragraph. On other days, Kebede found himself struggling to focus during the four-hour long class, his mind drifting while the other students discussed the current events from the past few days.

"Kfir, can you *please* answer the question," Shifra demanded of him during a complicated lesson on how to use prepositions correctly.

Kebede was gazing out the window with a blank expression on his face, ruminating about the two nights that changed the course of his life forever—the night his abandonment of Tigest and his five offspring became an irreversible reality; and the night the short but muscular man took Kebede and hundreds of others like him, ushered them into tightly crowded buses and then into an even more crowded airplane, which flew them via a city in Europe called Brussels to Israel. That night Kebede trembled with excitement so much so that neither his sorely parched mouth nor the perspiring bodies pressed against him fazed him. That night, Kebede, fortunate enough to be crammed next to a window for most of the two flights, bade farewell to the pitch black of Sudan and woke up to the rays of sunshine beaming down on the Land of Israel.

Out of darkness comes light. Or so he had hoped.

"*Nu*, Kfir. I'm waiting," Shifra shot Kebede with a look of disappointment.

A young and motivated *ulpan* teacher, Shifra was not going to let a bright pupil of hers like Kfir slip through the cracks. Kebede continued to gaze out the window, still unaware that Shifra had called on him. It had been several weeks since he had adopted the name Kfir, and he had yet to get used to responding to it. Only when Shifra walked over to Kebede's desk and stood silently in front of him did he finally snap out of it, returning to reality.

"Ummm . . . I don't know *how* the question was," apologized Kebede in broken Hebrew as he looked on ashamedly.

Kebede had always been a diligent student in school and was proud of the fact that he had completed sixth grade, more than nearly any of the other villagers and certainly more than most of the other new immigrants studying Hebrew in *ulpan* with him. But he was not accustomed to being scolded by a teacher, especially a female teacher. In the short time he had been Shifra's student, Kebede grew to rely on her approval to help him get through his otherwise dispiriting days, and he prided himself on being the star pupil of the *ulpan*.

"You don't know *what* the question was," corrected Shifra in her firm but patient voice. She turned her back to the blackboard and pointed to the question at issue, providing Kebede a second chance to redeem himself. And redeem himself he did.

Kebede smiled with pride.

If only Kebede could feel outside of *ulpan* the way he felt while he was inside—that he was literally living and breathing his lifelong Zionist dream—then he would be able to rest at night.

If only he could keep moving forward, then he wouldn't need to look back.

But every night without fail, Kebede tossed and turned as images of Azmera and Tigest haunted him.

Kebede—January 1985

Tigy. I don't even know where to begin. First off, have you heard from Azmera or Solomon? I told Solomon to contact me immediately upon arriving in Israel, but I haven't heard a word. I heard that no more Jews are being brought to Israel for the time-being. Do you know when they made it to the camp in Country X?

This morning my ulpan *class went to Jerusalem for the first time. In my whole life, I will never forget that moment when I looked at the Western Wall, or the* Kotel *as the Israelis call it. They say that you can leave your prayers with God by writing them down on a piece of paper and sticking it into one of the*

Wall's many cracks. At first, I thought about praying that you and the children might come join me safely here in Israel, but I wasn't sure. It isn't so easy here. Israelis get up on the bus when I sit down next to them, and they mock my accent in Hebrew even when I am certain that I am speaking correctly. The way of life is just so very different from home. Nobody takes things slowly here. It's always rushing, rushing, rushing. But I don't have anywhere to rush to, no tending to the fields, no children to take care of, and no house to keep.

It's not all bad, of course. There are some amazing people here, too. There are some wonderful Israelis who volunteer at the Absorption Center. They bring piles of old clothes they no longer need and all the immigrants like me go sifting through them to find the right size. I guess one of the male volunteers is around my height, because the piles are full of clothes that fit me. You wouldn't even recognize me in my fancy American clothes! Still, I'm a thirty-year-old man with five children, and I feel humiliated every time I must accept charity. My Hebrew is improving every day, and spending time in ulpan *is good for me. It's the best part of my day. But then I go back to reality, a reality where I have to take lessons on how to become more Israeli (or less Ethiopian), where people tell me that I'm not really Jewish, and where the cars zooming past my room make my head go dizzy. I feel like I'm not the man I used to be. And I feel alone. And that's why I didn't know what my prayer should be—for me to go back home or for you to come join me here. But then, being at the Kotel—a place I've prayed towards my entire life—got the best of me. It's so powerful there, this feeling of truly being home, that I forgot all the bad. So I wrote in my piece of paper, in my newly learnt Hebrew, my one simple prayer to God. Please come, Tigest. Please come soon.*

Yours, Kebede.

p.s. What a long letter I wrote! It's funny how I feel like I can talk to you so easily when I don't have to speak.

Chapter Eight

Azmera—January 1985

Solomon led the way as usual, but even though the jerrycan was nearly empty and easier on his back, his stride was starting to lose its spring. Azmera was trailing behind, depleted of energy on this tenth day of their journey. Her body was emaciated, and her bones protruded outward more than they ever had. She knew that Solomon was secretly saving extra rations of food for Azmera at his own expense, but she never admitted knowing so, let alone thank him. Their relationship had evolved from one of mutual mistrust and disdain to a burgeoning father-daughter-like relationship between uncle and niece. Solomon's striking resemblance to Azmera's father helped trigger the change, but his quiet expressions of care tipped the balance, fostering their unexpected relationship.

Their journey's landscape slowly began to show signs of change, with the Simien Mountains descending into rolling hills, and the rolling hills unfolding into desert plains. Solomon plopped himself down to the ground and signaled it was time to take a break. The sun was climbing up the horizon, and Solomon had stumbled his way upon a small water hole in the rocky ground—the perfect place to rest for the day until the sun set again. Water had become scarcer as they approached the border with Sudan, the arid desert both foreign and unwelcomingly harsh. To compensate, Solomon had calculatingly reduced their rations of water to just a few sips at a time, each spaced out by increasingly long intervals of trekking.

Solomon and Azmera stared down into the water hole. Their stomachs churned when they saw a green layer of scum floating on top, shielding the water—if it could even be called that—from their sight. With a resigned look of disgust on his face, Solomon reached his hand and the now empty jerrycan deep into the water hole, doing his best to well for something resembling potable water to restore their supply. He brought the jerrycan up into the air as he and Azmera leered suspiciously into its contents, floating bugs and all. There wasn't much of a choice, they knew. There were only two options—drinking potentially disease-ridden water or drinking no water at all. Solomon instructed Azmera to collect firewood or, in the desert's absence of wood per se, anything that had the potential to burn. But Azmera didn't move an inch. She couldn't. Her body was too spent to search for kindling, and without the kindling she would surely die of dehydration. She had resigned herself to her certain fate.

"I need you to stay strong for me, Meri," whispered Solomon, while squeezing Azmera's gaunt shoulder.

Meri was what Kebede used to call her. In his own stoic way, the nickname her father had bestowed upon her had always been his way of expressing affection and intimacy for his eldest daughter, letting her know that he loved her without actually verbalizing it. It was the first time Solomon had ever called her by the same nickname, and something about it made Azmera feel alive again. Or at least feel like she wanted to stay alive, for now.

Azmera turned to look Solomon in the eyes and saw a look of desperation she had yet to see in her uncle's characteristically determined face. Something in his gaze told Azmera that he was at his breaking point too; until this moment, Azmera had been sure that Solomon was unbreakable. But here he was, pleading for her help. He seemed so very human to her, so very much in need. Azmera lifted herself up with energy she didn't know she had and started to scan the terrain for anything that could get a fire burning. They needed water; the filthy water needed to be boiled, and they needed fire to do so. For the first time since embarking on their journey, Solomon really needed *her*.

Azmera was surprised to see that there were still some signs of life around her, despite the desert surrounding them. Dry brownish bushes stood low to the ground, providing small but prickly branches that made for good kindling. Azmera twisted and snapped off as many twigs as she could carry and headed back to Solomon, proud of her collection. For the first time since she had embarked on this journey, she was sharing the burden. She handed the twigs to Solomon and then headed out again to bring another load. With mere twigs to start a fire, they would need lots of them.

"We are almost there, you know," said Solomon in a tired voice as he held a tin pot of water over the small fire struggling to stay alit, "I know you are tired. I am too. But I need you to push on through for a few more days until we make it to the camp in Sudan. We must arrive there before the mission comes to an end, which could be any day now. Otherwise we could be stuck in Sudan while your father is waiting for you in Israel. And from what I've heard, we do not want to get stuck in Sudan."

Solomon's ominous message alarmed her less so than the length of it. It was by far the longest combination of words Solomon had ever spoken to her. Solomon's increased willingness to communicate with Azmera motivated her to step up the pace just as much as the threat of being left behind in Sudan. Plus, her father—her *Abat*—was waiting for her. She couldn't let him—or Solomon—down. Azmera lifted up the pot and took a sip of water, refreshed and surprisingly undisturbed by the fact that it was still boiling hot and worryingly discolored. She then gave a sip to Solomon. He took one sip and then poured the rest of the water into the jerrycan, secured the cap, and placed it to the side for later.

Hours passed, and Azmera and Solomon had drifted off to sleep—

neither the strong sun shining down on them nor the rocky ground beneath them deterred their bodies from getting the rest it sorely needed. Even while sleeping, however, Solomon was always on guard, and he woke up suddenly with the sound of footsteps approaching from afar.

"Wake up now!" whispered Solomon, as he nudged at his niece's shoulder.

Azmera tried to turn her back to her uncle, desperate to continue sleeping just a bit more, but his nudging was insistent enough that she knew she needed to comply. Azmera pulled her body off the ground. By now she had learned to abide Solomon's commands without a second thought. Her blind obedience at the beginning of their journey was out of sheer fear, but over time she grew to deeply respect Solomon and his keen survival instincts. Without him by her side, Azmera knew she had no chance at all.

The two traveling companions heard a rustling sound approaching them. Aside from the occasional family of baboons or warthogs, Solomon and Azmera felt like it was just the two of them in this world, not having passed a single village ever since venturing beyond the Simien Mountains. The rustling loudened, to the point where Azmera could with near certainty confirm that someone—not something—was headed their way. At this point in her journey, Azmera was more comforted by the sight of almost any animal in the desert, no matter how ferocious, than the sight of another human being. At least animals' intentions adhered to some natural order she could anticipate and defend against.

At the edge of the horizon, two tall men threateningly approached Solomon and Azmera. Solomon looked at his niece, his face straining to look calm while his eyes darted back and forth between the two strange men and his niece he was entrusted with protecting. As they neared, Azmera noticed their skin, much darker than what Azmera was accustomed to seeing. Their features, too, were much more pronounced—their lips bigger, their noses wider, and their foreheads broader.

"What do you want?" asked Solomon, trying to muffle the trembling in his voice by shouting, "We have nothing to give you. Leave us alone."

It was clear from their total disregard for Solomon's plea that the men did not understand him. The taller of the two whisked out a machete from his knapsack and held it out for all to see. He pointed the knife in the direction of Solomon's bag, which had served them well as their survival kit for the journey thus far. The contents of the bag were slim, but they included the most basic necessities: their jerrycan, a pot for boiling water, a bag of teff seeds which they would soak in water and eat for nourishment, *kolo* roasted grains, Solomon's Ethiopian identification card, some Ethiopian *Birrs*, a small pocket knife, a blanket for warmth, the plastic poncho sack that had come to Azmera's rescue in the thunderstorm several days before, and of course *injera*. The bandits surely wouldn't be making off with a fortune, but they would be stripping Solomon of every possession left to his name and, more importantly, of his and Azmera's lifeline until reaching their destination. Handing it over, no matter how sharp the machete, was simply not an option. Solomon decisively picked up his knapsack and strapped it onto his back, as if to shield it from any imminent attack.

Azmera stood behind Solomon not knowing how to react. She knew she should let Solomon handle things—he was the responsible adult, after all—but she had a sinking feeling that he couldn't fend off two men, one of whom was armed, all by himself. Solomon needed Azmera, but her thoughts were clouded by the stress of their predicament. Azmera stared at her uncle, desperate for him to tell her what to do, but his attention was focused elsewhere. He was clearly attempting to distract them as he spoke to the two men in a language they didn't understand while he rummaged through the contents of his knapsack.

When it dawned on Azmera that her uncle was rummaging for the pocket knife, she felt proud of herself for finally thinking clearly. Azmera recalled watching Solomon pack and re-pack his bag countless times throughout their journey, so much so that she remembered that he always placed the plastic bag on the bottom of the bag, followed in meticulous order by the blanket, the jerrycan, tin pot, teff seeds, *kolo*, ID card and money. Without fail, the last item Solomon put into his knapsack was the knife, eight inches in length, sharp and long enough to serve the purpose for which it was intended—cutting rope, cutting wood, and fending off attackers when necessary. But this measly knife in no way was intended to defend against two large, grown men with a machete the length of Azmera's arm.

The two men stood twenty feet away from Solomon. Dusk was approaching and the sun was setting behind Azmera and Solomon, painting the sky with a swirl of pinks, oranges, and blues. Azmera could see the bandits squinting to keep the sun out of their eyes, their vision impaired by the setting sun's rays. Solomon stopped rummaging in his bag and began shouting at the bandits to stay away. Standing behind Solomon, Azmera reached her hand into his bag and discreetly pulled out the knife, which had fallen from the top to the side of the bag. She slipped the knife into her robe and placed it under her armpit, careful to make small movements so as not to attract any attention. She knew that the two men's eyes were focused on Solomon and not her, or at least as much as the blinding sun allowed.

"Leave us alone, I said," commanded Solomon, his voice tensing up as he began to sense that his pleas were fruitless. "This bag is no use to you, and we need it to survive. Go along, leave us alone and we won't tell the soldiers we saw you."

Solomon knew by looking at the men's hardened features that they came from Sudan and not Ethiopia, and thus were at risk of being arrested by Ethiopian soldiers patrolling the border if caught. He also knew that they understood some of the Amharic he had just spoken to them as he watched their eyebrows perk up with apprehension upon the mention of the threat of soldiers close by.

The two men turned to each other and exchanged a few words unintelligible to Azmera. Their words' deep guttural sounds left no doubt that they were speaking Arabic. The taller man thrust out his machete and made a threatening gesture towards Solomon as he pushed his way past him towards Azmera. He grabbed Azmera by the neck and shoved her down to the ground, her frail body futilely struggling to fight him off her.

"Solomon! Help me! Please!" Azmera screamed, desperate for him to come to her rescue.

The man was now holding down Azmera's shoulders, his fingers digging so deeply into her skin that she could feel the bruises being formed.

Knowing he had little chance against the machete, Solomon chose to strike the easier target first—the unarmed partner standing to the side. This bandit had a feeble frame, with little muscle to conceal his bones, and his eyes and teeth were yellow where they should have been white. He was in such shock at how the situation had escalated so quickly that he was blindsided by Solomon's fist-punch directly to his Adam's apple. He fell to the ground with a loud thump, startling his partner in crime who still had Azmera pinned to the ground. Azmera's attacker let go of her to turn his head to see what had befallen his weaker half. While he wasn't looking, Azmera pulled the knife out from her armpit and hid it in the palm of her sweaty hand.

Azmera knew that this was her chance. Until now, the entire turn of events had flashed by her in a split second, and her thoughts struggled to keep up with the pace. But now everything was in slow motion. Her sense of hopelessness was replaced by a sense of clarity and purpose. She knew what she had to do. She raised her hand and forcefully thrust the knife into her attacker's neck, aiming for the thick, bumpy vein bulging outward. Azmera closed her eyes and mouth as blood spurted all over her, the familiar salty taste seeping into her mouth nonetheless.

Solomon rushed to Azmera and pulled her out from underneath the unconscious man laying above her.

"Meri, *wow*! Thank God you are okay!" said Solomon to Azmera as he hugged her tightly for the first time ever. "Now let's get out of here in case they wake up," instructed Solomon, not knowing whether he and his niece had injured or killed their two attackers.

A surge of adrenaline rushed through Azmera's veins. She felt more of a survivor than she ever had in her entire life. She wiped the blood off the knife on the inside of her robe and returned it to Solomon's bag, placing it neatly on top of the rest of their belongings, where it belonged. She took a deep breath, trying to process everything that had just happened and everything that she had just done. She exhaled, knowing that she had to keep moving. She and Solomon turned their backs to the men passed out on the rocky ground and set off in the direction of the setting sun. Its magnificent colors were like a magnetic force that pulled them in, closer and closer to Sudan.

Chapter Nine

Tigest—1969

Mother Nature had been gracious in the rainy season of 1969. The rain fell nearly every day, rendering a sense of hope that the upcoming harvest season would be more fruitful than the previous one. While Tigest was elated to see her and Kebede's teff and corn fields thriving, she knew that the rain and mud meant that no doctor, not even the Italian doctor with all his charitable intentions, would be visiting their village any time soon. And so, she alone watched her belly grow with every passing day. With every kick, Tigest felt her love grow for the unborn baby conceived out of tears. With every kick, she felt herself more willing to forgive her husband for what he had done to her the night the baby was likely conceived.

While at first indifferent to his young wife's growing belly, Kebede found his parents' joy at the thought of becoming grandparents highly infectious. His wife had also seemed to soften and, as her pregnancy progressed, Kebede began to look his wife in the eye, and she at him, for the first time. He even found himself daring to pat Tigest's bare belly where, beforehand, the only time he ever dared touch his wife was when he was preparing to mount her. It was an optimistic time by all accounts. The teff seeds and his own seed were slowly sprouting, and life seemed to be blooming all around them.

After months of eager anticipation, the month of October and the harvest season was upon them. The roosters crowing would wake Tigest and

Kebede early each morning, after which the young couple would set out with their sickles in hand to begin the arduous process of reaping in their precious teff crop. It was their first harvest season as a married couple. Both Tigest and Kebede knew that their livelihood depended on this joint venture, one made possible by Kebede's father's generous wedding gift of two acres of farmland on lease from Christians from the neighboring village.

Tigest squatted down to get to work. She knew exactly what needed to be done despite being a relative novice. She recalled the countless times she would stare at her parents, watching them work away, doing what their ancestors before them had done. Now it was her turn, but she found herself losing her balance when she assumed the squatting position, her swollen belly making her top-heavy and liable to topple over at any moment. Tigest carried on, though, partly because she knew that the work had to be done, and partly because in her stubbornness she couldn't bear to admit weakness to Kebede. She carried on with the sickle in one hand, and the other hand supporting her back, which was now throbbing with pain.

By her estimate, the baby was due in another month, but Tigest couldn't be certain. The Italian doctor hadn't returned to their village since he first diagnosed the pregnancy. And while she undoubtedly remembered that fateful day when Kebede stripped her of her girlhood, there was no way to know for sure if that was indeed the day the baby had been conceived. The date of conception could just as likely have been in the weeks following their wedding day when Kebede, bursting with hormones and an inflated ego, had forced himself inside his wife on a regular basis.

Until this harvest day, Tigest had felt relatively strong and robust despite her pregnancy, leaving her confident in her ability to harvest the fields with Kebede. But the throbbing pain in her back was growing stronger, and Tigest couldn't bear it any longer.

"Kebede, I need to rest a few minutes," declared Tigest as Kebede toiled away while large drops of sweat slowly trickled down his face.

Kebede had become more and more protective of his wife in the past few months, taking over tasks that he otherwise would have demanded be done by her. In fact, the past few months caught Kebede by surprise. When he got married, he was fulfilling his competitive drive to marry the most beautiful girl, regardless of whether he loved her. It was just one of many competitions Kebede played out in his head against his friends, Zenebe and Mualalem, even though they themselves weren't always aware of it. He wanted to love her, of course, but Tigest had made it clear from the very beginning that her heart was closed off to him. As a defensive response, Kebede naturally closed his heart off to her. He never expected, therefore, that he would soften together with, or more likely in response to, his wife. Kebede still remained relatively aloof and detached, but he began to radiate a caring tenderness which was previously foreign to him. And no matter how detached he may have been from his wife, one thing was certain. Kebede had grown to respect Tigest—to respect her character and integrity, and above all, her work ethic. She wasn't just a beautiful face to him anymore. She knew as well as he did how important the harvest was for their future. Kebede knew his wife wouldn't complain unless she had a good reason for doing so.

"Okay, Tigy, but first let me try to make you more comfortable," said Kebede as he gathered teff stalks, golden and straw-like, and bunched them together to use as a pillow for Tigest's head and between her legs.

For months now, Tigest could only sleep on her side, and Kebede had quietly observed how each night his wife slipped a folded-up shawl to place between her legs for support. Kebede could see that Tigest was trying her best to swallow her pain, to no avail, but he couldn't imagine that his wife was about to give birth. After all, his entire childhood he had heard his mother's stories of how she carried Kebede in her belly for ten long months, and they had only gotten married around nine months ago. Regardless, Kebede had no idea how to relieve his wife's pain, so he continued to gather the teff as he listened to his wife's muffled whimpers of pain.

Tigest lay on the ground grateful for her husband's caring gestures. She knew something was wrong when she felt the throbbing shift from her back to her stomach and pelvic area. With each tightening of her belly, Tigest belted out screams of agony, causing Kebede to abandon his task at hand. Still children themselves, both Tigest and Kebede were terrified, alone and not knowing what to make of the pain. Kebede considered running back to the village to seek help but didn't want to leave Tigest by herself, and she was in no shape to move from the makeshift bed Kebede had made for her on the ground. Kebede sat next to Tigest as she let out an agonizing shrill.

"I'm wet, I'm wet!" announced Tigest, as she pointed downwards for Kebede to see.

They now knew exactly what was happening, and Kebede knew he had no choice but to see Tigest and, God willing, his baby through. He pulled up Tigest's gown, for the first time with no resistance from his wife, and saw a head full of black, curly hair peeking out.

"Push, Tigest, push" shouted Kebede, overcome by excitement as he watched his wife bring life into the world.

Tigest breathed deeply. A beastly scream, one that resembled the labor sounds made by the calves Kebede had birthed in the past, accompanied Tigest's pushing, and then it was all over.

Kebede held the waxy baby in his arms, terrified she might slip and fall. He whispered into her ear, "Welcome to our world, Azmera."

Tigest paused for a moment as she heard her baby girl's name, a name her husband had bestowed upon her without any prior consultation. As Kebede gently placed the baby girl in her mother's arms, Tigest looked all around her—at the harvest that would sustain them and enrich their lives. She realized that Azmera, "harvest", was the perfect name for this beautiful creature cradled in her arms.

Tigest—April 1985

Time seemed to stand still after Azmera left home, her absence starkly present. Tigest found herself so consumed by longing for her daughter, and so engrossed in making it through each long day with her four children, that she barely noticed her belly growing like a balloon slowly being inflated. It took little Gabra's not-so-gentle reminders to harshly snap her back into the present.

"*Enati*, is this where the baby is?" asked Gabra as she pointed to Tigest's belly button.

Tigest had explained to her countless times before that the baby was growing inside her belly, but Gabra insisted that Tigest's belly button—the one that stuck out ever so slightly ever since giving birth to Azmera and even more so now that she was pregnant again—was the baby-to-be. Tigest tried her best not to be perturbed by her little girl for pestering her night and day with questions about the baby—the baby whose existence she still hadn't come to terms with—for it was Gabra's enthusiasm that made Tigest feel like this baby might be a blessing after all. Tigest prayed in her heart that the baby would one day get to meet her older sister and her father, but she glossed over her prayer, which she knew was unlikely to be answered, by sharing a warm smile with Gabra.

"No, silly, that's my belly button, just like yours! The baby is here, inside my big belly bump," displayed Tigest as she placed her daughter's hand on top of her belly just as it was starting to move.

"And when will *she* come out?" inquired Gabra, impatient with the nine-month waiting period, but certain as ever that the little baby growing inside was going to be a girl like her, and not a boy. She was surrounded by brothers and was desperately missing her only sister. It was only fair, she figured, at least as far as four-year-old logic goes.

The three boys were busy in the corner of the hut building a model *gojo* out of sticks they had collected outside, but they still made sure to eavesdrop every word that Tigest uttered. For them, their mother had all but disappeared ever since Azmera left. While she was still there physically, her soul was nowhere to be found. Daniel, the ten-year-old boy going on thirty, sensed that his mother wanted nothing to do with this pregnancy, so he diligently instructed the other two boys to not inquire about it. So, while Tigest's belly grew and grew, the boys did their best to pretend like nothing was changing. Fortunately for them, their inquisitive baby sister, Gabra, served as their source of inside information, and the boys' ears eagerly perked up to catch every word that came out of Tigest's mouth whenever Gabra got around to nagging, which was nearly all the time.

"In about two full moons from now," explained Tigest, despite her knowing that Gabra's concept of time was limited to not much more than yesterday, today, and tomorrow.

What Tigest didn't know was that this time around the moons were not nearly as aligned as she had expected them to be.

Six pregnancies had come and gone for Tigest, and she had five healthy children to show for it. Even though one of her babies was long gone and in heaven, she knew how lucky she was, hearing story after story of women suffering from multiple miscarriages and stillborn babies, and even of women dying in childbirth. And while she was aware of the risks involved in bringing life into the world, a part of her was certain that these sorts of tragedies wouldn't befall her again. She was too strong. As were her children. Of course, they were—they were a part of her and Kebede. In this, her seventh pregnancy, however, Tigest couldn't help noticing that things were infinitely harder on her body. She was consumed by exhaustion all the time, and no amount of sleep provided any relief. The physical labor of maintaining her household and raising four children without the help of Kebede or Azmera was more demanding on her body than she had anticipated. Her stamina for standing and working the fields was limited to a few minutes at a time before she would find herself catching her breath while hurled over in discomfort.

But no amount of exhaustion or pain could serve as an excuse for not getting things done around the house. If she didn't do it, no one else would. She was the sole provider for her four young children. And so, despite the pulsing back cramps, Tigest sat herself on the floor first thing in the morning as her three boys indulged in a few more minutes of sleep before a day's worth of chores. She furiously kneaded the *injera* dough, all the while fending off Gabra, the family's early riser, from climbing on her to kiss her belly. Since Azmera's departure, Tigest was neither physically nor emotionally able to initiate any warmth towards her children, so she welcomed these displays of affection from her youngest daughter. And while she was saddened by knowing that she was practically invisible to her growing boys, at least Gabra still felt loved enough by her mother to not completely give up on her.

But when Gabra climbed on her shoulders, sending a throbbing pain to her lower back, Tigest startled herself by screaming at the top of her lungs, "Gabra, GET OFF OF ME NOW!"

Gabra, four years old and with skin thinner than Tigest would have hoped for from her own flesh and blood, burst into tears. She was insulted and reeling from rejection following her mother's harsh reaction. Irritated by her screaming four-year-old, Tigest called for Daniel to wake up and calm down his little sister so that she could endure her pain in relative silence. Tigest watched Daniel, still half-asleep, obediently stroke Gabra's hair. For a moment, she was even able to forget the throbbing pain and take some comfort in how lovingly her oldest son was caring for Gabra. Ever since Azmera left, Tigest had been nearly blind to the fact that Daniel, all ten years of him, had grown into a little man. In this moment she was finally able to see him for who he had really become—strong and reliable like her husband, but also blessed with a heart and compassion for others like her Azmera.

The *injera* dough was still full of lumps as Tigest, her hands sticky with dough, lay on her side trying to conceal her moaning so as not to alarm the children. She recognized this pain all too well. It was an agonizing pain that shot up and down her back. At the same time, she doubted herself—after all, it had been over four years since she had last given birth, and a woman's memory is short-lived when it comes to the labor of labor. This was the case even more so for Tigest, who had been considered by the other women in her village to be exceptionally fertile. Her history of pregnancy successes lent her an air of confidence bordering on arrogance regarding all things having to do with creating life. So, she could never have fathomed giving birth at such an early stage in her pregnancy—by her estimate, at least two months before her due date.

But Tigest could deny the meaning of the pulsating pain in her back only for so long. When she started gushing water all over the knitted rug, turning the dirt and dust below it into a pasty mud that seeped through and caked itself onto her bare legs, she knew.

"Daniel, run to Rokenach's hut and tell her that we need her, and a sterile knife, clean blankets and water, *now!*" Tigest ordered her eldest son.

Daniel obediently darted out of the hut and raced across the village to the home of Rokenach, who humbly served as the village midwife. She had birthed hundreds of babies including all of Tigest's children except Azmera. Tigest trusted Rokenach with her life and the life of her children not just because she didn't have any other choice, but also because Rokenach made up for a lack of formal schooling with an abundance of experience and intuition. Of course, she had lost many women and many babies, but she had saved far more. For that reason, her services were in high demand—not only in their village but also in the neighboring Jewish villages, including the village where Tigest had been born and raised.

When Daniel arrived at Rokenach's hut, he discovered that her popularity meant that his mother would be left without a midwife, at least for now. Rokenach's daughter politely informed Daniel that her mother had traveled the two kilometers to the neighboring village, Tigest's birthplace, earlier that morning upon being summoned by another woman in labor. Daniel dejectedly walked across the village back to his mother, knowing how disappointed she would be to see him walk through the door alone. The ten-year-old boy knew next to nothing about birthing a child, but he was a caring son who idolized his mother and listened to every word she said to him. With his mother's desperate request in mind, he diligently began passing from hut to hut, pleading with the other villagers to come to his mother's aid. Clean blankets and clean water were quite the commodity, however, and only after visiting four different families did he manage to acquire a jerrycan of clean water, which he continued to lug on his shoulders to three more homes until he finally managed to get a sterile knife, clean towels and blankets. While he wouldn't be coming home to his mother with Rokenach the midwife by his side, at least he wasn't empty-handed.

Tigest's eyes said it all to Daniel as he walked through the door. Over the years, Daniel's mother had uncharacteristically adopted some of his father's stoicism. Tigest rarely displayed any signs of concern—especially not to her children. Ever since his father and Azmera had left for Israel, his mother appeared all but extinguished on the inside, making it virtually impossible for Daniel to know how to please her. But today there was no hiding it—Daniel could see his mother's eyes widen with fear. She was terrified of what was about to happen to her, her baby, and her family.

"Arghhhh," Tigest moaned in between excruciatingly painful

contractions that sent waves of pain now not only up and down her back but also through her pelvic region. Tigest could tell by the frequency and duration of the contractions that things were progressing quickly—too quickly.

"Daniel, this baby is coming into the world too early, and there's nothing I can do to stop it," Tigest muttered as she choked on her tears.

She sensed an overwhelming feeling of guilt rise in her throat, feeling that the words she uttered to her son were not exactly honest. There was so much she *should have* done to stop it. She should have taken better care of herself; she should have asked for help from her parents; she should have rested more; she should have put her baby's health first ahead of her other worries. So many *should haves*, so many regrets. But now it was too late to turn back time. This baby was coming into the world, for however brief or long God saw fit.

Daniel sat by his mother's side without a clue as to how to help her. He couldn't bear the sight of his mother suffering so terribly, nor could he bear the thought of this little baby not surviving. After all, it was the anticipation of a new baby brother or sister that comforted Daniel and his siblings when it felt like their family was otherwise falling apart. And so, in his designated role as the man of the house, he knew he needed to shield his little brothers and sister from witnessing the trauma of their mother suffering in pain. He promptly ushered them out of the hut, hoping they could fend for themselves until this was all over. The ten-year-old boy, who had tried his best to be helpful to his mother ever since Azmera left home, sat next to his mother feeling utterly helpless. The only tangible comfort he could provide to his mother was his hand gripping hers ever so tightly.

Tigest dug her fingernails into Daniel's palm, hoping to find some release from the agonizing pain of it all. For a fleeting moment in between contractions, Tigest thought of Kebede and how he had no idea that she was about to give birth to his baby. Ironically, she wished that the man who had abandoned her was by her side. Tigest found herself trying to hold back from pushing, as if this somehow would keep the baby inside her womb for a bit longer—a few more minutes, a few more hours, and maybe even a few more days—anything to give her baby a fighting chance. But then her body took over, succumbing to the contractions. She pushed, and then screamed, and then pushed harder, and screamed even louder. Daniel tried his best to hold back his tears—after all, he was Kebede's son—but each one of Tigest's screams caused his eyes to well up until they were hemorrhaging saltwater. His body trembled from head to toe, until the very last scream was followed by a deafening silence.

Tigest squatted on the ground and caught the tiny baby girl in her arms, her body covered in a sticky mixture of dirt, blood, tears, and amniotic fluid. Daniel's trembling hands grabbed the knife and reluctantly cut the umbilical cord. Tigest held this little creature in her arms and marveled with awe and fear at how small she was—smaller than any baby she had ever laid eyes upon, let alone held. Her wrinkly skin and bony frame were a testament to the fact that her body longed for more time inside her mother's womb. Her small chocolate brown chest was sunken in and concave, heaving up and down with an alarming frequency. Not knowing what to do to help her baby, Tigest drew her wax-covered body onto her bare breast with the hope that the warmth of her touch together with the first suckling of her milk might do some good. She motioned to her son to bring her the blankets. She knew that a baby so small and with so little fat on her surely needed help staying warm. As she held her new baby girl close to her chest, Tigest thanked God for each thumping heartbeat and each strained breath. Her new baby—a baby whose existence Tigest had all but denied until this moment—was deeply loved by her mother, who was now terrified of losing her.

"Daniel, run to the *Kes* and tell him that our baby has come early, and we need to go to the hospital in Gondar right away," instructed Tigest, knowing that time was not on her little girl's side.

Gondar was a grueling day's journey by car from their small village. While Tigest could make it to the town clinic in Debark in just a few hours, she knew that there was little they could do to help her daughter without a full-time doctor on hand and with lines that wrapped around in circles from dawn to dusk. The trip to Gondar, however, would be prohibitively expensive, and Tigest was in no state to collect *tzedakah* from the other villagers. Besides, despite all their hardships, Tigest knew that she was well-off relative to her neighbors. After all, she was married to the son of the former village *Kes*.

In all the years since having married Kebede, Tigest had learned to forgive her parents for having abandoned her—until now. Here she was with a baby in her arms straddling between life and death, no husband by her side, with four other young children to take care of. She felt angrier at them than she ever had. She belted out a roaring scream, sending Daniel darting out of the *gojo* to seek aid.

Several years before Kebede abandoned his family for Israel, his parents both died, with only a few months separating them from their respective last days on earth. His mother died from pneumonia, killing her before she was able to seek medical attention. His father died several months earlier. His position as the village *Kes* made him a visible target to the Christians from the region. He presumably was attacked and killed while on his way to Debark to purchase kerosene, although the family never found his body—his murder a mere presumption that grew more reasonable over time. Kebede's parents' death seemed to have little effect on Kebede, nor on Tigest, at the time; she had never stopped resenting them for the role they played in forcing her to marry their son, and they never seemed to warm to her, viewing her as unworthy of their eldest son. An unexpected consequence of their death was that it significantly diminished Tigest and her family's social standing in their village. This was even more so the case the day Kebede left Ethiopia for Israel, as Tigest herself had no roots of her own in the village. She had lived there now for half her life, but never made an effort to befriend other women—it was her own subtle way to rebel against Kebede and the life that had been forced upon her. Tigest felt like an outsider in the village—and with Kebede's departure, the other villagers treated her that way too.

It was for this very reason that Daniel, in his desperate attempts to come to his newborn sister's aid, ran out the door of his family's hut, and instead of running to the *Kes*, he ran past all the other huts, all the other goats and chickens, and the sprawling teff field that bordered the village. Daniel kept running the two kilometers until he reached the village of his grandparents, Tigest's parents. Tigest would take the children to her childhood village to visit their *Ayat* and *Setayat* at most twice a year, finding the four-kilometer hike with five children to be too challenging to undertake on a regular basis, even for her. Instead, Tigest made it clear to her parents that the burden of maintaining any meaningful relationship with her children was on them—after all, they were the ones who banished her from her home and village and sentenced her to a life with Kebede. Nonetheless, they rarely visited their daughter and grandchildren. They wanted to, but their visits always seemed so fraught with tension that avoidance became the easier option. And yet, Daniel, a boy who was proving to be even more resilient than his father, had memorized the way to his grandparents, a way marked by horse droppings and well-traveled trails of trampled-on grass.

Tigest's parents were shocked to see their grandson at the entrance to their *gojo* as sweat and tears ran down his soft complexion and bony cheeks. They hadn't seen Daniel or the rest of the family for months. And while Tigest's parents had received word from traders in their village that Azmera had already ventured on the journey to Israel, the news of Tigest's pregnancy and early childbirth came as a shock to them. They had so many questions to ask their grandson, but he had few answers to give them. So, instead of talking, Tigest's parents started doing. They quickly set out to solicit money or goods tradable for money from everyone in their village.

"Tigest and her little baby are in dire need of our help. Please don't forsake my daughter. She is still a part of this village, and we all need to take care of one another," pleaded Abaynesh from all of her neighbors, walking from hut to hut and begging earnestly one by one.

Abaynesh and Tigest's father, Avraham, were proud and humble people who typically shied away from asking for favors. But word of Tigest's situation left no room for their ego, only room for action. Remarkably, one by one, Tigest's mother and father managed to collect a significant sum of money; a gold Star of David necklace from Tigest's childhood best friend, Liya; several crinkled bills of *Birrs* from the village *Kes* and his grown son who had attended school with Tigest; and a total of three sacks of teff flour—practically more valuable than gold these days—collected a cupful at a time from those who had nothing else to give but nonetheless wanted to help.

Armed with cash and collateral, Tigest's parents marched determinedly towards Tigest's village, together with their grandson.

"If we sell the sacks of teff flour, we should have enough money for Tigest to take the bus to Gondar," reasoned Avraham, breathing a sigh of relief as he tightened his grip on Daniel's hand.

"True," replied Abaynesh, "but that baby's bound to catch something deadly being around so many strangers. We are going to need more money to hire a private car from Debark to drive us, but time is short," asserted Abaynesh. Her years of experience raising her own children had taught her that newborn babies were susceptible to a variety of illnesses, particularly a baby born as prematurely as Tigest's.

"We are going to have to sell it," concluded Abaynesh, as she looked at the cardboard jewelry box in her hands. The gold necklace inside was untarnished and unique with its exquisitely detailed Star of David charm. It was surely worth more than enough to shuttle Tigest back and forth to Gondar multiple times. But the lack of prospects for finding a willing buyer at a time when people's stomachs and pockets were both starkly empty rendered it practically worthless.

"Abaynesh, you tend to Tigest, and Daniel and I will keep walking towards Debark to see if anyone at the market is willing to pay a reasonable price for the necklace. If we don't come home by sundown with the money in hand, Tigest and the baby will have to take the bus to Gondar. There is no other way," asserted Avraham.

Abaynesh nodded obediently and parted ways from her husband and grandson, turning left on the trail that led to her daughter's village, while Avraham and Daniel continued to walk in the direction towards Debark. Named for the great generosity of spirit her parents hoped for her, Abaynesh felt like a part of her had been extinguished ever since she had arranged for Tigest to marry Kebede. She knew Tigest still resented her for that day, but she also knew that what she had done—arranging for her daughter to marry Kebede, the eligible bachelor son of the well-respected *Kes* from the neighboring village—was the best choice she could have made for her daughter at the time, even if Tigest was more than two years younger than she was when her parents arranged for her marriage to Avraham. The physical and emotional distance she had created from her daughter left her heart feeling as empty as her stomach these days. But as she saw the *gojos* made out of sticks and mud populating Tigest's village on the horizon, Abaynesh sensed a wave of relief strangely overcome her. After all these years, her maternal instinct to give to her daughter was being triggered again. And while she knew how her daughter justifiably felt aggrieved by her, she prayed to God that her daughter would be willing to accept her help and, if lucky, forgive her for all she had done.

The *gojo* Tigest now called home was eerily silent as Abaynesh approached it. Even her typically rambunctious young grandchildren were sitting on the ground outside their home in complete silence, their stunned faces a testament to what awaited Abaynesh inside. As she tiptoed indoors,

Abaynesh heard a low-pitched wailing accompanied by whimpering hyperventilation, and helpless cries; they came not from the newborn baby, but Tigest herself. Her daughter lay in a pile of blankets and towels smeared with blood and damp from the fluid that had safely housed the baby until a mere few hours before. Tigest looked up at her mother. All the tears she had heroically tried to hold back until now came flowing out of her eyes like Israel's Jordan River. No matter how old Tigest was, and no matter how many children she birthed and raised, it never ceased to amaze her how the sheer sight of her mother could make her feel like a little girl again. Despite her mother's betrayal of Tigest's trust, she was still the only person in her life that truly allowed Tigest to let down her guard.

"Tigest, my dear," said Abaynesh, her voice calm and resolute, "Daniel came to us and shared the news. I am so sorry, but now is not the time for pity or despair. We must do everything we can to save this little baby's life. Here—drink water, drink it all." Abaynesh shoved the water at her daughter only as a mother can do, "It will help your milk to come in. Now drink!"

Tigest listened to her mother and gulped down a jug of water so fast that droplets spilled out of the side of her mouth, wetting her clothes even more, and wetting the blankets wrapped tightly around her baby.

"Now," instructed Abaynesh, "in addition to nursing her as much as you can, you need to make sure that your baby stays warm. Keep her surrounded by blankets all the time, no matter how warm you think it feels to you outside." Tigest nodded, unable to speak without succumbing to tears. Her mother continued, "Best of all—place her on your bare chest while she nurses with a blanket over her and let her skin touch your skin. You need to hold that baby and not let go—your milk and your warmth is what will keep her alive. Your job now is to take care of the baby and my job is to take care of you and the children. Don't worry about anything else."

Tigest nodded again, surprisingly calmed by her mother's directives, and reassured that someone was by her side who knew what to say and do.

To her surprise, her mother provided even more relief when she informed her, "Your *Abat* and Daniel are on their way to Debark right now with a gold necklace we borrowed from Liya in hand, and with teff flour they managed to collect from the other villagers. Everyone did their best to give whatever they could to help you, Tigy. *Abat* and Daniel will do their best to sell it all in the market and should hopefully be back here in the next few hours with the money needed to get you to the hospital in Gondar."

Overwhelmed by a panoply of emotions, Tigest burst into tears, no longer concerned that her children waiting outside might overhear their mother's breakdown. She felt utter gratitude that her parents, and villagers and friends from her childhood, had come to her rescue after all these years of distance and detachment. Her heart couldn't stop racing when she understood that there was a chance, albeit a small one, that her baby might be in the care of a doctor by day's end.

As Tigest lay on the ground with her baby lying on her chest, Tigest thought how it was ironic that she now found herself praying to God for a crying baby after years wishing that her babies would stop crying and let her rest for a moment or relieve herself. She reminisced how she and Kebede always bestowed their babies with a name immediately after birth, the bestowal's immediacy an important recognition of the baby's personhood, despite its small size. With her boys, of course, they didn't publicly announce the name until after the *brit milah* or circumcision. Now, however, Tigest was terrified to give her baby a name. It would only make her more of a person to her than she already was, and more of a loss if she were not to survive.

The sun had been up for several hours, its rays beginning to warm the *gojo*. The baby was now a few hours old, but except for a few partial awakenings marked by a whimper and flailing of her frail arms, she had been fast asleep ever since birth, her heartbeat fluttering against Tigest's chest. Tigest felt her frustration mounting as the baby still hadn't managed to successfully latch on to her increasingly swollen breasts, despite her countless attempts. In her breasts lay the key to her baby's survival, but alas it could not be forced. Her baby had to be a willing participant to partake of it, and she currently was not. In fact, it appeared that Tigest's baby had very little fight in her. There was only so much Tigest could do to fight on her behalf.

"Merciful *Elokeem*," Tigest mumbled as she gazed up at the sticks and mud holding together the roof that had sheltered her family for all these years, her face puffy and swollen, "What did I ever do to deserve this?"

Tigest paused for a moment to catch her breath and looked down at her baby lying on her chest, "What did my baby ever do to deserve this?" Tears came streaming down Tigest's face as she grabbed on tightly to her baby's tiny hand. "I can't take it anymore. First Kebede leaves me, then Azmera, and now this. I am a strong woman, I am. But this is more than I can handle."

Tigest then directed her gaze back towards her mother, desperate for words of reassurance. Instead, Abaynesh simply stroked her daughter's hair and grabbed on tightly to her daughter's hand.

"*Enati*," Tigest whispered to her mother as if someone else might hear what she was about to say, "You know, Kebede had no idea I was even pregnant. He left for Israel before I even began to show, and anyway we barely ever spoke to one another. And now . . . now . . . what do I do if this baby doesn't survive? Do I tell him? Do I not? Will he blame me?"

"Don't you dare start going down that track, Tigy. Don't you think about anything but the here and now, nothing but this little baby," ordered Abaynesh with a certainty in her words that she lacked in her heart.

Abaynesh was shocked to hear that her daughter had never shared the news of her condition with Kebede—the revered son of the former village *Kes* so respected by all. She had always hoped and prayed that Tigest would warm to Kebede with the passage of time, and vice versa, and that she would ultimately forgive her mother for forcing her to marry him so many years ago. But Abaynesh couldn't ignore the many red flags indicating this was not the case, Kebede's abandonment of Tigest and his family and Tigest's and Kebede's lack of communication the reddest of all.

Tigest wiped the tears away from her eyes and tried her best to not cry, but every time she started to sing to her baby, the tears came gushing out all over again. Tigest thought to herself what her mother would always tell her when she was a little girl and was upset about something.

"When talking makes you lose control of your emotions," Abaynesh would tell her while holding her tightly in her arms, "then just be quiet until you've calmed down."

Tigest listened to her mother and stopped talking and singing, instead assuming a silence which finally gave her the strength to compose herself again. Once she stopped crying, she was able to shift her attention to her baby's movements, however few.

Tigest's body jumped with excitement when she heard her baby whimper loudly, louder than ever, so loud that it bordered on a cry. Tigest rushed to take advantage of her baby's wakefulness, and positioned her baby's small, pink lips close to her breast. To her great relief, the little creature in her arms opened her mouth. She was awake and ready to suckle from the source of life her mother so desperately longed to give her. With her mouth wide open, the baby frantically moved her head back and forth, letting out a cry of frustration until Tigest ever so gently guided her nipple into her baby's mouth. She reveled in that sweet moment when her baby latched on to her breast for the very first time, giving Tigest a small glimmer of hope that everything might be okay after all.

Chapter Ten

Azmera—January 1985

"The camp is not far away, Meri," explained Solomon as he looked back at Azmera dragging her feet, "We're almost there, you just have to be strong for just a bit longer."

"You," he paused to reconsider, "*we*—can make it."

Every time Azmera felt like she couldn't carry on any longer, Solomon had this remarkable knack for lifting her spirit and giving her the strength she needed to continue on. Solomon's skill for reading his niece was especially remarkable since he barely knew her before embarking on this journey. Yes, he was her father's brother, and would visit from time to time to celebrate a holiday or to chat with his older brother over three cups of *bunnah* coffee, but he never made the slightest effort to get to know Azmera, let alone speak to her. This had always been a particularly stinging affront to Azmera. She was his oldest niece, after all. But that was all in the past. Azmera had grown to deeply revere her uncle. She was in awe of his navigating skills, which he successfully displayed time and time again despite never having journeyed this far in the direction of Sudan. She admired his physical and mental toughness, which kept him going despite being weighed down by the heavy jerrycan and other contents inside his knapsack; and which kept her going even when she wanted to give up. She appreciated his kind and caring nature, which she never knew existed until now. With

Solomon by her side, Azmera felt much like a sheep being led by a shepherd, blindly but trustingly following her uncle wherever he took her.

"Listen carefully, Meri." Solomon squinted his eyes as he gazed at the dust and fog clouding the dirt path ahead of them. "In about one kilometer, we will reach the village of Metema. It's on the border with Sudan. Most of the Jews coming to Sudan up until now crossed the border by walking through the Atbarah River a few miles north of Metema, but they were in large groups and could fend off bandits more easily than just the two of us— plus, a large group passing through Metema wouldn't be able to go undetected like we can. I have decided to avoid more run-ins with bandits and walk to the camp through Dinder National Park where the only threat is from wild animals. Besides, my people tell me that there are very few Sudanese border patrol police manning the border by Metema there these days, so it's our job to find where we can slip in without anyone noticing."

The look of concern on Solomon's face alarmed Azmera. She listened attentively, knowing that, despite the strenuous journey, the cold and rain, and the bandits they had already overcome, their journey—and the relentless dangers it presented—was far from over.

"When we reach the village," Solomon whispered, even though the only eavesdropping ears were the desert's creatures burrowed under the sand, "your job is to blend in and not bring attention to yourself. If anyone asks, tell them that I am your father. Tell them we are Christians and came from Shinfa, the neighboring village, to mourn the passing of your grandfather."

Solomon passing for Azmera's father seemed to be a bit of a stretch— after all, he was much younger than her real father—but Azmera listened and committed to memory her new identity until she would reach the other side of the border.

As each day of their journey had passed, Azmera began to notice her body changing before her own eyes. Gone was all of her baby fat, and her legs, while always strong compared to those of the other girls in her village, were now thinly sculpted with muscles that popped out of her skin. Her stomach muscles were now visible to her eye whenever she would undress, and the biceps in her arms now resembled her mother's—muscles she earned from years of carrying babies and water from the stream. Azmera took delight in being able to keep up with Solomon's grueling pace without losing her breath, and in knowing that her uncle must have taken notice of her improved gait and endurance. Azmera, then, was unfazed by the final kilometer remaining before reaching the border town of Metema. With Solomon leading the way, Azmera walked down the path paved by rocks and sand, her feet sinking softly into the ground with every step.

"Fantastic, Meri. We are making great time," commended Solomon, whose words of encouragement reminded her of how she would fill up with pride every time her teacher, Alazar, would comment on how beautifully she could read—a skill foreign to most girls her age.

Behind them, the sun was just making its appearance on the horizon, marking the end of yet another night spent walking the land.

"This is just as I had planned," Solomon asserted proudly, "We will arrive in Metema right as the market is opening. That way, no one will suspect us."

They walked until they saw a road in front of them lined with shops selling jerrycans, kerosene, teff flour, and random, out-of-place items like T-shirts with English letters plastered on their front. Azmera noted to herself how much Metema resembled Debark. They were both transit towns with one main dirt road cutting straight down the middle of the town, with shops and *gojos* on the side and the local market at the road's end.

"I remember when I used to go to the market with *Abat* in Debark when I was a little girl," reminisced Azmera out loud, knowing that, with the mention of Kebede, Solomon was surely listening to her even though pretending not to be. "I remember how colorful and plentiful everything was. Those used to be my favorite days, you know—the days when I got to go to the market with *Abat*. It was like he was a different person when it was just the two of us. Kinder. More patient. He actually talked me to, and listened to what I had to say."

Azmera paused as she felt her heart twinge. "At home, he was always working, and never spent much time with us. I always got the feeling that he wanted to keep his distance from *Enati* . . ."

Solomon's gaze met Azmera's, letting her know that, despite his silence, he was listening.

"Plus, market day with *Abat* was the one day of the month where *Enat* didn't have a list of chores for me to do!" added Azmera with a smile.

As she spoke, Azmera looked despairingly at the market in front of her, saddened by the slim pickings of vegetables. There was no fruit. The onions were the size of garlic cloves and the few tomatoes for sale were dented all over with bruises. Walking through the market, she saw more empty stands than those manned by a merchant. The drought was making a mockery of the market and what it once was.

When she passed by a stand selling fresh *injera*, Azmera's appetite awakened, reminding her how hungry she was. She had grown accustomed to eating in rations long before embarking on the journey with Solomon, and her hunger pangs had dulled in intensity over time. But now, with the smell of fresh *injera* wafting into the air, her mouth began to water so much she had to be careful not to drool. Instinctively, she did as she always did when the need for food consumed her—she bit hard down on her lip, tasting her blood, sweet and salty, in her mouth.

Azmera hurried past the *injera* stand, knowing she couldn't stand much more temptation. She wandered throughout the market, past one merchant selling *kolo* and another merchant selling bags of teff flour. She reveled in the few minutes of leisure time Solomon had allotted to her to walk in whichever direction she chose. Much like in Debark, she felt eyes on her everywhere she went. She began to wonder to herself whether everyone around her knew that she was Jewish. She tried to calm herself down as she looked all around her at the merchants and the villagers who, in her mind, all seemed to look just like her. Of course, each person had their own unique characteristics—one tall and another short; one with a wide nose and one with a narrow one—but they all more or less seemed to dress the same and have the same skin color and same type of hair as she did. But then Azmera recalled how the boys from the Christian village near the stream used to taunt her whenever she would run into them on her way to collect water, calling her a "stinky Jew," even though as far as she knew there was nothing outwardly Jewish about her for them to identify. Azmera began to wonder if Jews really did smell differently, concerned that her assumed identity as a Christian might have unknowingly been compromised.

Azmera flinched when she felt someone grab her shoulder from behind, certain that she had been figured out. Instead, she was relieved when she turned around to find Solomon, offering her a piece of warm and fluffy *injera*.

"Girl, what's the matter with you? I tried calling out your name over and over, but you just seemed to be in another world," scolded Solomon.

Azmera was embarrassed when she realized that her sense that everyone's eyes on her was not due to her being Jewish but rather because her uncle had been calling out her name repetitively, with no response.

In an effort to change the subject, Azmera asked, "Are you offering me *injera*? We can afford to spend our money on it?"

Solomon explained to her that he had set money aside for this very purpose; if they were to play the part of father and daughter from the neighboring village coming to the market to shop, they would of course have to buy something, and what better than fresh *injera*, and another bag of fresh *kolo* already stashed away in Solomon's knapsack, to rejuvenate them before leaving Ethiopia and its food behind them.

Azmera held the *injera* in her hand. It was neatly folded into a puffy triangle and marked with tiny holes all over. She savored the smell for one more moment before devouring it. With each bite, she couldn't help but think of her mother and how she used to relish the sweet and tangy smell of *injera* wafting through her family's hut every time she prepared it. As she was about to take her last bite, Azmera thought to herself that this could be the last piece of *injera* she would ever eat. Surely, no *injera* could be found in the refugee camp in Sudan, let alone in Israel. Her nostalgia succumbed to her appetite as she swallowed the last bite with bittersweet delight.

"Okay, Azmera, the break is over," instructed Solomon as he wiped a sticky *injera* crumb plastered to his lower lip, "It's time to make our move."

They had successfully made their appearance in the village exactly as planned—father and daughter on an outing to the market—without arousing any suspicions. It was time they crossed the border.

Solomon began walking to the far end of the village, with Azmera on his tail. Not knowing what to expect on the other side, Azmera felt her heart beating through her shirt like a curled-up fist pounding from within.

"In just a few minutes, God willing, we'll reach the border with Sudan," announced Solomon.

Azmera thought to herself how arbitrary the border they were about to cross really was—just a few measly meters separated her from a foreign country, language, religion, and people. She knew nothing about Sudan except the frightening encounter they had had with the bandits earlier in the journey. It was an ominous introduction to the country they would now stay in until Israel came to take them home.

As they neared the edge of the village, Azmera looked ahead and saw nothing but a vastness flat and wide that seemed to go on forever. The grueling hills of the Simien Mountains had come to an end, and with the *injera* having replenished her body, her legs now moved with great ease, as if she were walking on clouds. While Azmera's legs had welcomed the change in topography, her chest quickly began to curse it—the desert land spewed dust directly into her lungs, sending her into a coughing fit just before they managed to reach the border.

"You have to get that coughing under control, Meri," ordered Solomon, "You are bringing unwanted attention to us."

Solomon explained to Azmera that in this region of the country, people's bodies surely had adapted to the harsh physical conditions including the dust in the air. A coughing spell could raise a red flag, Solomon warned, so Azmera did everything she could to keep herself from coughing. She held her cough down deep in her throat as her eyes welled up with tears.

They had escaped unwelcome scrutiny by the villagers in Metema so far. The only people who seemed to notice them were two teenage boys who had been unloading sacks of teff flour from a white pick-up truck covered in dirt stationed at the edge of the market. As Solomon and Azmera approached them, the boys uncomfortably stared down the girl, but Azmera was confident that their gawking was triggered by her looks rather than any suspicion of her identity. These two boys, bursting with hormones, had simply been hypnotized by Azmera's natural beauty, which was still apparent despite her stained robe and matted-down hair. There was no cause for worry.

"There's the border up ahead," pointed Solomon, with a rare air of excitement in his voice.

Azmera stared ahead at the border in front of her and thought to herself how curious it was that the border between two countries—especially two countries openly hostile towards one another—could be as invisible as the one standing before her. No army or fence marked the end of Ethiopia and the beginning of Sudan; instead, what lay ahead of her looked exactly like what she was leaving behind her—dry, brittle land with a vastness that made one gasp for air.

"Tell me, Solomon," questioned Azmera with an air of newfound familiarity, "How do you even know this is the border? I mean, it all looks the same to me."

"You're right about that—it does all look the same. But do you remember last year all those nights when your father and I would meet to milk the goats?" asked Solomon, "Your father and I would leave in the early evening to milk the goats so you'd have milk the following day."

Azmera remembered that each morning, she and the other children would thirstily wake up to a glass bottle filled with fresh goat milk, which they would then ration according to age and need for calories; the ration Azmera typically received was less than a cupful.

"You know, milking a goat isn't easy business, but you get used to it after a while. What I'm trying to tell you is . . . well, it doesn't take all night long to milk the goats, Meri . . ." explained Solomon, hesitant to reveal the secret he had kept all this time.

"What do you mean?" asked Azmera, not understanding what her uncle was trying to hint to her.

"What I'm about to tell you, girl, has to stay a secret. You understand? If word got out about this, it could endanger the lives of our family back in the village," cautioned Solomon, as Azmera eagerly nodded her head, thinking his demand for secrecy a bit silly—she had no one to tell anyway.

"Your *Abat* and I would meet every evening to milk the goats. That never took any longer than an hour," explained Solomon in a soft whisper, "Afterwards we went to the synagogue and met with the other leaders in the village and memorized by heart the way to Sudan. We learned different routes, not just one, just in case we needed to change plans. Every pebble, every hilltop, every river . . . we committed it all to memory. If anyone ever saw us, we just told them we were at *maariv*, doing our evening prayers."

Azmera was amazed to learn how her father had kept such a huge secret from her all this time. She wondered whether her mother was aware of it all.

As if he read her mind, Solomon responded, "Tigest knew. She didn't know all the details, of course, but she knew that we were meeting for more than just milking goats. She knew we were planning the journey. It was the village's big secret that everyone knew about."

And, with that, Azmera felt again betrayed by her mother for hiding this plan which had been in the works for more than a year. Betrayed by her mother for cooperating with the plan that would forever change her and her family's lives.

Solomon continued to explain how *Kes* Yonas, who headed the covert effort on behalf of his village, forbade those embarking on the journey to Sudan to carry a map with them, lest the map be discovered by the Ethiopian authorities on the way and raise any suspicions. Solomon explained how they were taught to find north by looking at the sun and the hour hand on his wristwatch, a purchase he had made in Debark months earlier; how he pored over maps well into the night; and how he and all the others had to pass a "readiness" test before they were given permission to leave.

"These meetings are still taking place, as we speak," Solomon whispered, even though no one else was around to hear. "The leaders change hands each time someone leaves. I was one of the leaders, and now here we are, ready to cross into Sudan," Solomon explained, breathing a sigh of relief as he let go of the secret he had been keeping to himself for such a long time.

Azmera listened, aghast at how complex and well-planned this journey really was.

The pair spent the rest of the day outside Metema—a mere hundred meters from the border—hiding behind a dry brush that managed to camouflage them only when lying down.

"We will camp out here for the rest of the day until the sun goes down," Solomon explained, his voice quivering with excitement. "For now, you need to get some sleep," he instructed.

Azmera tried her best to do as Solomon told her but couldn't. Her stomach was churning in circles, and she couldn't comprehend how her uncle could possibly sleep at a time like this. Even at the young age of fourteen, Azmera understood that what lay ahead of her could determine the course of the rest of her life. Once they crossed the border, there was no turning back—Ethiopia would be a part of her past, Sudan her present, and, God willing, Israel her future. Azmera had never had trouble falling asleep in the past, but the excitement of what lay before her, combined with Solomon's snoring, the dust in the air, and the scorching sun beaming down on her, made it next to impossible for her to sleep. Time seemed to stand still for Azmera as she lay there in the brush, awake by herself and terrified of being caught. As the day ended and the sun lowered into the ground, Azmera finally felt her eyelids growing heavy as she succumbed to a deep sleep.

"Wake up, Meri," shouted Solomon as he shook Azmera with both hands, "It's time to get moving."

Azmera struggled to wake up from the deep sleep she had just entered, her body like a sack of teff flour that could not be lifted from the ground.

"Just five more minutes, please!" begged Azmera of her uncle, a useless plea to buy her a few more minutes of slumber.

"We don't even have one more minute, girl. It's time to get moving. *Don't* make me say it again!" Solomon ordered.

Azmera knew from the tone of Solomon's voice that negotiating with him for a few more minutes rest was futile. She reluctantly dragged herself off the ground and brushed herself clean of the brittle grass stuck to her gray smock.

Nightfall had come and the stars shining brightly in the sky were all that were visible to see. The air was crisp and clean—a pleasant change from the hot sun beating down on them earlier in the day—and Azmera felt invigorated as she took a deep breath and stretched her arms high to the sky. They began walking, with Azmera tailing behind Solomon and the heavy knapsack on his back. Azmera mimicked Solomon's every move. When Solomon slowed down to a halt, so did Azmera. She watched as he scanned the horizon looking for border guards on duty. Solomon eyed one guard in the distance holding what must have been a flashlight and gestured to Azmera to take notice.

"Meri, come here," commanded Solomon in a whisper Azmera could barely understand.

Azmera moved closer to Solomon so that he could whisper directly into her ear.

"It's almost 22:00, which is when the Sudanese soldiers are supposed to change guard duty," Solomon explained, "We have a few more minutes before we cross."

With a slow nod of her head, Azmera signaled to Solomon that she was ready.

"Hopefully, the guards will be so busy changing duties that they'll miss us as we cross the border. From now on, not a word, you understand?" commanded Solomon, "And walk on your tiptoes. If you must cough, swallow it down. If you must sneeze, hold it in. For the next five minutes, you are quiet as a field mouse!"

The two continued to walk, this time slightly changing their direction to avoid the guard they had seen earlier. The moon above their heads looked like a thin smile rotated on its side. The night sky was so dark that Azmera followed Solomon by listening to his feet landing ever so softly on the ground.

Suddenly, Azmera heard Solomon's feet come to a stand, and she did the same.

"We made it, Meri," announced Solomon, this time in a tone a bit louder than a whisper, "we're on the other side."

Azmera breathed a sigh of relief, thinking to herself how crossing the border was easier than she had ever imagined.

"We made it!" cheered Azmera, as she ran to Solomon and hugged him, catching him off guard. "Now what?" his niece asked, her voice filled with optimism.

"Now we walk to the camp," announced Solomon with a heavy sigh,

"The journey is far from over."

Just as Azmera freed herself from her uncle's arms, she heard a clicking sound. The sound eerily brought back memories of how Ethiopian soldiers would pay a visit to her village and cock their guns announcing their arrival, threatening to kill each family unless they handed over all their money. She and Solomon turned around, shocked to see the barrel of a rifle pointing at their heads.

The soldier shouted something indecipherable to both Solomon and Azmera, but nonetheless the two stood with their arms in the air, pleading for their lives.

"Wait," begged Solomon in Amharic, while gesturing to the soldier to hold his fire.

Solomon grabbed for his knapsack, alarming the soldier, who then thrust the rifle up against Solomon's head. Breathing heavily, Solomon reached his hand into his bag. Azmera felt her legs warm with urine as she watched her uncle's death—and hers—unfold right in front of her eyes. Would *Enati* even know if she were to die right here? An image of her mother rocking her back and forth in her lap flashed through her head.

Solomon fumbled around in his bag searching for something. Azmera found it surprising that the soldier held his fire, exercising an extraordinary amount of patience under the circumstances; after all, for all the soldier knew, Solomon could be preparing an attack on him. Solomon pulled a crumpled envelope out of his bag and opened it up for the soldier, the slivered moon providing just enough light for him to see a wad of 1000 *birr* being offered him in exchange for their lives. Azmera's jaw dropped to the ground. She had never witnessed such a large sum of money in one place. The soldier, however, seemed far less surprised than Azmera. He snatched the money out of Solomon's hand like it was his entitlement. The soldier lowered his rifle and counted the cash in his large, muscular hands. Taking bribes from border-crossers was how this soldier sent money home to his family every month; the 1000 *birr* being offered to him would feed his wife and children for months to come. He turned his back on the Ethiopians and motioned for them to continue their way.

They had made it into Sudan.

Chapter Eleven

Kebede—February 1985

"*Yalla Chevre*, Let's go!" instructed Shifra, signaling to her students to climb into the bus waiting for them, its exhaust fumes lingering in the stifling desert air of southern Israel in summertime.

Shifra had just swallowed her last sip of Turkish coffee, leaving the "mud" at the bottom of the cup to be washed by the dining hall workers. She was anxious to get their big day started. It was 7 o'clock in the morning, but Kebede had already been awake for an hour and a half. As a boy, Kebede was a natural early riser, waking up with the sunrise to begin his morning chores before walking to school. Ever since coming to Israel, however, he found himself lingering in bed until minutes before his *ulpan* class began, opting to forgo the dining hall breakfast of cucumber-tomato salad and cottage cheese which, after three months of living in Israel, he still found unappetizing.

This morning, however, Kebede tossed and turned with the early sunrise. He was anxiously awaiting his class's trip to Tel Aviv, his first time ever to a large, metropolitan city. As his roommate, Mengistu, snored away, he got dressed in the dark, wearing the clothes he had laid out on his desk the night before. Kebede typically put little to no effort into choosing what to wear, accepting nearly all hand-me-downs given to him by the absorption center or other good doers. But today was different—today he was going to venture into Israel's most modern and vibrant city, and Kebede wanted to be dressed accordingly. He chose a Nike T-Shirt with a big *swoosh* across it and a pair of Lee jeans that, but for the second hand belt he wore that fastened them comfortably, would have fallen to his knees.

Kebede stepped outside his room so as not to wake his roommate. He looked up at the rising sun as he felt the cool morning air warm with every passing minute. Once he had been able to tell the time simply by looking at the sun. It had become a lost skill ever since arriving in Israel, and Kebede was now dependent on the watch given to him by the Jewish Agency to know when to eat and when to sleep. The watch, not his intuition, now ruled his life and daily routine. He had more than an hour until it was time to go, so he quietly snuck back into his room to grab his notebook and pen before heading back out to the balcony he shared with the other men on his floor. Sitting at a white plastic table dirtied with cigarette butts and half-empty plastic cups from the night before, Kebede began to write.

Tigy—

It's now officially three months since I became an Israeli, and today my class is going to Tel Aviv. Three months. It's hard to believe. It means it's been around four months since leaving. How is everyone? Has Solomon come to take Azmera? If so, have you heard from her? Has the Kes come to speak with you about when you should prepare for the journey? I hope you and the kids come soon. Here I am lonely. Yes, there are plenty of people surrounding me— students in my class, my roommate, and others living in the absorption center— but my days are empty without the kids asking me to tickle them one more time or tell them stories of what I was like as a little boy.

I can't wait until I get out of the absorption center. It's quite depressing here. Lots of the men drink vodka in the evening, and I'm surrounded by so many other Ethiopians that sometimes I forget I am in Israel. Still, I try to consider myself lucky—I have an amazing Hebrew teacher and can already get along quite well. From time to time, I sit with Shifra after class to practice my Hebrew. She has so many questions about life back in Ethiopia that I do almost all the talking, all in Hebrew. Shifra told me that her brother works for the Jewish Agency, and apparently, he hinted that they may not be bringing any more Ethiopians to Israel for now . . . I hope he's not right. I hope Azmera doesn't get stuck in Country X. Well, I better get going. The bus to Tel Aviv is about to leave. Please write to me soon.

Yours, Kebede

Kebede hurried to the parking lot where Shifra was waiting for him and the others. They had a full day ahead of them in Tel Aviv, and they needed to leave on time—a concept not all the new immigrants in the absorption center had fully grasped as of yet. Shifra had reminded her students the day before that the bus would be leaving at 07:00 sharp, but fifteen minutes after their scheduled departure time Shifra frustratingly found herself knocking on doors and dragging her students out of their rooms to board the bus.

In the week leading up to their trip to Tel Aviv, Shifra spent most of her time in *ulpan* teaching about the big city and what they could expect to see—the Mediterranean Sea, Bauhaus architecture, coffee shops, and the hustle and bustle that comes with any metropolis. Kebede was annoyed with his fellow new immigrants who were holding up the group; he didn't want to miss out on anything, and it would be all their fault if he did. When the full class was finally present, if not fully awake, Kebede boarded the bus for the long drive north to the coastal city. He felt like a little boy bursting with excitement for the new adventure awaiting him. With notebook in hand, Kebede scribbled down new words Shifra mentioned over the microphone during the ride; he took great satisfaction in feeling his Hebrew improve with every passing day, and he was willing to put in the hard work to make it happen. Later that night, while the others would sit outside on the balcony smoking and drinking cheap vodka they had bought from the Russian immigrants in the store down the street, he would study the words he had learned, committing them to memory so he could use them the next day in *ulpan*.

With his head pressed up against the window, Kebede took in the changing landscape and marveled at how quickly the yellow, rocky desert turned into green agricultural fields. But for his class trip to Jerusalem and a few errands he had run in Arad, a neighboring desert city, Kebede had not yet ventured out and explored his new country. For him, the four-hour bus ride to Tel Aviv was an adventure in and of itself, offering him the opportunity to eye the white-skinned drivers in the cars next to him; to read, and sometimes even understand, the traffic signs lining the side of the road; and, with a pocket map of Israel folded neatly into his notebook, to try to make sense of the country's geography.

Kebede could tell they must be approaching Tel Aviv when he felt the bus jolt to a halt. They had just joined the morning rush-hour on the Jerusalem-Tel Aviv Highway. Cars honked their horns relentlessly and motorcycles zoomed by the bus, circumventing traffic by zig-zagging their way through. The others shouted with excitement as they arrived at Tel Aviv. They looked out their windows onto a new world, but Kebede was surprised when he felt himself gasping for air, suffocated by all the chaos surrounding him.

"Look at how splendid," remarked a young woman sitting in front of Kebede as she stared out the window onto Rothschild Boulevard, a mesmerizingly beautiful tree-lined street onto which they had turned.

More noticeable than the trees lining the street for Kebede, however, were the coffee shops and restaurants filled with sophisticated-looking patrons, reading their morning newspaper over a cup of *hafuch*, Israeli-style cappuccino. As Kebede bashfully laid eyes on a young woman wearing denim cut-off shorts walking down the street, he wondered to himself if he would ever be like them. The young woman briefly looked at him through the dusty bus window and then quickly averted her eyes in another direction, as if he were invisible.

"*Yalla*, let's go, everyone. We're here. Get your things," instructed Shifra as the group impatiently unloaded the crowded bus.

They had arrived at Independence Hall, where David Ben Gurion, Israel's first Prime Minister, declared the establishment of the State of Israel in 1948. Kebede had learned all about this site from Shifra in *ulpan*, and here it was standing in front of him—the place where the Land of Zion had become a State. He and the others waited outside the modest-looking building for their guide to let them inside to begin the tour.

"I can't believe that this building—this plain, run-down building—was where it all happened," Kebede said to Shifra, having rehearsed the sentence in his head several times before uttering it out loud. He wanted to be sure that he made no grammatical errors in front of his revered teacher.

"It might be a plain building, *Kfir*," Shifra grinned as she used Kebede's new Israeli name, "but the story you will hear inside is simply fascinating. Just wait and see."

Kebede shook his head up and down whenever anyone used his new name as a reminder to himself that it was his duty to respond.

Anxious for the tour to start, Kebede's eyes jumped when the group's tour guide stepped outside the building, introducing himself as Uzi and inviting everyone to enter the building.

"He's named after a gun?" Kebede questioned his teacher.

"No, Kfir. You're right that there is a machine gun called an *uzi*, but the gun was named after the man who invented it, Uziel. It's a name from the Bible meaning 'the strength of God,'" said Shifra with a patient smile, "but keep up with the good questions!"

For Kebede, Shifra had a wealth of knowledge of all things Israeli and held the key to his integration in the country. Whenever the class went on group outings, he made a concerted effort to stand near her, feeling most comfortable asking her questions without needing to worry that she wouldn't understand his Hebrew or that she would make fun of his accent. And unlike the other new immigrants, Kebede wasn't interested in socializing with his classmates; he preferred to learn from Shifra and Uzi and practice his Hebrew than gossip or complain in Amharic. Kebede didn't care to interact with his fellow immigrants back at the absorption center either; while the others would tend to their children or sit on the balcony and drink vodka, Kebede would study Hebrew, or on more difficult days, think about Tigest.

Uzi ushered the group into the hall, his sculpted muscles visible underneath his crisp white shirt. The guide's golden-brown hair fell gently onto his face, tan from a lifetime of basking under the Mediterranean sunshine. The accompanying wrinkles added an air of maturity to his otherwise young face. Uzi was the quintessential Israeli—his looks, his job, his self-confidence and even his name exuded "Israeliness". Kebede intently listened to the man standing before him tell the history of the State of Israel not just because the story was captivating but because Uzi represented everything he hoped to be one day.

As a child, Kebede had learned from his father, who as the village *Kes* was a scholar of the Torah, that Israel had become a state and a modern-day miracle not long before he was born. He thought his father had taught him all there was to know about that glorious day on May 14, 1948, but Uzi proved to him that there was still much he did not know. He listened to Uzi recount all the fascinating details—about how the Hall itself was donated to the city by Meir Dizengoff, the former Tel Aviv Mayor, to be used as a museum; about how Ben Gurion declared Israel's independence a mere eight hours before the British Mandate was to come to an end; and about how Jews living throughout Israel cried with joy as they listened to the

Declaration over the radio news broadcast. The Zionist dream—Kebede's dream—had become a reality in this very building.

Kebede couldn't recall the last time he had cried, but it must have dated back to his boyhood. When Uzi finished his presentation and turned on the recording of Ben Gurion and the other leaders at the time singing *Ha'Tikvah*, Israel's national anthem, Kebede felt a tear softly run down his cheek.

When the singing of *Ha'Tikvah* came to an end, the group of more than forty Ethiopian immigrants stood in absolute silence, overwhelmed by all they had just learned.

"I told you so," whispered Shifra into Kebede's ear, as she placed her hand on his shoulder.

Kebede tried to pretend he was not bothered by the familiarity that came with Shifra's physical gestures, but he couldn't help but flinch whenever he felt her touch. Unable to find words to adequately sum up his morning at Independence Hall, Kebede simply looked at his teacher, his eyes still filled with tears. He softly nodded his head.

The silence dissipated into whispers and muffled coughs, no one wanting to be the first to break the intensity of the experience.

"*Bo'ou, Chevre*," announced Shifra, signaling to everyone that it was time to begin shuffling out of the Hall to head back to the bus for their next excursion.

Like always, Kebede made sure to stand close to his teacher, who was the last to leave the Hall as she expressed her gratitude to Uzi the tour guide.

"*Toda raba*, thank you very much, Uzi," Shifra said to him as she leaned in to give him a hug goodbye. Kebede discretely eavesdropped, not wanting to miss a chance to hear Hebrew spoken amongst "real" Israelis.

"My pleasure," Uzi responded with a smile, "but next time you bring one of your classes, please tell them to take a shower and wear deodorant before coming. I thought I was going to die because they smelled so bad!"

Not knowing what to say, Shifra uncomfortably nodded at Uzi. She turned around to make sure none of her students were in earshot of their conversation as she saw Kebede walk away with his head bowed down toward the ground.

Kebede rested his head against the bus window as they drove back towards Dimona. It had been a long day in Tel Aviv, complete with an outing to the beach, a delicious lunch of hummus and falafel, and a visit to the old city of Jaffa. It was still light outside, thanks to the long summer days that ended when the blazing sun descended into the Mediterranean Sea. Kebede closed his eyes, no longer interested in taking in all the sights and views the long drive had to offer. He couldn't stop replaying in his head what the tour guide had said to Shifra. He desperately wanted to believe that he had misunderstood Uzi, but Kebede was confident his Hebrew comprehension had gotten it right. Kebede felt dejected and small. After all, he indeed had not showered that day or the previous one—back home in Ethiopia, he was lucky if he was able to bathe in the river once or twice a week, and it never seemed to bother anyone before. And as for deodorant—the people from the Jewish Agency had provided him with some when he first arrived, but he had never used it before and saw no reason to use it now. Did all Israelis feel this way about Ethiopians? He felt less Israeli on the return trip to Dimona than he did when he left for Tel Aviv earlier that morning.

The bus left a trail of dust behind as it pulled into the absorption center. The sun had set somewhere around the desert city of Be'er Sheva, but Kebede was too disheartened to have noticed. The bus's headlights illuminated the darkness, and Kebede waited for all the others to unload before he slowly made his way off the bus. He dragged his feet in the sand as he walked towards his room. Kebede heard Shifra calling out his name from behind him, but he kept walking without looking back.

"Kebede, come join us," invited his roommate, Mengistu, after they returned to their room, hot and stuffy.

Mengistu pointed to the balcony where the other men had already positioned themselves for a night of smoking and drinking. Despite Kebede having already made it clear that he wasn't interested, Mengistu continued to invite his roommate to join him every evening before he went outside. This night, however, was different. Kebede took one look at his Hebrew notebook and carelessly threw it onto his bed. He then headed out to the balcony to drink his first shot of vodka.

Chapter Twelve

Tigest—April 1985

"*Enati*, wake up," Daniel whispered as he gently patted his mother on her shoulder.

As Tigest slowly began to open her swollen eyes, the boy tried to sneak a look at his tiny baby sister wrapped up in his mother's arms, but the pile of blankets keeping her warm left little for the eye to see. Tigest and the baby had fallen asleep while breastfeeding, with one of her engorged breasts poking its way out from under her robe. Avraham followed Daniel into the *gojo* and ran straight to his daughter to embrace her tightly, paying no attention to his daughter's breast. It was no surprise that he didn't feel uncomfortable by the sight of his daughter's bosom— Ethiopian women breastfed their babies publicly and unapologetically, their breasts perceived more as a source of life than anything sexual in nature.

"Tigy, my dear, we have good news," announced her father, with a hopeful look in his eyes.

The mention of good news brought Tigest back to life, anxious to hear what it could be. With a warm smile on his face and a tear running down his cheek, Avraham took a wad full of cash out of his pocket and showed it to his daughter. A modest man, Tigest's father wanted to give his grandson the spotlight, so he motioned to Daniel to tell his mother how they had managed to sell the gold necklace at a time when most people barely had enough money to eat.

"When we got to the market in Debark, there was barely a soul there. Hardly anyone was selling and hardly anyone was buying," Daniel recalled, his voice trembling with excitement at having been given the platform for all to listen.

"I was terrified we wouldn't be able to sell the necklace. I wanted so badly to help, to feel like I was being useful," Daniel said as he tried to hold back tears. "Anyway, *Ayat* and I walked all around the market, approaching every person we saw, but no one was interested. Things there seemed hard, way harder than in our village. We saw men on the street with their arms and legs missing, and we saw little boys and girls with swollen bellies and their ribs poking out of their chest running around begging for money. We saw so many people in need that I was sure we would never manage to sell it."

Daniel took a deep breath before he continued, "Things looked so hopeless that I broke down crying. I felt like I was failing you and failing the family and I just couldn't stop crying," Daniel glanced at his grandfather who nodded approvingly, "I was so ashamed to cry that I made *Ayati* swear to me that he wouldn't tell you," Daniel hesitated and then looked directly at his mother, "But now here I am, telling you."

Tigest felt her heart melting as she listened to her little boy. She grabbed his hand and squeezed it gently while he continued.

"After an hour wandering around the market, *Ayati* and I had given up hope and started to head back home empty handed. When we got to the end of the Debark road, *Ayati* stopped walking and said he thought he heard something strange. We both stopped and listened and then heard muffled voices speaking in a language we couldn't recognize. We walked off the Debark road to one of the side trails leading to our village, and there we saw two *faranjes*, two white men, sitting on a rock eating *injera* together with an Ethiopian man. I tried to wipe the tears from my face as we approached them, but they clearly saw that I had been crying. The two *faranjes* didn't speak a word of Amharic, of course, so their friend translated for them, asking me why I was crying. I told them the whole story, of how you had given birth to my baby sister and how she was sick and needed to get to a hospital as soon as possible, and how we had come to Debark to try to sell the gold necklace so we could pay for the trip. When I held out the necklace, hoping that maybe I had finally found a buyer, the two *faranjes'* mouths dropped to the ground. They saw the Star of David and immediately, in hushed voices, told us that they are Jews from America. They didn't say anything about what they were doing in Ethiopia, and we didn't ask, but *Ayat* told me afterwards that they knew that we knew. Anyway, I guess they were so moved by our story and wanted to help, so they gave us some money without even taking the necklace. But most amazing of all is that they offered to take you and the baby in their private car. They are waiting for you outside right now."

Tigest had thought she had heard the humming of an engine when Daniel and her father entered the hut, but she dismissed it at the time as an impossibility and attributed it to her foggy postpartum brain. Tigest handed her baby girl to her mother before leaning on her father and son to help her stand up from her bed. A gush of blood came rushing down Tigest's legs as she stood upright, this being the first time standing since giving birth. She hastily grabbed a towel to wipe herself and then took her baby back into her arms, softly hushing in her ears as she walked out of the hut into the light of day.

Parked on the dirt road next to the hut was a dust-covered, white Toyota Land Cruiser with two white men sitting in the front, and an Ethiopian man in the back. Tigest could count on both hands the number of times she had ridden in a car, but this would certainly be the first time she had ever been in a car as luxurious as the one standing before her. With her baby cradled in her arms, she opened the door and climbed into the backseat to sit next to the Ethiopian man and friend of the *faranjes*. She didn't know what to say to them or how to ever express her deep appreciation for their generosity, so with a cracking voice she gently muttered in English "thank you," one of the few phrases she remembered from her trips fetching water from the river as a little girl.

"There's no time to waste. Let's get you and that baby to the hospital!" said the driver, who, via their interpreter in the back seat, Abaye, introduced himself as David from Chicago, a middle-aged man with creases in his forehead so thick they resembled books stacked one on top of another.

"My name is Josh," stated the man sitting next to David, his face plump but friendly, "I'm from New York."

Tigest nodded in acknowledgment after the translation was complete. She managed to catch the *faranjes'* names, but their places of origin were completely foreign to her, and thus went in one ear and out the other.

Tigest rolled down her window and held out her hand to Daniel, who was anxiously tapping his foot. She flashed him a smile as she gently nodded her head. They were small gestures meant to reassure her son that everything was going to be okay, even though she herself wasn't sure. Abaynesh and Avraham approached the window and, without muttering a word, their eyes told Tigest that she needn't worry about her four young children—they would be cared for until she returned from the hospital. David backed the car up to turn around, giving Tigest one last chance to get a glimpse of Desta and Amara, now huddled around their grandfather, and Gabra sobbing inconsolably in Abaynesh's arms.

The drive to Gondar was a long and jarring one. The seventy miles separating Tigest's village from the hospital took several hours of treacherous driving on one-lane dirt roads. At times, the road was so close to the edge of a terrifyingly dramatic cliffside that, with each bend in the road, the *faranjes* feared for their lives. The bumpy drive was calming for the baby, though. Safely nuzzled into her mother's chest, she would let out a whimper whenever the car dipped deep into a ditch or came to a halt at a checkpoint manned by soldiers.

"Don't worry, Tigest," Abaye said to Tigest, this time communicating directly with her instead of interpreting, "when the soldiers at the checkpoints see David and Josh—two American *faranjes* with money—they'll let us through with no problem."

Not having ventured outside of her village often, especially by car, Tigest didn't know what perils awaited her on the road to Gondar. Abaye and the *faranjes*, on the other hand, seemed entirely unconcerned when they pulled up to a military checkpoint randomly positioned in the middle of the road.

"Stop," shouted the soldier as he pointed a Kalashnikov rifle towards the driver's-side window. David slowed down the car. He calmly and deliberately searched in his wallet looking for their ticket free.

"He looks like a child!" muttered David to Josh under his breath, as he rolled down the window to reveal his white skin.

Just as Abaye had expected, the soldier took one look at David and Josh and laid down his weapon. Tigest felt a taste of disgust in her mouth as she watched the soldier linger by the car, clearly waiting for a handful of money before letting them continue their journey. While she had heard Kebede and Solomon discuss politics from time to time, complaining how corrupt the Marxist Mengistu regime was, Tigest rarely bore witness to it. And while she wasn't surprised as she watched David hold out 100 *Birrs* to the soldier, she felt ashamed of her country. Her feeling of shame quickly dissipated, however, replaced by relief as the soldier sent them on their way.

"That's what I call *green* privilege," Josh laughed as David focused his attention on the bumpy, narrow road ahead of them. Abaye translated Josh's apparent joke for Tigest, but neither he nor she seemed to understand it.

"We've been in Ethiopia on and off for over a year now, so we know how to get around," explained David as he looked back at Tigest in the rear-view mirror.

Tigest wasn't sure at first whether David's comment was an invitation to talk, but then she recalled her trips to the river as a little girl and how eager for conversation the *faranjes* seemed to be whenever she happened to spot them.

"Are you here with the Jewish Agency?" questioned Tigest.

Abaye shot her a look of disbelief before translating the sentence for the *faranjes*. Tigest knew that she must have surprised the men with such a probing question after having remained silent for most of the ride. However, she knew that they knew she was Jewish, so she felt no need to dance around the issue. Besides, she sensed that they were intrigued by her and their mission to come to the aid of her sick baby girl.

"Sort of," answered Josh, the designated spokesman while David focused on the winding road, "We are part of an organization called the AAEJ, the American Association of Ethiopian Jews. We're working together with the Israeli Government and the Jewish Agency to help bring the Jews of Ethiopia home to Israel."

Tigest listened carefully, hoping to gather any useful information from him about Azmera.

"We were actually on our way back to Addis when we ran into your son," Josh continued. "You know, we've seen a lot of desperate people in our time here and seeing so many of them hardens you somehow. But he was different—we just couldn't say no to his desperate face, especially when he showed us his Star of David necklace. All he wanted to do was help his baby sister live. We just had to help him. What do they say in the Talmud? *Kol Yisrael Arevim Ze L'Ze*, or something like that. The people of Israel are responsible for one another—no?"

Tigest nodded her head gently as she pulled her baby a bit closer to her chest. She had no words to describe how amazed she was to learn of white men coming from faraway places to her tiny corner of the world for the sole purpose of rescuing Ethiopian Jews, just because they were Jewish. Ever since she was a little girl, Tigest had a deep awareness of her Jewishness, but only now did she understand how it connected her to Jews from all over the world—people from different countries, who spoke different languages, and had a different skin color. But all Jews.

"I don't know what to say other than thank you," said Tigest quietly, "I don't know what we would have done if you hadn't come to our aid. If my baby survives, God willing, it will be because of you."

Josh and David listened intently as Abaye translated every word Tigest had said. Tigest knew how touched they were by the warm smiles broadening their faces.

By now Tigest felt she had gained their trust, so she continued, "Now that you're helping me with my baby daughter, maybe you can help me with my eldest. She left for Sudan around four months ago. Is there any chance you can find out for me what happened to her? I haven't heard a thing from her since she left, and it's killing me with each passing day."

Tigest watched Josh pause to calculate in his head. It was now the end of April. If Tigest's daughter had left for Sudan around four months ago, he thought to himself, she would have arrived sometime in January at the earliest. Tigest could tell he didn't have good news for her as he slightly lowered his head to the ground, debating what he should or should not say considering Tigest's condition.

"There's no way to know for sure," mumbled Josh, uncertain of his words, "By my estimate, your daughter would have arrived in Sudan after Operation Moses came to an end."

Tigest had no idea that the operation everyone talked about in muffled speech even had a name. Tigest's heart skipped a beat as she waited for Josh, who paused for a moment and gazed out the window.

"If she didn't make it in time for the big airlift, then she would have been left behind in the camp. I hope your daughter is strong," Josh cautioned, as he turned his head around and stared Tigest straight in the eye.

"I'll be straight with you. The conditions in the camp are horrendous. Lots of people die. But if she survived, and that's a big if, then there's a chance she got on a plane to Israel around a month ago during a much smaller operation called Operation Joshua." Josh smiled, clearly taking pride in the operation that was also his namesake before continuing, "If so, she should be in Israel by now."

Tigest's thoughts shifted from her baby girl in her arms to her eldest baby girl. Her postpartum brain was still not in full working order, but she tried her best to hold on to every single piece of information Josh had offered her. Each word he uttered somehow brought her closer to Azmera. Josh didn't know Azmera, but Tigest did. Meri was strong, about as strong as they get, and Solomon was even stronger. Together, she thought to herself, they most definitely would have survived. She felt the muscles in her shoulders loosen as she realized that her eldest daughter must have made it to Israel. She had to have survived. Her heart simply couldn't bear the alternative. As David pulled the car up in front of the hospital in Gondar, Tigest knew that now it was time to do everything possible to make sure that her youngest daughter—the one who now needed her most of all—would as well.

Chapter Thirteen

Azmera—January 1985

Azmera was in Sudan, but she wasn't nearly as close to her destination as she had hoped. Until now, she told herself that she just needed to cross the border, but the vast desert expanse ahead of her made it clear that their destination was still very far away.

"Meri, this all around you is Dinder National Park. The good news is that here we don't have to worry so much about running into bandits or soldiers. That's why we crossed the border at Metema and not over the river like most others do," explained Solomon, "the others before us walked to Sudan in large groups, so it was easier for them to fend off any bandits. It's just the two of us, so we are safer walking through Dinder, even if wild animals are all around us."

Solomon stood erect with his gaze focused on the majestic savannah before him, marked by a sea of coarse yellow grass and trees that stood far from one another as if warding off disease. Solomon's voice was assertive but enthusiastic. He bent his knee down on the ground, gesturing for Azmera to do the same.

"Now listen carefully," Solomon said, "If we walk at a good pace all day, then we'll make it out of Dinder within two days, leaving most of the dangerous animals behind us. And so long as we're in the park, we can walk at all hours of the day without worrying we might run into anyone who might cause us problems."

Azmera listened intently, feeling like she was back in school listening to her teacher provide instructions for solving a math problem. She appreciated Solomon's forthrightness, making her feel like his equal partner in a joint endeavor. She nodded her head slowly, not sure of whether she was capable of meeting Solomon's demands, but desperately wanting to.

"Now, Meri," Solomon continued, "I know you're tired. And I know you're hungry. I know. So am I."

Azmera was taken aback by her uncle's admission that he too was suffering from the many hardships of the journey. Of course he was, she knew, but his saying so made him more relatable than ever before.

Azmera unwittingly flashed Solomon an understanding smile as he continued, "But I bought a big bag of *kolo* in the market in Metema while you were wandering around, so that will give us the energy we need, at least for the next few days. And if we keep up a good pace for just a bit longer, I think we can make it to the Qadarif within five days. Just five more days, Meri. I know you can do it."

Solomon had known that time was not on their side ever since the night they left their village many lifetimes ago, but he now sensed an even greater urgency than before. While they were maintaining the pace he had hoped for, he knew they were competing against an hourglass that was running out of sand with each passing day. At the same time, he knew that there was a limit to how much he could pressure his niece. While both her resourcefulness with the bandits and her natural endurance caught him by surprise, he couldn't forget the fact that she was still a young girl. There was a very fine line between pushing her and breaking her.

"What kind of wild animals should we expect to see?" asked Azmera in an abnormally high pitch, a failed attempt to disguise the fear in her voice.

While Azmera felt right at home next to the baboons and the ibex in the Simiens—she knew what dangers they presented, how not to threaten them, and what to do if they charged at you—she had no experience with other wildlife. She wanted to be prepared.

"Lots of antelopes in this part of the park. Big ones, small ones, all different kinds," explained Solomon, "They usually travel in herds, so the biggest threat is that they trample us. If you see them running towards you, get out of the way."

Azmera nodded, reassured by how very simple Solomon made it sound.

"Anything else?" asked Azmera, wanting to make sure that Solomon was not leaving anything out. "Please, I'm not a little girl. I can handle it," she pleaded, her eyes locked on her uncle's.

As the sentence came out of her mouth, Azmera wondered to herself if she really meant it.

"Look, Meri. I don't want to scare you, but as far as dangerous animals go, there are lots of lions here. And buffalos, which are more dangerous than you'd think. Plus, there's the occasional hyena, leopard and cheetah." Azmera gulped down her fear as Solomon continued.

"If you see them, don't let them see you. If they see you, back away slowly. Slowly is the key. Do not run. If they charge at you, scream at the top of your lungs, and make yourself big, as big as you can." Azmera felt her heart racing as Solomon explained to her what to expect. "In the meantime, don't think about them, and let's get going. You and I have to talk as much as possible to keep the animals away."

Azmera doubted that she and her uncle would have enough to talk about for the next two days, but she welcomed the opportunity. Finally, her uncle would be forced to talk—*really talk*—to her.

The sun's rays beating down on Azmera's body made it difficult for her to appreciate all the beauty surrounding her, let alone be an active participant in the conversation forced on them by their circumstances. She was grateful, then, that her uncle did most of the talking at first, allowing her to focus on her feet beneath her treading as fast as Solomon's pace dictated.

"Your father sent letters, you know," Solomon grunted as they trekked through coarse grass that scratched their legs through their clothing. Not wanting to let her uncle see her excitement at the mention of her father's name, she remained silent and let him continue. "He sent me a letter when he arrived in Israel, about a month and a half ago. He's living in an absorption center for Ethiopians in the desert. Your *Enat* also received a letter from him. We shared them with one another so we could stay informed of where he was and what he was doing."

"Yes, my *Enati* told me," replied Azmera, not wanting Solomon to know how little she knew. "Does he know that we are on our way?"

"No. Everything happened so fast, Meskie and I were working in the fields when *Kes* Yonas came and told me about the rumors that the operation was about to come to an end. There was no time to think or plan," Solomon recalled.

Azmera's ears perked up with the mention of Solomon's wife, a girl not much older than Azmera herself. She desperately wanted to ask her uncle about his wife but wasn't sure how he would take the probing. On the one hand, he had opened up to Azmera in recent days; whether it was because he wanted to ward off the wild animals or because he felt a kinship to his niece didn't really matter, at least not to her. On the other hand, asking Solomon questions about his wife felt off-limits to Azmera, mostly because he *never* talked about her. Ever since marrying Solomon nearly six years ago, Meskie, while technically part of the family, had been practically invisible to her.

"Why didn't Meskie join you on the journey?" Azmera asked her uncle, deciding to tread gently into the subject. Until now, Azmera had been so consumed by the devastation of her mother's abandonment and her own loss that she failed to consider that her uncle might also be mourning something or someone. Solomon's gait widened, nearly forcing Azmera to run to keep up.

"That's really none of your business, is it?" her uncle replied with a stern tone reminiscent of the first days of their journey. "But if you have to know, she wasn't feeling well and simply wasn't up to making the journey."

Azmera replied with a nod of her head, finding her uncle's reply curious and unsatisfactory at the same time. After all, she had seen Meskie not long ago while fetching water from the river and she had looked perfectly healthy to her.

Azmera changed the topic to put an end to the awkward silence pervading the air. "What did *Abat* tell you that he didn't tell *Enati?*" inquired Azmera, trying to conceal the fact that she knew much less about her father's whereabouts than Solomon thought.

As she impatiently waited to hear Solomon's reply, her mouth dropped to the ground. A massive herd of antelopes was running towards her. Something about their gracefully long and slender legs bounding through the plains reminded her of herself. She stood in awe as she gazed at the majestic beauty of their synchronized running on display in front of her.

"Meri, get out of the way!" shouted her uncle, reminding Azmera that, while a harmless animal on its own, dozens of antelopes joined in a sprint towards you was quite dangerous.

Azmera rushed to the side and stood next to Solomon, still hoping for any information he was willing to provide regarding her father. As the last antelope leapt past them, Azmera felt grateful for the sudden appearance of the herd. Not only did its splendor allow her an escape for a moment, however brief, but it also gave her the first opportunity to rest since entering Sudan. Solomon and Azmera waited for the cloud of dust to clear the air and then continued on their journey.

"You see, Meri. There is wildlife all over the park. We must keep talking lest we surprise them. There is nothing worse than a dangerous animal caught by surprise," warned Solomon.

Azmera brushed off the warning about dangerous animals and instead focused on the opportunity they provided her. By now, she had learned to read her uncle well. She decided to stay silent despite his warning, knowing that if she weren't to talk, then he would be forced to respond to the question she had asked before the antelopes interrupted her subtle attempt at interrogation.

"Back to your question—your *Abat* is studying Hebrew and doing fine. He arrived not long ago, so I haven't received many letters," Solomon shared what he knew, which, to Azmera's disappointment, was not much more than what she already knew from her mother. "But before he left, he left me responsible for ensuring that you make it to Israel safely."

Azmera slowed down for a moment as she wondered why her father would have entrusted her care to her uncle when she had a mother who knew how to care for her better than anyone else in the world.

"With all due respect, *Ah Goht* Solomon, why you and not my *Enati*?" asked Azmera, not sure she wanted to know the answer.

"He didn't really say," Solomon replied, "He just told me that Tigest wouldn't be up to the journey with so many young children to care for."

Azmera felt her left knee buckle from underneath her, but she continued walking despite the shooting pain running up and down her leg. She wondered if her father knew her mother was pregnant with another baby, but she wasn't sure if she wanted to know the answer. Her father's abandonment of his family for Israel was hurtful enough; abandoning her mother when he knew she was about to bring another child into the world would have been inexcusable, no matter how fervent a Zionist he was.

Azmera could tell by Solomon's silence that he was the one now waiting for her response, but she did not comply, at least not immediately. After all, as far as she knew, Solomon didn't know about her mother's pregnancy. Tigest was around halfway into her pregnancy when Azmera and Solomon left on their journey, showing just enough for those close to her to notice—particularly those who cuddled with her first thing in the morning. The pregnancy at the time could easily be concealed from others by wearing her daily dress—a loose skirt and shawl draped over her stomach. Besides, Azmera recalled her mother's pregnancy with Gabra four years ago and how she and her father would carefully avoid the topic whenever Solomon came to visit, even when Tigest's stomach was the size of a watermelon. For reasons still unclear to her, it seemed that her parents had no interest in sharing the blessings of their pregnancies with Solomon, nor did Solomon have any interest in blessing them.

"I guess *Abat* was right," replied Azmera with a forced sigh, "The journey would have been next to impossible with little Gabra."

While the journey indeed would have been more challenging with her four-year-old sister, Azmera had heard of plenty of families who had managed the trek to Sudan with young children on their backs. Surely Solomon and Tigest could have managed together, especially with the help of Azmera and Daniel. Her father, then, may in fact have known of the pregnancy. There would have been no other reason to send Azmera on her own with her uncle. Solomon, on the other hand, wanted to believe the excuse Kebede had given him, ignoring the possibility that there was another reason keeping Tigest from joining them on the journey.

Solomon—January 1985

Ever since Azmera mentioned Meskie—back where the lifeless trees touched the barren Sudanese ground—Solomon couldn't stop thinking about her. Meskie, his wife of over six years; the love of his life. He had married her when he was a ripe twenty years old, having waited patiently for the girl to turn fifteen. Unlike Kebede, he had courted Meskie long before asking for her hand in marriage. He would walk her to her school in the next village or surprise her while fetching water from the river, despite his father's inevitable scolding for having missed an hour of tilling the fields. Theirs was an innocent love, one between a boy who had just become a man and a girl who was not yet a woman. On the day before they married, at nightfall, they went to the teff fields and held each other in their arms for the very first time. Solomon recalled how his body trembled as Meskie drew her body in close to him, gently patting his cheek.

For Solomon, he had all the time in the world to take his newlywed wife to bed. He didn't pressure his new wife, letting her initiate whatever physical contact there would be between the two. As the months went by, Meskie became more and more intimate with her husband, until the day she took her husband to the trees lining the teff fields. There she coyly undressed her young body for her husband to see in the light of the moon. On that night, months after their wedding, they consummated their marriage. Solomon remembered how his body quivered with excitement as he touched all of her for the first time. He also remembered the excitement for what now certainly lay ahead of them—children. Solomon's instinct to bring life into the world had become even stronger when the life of his parents came to an end all too soon, his father passing away not long after the wedding, and his mother several months later.

Ever since he was a little boy who loved to dig holes outside his family's hut, Solomon had looked up to his big brother Kebede. Six years his senior, Kebede was his role model for nearly every aspect of life. So, when he saw the ease with which his brother and his wife brought children into the world, he assumed that would be the case for him too. If Kebede and Tigest could bring children into the world despite their loveless marriage, then surely the strong and loving foundation he had built with Meskie would guarantee them a home full of little babies.

When Meskie came to him and announced that she was pregnant,

Solomon dreamt of a little boy who would be his shadow, just as he had been his father's. Solomon relished watching his wife's body change, not just for what was growing on the inside but also for what was growing on the outside. As her hips gradually widened and her breasts swelled, Meskie looked more and more like a woman and less like the skinny and bow-legged girl whom he had married.

Solomon recalled how bone-tired Meskie was at the beginning of her pregnancy. She would go to bed at sunset, leaving the tidying up and any other remaining chores for the day to her husband. She recoiled with pain whenever he tried to touch her in bed. One day, Meskie returned from fetching water by the stream and told him that she felt like her old self again, full of energy and free of pain. For weeks, Meskie took delight in her rejuvenated and feather-light body. To Solomon's relief, she resumed tending to the goats and tilling the teff and corn fields just as she had before; and to his delight, she resumed initiating intimate contact with her husband. But then came the day when Meskie said her belly didn't seem to be growing like she expected it would. Solomon looked at his wife's belly in the glow of the morning light and reluctantly agreed with her.

Solomon recalled listening to his wife sobbing at night after she thought he had gone to bed, her cries slightly muffled by her nightgown pulled up over her face. For days, they pretended as if everything were normal when they both knew it was not. He remembered the morning when he and Meskie woke up to a bed covered in blood, and the agonizingly long days that followed. For months that followed, he couldn't stop thinking of how Meskie screamed as she pushed the dead baby out of her belly. She held the baby boy in her arms, the baby that had given them so much hope only five months before, the baby who never had the chance to be his father's shadow. And while he watched on the sidelines as his wife mourned their terrible loss, he felt his entire body fill with rage—rage towards God for taking away his baby without reason and rage towards his brother for unfairly bringing so many babies into the world before he was able to bring even one.

Solomon recalled how he listened to Meskie share the horrible news with her parents and how she could barely get the words out of her mouth.

"The baby died," she said, as tears rushed down her cheeks and she collapsed to the ground.

She moved into her parents' home for two months to recover, and every day Solomon would walk to the other side of the village where they lived to massage her feet and to perform the coffee ceremony—a ritual typically relegated to women—so he could sit by his wife's side and let the bitterness of the coffee open her heart. At night, he prayed that his wife would come back to him—that the devastating loss would not destroy her, at least not completely. And then he saw her smile for the first time since that dreadful day; a smile, brought on by Solomon sneaking up on her from behind, that remained forever etched in his heart. It was the first time he truly believed that they could make it out of the depths of despair into which they had fallen.

Solomon recalled that hopeful day Meskie decided she was ready to come home. He watched his wife slowly come back to life, until one day it seemed like everything was back to normal. He remembered the joy he saw on her face when she told him she was pregnant again. He also remembered the anxiety Meskie felt every day, so much so that she couldn't enjoy the new seed that had been planted inside her. A few weeks into her pregnancy, Meskie found a bright red stain on her undergarments. She unraveled so quickly that Solomon was certain she was about to fall apart. Yet she didn't. Solomon marveled at his wife's inner strength to somehow keep on living. Soon thereafter, though, Meskie told him she wasn't able to visit Kebede's family—at least not for now. The pain of seeing Tigest pregnant again, this time carrying their fifth child, would have been like a dagger to her heart, she explained. She begged him not to tell his family what had happened to her. She didn't want anyone's pity, especially not from the uber-fertile Kebede and Tigest. A sad and longing silence haunted their *gojo* at night, evoking the feeling that there was a void in their lives that needed filling.

Solomon remembered making love for the first time after the loss; he felt like a virgin all over again, quivering with excitement. He began attending synagogue with more purpose than ever before, praying to God that his wife would be blessed with the child for which she was so desperate. And he was certain his prayers had been answered when, several months later, his wife announced to him her third pregnancy. Solomon felt deep in his heart that this time things would be different.

Solomon recalled how he held his breathe with anticipation as he watched his wife's belly grow, and how they breathed a sigh of relief when they passed the point of her first miscarriage. Meskie barely left their *gojo*, and when she did reluctantly venture out, she wore a loose-fitting dress that hid her condition. Solomon gently kissed and rubbed Meskie's belly while they planned for the future, and he saw a glow in his wife's face that he hadn't seen in months. One beautiful morning his wife unexpectedly volunteered to walk to the stream to collect water; she needed to get some fresh air after being cooped up inside the hut for so many months, she explained. She smiled at him as she walked out of the hut and he smiled back as he watched her go. But then he heard screaming from down below in the valley; he threw the hoe down into the partially-tilled field and sprinted to see what had happened. He saw his wife sprawled on the ground sobbing uncontrollably. A concerned young girl standing next to her explained how she had seen Meskie tumble down the rocky hill notorious for its poor footing, landing hard on her side. Solomon tended to Meskie's scrapes and bruises before carrying Meskie up the hill back to their home. His wife moaned from pain as she clutched her stomach tightly. Solomon sent Kebede to call for Rokenach the midwife and they anxiously awaited her arrival. When Rokenach walked into their hut, they felt a sense of relief—everything would be okay this time around. Time stood still as he watched the revered midwife check for the baby's heartbeat. Solomon kept his eyes affixed on Rokenach's face, searching for even the slightest cause for optimism. Rokenach placed her hand up into his wife; when her face soured, he knew something was wrong. He nearly vomited when he heard the words that splintered his heart and crushed his wife's: "placental abruption", the midwife said; although neither he nor his wife really understood what that meant— they knew it was bad.

Solomon recalled how Rokenach explained to them that the fall had caused the placenta to separate from the uterine wall and how the baby was not receiving enough oxygen and would die a slow death inside of her. The midwife explained that the only option to save the baby would be a Caesarean section, but that she was not equipped to do so here in the village; they could try going to the hospital in Gondar, she explained, but they wouldn't make it there in time to save the baby. She then explained how even if the baby came out alive, at approximately six months gestation there was no way the baby would ever survive.

He watched Rokenach hesitate for a moment before turning to Meskie and softly muttering, "I'm very sorry but there's nothing I can do to help."

His chest ached as he looked into his wife's eyes, overflowing with tears. As a man who always knew how to fix things, Solomon burned with frustration for not being able to do anything to help his wife, and his baby.

In the months that followed, Solomon spent his days planning how he could bring his wife back to him. At night, after he tucked his wife into bed, he began to join his brother in the meetings at synagogue; it was there that he decided that there was no future for him or his wife in Ethiopia. They needed a change; they needed to return to Zion. He begged his wife to join him on the journey to Israel, but she begged him to leave her behind, telling him that she was no good to him if she couldn't bring children into the world. Solomon kneeled at his wife's feet with tears in his eyes and told her that she was the only woman for him, the love of his life. He watched her face soften as he spoke. She gradually retreated from her position, declaring her love for him, and allowing him to declare his love for her. But his wife stated a truth he desperately tried to pretend did not exist—that she in fact was in no state, neither emotionally nor physically, to make the arduous journey to Sudan. Together as man and wife, they made the painful decision that he would go to Israel first to plant the seeds for their new life—for a better life—and Meskie would join him whenever she felt she had regained her strength. He remembered that dreadful night when he said goodbye to his wife, softly planting a kiss on her lips as he walked out of their empty home. He walked the short distance to his brother's hut, and his stomach knotted when the door opened to the faces of his five rambunctious nieces and nephews.

Azmera and Solomon—January 1985

Solomon looked at Azmera. She had been speaking for the past few minutes about some thing or another, but Solomon hadn't listened to a word, his mind deluged with memories of Meskie and all the loss they had suffered. As much as he hated to admit it, Azmera was a much better travel partner than he had ever expected. Solomon had so badly wanted to resent his niece as he did the night they left their village—to take his anger out on her and to use her as his punching bag—but something about her made him soften. She listened to his every word as if it were the Torah—like he was her father and she, his daughter. And he liked the way it felt. So it was that here in the middle of Dinder, with a magnificent expanse surrounding them, Solomon realized that not only did his niece need him by her side, but he needed her by his. She reminded him that things could get better; that one day he and his wife could have the life of their dreams. That one day they could have a family. And if one day he became a father to a girl like his niece, he would be truly blessed.

"Solomon!" whispered Azmera with an exasperated look on her face, "Did you hear what I just said?"

Solomon looked back at his niece with a blank stare, not knowing how to answer.

"I told you that I heard rustling over there," explained his niece as she pointed to a thicket of lifeless trees crowding the side of the makeshift trail. "Quiet! Don't move!" whispered Azmera, sensing that she had caught her uncle off guard, as if he had been daydreaming—highly out of character.

Since crossing into Sudan, Azmera had been terrified of a surprise encounter with a dangerous animal. This fear, however, slightly dissipated with the relatively harmless sighting of the antelopes. In her mind, the surprise encounter she had dreaded was now behind her. Until it wasn't.

Azmera and Solomon stood motionless in the middle of the trail, making every effort not to breathe, let alone cough or sneeze. Solomon signaled to his niece to crouch down on the ground. Azmera immediately obeyed, relieved to have her uncle back in control of things, as should be. Time stood still as they sat still. The rustling coming from the thicket suddenly grew louder. As they heard the trampling of dried-up leaves and broken twigs, Azmera had to restrain herself from screaming and dashing for cover. She was certain that her thumping heart would instantly give them away, but she stayed by Solomon's side and closed her eyes, wishing for it all to be over.

Azmera focused her gaze on the ground, not wanting to see what was about to come out of the thicket. Solomon held his hand out to hers and grabbed it tightly; his hand felt just like her father's hand, muscular but weathered. When her uncle's hand dropped to the ground, Azmera lifted her head to meet the predator surely standing in front of her. To her surprise, however, she saw a small herd of male buffalos running away from her. Their curved horns sparkled under the sun's rays and their muscular legs left a trail of dust behind them.

"It's not over yet," cautioned Solomon, "Don't move an eyelash."

When the noise of the stampeding buffalo muffled into silence, Azmera perked up her ears to check if there were any more sounds hidden in the brush. The thicket was indeed quiet, the tranquil chirping of birds in the trees overhead the only sound to be heard. Solomon signaled that the worst was behind them when he slowly stood up and scanned the surroundings. "

Meri, those buffalos are crazy animals, some of the most dangerous in all of Africa," he explained to his niece. "If they would have heard us, they would have charged at us, and we would have been crushed to pieces—literally."

Azmera had never heard of buffalo, nor was she aware of the immense danger from which they had narrowly escaped.

"And the most dangerous part of all with these types of buffalo is when they travel alone," Solomon continued, "That's when they are most on their guard and that's why I told you to wait even after we saw the herd run away. Just to be on the safe side."

After holding her breath for what seemed to be an inordinate amount of time, Azmera let out a wheeze, followed by another and another. Before she knew it, her breathing was out of control, hurried and shallow and gasping for air. She was hyperventilating for the first time in her life and had no idea how to stop it.

"Meri, hold your hands up over your head and try to take a deep breath," instructed Solomon calmly and assertively.

He had learned how to stop his wife from hyperventilating following each miscarriage and the subsequent breakdowns she experienced. Barely able to hear her uncle over her wheezing, Azmera looked at her uncle and followed his lead, placing her hands high over her head. Each deep breath she took was followed by several shallow and wheezing ones until she finally restored her breathing to a normal, steady state.

With tears in her eyes, Azmera looked at her uncle and said, "I don't know what just happened to me."

Solomon looked back at his niece with a warm and sympathetic face and replied, "It can happen to all of us. Especially when you feel like you have no control over things. But we're back in control now, and we need to keep going."

Solomon reached into his bag and pulled out a handful of *kolo* to share with Azmera. There was no time to sit down and savor each delicious crunchy bite—time, as always, was running out. She was no longer hyper-ventilating, but Azmera still couldn't shake the anxiety wreaking havoc on her body. She had survived the stampeding antelopes and the charging buffalo, but she had no idea what to expect next time—and by now she knew there would inevitably be a next time. Azmera ravenously shoved the *kolo* down her mouth, the savory flavor slightly alleviating her angst. They continued their journey, leaving the yellow savannah and parched trees behind them.

Azmera had just begun fetching water from the river when she first overheard her father and Solomon talking about Qadarif and the Tawawa Refugee Camp. Ever since, Tawawa had become a household name of sorts—everyone she knew was familiar with it as the refugee camp for most of the Ethiopians fleeing their country, both Jewish and Christian. And while she knew that Tawawa was a necessary transit stop along the way to Israel, she dreaded going there, having heard far too many rumors of the wretched conditions and rotting corpses strewn throughout the camp. She was relieved to leave Dinder and its predators behind her, but she regretted not having taken advantage of the opportunity to get to know her uncle better while fending off the wild animals. In the two days they had trekked through Dinder, she found herself talking mostly to the air, with her uncle clearly in a different place. Now with no immediate threat of attack by beast, Solomon would carry on with his silence, a silence which Azmera was beginning to sense was marked by sadness more than stoicism.

Azmera looked at the dirt road paving the way to their next destination. The searing air was clouded with dust and sand, making it next to impossible to see anything farther than just a few feet ahead. She took some relief in knowing that the road, however rugged, would guarantee that they were headed in the right direction. She took even more relief in the fact that the road, or what she could see of it, was lined with squat baobab trees, serving as much-needed shade from the desert sun shining down upon them.

"Meri, you see up ahead where to the right of the road the path leads down into a valley? That's where we are headed," announced Solomon.

"But why?" questioned Azmera, no longer attempting to hide the frustration in her voice.

"Why do you think so?" her uncle said in a disappointed tone, "We'd be caught in an instant if we walked the whole way to the camp on this road. Either by the Sudanese military or by more bandits looking for easy money. I'm sorry, Meri, but there's no choice."

Azmera squinted her eyes to get a look at what awaited them down in the valley. Her stomach tied in knots when she saw that it was as sparsely vegetated as the peaks of the familiar Simien Mountains back home. There would be nothing to shield them from the sun for the next three excruciatingly long days of walking.

"Meri, there's a small town not too far from here called Doka. We have to go there to fill up on water before we can start the final stretch to the camp," informed Solomon.

Azmera sensed an air of anxiety in his voice but brushed it off. Her uncle—her leader—couldn't be weak. Solomon lowered the knapsack from his shoulders and took out the jerrycan. He offered a sip of water to his niece, who noticed how light it felt when picking it up towards her mouth. Until now, Solomon had allotted her one liter of water per day, broken up into small sips taken on an hourly basis. But now such generous rations were a luxury, at least until the water was replenished. In the meantime, Azmera felt the scorching sun sucking the life out of her.

"When we get to Doka, you need to pretend that you have come from the refugee camp to stock up on supplies, you understand? Word has it that the army is cracking down on new arrivals from the border, so as far as you're concerned, we arrived in Sudan two years ago," instructed Solomon, as he held out two counterfeit refugee identification cards with fake names and registration dates written in Arabic. "Now, there's no hiding we're Ethiopian, but do not let anyone know you are *Beta Israel*. Sudan is a declared enemy of Israel, which means they hate Jews."

Azmera nodded, amazed at how the contents of Solomon's bag continued to surprise her. With the ID card now safely placed in her knapsack, she thought to herself how odd it was that the Jewish State's staunchest of enemies was to be the country that would house them until they were taken to Israel.

The visibility improved when they reached the valley. Azmera could tell they were approaching Doka when she saw a group of women covered from head to toe in scarves and robes, leaving only their dark faces for the world to see. Like Azmera and her uncle, the women were walking off the road despite the sun beating down on the layers of clothing melted to their bodies. Azmera looked at the women with pity for having to spend their entire lives in the sizzling desert covered from head to toe in clothing, no matter how debilitating the heat. She also wondered to herself why they felt the need to walk away from the road's tempting plethora of shade. After all, from their dress and color of skin, it was clear that they were Sudanese in origin and therefore not at risk of arrest by the police. Little did she nor Solomon know, however, that a civil war was raging in Sudan at the time, putting women at risk of harassment—or worse—from both the police and the army. Traveling together as a pack, far from the road, was the best way to ward off any unwanted attention.

"Azmera, you see those women up ahead? They are carrying jugs on their heads, right?" asked Solomon, a rhetorical question that demanded only a slight nod from his niece. "They clearly are out to fetch water. We need to befriend them, and if we're lucky then maybe they'll show us their water source. If we manage to get water with their help, then we can bypass Doka entirely, avoid any questioning by the police and keep to our journey."

Azmera watched the women gather closely together as she and Solomon approached them, their eyes alert and their bodies erect. They seemed to loosen their guard, however, the moment Azmera was close enough for them to realize that not only was she a woman, but a young one at that, and therefore no threat to them.

"*Salaam alekheim*, Peace be unto you," greeted the eldest of the women in Arabic, appearing to be around Tigest's age. Two poorly healed, raised scars ran deep on her cheekbones.

"*Salaam*," responded Azmera, with the same greeting in Amharic as she flashed a smile and gently nodded her head.

Azmera couldn't help but wonder what had caused those deep scars and had to hold herself back from asking whether it was from an accident or if it had been done to her on purpose. Azmera instinctively knew she needed to take the lead. The Sudanese women in front of her would be much more likely to help her—a poor and emaciated-looking fourteen-year-old girl—than her uncle, a strong and potentially hostile grown man.

"We need water," stated Azmera in Amharic.

Knowing that the women couldn't understand her, Azmera grabbed the near empty jerrycan from Solomon and held it out for them to see. The woman with the scar gestured to Azmera to join her, so she and Solomon followed the group of women without knowing where they were leading them. One of the women in the group was in the advanced stages of pregnancy, her belly poking out from the loose robe attempting to conceal it, and all the other women matched her slow gait step by step so as not to leave her behind. Azmera could sense Solomon's growing frustration with the slow pace, but Azmera used this as an opportunity to study the women surrounding her.

Their dress was far more colorful than the clothes she was familiar with back home. She noticed the scarves wrapped around their heads and couldn't help but wonder what was hidden underneath. Azmera glimpsed one of the women, who turned back to peek at Azmera from time to time, apparently studying Azmera the same way that Azmera was studying her. Azmera wished she could initiate a conversation with them, but the language barrier limited their interaction to mere body language and the few words in each other's language they shared in common. Nevertheless, it had been days since Azmera had had any real social interaction with anyone, let alone females, and something about their presence made her feel safe.

"Meri, I was wrong. I have no idea where these women are taking us and they are walking slower than your baby sister!" vented Solomon in a harsh whisper, "We can't tell them we're in a hurry because that would raise their suspicions. I say we leave them, and we go on our own to Doka, where we'll make do."

"No, uncle," replied Azmera forcefully, "Trust me. I trust them. Besides, they know the land way better than we ever will, and like you said, if we succeed, they will save us from making a trip into town."

It was a rare occasion for Azmera to not blindly follow Solomon's orders; she felt empowered yet uneasy with her new role at the same time. Solomon stared back at Azmera with a dumbfounded expression, not knowing how to respond to his niece's failure to heed his commands. Instead of pushing back, he decided to let her win. He decided to trust her intuitions. He decided to let go.

Solomon felt like they had been walking forever but was surprised to see that only twenty minutes had passed when he looked down at his watch. The infinite Sudanese desert provided few landmarks for tracking the way, and the desert heat combined with the sandy footing made each step taken feel like a dozen. When the women's leisurely walk came to a sudden halt, Solomon was prepared to tell Azmera that they were going to do it his way and leave these kind—but slow—women behind them. To his surprise, he looked up and saw the woman with the scar tying her jug to a rope that went deep into the ground. It had never dawned on him that well water would be available in the middle of the Sudanese desert, but here it was. Solomon looked on with disbelief as he watched the woman pull her clay jug, full of water, back up to ground level. In all the preparation he had received, in all the late nights he had spent studying by candlelight maps of rivers and water sources, he had never imagined that this discovery of water in the middle of the desert was possible. Solomon felt humbled as he watched these Sudanese women prove to him that perhaps he didn't know as much as he thought he did.

Each woman took her turn lowering her jug down into the well, leaving Azmera the last to partake of the underground water source. The woman with the scar held out her hand gesturing to Azmera that she needed the jerrycan. Azmera handed it to her, feeling a sense of relief that the unfamiliar task of welling the water was no longer her responsibility. The woman with the scar proceeded to fill the jerrycan with water from her own jug. With a gentle smile that crinkled her scars, she returned it to Azmera.

With that, the women gathered their things and turned around to head home, the heavy clay jugs anchored squarely on the tops of their heads. Solomon, not having uttered a word to the women, didn't know how to thank them and again deferred to Azmera, who simply turned to the woman with the scar and smiled. Azmera couldn't help but think of her mother when the woman came closer to her and embraced her tightly—it was the kind of hug that only a mother knows how to give. Azmera looked at the woman and pointed her hand to the sprawling desert land that lay before them, signaling that it was time to continue their journey. Azmera thought to herself how easy it is to communicate without words when there are two willing parties involved. She wished in her heart that the same would be true when she would arrive in Israel.

With their renewed supply of water and Azmera's renewed sense of confidence, she led Solomon past Doka, careful to stay off the main road lest they have any uninvited encounters. They had around two more days of walking ahead of them, and for the first time since they started their journey, Azmera could feel the end nearing. Despite the searing blisters on her feet and the cramps racing up and down her legs, for the first time Azmera believed that she could carry on until they reached their destination.

Chapter Fourteen

Tigest—April 1985

Tigest had been to Gondar several times throughout her adult life, but she never ceased to be impressed—and overwhelmed—by the masses of people everywhere she looked. That feeling was even more amplified the minute her escort jeep pulled up to the city's main hospital. The large three-story building was a rare sight for Tigest, and she looked down at her daughter nestled into her chest and felt optimistic that this—one of Ethiopia's best hospitals—would be the place that would save her baby's life.

"This place looks like a shit-hole," mumbled Josh under his breath to David, "That baby doesn't have a chance here."

David didn't respond at first, and instead stared at his friend with contempt.

"Don't translate that, Abaye," instructed David, "Despite his heart, Josh is a spoiled American. No matter how long we stay here, he simply cannot get used to life in Africa."

Abaye turned back to look at Tigest and saw that she was too busy comforting her crying baby to have paid attention to the conversation taking place in the front of the car. Abaye climbed out of the car and opened the door for Tigest, holding out his arms for the baby as Tigest climbed down from the jeep. Tigest hesitated before handing over the baby to him, this being the first time her baby was in a stranger's arms, even if just for a moment.

The line that wrapped around the outside of the hospital unceremoniously greeted Tigest and her baby. Emaciated old women who looked like they were already on their way to the grave, screaming children with broken bones, and young men with missing limbs stood in line. No numbers were handed out, and there was no one to tell them whose turn it was to enter the hospital next. Utter chaos ruled. Tigest and her baby reluctantly joined the sea of invisible patients, making her the last in line.

"This is simply ridiculous," shouted Josh, this time making sure his voice was heard loud and clear to whoever would understand, "At this pace, her baby will die standing here in line. We have to do something about this."

David gave a nod to Abaye, signaling that this time he was free to translate what his friend had just said. For better or worse, being a "spoiled American" meant not accepting anything sub-standard, and Josh was about as spoiled an American as they come. A native Manhattanite, Josh was a litigation partner in a leading corporate law firm in New York City and was pushy, loud, and unapologetically condescending, but also charitable, ideological and good intentioned. David had befriended Josh through their work with the AAEJ. While David found Josh's demanding personality to be exasperating, he knew that with Josh by Tigest's side, they would have a doctor tending to them within the hour.

Josh pulled Tigest out of the line and dragged her into the hospital waiting room. The room was so crowded with patients that there was little air left to breathe.

"Can't someone open a window here, for God's sake!" shouted Josh to no one in particular, finding himself suffocating from the stagnant air. No one paid any attention to his plea.

Tigest covered her baby's mouth and nose to prevent—as much as possible under the circumstances—the transmission of germs surely floating all around them. Another line of twenty people stood waiting patiently to be served by the two hospital nurses manning the reception desk. In front of

Tigest stood a ten-year-old boy heroically holding back tears as his severed leg hung by a thread, his mother trying her best to be strong for her soon-to-be amputee boy. His young blood was gushing all over the floor, but no one tried to clean it up. Once more, Josh pulled Tigest out of the line, and dragged her to the front of the reception desk. Tigest was thankful for Josh's assertiveness, but she couldn't erase the ten-year-old boy from her head—he was Daniel's age, and in the best of scenarios he was bound to lose a leg, if not bleed to death.

"You must admit this baby right away," demanded Josh to the hospital nurse, "She will die if a doctor doesn't see her soon!" Abaye hurriedly translated Josh's command into Amharic, but the nurse stared back at him like he had lost his mind.

"I'm sorry, sir, but she is going to have to wait in line with the others. Everyone here has their own tragic story to tell. It's not my job to decide who gets to be seen first," replied the nurse as she signaled to the next patient in line to move forward.

Josh looked around him and understood what the nurse meant—far too many of the patients standing in line were straddling life and death, and far too many of them would surely be sucked into death's abyss as the hours went by. Still, he couldn't accept the nurse's casual attitude towards the value of life, especially that of an innocent baby brought too soon into the world through no fault of her own.

"I hoped it wouldn't come to this," Josh continued, this time with a more forceful tone, "But you see, I am a diplomat at the American Embassy. Here's my credentials." Josh confidently held out an identification card proving that he was in fact what he claimed to be. "You can call the Embassy if you want to check, but as you may know the phone lines have been out in Addis for the past few days. This woman is a valued employee of the Embassy, and her baby needs to see a doctor immediately."

The nurse looked at Tigest, who on first impression appeared to her to be a simple peasant. But then she looked again at Josh, her face awestruck. Here was a diplomat—an American diplomat at that—standing before her asking for her help. She flashed him a subservient smile, stood up from her desk and ushered Tigest and her baby down the hall to the maternity ward, with Josh and David trailing behind them.

"Josh, you are one crazy bastard!" whispered David as they approached the maternity ward.

"Tell me about it," mumbled Josh with a smirk on his face, "That bit about the phone lines being out in Addis . . . I made it up on the spot, of course, but it worked. And that ID card you got us—in all our time here, it's the first time I ever had to use it. It looks so damn fake to me, but it worked like magic!"

A lean and muscular doctor greeted them as they entered the maternity ward. Josh couldn't help but think to himself how his body was the ideal body type in America—one evoking his wife's numerous workouts played on their new VHR machine back in Manhattan. In Ethiopia, the doctor's physical appearance indicated his social status, making him a constant target for begging and soliciting by those less fortunate than he. The doctor tried to maintain compassion for his fellow man, but the relentless sight of poor and hungry souls pleading for his help, both inside and outside the hospital, had hardened him. The doctor's English was heavily accented, but he was nonetheless able to communicate with Josh, who continued to bulldoze Tigest's way into getting the care her baby needed.

"Not sure what the nurse told you, but this baby needs help now. Born this morning, two months early according to the mother. Trouble breathing. Managed to nurse once or twice on the way here, but her heartbeat is abnormally fast—again, according to the mother."

Tigest took comfort knowing that Josh was acting on her behalf; she knew she would still be back in her village but for his and David's help. The doctor listened to Josh's account of the baby's short medical history and couldn't help but glimpse the Rolex watch glistening on his wrist.

The doctor knew that the man before him was a man of power that could open doors to him that were otherwise closed. The doctor, however, knew it would be highly inappropriate at this stage to share with the fancy diplomat his dream of moving to America and getting out of this hell-hole of a hospital; instead he scribbled a one-page form and admitted Tigest and the baby into the neonatal intensive care unit. Tigest hesitated before handing the baby over to the doctor—while she knew that her baby would now be taken care of, she was terrified to think that this very moment might be the last time she would ever hold her baby. The nurse promptly weighed her in at a scant 1.8 kilograms (4 pounds), and Tigest held back tears as she watched her daughter's face disappear under an oversized oxygen mask covering all but her tiny eyebrows. Her baby was then placed into the only available incubator, a recent acquisition that David later informed Tigest had been donated by an American aid organization.

"Josh. David. I don't know what to say," sighed Tigest as she held back her tears, "I don't know how I'll ever repay you. You have given my baby a chance at life. She doesn't have a name yet, but if she lives, I will give her a name that reminds her every day how lucky she is to be alive."

With a warm smile atypical of his abrasive, Wall Street character, Josh pulled Tigest in for a hug. "It was our privilege and pleasure to help you. Now, you get this baby healthy and then get the hell out of Ethiopia," Josh said with a chuckle.

Josh and David stepped outside the NICU for a moment, giving Tigest the opportunity to take in her baby's new home. The room was poorly lit, but Tigest managed to spot a rat running across the back of the room. Tigest counted a total of twenty babies in incubators like her daughter's, but she saw only one nurse, an older woman who sat in a wheelchair and wheeled herself from one incubator to the next. When the nurse finally did stand up, Tigest could see her hunched back painfully protruding outwards, her spine lopsided and lumpy. Suddenly, Tigest saw a doctor rush into the room with what looked like an extremely premature baby. The nurse admitted the baby into the unit, but the baby stopped breathing in the nurse's arms several minutes later. The new mother stood by hysterically screaming for someone to come to her baby's aid, until she understood that her screaming was in vain. Tigest's heart ached as she placed her hand inside her daughter's incubator and gently stroked her cheek.

With Tigest inside the unit tending to her baby, David and Josh walked down the hallway to catch some air. "There's got to be somewhere to buy coffee in this Godforsaken place, no?" David said, his patience running thin from not having consumed caffeine all day long.

"I'm sorry to have overheard your conversation, but there's a cafeteria for doctors down the hall," interrupted the doctor from before, "Come. You will be my guests. My name is Dr. Berhanu Abra, by the way."

The three men sat down on white plastic chairs pulled up to a white plastic table covered with a cheap tablecloth decorated in blue flowers. A young woman approached their table and, following the doctor's instructions, served them freshly brewed coffee.

"You know, the coffee here is usually stale and lukewarm, but I asked her to treat you two like you deserve," shared the doctor, sporting an overly friendly grin on his face.

Sensing that the doctor was trying to capitalize on the situation, Josh decided to take advantage of the opportunity and do the same. "My brother's wife gave birth to a baby boy at 32 weeks two years ago," Josh told the doctor, "It was a tough time. The baby was in the NICU for over a month to get him strong enough, but there was never any fear that he wouldn't survive."

"Your brother and his wife were lucky to be living in a country as wonderful as America," replied the doctor, "Here, a baby born at 32 weeks has about a thirty percent chance of surviving. Maybe closer to forty percent if the baby is a girl, but closer to twenty percent if the baby is a boy. Girls are born fighters from the get-go. Of course, this is only relevant if the baby makes it to the hospital in the first place."

"So, you're saying that our friend's baby has around a forty percent chance of surviving?" asked David with a concerned look on his face as he carefully took a sip from his coffee.

"I'll take those odds," interrupted Josh as he held out his fancy watch for the doctor to see. "Tell me, Dr. Abra. The woman and her baby—their wellbeing is very important to all of us at the U.S. Embassy. You take care of them, and I am sure that we can find a way to take care of you, too." Josh amazed himself by his ability to manufacture lies out of nowhere, and in doing so, manipulate the doctor in front of him like a marionette.

"Well, funny that you mention it," answered the doctor with an uncomfortable yet eager look on his face, "But I've been trying to get a visa for myself and my family to go to the States for years now, with no success. Ever since the Dergue came to power, it's been virtually impossible for Ethiopians—even a hardworking and skilled doctor like me—to get a visa to your great country."

"We can help you," replied David, after having decided to join in on this masquerade, "You treat that baby girl like it's President Reagan's grandchild and we'll pull some strings down at the Embassy."

David and Josh glanced at one another, not sure what the next step of their improvised ruse would be.

"I will. I will. I promise I will treat that baby like royalty," nodded the doctor enthusiastically. "Umm... but then what? Do you have a business card for me to contact you?"

"You know, we were on a week off from work, so we didn't take our cards with us. We came to Gondar as a starting point for hiking the Simien Mountains. But here, this is how you can reach us," Josh said as he scribbled down his phone number at the AAEJ office back in Addis Ababa.

To be fair, Josh did feel a bit guilty to be so blatantly deceiving the doctor into believing he could help him emigrate to America. He seemed like a decent person who was just looking to find a break like everyone else. At the same time, he didn't see any other way that baby would have a real chance. At the very least, he reassured himself, he would send money to Dr. Abra once he was able to.

"When that baby makes her way home alive and kicking, you call me and we'll do what we can to help you get a visa," Josh stated as he took his last sip of coffee.

"I sure will, sirs," answered the doctor eagerly as he looked down at the number handed to him, "I sure will."

With that, Josh and David shook hands with the doctor before they headed back down the poorly lit corridor to Tigest. Dr. Abra remained seated at the table, optimistic about his future in America but concerned that he would not be able to meet the diplomats' demands of him. The lights in the cafeteria flickered on and off for several minutes, bringing to a halt all the hustling movement around him. He couldn't help but feel ashamed that Josh and David had borne witness to the hospital's horrendous conditions. When the electricity finally stabilized, he stood up and returned to the NICU. He had work to do.

"Tigest, it's time for us to leave you and your little fighter," Josh turned to Abaye who then translated for Tigest. "But don't you worry—Dr. Abra is going to take excellent care of your little girl. We've made sure of that. And if he asks you any questions, remind him that we are diplomats at the U.S. Embassy and that you work for us. And if he asks for more details, you tell him to call us on the number we gave him."

Honesty had always been a virtue Tigest did her best to live by, but she felt only slightly uneasy playing a role in the scam Josh and David were running. She knew she had to do whatever she could to save her baby's life.

"Remember your promise, Tigest. Get out of this country as soon as you can. And who knows? Maybe one day, God willing, we'll meet again in Israel."

Josh pulled Tigest in for a hug with David standing next to him waiting for his turn. Tears slowly rolled down Tigest's face as she gently lowered her head in a sign of respect. She turned to Abaye, her trusted interpreter, and in words made barely decipherable by her muffled tears she mumbled, "I will never forget what they have done for me and my baby. Please let them know that. God bless them."

David, Josh and Abaye walked out of the NICU into the madness of the hospital, leaving Tigest and her baby girl alone for the first time since she had sent Daniel out for help many hours ago. Dr. Abra walked into the room and brushed shoulders with Tigest before approaching the hunchback nurse. He whispered something into her ear and then, with a nod of her head, the two of them got back to work, diligently tending to Tigest's baby.

"Today she's up to two kilos (4 pounds, seven ounces)," announced the hunchback nurse as she picked Tigest's baby up off the cold metal scale, "You've done a good job squeezing out milk for your little girl. I think it's time she graduates from the feeding tubes to your breast."

Tigest watched with surprise as the nurse, despite her deformity, held on to her baby with warm and gentle hands.

"Have you chosen a name for her yet?" questioned the nurse, although she quickly understood when she saw tears in Tigest's eyes that she had not.

The nurse was accustomed to caring for nameless babies—that way there would be no nicknames and no songs to sing with the baby's name in rhyme. It made it easier for the parents to remain emotionally detached so long as their baby's survival wasn't guaranteed.

The following day, Tigest noticed that her baby's breathing had slowed down to an alarmingly sluggish rate.

"Help! She's barely breathing!" Tigest shouted to the room filled with helpless babies and their helpless mothers.

Dr. Abra rushed into the NICU to care for her. He grabbed her out of the incubator and held on to her with a roughness that only someone who holds babies for a living can get away with. As the doctor hurriedly undressed Tigest's baby, he instructed the nurse to pinch the baby's feet, miraculously restoring her breathing to a normal pace within seconds. Tigest sat and watched in disbelief as the medical staff took care of her baby. She had been so optimistic just the day before—her baby was gaining weight, and things were progressing better than she could have hoped for—but she understood that her baby's breathing problems meant that they were not yet in the clear.

The days and nights in the NICU seemed endless for Tigest, who was a constant by her baby's side. It was the first time since Azmera had been born that Tigest was responsible for caring for only one child. Despite the constant anxiety weighing heavily down on her and all the other parents in the NICU, Tigest strangely felt a sense of freedom she hadn't felt in years.

The mask covering Tigest's face muffled her words as she sang sweet lullabies to her baby. The chaos of the NICU offered Tigest very little time to process all the changes that had taken place in the two weeks since she had given birth. Now, with her baby nestled in her arms, she could see one small roll of fat developing underneath her baby's chin that she was certain had not been there just a few days prior. While she reveled in each of her daughter's milestones, however small, she had no one to share them with. The other mothers standing guard next to their own babies were far too preoccupied to make any contact with anyone but the doctor or nurse. Plus, there were plenty of babies in a far worse state than hers and it would have been cruel to rejoice in her daughter's slow entry back into life when other babies were gradually departing it. On top of it all, Tigest knew that the other mothers resented her for the special attention showered on her baby by Dr. Abra and the hunchback nurse. She took no offense at their angry stares, knowing she would have felt no different if in their situation.

Breastfeeding, like having children, had always come easily to Tigest;

this baby, however, had made it clear from the get-go that she was an exception to the rule. When she latched on to her mother's breast, Tigest would wince in pain as the suction from her baby's lips would re-open sores that hadn't had more than a few short hours to heal. Nursing sessions took upwards of an hour, and while her milk slowly brought her daughter back to life, she felt like her daughter was sucking the life out of her. Water was hard to come by in the hospital, even for someone in Tigest's state. There was no running water in the NICU, but on a good day the hunchback nurse would sneak a cup or two into the room for Tigest.

As the days went by, Tigest developed a sort of routine marked by three-hour intervals. Sleep was a luxury relic from the past; if she were lucky, she would doze off for an hour or two in the NICU while sitting on a plastic chair that dug deep into her bones. The baby was now officially capable of breathing on her own and, as a result, the oxygen mask came off, allowing Tigest to peek in at her daughter's button nose and cheeks, which were growing chubbier by the day. In between each breastfeeding session, Tigest would step out of the NICU to get some fresh air. Once a day she would step outside the confines of the hospital and, using the money Josh and David had given to Daniel, she would buy *injera* with *shiro* chickpea stew from a vendor on the street. It was cheaper and fresher than the food for sale in the hospital, and it refueled her body for the time-being. She would then check with the front desk to see if she had received any mail from her parents. A week into her stay, she had sent a letter to her family letting them know that the baby was in good care and was improving daily. She kept the letter optimistic, deliberately avoiding the many setbacks her baby faced with the hope that it would prompt a similarly optimistic response from her family. There was, of course, no way of knowing if her letters were ever received, let alone sent. But she missed her older children and desperately wanted to hear that they were faring well without her. Sadly, each day she left the front desk disappointed to discover that no mail had arrived for her.

One morning, Tigest woke up to the sounds of her crying baby, hungry for her next feed. The air that day was so humid that she could almost drink from it. She wiped the drool from her chin and stood up from the plastic chair, her body stiff and sore. Now three weeks old, the baby's latch was much more efficient, cutting the nursing sessions in half, much to Tigest's relief. When the baby's eyes slowly dozed off for yet another nap that day, Tigest stood up again to place her baby back into the incubator. Her head light and foggy, the next thing Tigest knew she found herself lying on the cold, hard ground, with the baby screaming next to her. The hunchback nurse ran over and struggled to bend down to pick up the baby. Tigest heard muffled sounds of her baby's screaming and the nurse's hushing while she lay on the ground, confused and terrified of what she might have done to her baby. She slowly dragged herself up from the ground and saw the hunchback nurse and Dr. Abra examining the baby to check whether any harm was done.

"Is she okay?" sobbed Tigest, now in hysterics, "Dear God, I dropped my baby. I dropped my baby! Please tell me she's okay!"

"Nurse, go get Tigest something to eat and drink and make her sit down and rest," ordered Dr. Abra, "Her body is physically spent, and we can't afford to have her fainting on this baby again."

The nurse, knowing the stakes for the doctor and, in turn, for herself, complied. She whisked Tigest away to the staff cafeteria where she bought Tigest a juice shake and a serving of *injera* with a platter of grayish chicken. Despite Tigest's uncontrollable bursts of crying, the nurse forced Tigest to finish every ounce. Beyond the financial incentives Dr. Abra had guaranteed should Tigest's baby survive, the hunchback nurse felt a special kinship for Tigest. Nearly all the other mothers who came to the NICU with their sick babies had a husband and family by their side, ensuring that the mother was well cared for while she cared for the newborn baby. Tigest was different. She was all alone. And while the nurse was careful not to pry too much into anyone's business, she felt a deep sense of compassion for Tigest every time she watched her doze off to sleep on the plastic chair as if she were on guard protecting her baby. When Tigest fainted, the nurse had to hold herself back from crying—it wouldn't have been professional to let the other mothers see her get too emotional, even in the worst of crises. And while her hunched back had kept away the suitors her entire life, she had always felt in her heart that she was a mother without children. She had worked for more than twenty years as a nurse, but watching Tigest agonize over what she might have done to her baby pinched her heartstrings more than she expected.

After Tigest's stomach was sufficiently replenished, the two women sat in silence for several minutes. Tigest kept shaking her head from side to side as if she were still processing the irreparable harm she may have caused to her baby girl.

The hunchback nurse held out her hand towards Tigest and stroked it gently with a shake of her head. "You know, I've seen lots of babies come and go here," said the hunchback nurse softly, "The mother has to be strong for her baby, but if she doesn't take care of herself, she'll be good to no one."

Tigest looked back at the nurse with a blank expression. She appreciated the advice and the genuine concern, but she didn't see how things could be any different. Kebede and Azmera were long gone, and her parents were busy caring for her other children. Caring for herself was a luxury she couldn't afford.

When Tigest returned to the NICU, she was relieved to see her baby girl in one piece taking a nap in her incubator.

"Mother's instincts," shouted Dr. Abra cheerfully from across the room, where he was checking in on another baby.

Tigest looked over at the doctor, not sure she understood what he meant.

"Neither the nurse nor I saw what happened," explained the doctor, "but you must have held your baby in your arms until you hit the ground.

Even when unconscious, the mother's instinct to protect her baby is still intact."

A tear rolled gently down Tigest's eye as she waited for final confirmation that she had not caused any harm to the baby.

"I checked your baby from head to toe, and she's fine. You can relax now. But take better care of yourself or it will happen again," commanded the doctor with a reassuring grin on his face.

While somewhat comforted by the doctor's words, Tigest couldn't help but wonder how she would ever manage to take care of herself when she had so many souls depending on her to take care of them.

"Today she's up to 2.5 kilos (5 pounds, 8 ounces)," shouted the hunchback nurse over the sound of Tigest's crying baby lying on the cold metal scale.

The baby was now four weeks old and gaining weight at a steady pace. Tigest had just come back from the market in Gondar where, with the money from Josh and David, she had bought a bag of *kolo* and five fluffy pieces of *injera* to last her for the next few days. Ever since the fainting incident, Tigest had done her best to eat when hungry and drink when thirsty, even if it meant using all the money she had. Sleep, however, still eluded her. No matter how many hours she spent dozing off in the plastic chair, it never relented from digging into her back.

"She's gaining weight so well that you two will be heading home in no time," announced Dr. Abra.

While he did his best to remain professional in all things concerning the baby's health, he found himself counting down the days until it would be medically sound for the baby and his mother to be sent home, and in turn, for him to receive his visa to America. Tigest smiled at the good news, but in truth she was terrified to return home. No matter how long and exhausting the days were in the NICU, she had the hunchback nurse and the doctor by her side whenever she needed them. She didn't see how it would be humanly possible for her to care for four young children and a newborn baby upon return to the village, all the while tending to the teff and corn fields and caring for the goats and chickens.

Tigest picked her baby up off the scale and looked into her deep brown eyes. With each passing day, the baby was becoming more and more alert, spending more and more time staring back at her mother while cuddled in her arms. And while Tigest couldn't help but fall in love with her, she also couldn't help but feel like it was a mistake to have brought her into the world—into a world with war, famine and drought all around her, a world without a father and without a future, at least not in Ethiopia. But there was no undoing what was done—for better or for worse, her baby had climbed her way out of limbo.

With her baby cradled in her arms, Tigest decided it was time to connect to her offspring on a deeper level—it was time to bestow upon her a name. Until now, Tigest and Kebede had carefully chosen names for their first five children, avoiding names that revealed their Jewish identity. Of course, Biblical names were acceptable so long as they could easily be mistaken for Christian ones. She contemplated the options but couldn't shake off the feeling that this time around there was no need to avoid a name that would give away that she was a *Falasha* Jew. In fact, looking down at her helpless baby girl, Tigest hoped now more than ever that her days in Ethiopia were numbered. In Ethiopia, she would be forced to raise five children on her own while combating poverty, famine and the Dergue regime's attacks on *Falashas* like herself. In Israel, she would have Azmera and Kebede by her side, and a country and people welcoming her home. The choice was obvious. There was no life for her or her family here.

With that, Tigest whispered softly into her daughter's ear lest anyone else hear, "Chaya, I'm your *Enati*. Welcome to the world, my sweet bird." Her name meant "life" in Hebrew—Tigest had fulfilled her promise to

David and Josh to bestow upon her daughter a name that reminded her how lucky she was to be alive.

Tigest couldn't deny Chaya's resemblance to her father—her striking features matched his, even as a newborn baby. She patted Chaya's high cheekbone and felt a tear slowly roll down her own, "I just wish your *Abat* and Azmera were here to meet you."

Three days later, Dr. Abra eagerly ushered Tigest and Chaya out of the NICU and towards the hospital front doors. Before leaving the hospital, she swung by the hospital's front desk just to make sure that she hadn't received any letters. Four weeks had passed since arriving at the hospital and, while she hadn't received a single letter, she hadn't given up hope. She watched as the receptionist humored her while she leafed through a thick pile of envelopes, none of them addressed to Tigest. More than anything, she had hoped her parents would have written her with word from Azmera. She hadn't heard from her eldest daughter since she had left their home months ago, and now that Chaya was healthy enough to go home, Tigest could focus her worries on her other children.

With her sleeping baby wrapped snugly inside her shawl, Tigest stepped outside the hospital. She was now the sole caregiver for the tiny creature breathing against her chest. In the few minutes that had passed since exiting the hospital, Tigest had witnessed a grown man defecating in the street and way too many begging children to count. While their vacant stares and sunken cheeks pinched her heart, she had no money to spare—she needed every *birr* remaining to pay for her bus ticket back to Debark. Tigest was accustomed to the poverty in her village, marked by food and water shortages and hard work in the fields; she still hasn't gotten used to the sight of poverty, disease and filth that pervaded the city. It was a whole different level of misery, she convinced herself. She had to get her baby away from the rats of Gondar and back home to the field mice of her village. Tigest looked down at Chaya, who was sleeping peacefully inside her mother's shawl, and felt an enormous surge of gratitude. She was on her way home with her baby girl intact.

Dr. Abra watched impatiently as Tigest and her baby walked down the street toward the bus station. When she was finally out of sight, he walked over to the front desk and picked up the phone. He felt his heart thump as he dialed the number scribbled on the note, now crumpled from weeks spent in his pocket. The phone rang once, and then twice, and then three times.

"Pick up, pick up!" the doctor uttered under his breath.

The doctor let the phone ring until the nurse manning the front desk timidly approached him, informing him that she needed the phone back. Dr. Abra slammed the phone down onto the receiver and walked back to the dimly lit maternity ward, his head and spirits cast down towards the ground.

Chapter Fifteen

Kebede—March 1985

Dear Tigy,

Yesterday in ulpan *(you remember, right?—It means Hebrew class), we heard on the news about a horrible attack on Israeli soldiers. By the way, that's something really amazing about Israel—every hour, everyone stops what they are doing to listen to the hourly radio broadcast. Anyway, apparently a terrorist drove a truck loaded with explosives into an Israeli tank in southern Lebanon. Twelve Israeli soldiers were killed. I remember thinking two things when I listened to the radio. First, I remember thinking how proud I was for being able to understand almost everything the broadcaster said in Hebrew. I know I shouldn't have been thinking of myself at such a moment, but that's what I felt. Second—I was angry. And I wasn't just angry because so many young Israelis were killed for no reason by an enemy who doesn't want us to exist. I felt angry over everything—angry at myself for having had too much to drink the night before (and the night before that), angry at you for not seeming to care when I left for Israel, angry at Solomon for not having yet arrived in Israel with Azmera, angry at Shifra for calling me Kfir, angry at the others in the absorption center for not trying hard enough to learn Hebrew, angry at myself for abandoning my family, angry at Israel for bringing me here and then treating me like I don't belong, and last but certainly not least, angry at God for making me feel so angry at the world.*

I'm having a hard time here, Tigy. Every night I sit in my room with my notebook and try to study what we learned that day in ulpan, *but then I hear it. I hear the others sitting outside on the balcony chatting away, the alcohol having numbed their anger, erased all their worries and blurred all their memories, at least for the night. Some nights I manage to stay in my room. But other nights I go outside to join them. I never intend to have more than one drink. But then one of the guys offers me a shot of arak, and another shot, and another. Before I know it, I'm crawling my way back into bed and I have four hours to sleep before I must wake up for* ulpan. *Shifra, my teacher—I think she knows, but she hasn't said anything to me about it. I think she pities me. I've never felt pitied in my entire life. I used to be a strong man. That's what I was named for. That's what my father raised me to be. People used to respect me. I don't want you to come here because I know there's no way you'll want to be with me in the state I am. So, take this as my warning—Tigest, dear Tigest, Stay in Ethiopia. Stay far, far away from me. It's for your own good.*

Kebede

Kebede lay in bed with his tattered notebook in hand, wondering what Tigest would think if she were to receive the letter he had just wrote. In their nearly fifteen years of marriage, he had never opened to her like he did in the letter resting in the palm of his hand. Since coming to Israel, he had discovered there was something about writing that was different from talking—something more anonymous and intimate all at once. Every time he wrote a letter to his wife, Kebede was able to put into words thoughts and feelings that he didn't know existed beforehand. There was something cathartic about writing, even if he knew that in the end no one would ever actually read the letter. In fact, it had been weeks since he placed one of his letters in the red mailbox outside the small grocery store, the same grocery store where he would buy coffee—which paled in comparison to the *bunnah* at home—and other basic supplies. While he was terrified of Tigest coming to Israel and seeing him the way he was, he desperately needed her back in his life. She couldn't know, then, how unraveled he had become in the past few months. Kebede had tried several times writing optimistic letters where everything was perfect and nice, but they felt forced; he knew Tigest would see through it and know something was wrong. So, he stopped sending letters altogether. But that didn't keep him from writing them. He crumpled up the letter in his hand and slammed it into the trash can next to his bed, and then headed outside to join the others on the balcony for just one drink.

Kebede—April 1985

"Kfir, I asked you a question!" shouted Shifra in Hebrew at her once prized student, now dozing off in the middle of class, his drool forming a small pool on his desk.

Kebede shook his head and pulled his body upright in the wooden chair attached to the desk. It was entirely too small for his tall frame. He awkwardly straightened his legs, making a futile attempt to find a comfortable position in an uncomfortable chair.

"Umm . . . ," mumbled Kebede, trying to buy time to compose himself after a late night of drinking.

Before he had a chance to answer, a boy sitting next to him who looked no older than Azmera raised his hand and offered the correct answer to Shifra's question. The boy was one of the few new arrivals to the absorption center, having landed in Israel only days before.

Kebede couldn't help but feel a twinge of envy towards the boy who spoke Hebrew fluently and effortlessly, even though he had just arrived. He looked at the clock, anxious for the morning break to come so he would have an opportunity to question the boy about his journey. There had been rumors circulating throughout the absorption center that there had been a small covert airlift from Sudan bringing *Beta Israel* still left behind in the camps to Israel, but no one had officially confirmed it. He wondered, then, if perhaps the boy could be a valuable source of information.

"Before we take our morning break, I want to play you our song of the week," announced Shifra.

Her enthusiasm for teaching Hebrew was only slightly greater than her enthusiasm for introducing Israeli music to her students. She had a penchant for a quirky Israeli musician named Meir Ariel. Kebede, however, found his music, no matter how pleasant the melody, to be frustrating—the singer's play on words was nearly always lost on Kebede. Yet, despite the music's foreign sound, each song he learned made him feel a bit more Israeli, even if the music's Israeliness called to mind an Ashkenazi kibbutznik reading Amos Oz by a desert campfire more than it ever would himself.

Shifra handed out printed copies of the lyrics to the song of the week, *Agadat Deshe* (The Lawn Tale), and Kebede began to skim through the words. As always, Shifra read through the lyrics verse by verse together with the class before she turned on her black boom box to play the much-anticipated song. And while Kebede did not understand every word in the song's complicated lyrics, he was surprised at how much he did understand—a boy and a girl lying together on the lawn, embarrassed by their romantic feelings for one another. When Shifra finally played the song, Kebede listened to the beautiful lyrics and melody, and his heart sank. Meir Ariel had managed to perfectly describe in a poetic combination of words everything that he and Tigest never had together.

When the song ended, silence pervaded the classroom; the song apparently touched the heartstrings of all his classmates. No one moved or said a word until Shifra announced it was time for their morning break. Kebede extricated himself from his desk, anxious to catch the new boy outside on the balcony.

"Kfir, I need to talk to you," called out Shifra just as Kebede was exiting the classroom.

Kebede knew it was a matter of time before his teacher would initiate a conversation about his performance in class recently—in fact, he was surprised she hadn't done so long ago—but Shifra had kept her distance the past few weeks, joining the other *ulpan* teachers during the break for a smoke outside the dining hall. The anticipation of hearing a twinge of disappointment in her voice made Kebede's stomach churn. Kebede paused by the door and debated whether he should come up with an excuse to get out of the room as soon as possible, but he knew this conversation was inevitable. He might as well get it over with.

"I've been noticing that you've been coming to *ulpan* late recently," Shifra spoke with a concerned but stern voice, "And your Hebrew has not been improving as I expected of you."

Kebede looked back at Shifra—not much older than himself—and felt like he was a little boy back in Ethiopia being scolded by his teacher. Kebede remained silent, not knowing what to say or how to justify his sudden change in performance.

"*Nu*, come on, what do you have to say for yourself?" Shifra demanded.

Kebede gazed at the floor and noticed for the first time that it was ever so slightly sloped, which explained why every time he dropped his pencil it would quickly roll over to the left side of the room. No matter how much Kebede respected Shifra, and no matter how much he valued her opinion, he couldn't overcome the fact that she was a woman. He could not show her any weakness.

"I just haven't been feeling well recently," mumbled Kebede, his eyes cast downwards in a deliberate attempt to avert contact with hers.

"There's more going on than that, Kfir," Shifra exclaimed as she stared disappointedly at her once prized pupil, "I'm not stupid, you know. I can smell the vodka on your breath in the morning. I can't imagine all that you must be going through, but I'm here for you if you need to talk."

Kebede felt his eyes welling up with tears, so he tilted his head downwards even more, his chin now nearly touching his chest. She was right, of course, but there was nothing to say. He turned his back towards his teacher and walked out the door. Shifra sat down at her desk, slowly shaking her head from side to side.

"Hey, you!" shouted Kebede to the new boy who was sitting on the balcony drinking sugary juice out of a flimsy plastic cup.

Kebede looked at his watch. Assuming Shifra would linger over her cigarette like she had been doing recently, they had ten more minutes before the morning break came to an end. He had already been a half-hour late that morning. He couldn't be late again. The boy hesitated before turning to look at Kebede, as if he wasn't sure that someone could possibly be interested in talking to him. He had arrived in Dimona two days prior and Kebede hadn't seen him speak to anyone outside the classroom.

"*Salaam*," answered the boy with a polite nod of the head.

Kebede was taken aback at the sound of the boy's Tigray accent in Amharic, but it certainly explained why he had been keeping to himself. Until now, the absorption center had housed only Ethiopian Jews from the Amhara region of Ethiopia, but this boy's arrival all the way from the Tigray region was a sign that things—both inside Israel and outside—were changing.

"Tell me, boy, what's your name?" asked Kebede as he smiled gently at the boy.

The boy, short in stature and still emaciated, responded in thickly-accented Amharic, "My name is Tsege, but I plan on changing my name to Tzur."

Kebede wondered to himself how this young boy was so confident in his new identity when he himself was anything but.

"My name is Kebede. When and how did you arrive in Israel?" inquired Kebede.

He had a feeling that the boy was struggling to understand him, and that became clear when the boy replied in Amharic asking if he could respond in Hebrew instead. Kebede immediately acquiesced, excited at the opportunity to practice Hebrew outside of the classroom with a fellow immigrant.

In what sounded to Kebede to be perfect Hebrew, the boy explained in a quiet whisper, "I was in Sudan at the Tawawa refugee camp. I arrived around the end of December together with my mother and younger brother, but we didn't manage to get on a flight during the big operation."

Kebede nodded his head and encouraged the boy to continue, hoping for even the slightest bit of information that could help him locate his daughter.

"The journey to Sudan was not easy for us, especially for my mother," explained Tsege, his eyes cast downwards, "When we got to Tawawa, she was very sick. She was treated by the clinic, but things didn't look good. We couldn't leave her side, so we stayed in the camp even though a man offered to put me and my brother on the bus to Khartoum, and then to Israel, with all the others."

Kebede felt the alcohol from the night before wearing off as he watched the boy hold back tears. He was in awe at how open and raw Tsege was with him—a perfect stranger—especially considering how he himself was unable to open himself up to Shifra, his beloved teacher.

"The operation came to an end suddenly sometime in early January. I don't remember when exactly, but I just know that my mother died a few days later," Tsege looked up at Kebede with lost eyes as he continued, "We stayed in the camp not knowing what was going to happen to us."

Kebede's ears perked up with every bit of information Tsege shared with him, as if he and Kebede were slowly putting together a complex jigsaw puzzle.

"Yes, we heard rumors that the big operation came to an end because some journalists and politicians just couldn't keep their mouth shut," exclaimed Kebede, trying hard to contain his frustration. "Tell me, how many *Beta Israel* were left in the camp? You see, I think my daughter might have been left behind after the big operation."

Tsege's eyes now darted away from Kebede's. Kebede sensed that all his interrogating, with no sympathy for Tsege's own losses, had shut down the boy.

"I'm terribly sorry for your loss, Tsege," added Kebede, trying his best not to sound too eager to get on with his questioning, "Everyone here at the absorption center seems to have lost someone or left someone behind. It's just the way it is, and now you and your brother are going to have to create a new life here in the Holy Land without your mother."

"No," Tsege whimpered, "My brother. He didn't make it. After the big operation, he got sick with malaria. The people at the clinic tried to treat him, but he was too sick. He died one month after my mother died. I remember—I had just finished thirty days of mourning, and then I had to start them all over again."

Tsege stared at Kebede, his big brown eyes swimming in a sea of loss. The boy shook his head slowly from side to side, trying to convince himself that his story wasn't real. Kebede felt for him, he truly did, but after a few months in the absorption center, he couldn't help but feel a bit hardened to all the grief around him. More than anything, though, Kebede felt guilty—guilty for having left his entire family behind him and guilty for feeling sorry for himself when in fact he was one of the lucky ones. After all, he hadn't lost anyone—yet.

Kebede held out his arms to hug Tsege and squeezed him tighter than he himself had expected. It was his first hug in months. The much-needed physical contact prompted Tsege to continue talking.

"Back to your question, there were many of us left at the camp after the operation came to an end. I'm not sure how many, though. I was so preoccupied with mourning my mother and caring for my brother, it's hard for me to say. What was your daughter's name?"

"Azmera," Kebede said with a proud look on his face. "No, no . . . that's a unique name. I would have remembered it had I heard it," answered Tsege to Kebede's disappointment.

He was right, though—Azmera was a unique name—a special name for a special girl. Kebede's heart ached. He continued with his interrogation, not willing to give up hope just yet.

"She would have been with my brother, a young man named Solomon. Actually, he looks quite a lot like me," Kebede said as he awkwardly posed for Tsege.

Tsege studied Kebede's face. He knew there was something familiar about Kebede when he saw him hurry into the *ulpan* with a look of shame on his face earlier that morning. Something in his eyes and his cheekbones reminded him of someone, but he couldn't manage to place it. The number of people he had encountered in the past year of his life far surpassed the total number of people he had met in the eighteen years preceding it, and most of the names and faces were all long forgotten.

"I don't want to get your hopes up," Tsege replied, "but there *is* something familiar about your face."

"*Yalla, chevre,* come on, guys!" shouted Shifra, signaling an end to their morning break.

Kebede and Tsege gazed at one another, both grateful for the short encounter made possible by their *ulpan* teacher's smoking habit. Kebede returned to the classroom with a lightness in his step. He couldn't know for sure yet, but he held out hope that Solomon and his daughter had been on the plane with Tsege. They just might be in Israel.

Kebede listened to Tsege read out loud the article that Shifra had given them to read. It was about the big operation, termed "Operation Moses" by those in charge.

Shifra interrupted Tsege in the middle of the paragraph to eagerly share with the class, "I can't help but find the name chosen for the operation to be ironic—after all, Moses never made it to Israel."

Shifra chuckled softly to herself but stopped when she realized that the irony wasn't nearly as amusing to her students—all of whom had family members left behind—as it was to her. While Operation Moses may have brought her students to Israel, it had failed so many others. Shifra felt mortified by her ignorance and insensitivity when she had always prided herself on being just the opposite. Tsege continued to read, and Kebede felt envious as the boy successfully pronounced every word correctly with just a hint of a Tigray accent. Kebede knew that his role as Shifra's prized pupil was long gone, but it didn't seem to bother him nearly as much as he thought it would. Tsege had given him what he needed far more than Shifra's approval—hope.

The students shuffled out of the classroom at the end of the day, the women headed to the market and the men to the balcony for their ritual cup of coffee to pass the lazy afternoon hours before the evening drinking hours arrived. Kebede joined them, desperately in need of caffeine to waken his body after a late night on the balcony the previous night. He would drink an afternoon coffee with the others, he told himself, but tonight he would resist the urge to drown his sorrows in another plastic cup filled with vodka. After all, any day now he could be reunited with his daughter.

Spring was the shortest of seasons in the desert city of Dimona. Winter came in like a lamb, and summer like a lion, but springtime was barely noticeable. Even as early as April, the desert sun had Kebede rolling up his sleeves and putting on his trademark Israeli sunglasses. He had bought them after he saw Israeli soldiers nonchalantly standing at bus stations with glasses plastered to their heads. Kebede sipped his coffee with the others on the balcony. This was his favorite part of the day—a day's worth of learning was behind him, lending a sense of accomplishment, and he could still manage to delude himself into believing that he wouldn't partake in any nighttime debauchery. Occasionally during the afternoon coffee hour, the men would begin to sing. One of them, often his roommate Mengistu, would initiate an impromptu melody as he hummed away until the others improvised and joined in. They would make up the words as they went, singing of their lives back home and their journey to Israel. If the evening's drunkenness served as an escape from their reality, the afternoon coffee hour did just the opposite, allowing the men to reminisce and feel a sense of comradery with one another. Kebede didn't always join in the singing, but he listened intently to the stories his fellow immigrants had to share. It made him feel a bit less guilty knowing he wasn't the only one who had left behind his wife and children, for whatever reason. But on this day, while Mengistu was just getting the song started, the men were cut off abruptly when an unexpected visitor hesitantly approached the balcony.

"Gentlemen, excuse me for interrupting your beautiful song," apologized Oren, the manager of the absorption center.

Oren stood at the entrance to the balcony and peeled off the skin from his cuticles, hoping no one would notice. It was his method of coping with everyday anxiety—and while it may have left his fingers bloodied, he reasoned that there were far worse habits to be had. The immigrant men listened intently—after all, Oren was highly respected, a salt-of-the-earth Israeli who truly cared for the well-being of his residents. He was the sort of manager who checked in on them, asked them how their families back in Ethiopia were doing, and even tried to use newly learned phrases in Amharic from time to time. If he wanted to talk to them, they were going to listen.

"This isn't easy to say," shared Oren, his eyes avoiding direct contact with any one person, "But I need to tell you that if you want to be Jewish in the eyes of the Israeli Rabbinate, you will have to undergo a small ritual circumcision."

Kebede sat on the balcony dumbfounded together with the others. None of them understood what Oren was talking about. They had been Jewish their whole lives. They had been persecuted for being Jewish their whole lives. More than anything, though, the State of Israel had initiated a mission to bring them to the Jewish homeland precisely because they were Jewish. If that wasn't Israel's recognition of their Jewishness, then what was?

"You must be mistaken. We are Jews and we already had a *brit milah* (circumcision) back in Ethiopia. Plus Rabbi Ovadia Yossef recognized the *Beta Israel* as Jews!" argued Kebede, the unofficial spokesman of the group, who understood the significance of the Chief Sephardic Rabbi of Israel's recognition of his people.

"I know, and I think you are Jewish just as much as me or anyone else in this country. But it's not a mistake," retorted Oren apologetically but firmly, "I have been specifically instructed by the highest officials of the Israeli Rabbinate, including Rabbi Ovadia Yossef, that all Ethiopian males must undergo a symbolic circumcision—even if you had a *brit milah* in Ethiopia. You'll need to do a symbolic circumcision where the *mohel* will draw a small amount of blood from the genital area, what's known as a *hatafat dam.*"

The dark-skinned men standing on the balcony now were the ones anxiously picking away at their cuticles. They waited for Kebede to respond, but his lips were frozen, and his eyes were locked on the dust-covered tile floor below him.

"Listen," comforted Oren, "This is just a technical procedure that you can get out of the way within seconds. I know it's painful and insulting, but

I don't think you have any other choice but to go ahead with it. The *mohel* will be here tomorrow after *ulpan* for the procedure. I wanted to give you time to prepare for this." Oren looked at his residents, their heads downcast. Their silence spoke volumes. "You know how much I care about all of you. I wouldn't tell you to do this if I didn't think it would help you in the future," reasoned Oren.

Kebede turned to his Ethiopian brothers and spoke to them in their language. Oren did not need to understand.

"I don't know what to say, but it looks like we really don't have a choice." reasoned Kebede. "Our lives in Ethiopia are a part of the past, and now we must look to the future. Our future is to live as Jews in the Jewish homeland."

The men nodded reluctantly in response. They spent the rest of the afternoon sipping their coffee in complete silence, as they listened to the birds chirping in the distance.

Kebede and his peers drank in excess, even for them, that night. The next morning, Kebede struggled to listen to Shifra as she reviewed the past and future tenses. He couldn't believe that Oren, who wore a colorful knitted *kippah* on his head and spoke endlessly about *Am Yisrael* (The Jewish People) and mutual responsibility for one another, could ever have agreed to endorsing such a humiliation. He wondered if Shifra had been in on this as well and realized that maybe she had been trying to warn him earlier. He felt the muscles in his body tense with anger. He couldn't help but think of his three boys back at home, patiently waiting to come to the Jewish homeland to join their *Abat*. He couldn't fathom anything more degrading than what he was about to be forced to do. And what they, too, would be forced to do.

After *ulpan*, the immigrant men lingered outside their classrooms' hallway, not knowing which way to go—back to their balcony where they would drink coffee as if it was just another typical lazy afternoon, or to the clinic where Oren had instructed them to go. Kebede took a deep breath and headed in the direction of the clinic. He had decided he was going to go through with it, despite his strong objections. It had been months since Kebede had taken on a leadership role, and he felt his chin rise a notch when he noticed the others following behind him.

When Kebede arrived outside the clinic, he spotted a bearded Haredi man covered from head to toe in black polyester. Since arriving in Israel, his interactions with *sabra*, native-born Israelis, were limited to visits from officials from the Jewish Agency and the Ministry of Absorption, and the occasional volunteer who made the long trip to Dimona to lend a helping hand.

"You understand Hebrew?" questioned the man.

The man fidgeted with his hands as he spoke. Kebede could tell he was uncomfortable standing there and he took some pleasure in the man's discomfort.

"Yes, we speak Hebrew," replied Kebede after a long and uncomfortable pause.

"Good. My name is Moshe and I come on behalf of the Rabbinate," explained the man before he continued, "I'm here to do a small symbolic circumcision so you will be Jewish in the eyes of the Israeli Rabbinate. I am a licensed *mohel*." Moshe held out a crumpled certificate, but no one was interested in checking it.

The men stared back at Moshe. Until recently, they thought they were the only Jews in the entire world; now, they were being told they weren't Jewish enough. But they knew that cooperating was the only option. With his chin down, Kebede approached Moshe and informed him that he would volunteer to be the first one to undergo the ritual, and that the others would follow him. Kebede trailed behind Moshe who led him into the clinic usually used for tending to scratches on the knees of children and the occasional fever, but now designated for stripping grown men—of their clothes and their dignity. Kebede lowered his pants and felt his body cringe as the *mohel* inspected his genitals. He winced when he felt a pin prick his penis. A drop of blood slowly rolled down his leg. Kebede refused to look Moshe in the eyes as he wiped the blood away. He walked out the door and, with his head fixed to the ground, motioned to the others to stand in line for their turn.

Kebede returned to his room, careful to avoid eye contact lest anyone see his eyes red and tearful. He reached into Mengistu's closet to snatch the bottle of arak hidden on the top shelf and poured himself a generous portion to help him make it through the evening. He lay down in his bed and grabbed a piece of paper to write another letter to Tigest. Another letter warning her not to come. Another letter he would not send.

Chapter Sixteen

Azmera—January 1985

Dear Enati,

I have so badly wanted to write to you to let you know that I was okay, but there was no time until now. One week ago, we arrived at the camp in Country X. The journey here was very difficult, but Solomon took good care of me, and we made it together. You would be proud of how brave and strong I was. Solomon even said that we made it to the camp one day earlier than he had calculated. When we arrived at the camp, there was complete devastation all around us. Dead bodies were strewn all over the place, with swarms of flies hovering over them; children lay on the ground, too weak to stand, with their glassy eyes sunk deep into their bony cheekbones; women standing in line for flour, so skinny that their knee joints were wider than their legs. And worse. Solomon explained to me on the way that we are going to the best of camps in all of Country X. I can't imagine anything worse than what I have seen here.

While we thank God that we survived the journey, we were shattered to discover that the operation came to an end just as we arrived. The Kes was right about the operation coming to a sudden halt. Here, no one expected it, and when word got out that the last bus was leaving for Khartoum, all chaos erupted. Hundreds of people in a panic rushed the bus. Solomon and I—we knew we didn't have a chance. We had arrived at the camp the night before and hadn't even registered yet, so no one even knew we were there. Lots of Beta Israel were left behind, although it's hard to say exactly how many. I wouldn't be surprised if there are Ethiopian Christians who are claiming to be Jewish just to get out of this place—I'd probably do the same if I were them. From what we've heard around the camp, though, a Falasha-Finder *has to vouch for your Jewishness before you can board the bus, so the Christians had no real chance of getting out.*

Enati—please believe me that I've tried my hardest to be strong like you, but I must admit that I am in complete despair. I am stuck here and have no idea what the future holds for me. The first week after the operation came to an end, we would wake up early in the morning even before the sun had risen hoping that another bus was on its way, but after a while we all gave up hope. There's not enough food here and everyone seems to be getting sick. Once a week, we get a sack of flour to make a flatbread that makes me long for your injera, *and a piece of goat meat, but we don't eat it because it's not kosher. Every week, I feel like my faith is being tested when I am forced to turn down the meat. Solomon doesn't let me drink from the water until we've boiled it. I'm usually so thirsty that I drink the boiling water before it has even cooled off. We try our best to stay clear of the Ethiopian Christians—we were told that a few months ago they found out that we sometimes receive outside help, so they tried to burn down our people's tents and huts to extort money and food from them. For the most part, though, the Christians tend to stay on the other side of the camp. I do my best not to draw attention to myself when I stand in line for our water and food rations, and so far, none of the Christians have caused me any trouble.*

I have trouble sleeping at nighttime. I think about you and the children, and dream of seeing you all again soon, wherever it may be. Sometimes I'm so hungry that I dream about your injera, *dreams so real that I can practically taste it in my mouth. Before coming here, I thought that I knew what it meant to be hungry, but now I have a new appreciation for what hunger truly is. Enati—I don't want you to worry about me, I'll be fine, really. But I'm telling you all of this so that you know not to come to Country X, at least not for now. The children, especially the new baby, simply won't survive it. I'll do my best to write as often as possible, although I have no idea how long the letter will take to reach you, if ever. I wish you could tell me how you are doing, and how the pregnancy is coming along, but I know that's not possible. And please know that I am not angry with you anymore for sending me away. I just pray that one day we'll be together again.*

Your loving daughter,
Meri

Azmera neatly folded the letter in half and stood up, her eyes blinded momentarily by the blazing sun.

"Where are you going?" asked Solomon as he sat over a fire waiting for their two-gallon ration of water to boil.

"I have to go back to camp headquarters to return this pen I borrowed yesterday," Azmera mumbled, her brain now exhausted from writing the letter, "and hopefully they'll be accepting letters today. I want to send word to my mother."

Tawawa's headquarters was largely avoided by the Jews not because of the inept camp management, but because it was centrally located amid hundreds of Ethiopian Christians, making access to the basic services offered by the camp a near impossibility for the *Beta Israel*. Azmera, however, couldn't stop thinking of her mother, especially after she had just seen another mother holding a lifeless daughter in her arms the day before. Azmera had been washing and scrubbing her clothes by her tent when she saw the grieving mother walk by. She recalled looking into the mother's eyes—they were completely vacant. Their light had been extinguished with the passing of her baby girl.

"We must not practice our faith around the Christians," Solomon had instructed upon arrival to the camp.

Solomon's directive included the burial of loved ones and other Jewish rituals. As time went by, Azmera learned that her people were so secretive that they often buried their dead children in the dirt ground inside their huts or tents so they could provide them with a proper Jewish burial. She could only imagine how the mother staring back at her must have wanted to cry like a ravenous hyena, but that could have put her other children, and her dead daughter's burial, at risk. Azmera watched the young mother walk towards her hut with her baby girl in her arms as if she were alive. Azmera abruptly stood up, leaving her dirty, wet clothes on the ground, and decisively headed towards the Christian side of the camp. Her own mother must be dying to hear from her.

As Azmera walked past Christians with crosses tattooed across their foreheads, she felt their eyes staring her down. The sight of a white-skinned *faranje* adorned with a Red Cross vest gave her some comfort, although she had no real confidence that they would be able to stop any attack on her should it take place. She had only been in the camp a short while, but it took her no time to see how overwhelmed, and useless, the Red Cross staff truly were. Their bloodshot eyes gave it away—a mix of apathy towards anyone daring to ask them for help combined with guilt for feeling that way. Still, the presence of a white-skinned person largely forced the dark-skinned Christians to behave; with her borrowed pen in hand, Azmera walked confidently past their tents to the headquarters office.

Azmera was disappointed when she saw a line wrapping its way around the building. The camp had recently erected a makeshift awning to provide shade from the scorching sun, but the line was so long that she was left standing far beyond its reach.

"But all I have to do is return a pen!" explained Azmera to a Sudanese man working the line.

"Everyone here claims to *just* need this or that," the worker replied in near perfect Amharic, "You'll have to wait just like all the others."

Azmera debated leaving the line and heading back to her tent with the borrowed pen, but she remembered the promise she had made the day before to the young woman manning the office, and the offer she had made to her in return.

Azmera had waited in line in the blazing sun for hours with the hope that someone wearing a Red Cross vest would be able to help her, and her patience was running thin. She felt lightheaded when it was finally her turn.

"I need a pencil to write my mother," explained Azmera impatiently in Amharic to a flustered young woman with flaming red, curly hair.

The young woman stared back at her with a confused look on her face. "Can you repeat that again?" asked the young woman in slow Amharic that sounded unfamiliar but correct, nonetheless.

Azmera repeated herself and it became clear that the young woman understood her when a small smile crept up on her freckled face.

"You know, you're the first girl here who's ever asked me for a pencil. That's why I was confused at first," explained the young woman. "Most girls here don't know how to read, let alone write."

Growing up, Azmera knew she was fortunate that her parents allowed her to go to school even if her attendance was sporadic, but until now she hadn't realized how rare a privilege it was.

"I don't have any pencils here, but I do have a pen. I wish I could just give it to you and let you write as often as you want, but we don't have nearly enough pens here and we need them all to register the new arrivals," explained the woman, who introduced herself as Biddy from Ireland. "I'll tell you what. You write to your mother all you want today and bring the pen back tomorrow. In the meantime, I will do my best to locate a sharpened pencil for you, and if you're lucky, I'll bring you a pad of paper too."

Biddy offered Azmera the pen and a blank sheet of white paper and a smile, easing Azmera's lightheadedness if just for a moment.

As Azmera approached the awning, she found relief in the shade from the late morning sun. The line for the headquarters suddenly branched into two. The longer line was for the camp's refugees waiting to meet with Red Cross staff. The other, shorter, line was for receiving mail and photocopying documents, for those fortunate enough to have them. Azmera absurdly needed to wait in both lines—the first, to return the pen to Biddy, and the second, to mail her letter to Tigest. Excited to see that the mail line—which was open on a sporadic basis at best—was open, and anxious to get her letter to Tigest on its way, Azmera stepped to the side to join the shorter line. With any luck, the Red Cross line would slowly dissipate throughout the day as the temperatures rose, sending most everyone to hibernate inside their tents until the desert air started to breathe again.

"Stamps cost 1 *qirush*," announced an Ethiopian man as Azmera approached the front of the line.

The man was missing most of his teeth and his forehead was far too large for his face. He was one of the lucky few who, as veteran refugees, found work in the camp, earning them 10 Sudanese *qirush*, or one dollar, per month. This man, despite his sour demeanor, had apparently been charged with receiving and delivering mail. Most of the money Azmera's mother had stuffed into her knapsack had remained untouched on the journey to Sudan. Solomon had covered all the expenses incurred, not once asking for his niece to contribute her share. She proudly held out three *Birrs*, hopeful that the man would accept the equivalent sum in the currency from the country they had both fled.

The man in front of her rolled eyes, but reluctantly accepted Azmera's payment in *Birrs*; it of course complicated his accounting at the end of the day. He handed her a stamped envelope and waited for her to scribble the mailing address on it. "Tigest Avraham; Debark, Ethiopia," Azmera wrote, satisfied with herself for displaying her fine writing skills in front of an elder male who very likely could not read himself. She had never heard anyone refer to her mother as anything more than just Tigest or *Enati*, but she knew that she needed to include her family name—to be exact, Tigest's father's name—for the letter to reach its intended destination. She handed the mailman the letter and paused to look him in the eye for confirmation that they had completed the transaction.

As she walked out of his office, the mail man held the envelope up for the next person in line to see.

"Tell me to whom this letter is addressed to," he demanded, hopeful that the authority rendered to him as the camp mail man would outweigh the embarrassing disclosure of his illiteracy.

Anxious to comply, the man standing in front of him squinted his eyes and whispered, lest the others in line hear, "To Tigest Avraham."

The mail man perhaps couldn't read but he knew that the name Avraham was likely a *Falasha* name. Plus, he was certain he had previously seen Azmera—the girl who could read and who had annoyingly complicated his accounting—walking from the far end of the camp. She must have come from the untouchable part of the camp where everyone knew the Jews were located.

"Thank you. I need to go on a break now. I will be back soon," the mail man abruptly announced.

He walked to the back of the office with Azmera's letter in hand for his second break of the morning. Once he confirmed that no one was watching him, he took Azmera's letter and tore it up into tiny pieces. He looked over his shoulder as he threw the shredded paper into the trash can in the corner. He may not have had the courage to outwardly attack the *Falashas* flooding the camp, but this much he could do—again and again.

✡

Satisfied with herself for having sent word to her mother, Azmera joined the line outside for the Red Cross staff to return the pen and, if lucky, to receive a pencil in exchange. Just as she had hoped, the line had shortened significantly with the sun's strengthening rays. In the week she had been at the camp, Azmera had noticed that the Red Cross staff wearing red vests rotated on a frequent basis, so she was surprised when she saw Biddy, with her flame-red locks of curls, counseling a Tigray woman with one lazy eye.

"You kept your promise!" shouted Biddy with joy in broken Amharic. The woman with the lazy eye walked out of the office, her good eye showing disappointment at the outcome of her visit. "I was sure it would be yet another case of a disappearing pen," laughed Biddy, her contagious grin bringing a smile to Azmera's face.

"I always do my best to keep my word," answered Azmera, hopeful that Biddy had remembered her promise as well.

"Well, you're in luck, my dear. I asked all my colleagues for a pencil yesterday, but no one had one, so I gave up on the search. But then this morning, I opened the desk drawer and, look what I found hiding in the back!" Biddy replied, finding it hard to contain her excitement.

The Irish woman had been working at the camp for over a year now, and she knew this was a rare occasion where she could provide tangible help to one of the refugee clients she was charged with serving. She handed Azmera a long, yellow pencil with its tip freshly sharpened and a gently used notebook for her to write in.

"I wish I could give you a sharpener too," Biddy explained, "but we need it for the office. That will just give you an excuse to come back and visit!"

Azmera didn't exactly understand Biddy's eagerness to help her at first, especially when there were hundreds of others waiting for her assistance, but then she recalled her mother's saying from when she was a little girl: *You can't help everyone, but everyone can help someone.* Azmera smiled at the pretty Irish lady and promised to return soon to visit, and of course to sharpen the pencil.

Azmera—Early March 1985

Dear Enati,

Have you received any of my letters? I've been sending them to you on a weekly basis ever since arriving at the camp over a month ago, but I'm starting to worry that you haven't received any of them. To think that all the money you gave me has been going towards buying stamps! I know you won't be able to write me any letters until I reach Israel—but I hope you at least received mine.

Things here are very bleak. I am hungry all the time, and I have lost all the muscle I gained from the journey to Country X. Solomon says I look like a skeleton. He tries to take good care of me, always giving me the last bite of flatbread even though he is equally hungry. He still thinks that the Israelis will come take us soon, but with each passing day it's clear that we are not going anywhere, at least not for now.

I forgot to tell you in my first letter, but Solomon lied when we arrived at the camp and told the registration office that I was his daughter so that we could stay together in the same tent. It makes me sad to say, but in lots of ways Solomon has been more of a father to me in the past few months than Abati ever was—especially in the past few years. He treats me like the child he never had. Most of the refugees in the camp live in gojo *huts, like our* gojo *back home, but in the past few months the camp has been so overwhelmed with new arrivals that it ran out of supplies for building more, so they placed us in a weathered tent. Our tent looks like it has seen more winters than I have. At nighttime, the desert air penetrates sharply through the tent's thin cloth, making it impossible to stay warm. During the day, the tent traps the desert heat inside, making it suffocatingly hot, so much so that I often prefer to stay outside in the sizzling sun. At least then I can breathe the fresh air.*

Solomon and I share a tent together with another Beta Israel *family. Unlike us, they all made the journey to Country X together—the father, mother and three young children—and they arrived several months before we did. They were devastated to have been left behind when the operation came to an end— apparently, they couldn't sufficiently prove they were Jewish to get on the plane, despite the father's begging and several others vouching for them. I have no doubt, though, that they are Jewish. They come from Ambover village, and the father, Alex, is the* Kes *there and wears a white turban on his head. They sing the prayers in Ge'ez with us before Shabbat and dream of going to Jerusalem just like we do.*

They also mourn just like we do.

The first few weeks together, I really enjoyed spending time with the three children and teaching them how to write their names with sticks in the sand. The long days passed by more quickly with them around, even though it meant that there wasn't enough room for all of us to lie down at night in the tent.

But then the youngest boy, Kaleb, started to cough uncontrollably, especially at night. I remember cursing him and his cough for keeping me awake as I shivered under my blanket. I'll never forget how deep his cough was, as if he were desperately trying to empty his lungs. At first, his mother resisted taking him to the clinic out of fear that someone might discover they were Jewish, but when he started to cough up blood, she realized she had no choice. The mother, Alam, took Kaleb to the clinic.

Only Alam returned.

The family mourned inside the tent for the entire shiva, even when the heat inside was so oppressive that it nearly killed all life around it. During those seven days, Solomon and I did our best to comfort them by making flatbread and fetching extra water for them, but I'm not sure there was any comfort to be found no matter what we did.

While we might have a bit more room in the tent to lie down at night, now there's a silent sadness pervading the air in place of Kaleb and his siblings' laughter and games. Ever since he died, Alam has stopped living. She just seems to be going through the motions, doing whatever she needs to get by. Alex and his children, though, have started to come back to life. I even make the children giggle from time to time when I tell them a story about how we used to pretend to be baboons when I was little, but there's still a real sadness in their young eyes. I think, even more than the loss of their brother, they are mourning the loss of their mother. Watching her suffer so deeply makes me realize that, despite all our family's hardships—despite the hunger, despite the separation, and despite our uncertain future—we are so blessed.

Enati—I wish I could know that you were receiving these letters, and I wish you could write back to me—but I know it would be too dangerous. Please tell me that you and the children, and the baby, are doing fine. I desperately need to know that you know that I am okay, and even more so, I need to know that you and the children are okay.

Your daughter, forever,
Azmera

"Solomon, have you sent any letters to Meskie?" asked Azmera as she poured boiling water into a bowl of flour to prepare their daily meal.

Nearly two months had passed since arriving at the camp, and both Solomon and Azmera were becoming unrecognizable to one another, their bones protruding out of their pale brown flesh. And while Solomon's mind slowed down together with his body, he nonetheless appreciated the diligence with which his niece wrote to her mother, even though she too was becoming weaker and weaker in the body and mind with each passing day. Remarkably, with every letter Azmera sent, her spirits seemed to lift ever so slightly off the sandy desert ground. In those very first days after they arrived at the camp, Solomon watched Azmera furiously writing away, and he consciously decided to refrain from telling her that her efforts were futile. He knew that an Ethiopian Christian was manning the mail station, and he had heard from the other *Beta Israel* at the camp that they suspected him of throwing away their mail if he sensed that the deliverer or the recipient was Jewish.

Solomon knew all of this but didn't tell his niece, even as he watched her make trip after trip to the other side of the camp to put letters in the mail that were never going to get sent.

"No, I haven't, but Meskie doesn't read or write well," responded Solomon.

In truth, he hadn't bothered sending his wife a single letter, not because of her illiteracy but because he knew it would never reach her anyway. Instead, he remained optimistic that the Israelis would come soon and whisk them away like they had the others before them. The first thing he would do upon arrival, he told himself repeatedly, was write to his wife and tell her how much she meant to him, with or without a baby in her arms.

"I'm sure Tigest received your letters and wants to respond, but she can't take the risk of sending a letter to Sudan," he explained as Azmera nodded.

Azmera knew that her letters to Ethiopia were sent under the guise of an international organization—the International Red Cross—and thus would arrive safely to Ethiopia without any mention of Sudan on the envelope or on the letter inside; Tigest, on the other hand, had no way to safely send word to her daughter.

Azmera nodded, her head slowly melting away in the desert sun. She had become quite forgetful in the past month at the camp, oftentimes not recalling what had been said to her seconds before. To save face, she would simply nod her head, preferring to feign agreement to the unknown than to reveal the shame of her mind betraying her. She turned to look at Alam who was holding her two children in her arms, quietly singing to them the story of their births; the youngest on a rainy day inside their hut and the oldest as Alam was walking to the river to collect water. Azmera felt chills run up and down her spine as she listened to Alam sing, much like Tigest used to sing to her.

Unlike her memory of her mother, thin but strong, Alam's emaciated frame looked like death was calling. Her brown lifeless eyes, however, slowly came back to life with the rolling laughter of her children. She knew that Alam wanted to die when she lost her son just like her own mother must have felt when she left for Sudan, but she also saw that Alam's two living children brought her back to life.

Azmera felt a smile creep up on her face with the realization that, letters or not, she had to trust that her mother was fine. Her mother had to be fine because her siblings didn't leave her a choice but to be.

"Solomon, we need your help," announced Alam, standing beside her husband, a tall man whose face was as narrow as his neck.

Ever since the tragic death of their son, Solomon and Azmera had provided help to Alam and Alex wherever possible, creating a mutual trust and respect between the two families. But this was the first time that they had actively solicited Solomon's help. Solomon was lying down inside the tent next to his niece. Both had been in a vegetative state for several hours already despite it being the middle of the day. Solomon had been nursing a pounding headache that seemed to intensify every time he lifted his head up from the ground. Azmera had tried several times to give to him her rations of food and water, but he proudly refused, leaving Azmera no choice but to watch her uncle slowly deteriorate together with the others. He forcefully propped his body upright to make eye contact with his tent-mates, their unprecedented call for help worthy of his proper attention.

"God willing, if and when the Israelis come, we can't get left behind like we did before," explained Alex, his hoarse voice at a whisper so as not to strain it, "We got left behind the last time because they didn't think I was Jewish . . . and I will never forgive myself for what happened afterwards. If we would have gotten on that plane, my son Kaleb would be alive today."

It was the first time that Solomon had heard Alex speak except for when they recited the prayers together on Shabbat. Until now, Alex had played a behind-the-scenes role in their family, expressing his love by quietly performing daily chores to allow his wife the space she needed to mourn for her son.

"But you're a *Kes*! Why didn't they think you were Jewish?" questioned Solomon, his strength partially rejuvenated by Alex's call for help.

"I have this feeling that you are a man to be trusted. Please don't prove me wrong," said Alex, his eyes looking straight into Solomon's as if they were assessing his integrity.

Solomon nodded assuredly.

"I am not really a *Kes*. I'm not even circumcised," Alex admitted, his face lowered to hide his shame, "I am *Falush Mura*."

Solomon had heard of the Jews of Ethiopia who had been forced to convert to Christianity many years before, but he had never met one face to face. If Alex was *Falash Mura*, Solomon wondered to himself, how did he know how to recite all the prayers before Shabbat?

"Alam comes from the Jewish village of Ambover and was raised as a Jew," Alex explained, "I am from Gondar City and was raised as a Christian, although my family has proof that we used to be Jews. We met when we were young and fell in love. She listened to her heart and married me, but Alam's parents did not approve of the marriage and cut off all ties with her. We had no choice but to live in Gondar on our own. But Alam still wanted to raise our children Jewish. We did, but in hiding. I learned all the prayers and we even brought a *Kes* from Wolleka to perform the *brit milah* for our three sons when they were eight days old. One of them of course is no longer with us."

Solomon stared back at the man, shocked more by his openness than by the revelation of his identity. "But how in the world do you think I can help you?" questioned Solomon, both perplexed and flattered by Alex's faith in him.

Alex cautiously removed his white turban—the same white turban adorned by *Kes* Yonas from Solomon's village—revealing a small, faded tattoo of a cross etched on his forehead. Until now, the turban had been a permanent fixture on Alex's head; while Solomon was used to seeing *Kessim* wearing turbans, he had found Alex's to be curiously downward-facing, covering more of his forehead than he was accustomed to, but he had never put much thought into it.

"This tattoo gives my identity away immediately and will destroy my family's future," Alex explained with a look of desperation in his eyes, "I need you to cut it off."

Solomon felt a rush of blood to his head and held out his hands to keep himself from collapsing.

"You *what*?!" exclaimed Solomon with a look of disbelief on his face.

"Cut it off might not be an accurate use of words," explained Alex, "but scrape it off, rub it off, whatever it takes to make it go away, I need you to do it as soon as possible so that the wound will heal before the Israelis come again, God willing. I see that you are a strong man, and you are the only one here I trust to do it."

Solomon paused for an uncomfortably long moment before responding.

He had heard of Christians in the camps trying to pass off as Jews to secure a better life for themselves and their children in Israel. While he understood their motives, he also knew what kind of harm they could unknowingly inflict on the *Beta Israel*, authentic Jews like himself, both within Israel and without. After all, there were already enough white Jews claiming that the black Jews were a farce, or so he heard. The last thing he wanted to do is provide aid to another Christian masquerading as a Jew.

Solomon paused to reconsider. He wasn't really a Christian though, was he? He was a Jew whose family had been coerced to convert to Christianity decades ago. And he was married to a Jewish woman, rendering his children Jews according to Jewish law. He was raising his children as Jews, and living his life as a Jew. And, of course, he had already lost so very much. Solomon knew from experience that grieving for a dead child is a parent's worst nightmare, but he couldn't imagine the depth of Alex's guilt for believing that it was he who was responsible for his son's death.

"I'll do it," responded Solomon, his voice trembling.

Alex let out a deep sigh of relief and handed him a knife that he had hidden underneath his thin mattress.

"Alam, take the children for a walk," commanded Alex, his voice stern to mask the fear and adrenaline rushing through his body.

Alam grabbed her two boys' hands and gestured to Azmera to join her, leaving the two men alone together. Solomon placed the knife in boiling water and reassured himself that what he was about to do wasn't so different from back in the village when he would brand his goats. When the knife was fully sterilized, he took a deep breath and pressed the knife deliberately into Alex's forehead, careful not to cut too deep and hit his skull, but nonetheless deep enough to accomplish his mission of concealing the tattoo. He made small but decisive cuts over the tattooed area. Alex winced as he saw dark red blood oozing down his face, but he remained still and quiet, determined to allow Solomon to finish the job. One tear trickled slowly down Alex's cheek. When Solomon deemed the carnage of Alex's forehead to be sufficient, he looked into Alex's eyes. For just a moment, they felt each other's losses, even the unspoken ones.

Solomon stepped back to look at his bloody masterpiece, confirming that no evidence of the tattoo remained.

"Your tattoo is gone," Solomon announced, his voice choking back tears, "When the time comes, you'll be able to take your family to Israel."

Azmera—Late March 1985

Nearly a month after Solomon had cut off Alex's tattoo, the scabbing on his forehead was healing nicely, leaving behind fresh pink scars. Alam was still grieving her son's death, so Solomon had designated Azmera to oversee nursing Alex's wounds. Solomon knew that his niece needed something to help pass the daily monotony of collecting water, washing clothes, and making flatbread. Indeed, she found that making the requisite trips to the camp's clinic to acquire sterile cotton balls and alcohol helped pass the time, otherwise as stagnant as the desert air in the middle of the day. It had been almost a month since Alex had last left the tent. He didn't want the desert sand to cause an infection on his forehead, nor did he want to attract any unwanted attention to him or his family.

"You have *another* cut on your leg?" asked Sam, the British medic in the clinic, as he stared down at Azmera's bloody scrape on her knee.

In addition to cleaning Alex's wounds, Azmera had joined the effort to hide Alex from outsiders by intentionally and regularly scraping her knees and elbows as a pretense for receiving medical supplies. While the clinic's medics were overwhelmed by the sick and dying, Azmera sensed that they found some relief in simply giving her the sterile cotton balls and alcohol they thought she needed for her wounds. Unlike so many others visiting the clinic, she had something they could heal.

Armed with cotton balls and alcohol, Azmera made the trip back to the *Beta Israel* side of the camp. On the way, she passed a line snaking its way through the middle. Starving mothers and children with heads disproportionately too big for their gaunt bodies crouched down on the ground while waiting for their next bag of flour. She, too, needed to replenish her supply of flour, but she couldn't bring herself to stand in yet another line in the blazing sun. She was hopeful that when she returned to her tent Solomon would agree to take over her duty just this one time.

"Meri! Where have you been? I've been looking all over for you!" shouted Solomon impatiently, the first time he had raised his voice at his niece since arriving at the camp.

"I went to get supplies to tend to Alex's forehead," explained Azmera, not understanding the sudden importance of her whereabouts.

"I saw some new arrivals at the camp today," explained Solomon, his voice trembling with excitement. "One of them was Alazar, your teacher from back home. I didn't even recognize him—he looked like a walking skeleton—but he recognized me. He told me that he had come from Um Rakoba, the camp I told you about with conditions way more horrific than here."

Solomon paused to make sure Azmera was listening to his every word. "He said that someone gathered up all the Jews left at Um Rakoba and brought them here. He was told to be prepared to leave the camp at any moment. You understand what this might mean?"

Azmera nodded her head slowly as she tried to process the news her uncle had just delivered. If this was true, then it meant that she could be in Israel any day now. She felt her stomach churn in circles, not sure whether it was because she was excited or terrified, or both.

✡

"Meri, wake up!" whispered Solomon just as Azmera settled into a deep sleep.

Desperate for rest, Azmera tried to roll away from her uncle, but she knew that his incessant shaking would ultimately win.

"What's going on?" murmured Azmera as she wiped away the sleep from her eyes.

"They're here," Solomon announced, his voice in a whisper, "It's time to go."

Azmera popped out of bed to see Alam and Alex readying their children. Solomon approached Alex and took one long look at his forehead.

"All evidence of the tattoo is gone, although the scarring still looks fresh," commented Solomon, knowing that Alex's nerves needed calming before he interacted with anyone outside the confines of the tent. "Still, I don't think you should wear the turban to cover it up because it will only draw more attention to you as a *Kes*. The Israelis might question your knowledge of the *Orit*."

Alex reluctantly nodded his head in agreement—he knew he wasn't as well-versed in the Torah as an actual *Kes* would be—before Solomon continued, "But you should be prepared to answer questions as to what happened to your forehead, so it doesn't look suspicious."

Ever since Solomon had chopped up his forehead, Alex had struggled to come up with a reasonable explanation for something so gruesome looking on his forehead. The most convincing of explanations he managed to think of was so convoluted that he hoped the Israelis would buy it—he had gone to the camp's junkyard to search for pieces of steel for strengthening his family's tent, but while there, he fainted and fell flat on his face, landing on a pile of sharp scraps of steel. The junkyard pile of steel did in fact exist, and refugees frequented it all the time to snatch pieces of metal for whatever use they saw fit. Fainting spells, too, were common occurrences at the refugee camp where starvation was rampant and the heat oppressive. It wasn't the most probable of explanations, especially because the rest of his face remained unscathed, but it was the best he could come up with.

Alex and his family were still busy readying themselves for the journey ahead of them. Solomon grabbed his bag and decisively walked out of their tent—his niece trailing behind him—for what he hoped was the last time. The sky was black as coffee, illuminated by stars sprinkled over it like tiny granules of sugar. Azmera had never before been outside her tent at this late hour, and she paused to take note of how the chaos and despair that pervaded the camp during the day was replaced by a tranquil stillness at night. Solomon led Azmera to the outskirts of the camp, where a large group had already convened. Mothers were doing their best to muffle their babies' cries, while the older children were tasked with keeping their younger brothers and sisters as quiet and still as the night air. Solomon was relieved when he saw Alex and Alam hurriedly join the group with their two children in their arms. He had felt a slight pang of guilt when he left them behind minutes earlier in the tent, but he couldn't risk getting left behind himself. His life and Azmera's was at stake.

"Four hundred and seven, four hundred and eight," counted a man whose seriousness emanated in a way that reminded Azmera of her grandfather, Rahamim.

It was the third time someone had come to count them, as if they were checking to make sure they didn't miss anyone. Solomon pulled Azmera off the ground when an Ethiopian man wearing clothes more fitting for a Westerner approached them.

"Where are you from?" questioned the man, as he began his interrogation into Solomon and Azmera's legitimacy as Jews.

The pair answered a litany of questions to the man's satisfaction. Then he motioned for the two to continue moving ahead towards the line of trucks waiting, their lights dimmed, and their motors switched off.

Azmera and Solomon climbed up the truck and squeezed their frail bodies into the cramped cabin, their ribs so compressed on all sides that they could barely breathe in the cool desert air. Azmera felt her heart and Solomon's racing with excitement, his chest pressed up tightly against her back. The truck's cabin seemed to be at maximum capacity long ago, but another woman and her young child managed to squeeze their way into the remaining cracks and gaps. The air was thick and stagnant, the odor overwhelming. Azmera stared at the ground, focusing all her energy on not vomiting up the little food she had consumed that day. Solomon grimaced as he stood on his tiptoes, his calf muscles burning from the strain. He was hoping to see Alex and Alam amongst the masses of people boarding the truck next to them, but the foggy night air and the sea of people in front of him made it impossible to tell who was there.

To his despair, Solomon heard a muffled cry from behind him; it stood out from the cacophony of crying muffled by mothers and fathers. It belonged not to a baby or young child, but to a grown woman. The cry was the same deep moaning he had become familiar with in his tent weeks ago. The cry belonged to Alam.

"No, Alex, no!" Alam shouted, her voice sending echoes through the air.

Alam's shouting was quickly muted by the sound of the engines humming, the trucks now preparing to leave the camp and its misery behind. They pulled out one by one, leaving a trail of dust behind them illuminated by the taillights. Solomon stood on the tips of his toes once more to take a final look at the hell he was leaving behind. When the dust cleared, he saw Alex, with his scarred but healed forehead exposed, standing alone, watching his wife and two remaining children drive off into the distance.

✡

Azmera shut her eyes tightly as the truck zoomed over bumps and ditches in the dirt road, spraying sand and dust into the air. With each jarring bump or turn, she felt her stomach drop to the ground. Azmera felt grateful for the loud revving of the engine. It managed to drown out the gagging sounds made by the other children standing next to her as they vomited on the feet of their nearest neighbor. When the truck slowed to a halt, Azmera breathed in deeply before opening her eyes to the sight of a vast strip of land, evenly paved with dirt. She and Solomon anxiously awaited their turn to climb down from the truck, resisting the urge to push the others in front of them. Azmera felt relieved once her feet touched ground; her stomach would return to normal, and her limbs would have the freedom to move again.

Azmera and Solomon followed the lead of the others in front of them and sat on the dirt ground and waited. But for the full moon shining brightly in the sky, Azmera would have completely lost all concept of time; the events of the past few hours had flashed by in an instant. Azmera felt her mind and body ease for the first time since leaving her tent, having been on high alert ever since. She felt her eyes grow heavy and rested her head on Solomon's shoulder, only to wake up minutes later to the deafening sound of a plane landing next to her.

"This is it," announced Solomon, as they stood up after being called to board the camouflaged plane on the strip of land in front of them.

Azmera felt her legs tremble as she and her uncle climbed up the metal steps to board the enormous metal flying machine. She and Solomon found seats together, their seat backs uncomfortably upright and rigid. They waited as they watched hundreds of others like them, men with and without their families, young children, teenagers, and the elderly, file their way onto the plane. There was a patient nervousness in the air. Each person had waited so long for this moment to come, but now that it was finally here the long minutes leading up to takeoff felt longer than the journey to Sudan and their time at the Tawawa combined.

When the plane finally turned on its engine readying for take-off, Azmera felt her stomach turn. She felt more terrified in this moment than she had in the months since leaving her village. Fending off bandits, the elements, wild animals, and armed soldiers all paled in comparison to flying higher than the clouds in a machine made of metal and steel.

"We're going home, Meri," whispered Solomon, trying to contain his excitement.

Azmera gazed into the distance, visualizing her mother waiting for her back in Ethiopia and her father waiting for her in Israel. As the plane took off into the black Sudanese sky, she wasn't sure whether it was taking her away from home or bringing her towards it.

Chapter Seventeen

Azmera—Late March 1985

Solomon squeezed Azmera's hand as they carefully walked down the steep stairs to deboard the airplane, the desert air cold and brisk against their skin. The sun was just peeking its way above the horizon, bringing an end to the eventful night that had brought them to wherever they were now standing. Azmera looked in all directions for a sign of Jerusalem, but other than the blue and white Israeli flag proudly waving in the sky, there was none. The desert mountains surrounding them looked nothing like the Land of Milk and Honey Azmera had envisioned.

"Welcome home, everyone. You have arrived to Ovda in southern Israel," said a handsome young man in Hebrew, wearing an olive-green uniform with three stripes on both of his shoulders. His job appeared to be directing the hundreds of new arrivals to their next destination. "Please continue straight ahead to the tables set up in the shade. A representative from the Ministry of Absorption will be waiting to meet with you."

Azmera stared back at the man and felt herself blush out of nervous embarrassment for not understanding a word he had just said. There apparently was no designated interpreter for now, and Azmera quickly understood how fortunate she was to have Solomon by her side. The others didn't seem to have a clue what to do but follow the herd. As far as Azmera was concerned, her uncle was practically fluent in Hebrew, having studied it for months before leaving for Sudan. Surely, he would know how to get around.

As they neared the tables lined up waiting to receive them, Azmera noticed a man with dark skin busily floating from table to table to assist the white staff members in communicating with their new clientele. When it came time for Azmera and Solomon's turn, a white woman with gray, spiky hair looked Solomon directly in the eyes.

"So, this must be your wife?" she inquired, as she turned and pointed at Azmera.

Excited at the opportunity to use his new Hebrew skills and far too proud to ask for an interpreter, Solomon replied in Hebrew. "No, no, no," responded Solomon while deliberately avoiding eye contact, "She is the daughter of my brother, Kebede Rahamim. He is already here in Israel, in a city called Dimona." Solomon struggled to answer the next few questions with confidence, but he insisted on replying in Hebrew nonetheless.

"Now, smile for a picture," the woman commanded as she hastily snapped a picture of the man and the girl, both with dumbfounded expressions on their faces, hardly the smile she was looking for. After years of waiting, Solomon couldn't believe how expedited their entry into Israel was. "Most of the absorption centers are already full, including the one in Dimona, so you have been assigned to the Karmiel Absorption Center," informed the woman as Solomon nodded his head reluctantly, "Here are all the documents you need, including your identity number. The bus waiting to take you to Karmiel is over there," she said with a hurried smile, as she pointed to a parking lot with exhaust fumes and cigarettes painting the spring air with smoke. "Welcome to Israel."

"Where are we going, uncle?" asked Azmera as she trailed behind her uncle.

"To a city called Karmiel," Solomon replied. "I told them that your *Abat* is already here, but we are going to Karmiel, not Dimona. I hope it's near him at least."

Despite his best efforts, Solomon's words revealed his lack of confidence. In truth, he had found the spiky-haired woman's Hebrew next to impossible to understand; her speech hurried, and her words mumbled. Had she not pointed in the direction of the parking lot, he would not have understood where to go next. But pride can be a curious thing, especially for a man as proud as Solomon. He walked towards the bus with their documents in hand, replaying in his head everything he had said to the woman in Hebrew. He could only hope that he hadn't misspoken or misunderstood what she had said.

Azmera hadn't slept since before leaving Tawawa the night before, so the eight-hour drive north to Karmiel provided her with a welcomed opportunity to rest her eyes. The moment Azmera had set foot on Israeli soil, the muscles in her body loosened and her head lightened. She no longer had to keep up her guard. She could finally shut her eyes without fear or discomfort, even if it meant missing out on the new world passing by her at the alarmingly fast pace of fifty miles per hour.

Solomon, on the other hand, couldn't calm his mind enough to give his body the rest it needed. As he watched the scenery change from rocky desert mountains to green rolling hills to the coastal sea line, he started to worry. In his letters, Kebede had relentlessly complained of Dimona's hot desert sun and the cold desert nights. At the time, Solomon had no pity for his older brother; after all, his worries were objectively far greater than uncomfortable weather. Solomon anxiously watched as the landscape faded into the background, leaving behind psychedelic streams of exhaust fumes. His heart sunk heavily into his stomach. He feared that Karmiel was nowhere near Dimona, and nowhere near Azmera's father.

A chorus of honking horns woke Azmera from a deep sleep. She gazed out the window with amazement as she saw a sea of cars surrounding their bus, all impatiently waiting for a traffic jam to clear. To her left was a stunning view of the tranquil blue Mediterranean Sea. Azmera's grasp of geography in Ethiopia was weak, far weaker than her grasp of Israel's geography; she too could tell that they were moving northwards, as the long narrow map of Israel hanging in their village synagogue had been etched in her mind ever since she was a little girl. The bus jerked in stops and starts that made Azmera's stomach churn. She turned to her uncle, who was too busy picking his nails to notice that she had woken.

"Is this Karmiel?" questioned Azmera, excited to get acquainted with her new home.

Solomon paused for a moment before answering, "I don't know," surprising his niece and himself with the admission of not knowing even more than the not knowing itself.

"Here, take a sandwich. They passed them out while you were sleeping," Solomon said as he handed his niece a long sandwich wrapped in plastic wrap, grateful to be able to change the subject.

Azmera clumsily unwrapped the plastic to discover a long white roll with beige seeds sprinkled on top. Inside was a fluffy egg omelet and thinly sliced tomatoes. A beige paste-like spread, "hummus" according to the Israeli who had passed out sandwiches earlier, held the sandwich together. When she bit into the sandwich, Azmera realized how hungry she had been. She devoured it, relishing each bite of this new cuisine. When she finished, she carefully inspected the plastic wrapping for any leftover crumbs or licks of the paste-like spread. Her attention quickly turned from her sandwich to two men standing in the middle of the road next to their dented cars. They frantically gestured with their hands as they screamed at one another. Azmera had never witnessed such a shouting match in her entire life. She swallowed down her nerves as the bus began to pick up speed, leaving the car accident and the two men behind.

The bus continued to weave along the winding roads, and Azmera gazed out the window at a tree-covered mountain range. The buildings to her side grew more tightly packed and the bus slowed down as it made its way onto a residential street. Azmera could feel that they were approaching their new home. It suddenly dawned on her that the other passengers on the bus would be her new family, or at least her new neighbors. She excitedly scanned the bus for Alam and Alex and their two boys, to no avail.

"What happened to Alam and Alex?" Azmera inquired of her uncle, who was surprised that his niece was just now remembering her beloved tent-mates.

Solomon's face was glued to the window as he gazed in awe at the passers-by on the street pushing baby strollers and riding bikes.

"Alex didn't make it," Solomon uttered, his voice monotone and softer than usual. "I didn't tell you at the time because you weren't feeling well. Alam and her children got on the truck to the airstrip, but Alex wasn't allowed to join them. Alam and her kids are on the way to an absorption center just like us, but without Alex," Solomon confessed, as an oval tear rolled down his cheek. He was no longer able to contain his guilt for not having stayed behind to help his scarred friend stay together with his family.

"What?" Azmera asked in disbelief. "How could they separate a family like that, especially after all they've been through?" she cried, despite knowing the simple yet harsh explanation already.

"The *Falasha-Finder* must have known that he wasn't Jewish, Meri," replied Solomon as he shook his head from side to side, "I tried to help by removing the tattoo, but I should have helped more. I should have stayed behind to help him get through."

Azmera felt her eyes well up with tears as the bus came to a halt. She looked out the window at the gray cement building standing in front of her and turned to Solomon.

"What will become of Alex? And what will become of Alam and her two boys? Who will take care of them?" she asked her uncle, not expecting a response. Azmera felt paralyzed as the others on the bus eagerly got up from their seats to get off the bus, their smiles and tears of joy on display at the sight of their new home. Despite the commotion and excitement, all Azmera heard was silence.

When the others finished unloading the bus, Solomon grabbed his niece by the shoulder and gave her a gentle nudge. "Come, Azmera. It's time to get off the bus. It's time for our new lives as Israelis to begin."

Azmera nodded her head slowly in agreement and reluctantly pulled herself out of the bus seat. She wasn't sure how she could possibly celebrate her new life beginning when Alex's had been destroyed.

"You're sure that Dimona is nowhere near Karmiel?" questioned Solomon as he learned that his fears had been confirmed.

"Yes, I'm positive. Dimona is in the south of Israel. I'm sorry, but practically all the absorption centers are full. We barely have room for all of you here in Karmiel," answered Yehudit, a secretary at the Karmiel Absorption Center. Her skin was so white that Solomon could practically see through it. Azmera tried to listen in on the conversation but couldn't understand more than a few words here and there. Nonetheless, she could sense from Solomon's sunken head that they were nowhere near Dimona.

"How can we find him?" continued Solomon, frustrated with his inadequate Hebrew.

"Well," explained Yehudit, "We can call the office in Dimona. But they have hundreds of Ethiopians there. Do you know if he kept his African name or if he changed his name to an Israeli name?"

Solomon looked back at Yehudit and wondered what she meant by an "African" name, as if the entire continent of Africa, with its hundreds of languages, tribes, cultures, and religions, bestowed the same names to their children.

"I don't know if he changed his name, but his *Ethiopian* name is Kebede," Solomon replied in a tone that failed to mask his frustration with the situation.

"Well, I can give you the number for the Ministry of Absorption, they should be able to tell you if he's been placed in Dimona," Yehudit explained as she scribbled down a number on a yellow note, "Call them between the hours of 8:00–12:00 on Sundays, Tuesdays and Thursdays or from 13:00–15:00 on Mondays or 14:00–17:00 on Wednesdays." Solomon concentrated intently as Yehudit continued, "There's a pay phone for you to use in the *moadon* club."

Kebede tried his best to commit to memory the convoluted office hours for calling but found memorizing numbers in Hebrew together with the days of the week to be impossible.

"In the meantime, what is your relation to the girl?" Yehudit questioned as she looked over at Azmera, who had long given up on eaves-dropping in a language she couldn't yet understand.

Solomon paused, not knowing how to respond. He had told the spiky haired woman upon arrival that he was Azmera's uncle, but that message apparently hadn't found its way to Karmiel. If he told the truth, there was a risk that his niece might be sent to a boarding school, like so many of the Ethiopian youth who had arrived without their parents. If he claimed to be her father, on the other hand, he might jeopardize any efforts to reunite Azmera with his brother, her true father.

"I am her father," Solomon answered as he looked Yehudit straight into her blue eyes.

Kebede might be Azmera's true father, but he had entrusted him to care for his daughter and that is exactly what he was going to do. Azmera needed him now. Kebede would have to understand.

Azmera followed Solomon to a cinder-block dormitory building surrounded by wild grass reaching as high as a tall man's knees. The walls were decorated with bulletin boards with posters and notices written in Cyrillic letters. A blond man named Alon waited at the entrance to the building and introduced himself as the manager of the Karmiel Absorption Center, as the new arrivals shuffled through the door.

"This was used as an absorption center in the 70s for the immigrants from the Russian *aliyah*," he explained apologetically.

Unable to understand, Azmera instead directed her attention to Alon's clothes. He was wearing short shorts, sandals and a T-shirt with the collar cut off so that it exposed his muscular shoulders. Azmera looked down at the gray smock she still had on. It was the same one she wore the night they left Sudan. She couldn't help but feel curious about the way Alon and the other young Israelis dressed.

Solomon listened intently to Alon as he continued his introductory speech, "Please forgive us, we just received word two days ago that there was going to be another airlift. Nearly all the other absorption centers are completely occupied, and we didn't have time to get fully ready."

Solomon looked down the hallway and saw strong men carrying bed frames and stained mattresses, placing them in room after room. Despite the look of things, he was quickly reassured by Alon's guarantee that the absorption center would clean the dust off the shelves and hire a local interpreter by the following week. After all they had been through, Alon explained, a warm place to sleep and plenty of food to eat would surely suffice, at least for the next few days.

Despite being Azmera's purported father, Solomon was placed in a room separate from his niece, just a short flight of stairs above her. Families with young children were not separated, but a fourteen-year-old girl could not be placed in the same room alone with another man—even if it was her father—or so it was explained. Azmera felt anxious as she parted ways from Solomon and walked towards her assigned room. A large brown duffle bag was waiting for her on the bare bed frame. Inside, she discovered a plethora of bed and bath supplies—sheets, pillowcases, towels, a bar of soap, a plastic bottle and container both unidentifiable to her, a hairbrush, a thin, long brush with short bristles, a tube of red and white paste and a package of pads with stickers on the bottom.

The Israelis may not have had enough time to bring an interpreter, she thought to herself, but they sure did prioritize hygiene. Azmera curiously inspected the different plastic bottles, not quite certain of their contents. Just then, a girl not much older than her walked into her room.

"*Salaam*. I'm Adeneko," murmured the girl, her eyes cast on the ground.

Azmera nodded her head in Adeneko's direction, "I'm Azmera. I'm from a village outside Debark. Where are you from?"

While Azmera couldn't shake her unease at sharing a room with a perfect stranger, she was nonetheless excited at the prospect of a new friend. Adeneko, however, was already curled up in a ball on her bed, obviously uninterested in getting acquainted with her new roommate. Azmera was grateful, then, when Solomon gently knocked on the door and called her to join him outside in the hallway.

"I think the Ministry of Absorption should be open now," informed Solomon as he headed in the direction of the payphone with phone coins in his hand, "We should try to call and inquire about your father. While you were setting up your room, I went to speak to Alon and he agreed to help me speak with the office. He also exchanged for me all my remaining *Birrs* for *shekels* and even gave me phone tokens for the pay phone." Solomon's voice exuded an air of confidence that had all but disappeared in the past few days. "You know, Meri, we don't need our *Birrs* anymore. You should do the same with your money."

Azmera glanced at the 50,000-shekel bill in his hand. It looked fake to her with its Hebrew writing and crisp fold. Did Solomon really want her to get rid of every *Birr* in her possession in exchange for that?

Alon was standing in the *moadon*, greeting the newcomers with a warm smile as he waited for Solomon to bring his "daughter" to make the phone call. As they walked through the door, however, Azmera was distracted by a pile of pamphlets printed in Amharic. It was the first source of information she could comprehend since arriving in Israel. She grabbed two pamphlets, one for now and one in case the first one got lost, and quickly became engrossed in its contents. The pamphlet described her rights as an Israeli citizen, and her many entitlements as a new immigrant, or *oleh*, including a monthly cash allowance far surpassing her parents' yearly income back in Ethiopia.

Azmera read the pamphlet over and over, finding comfort in the Amharic words in front of her. She knew there was no point in attempting to listen in on Alon and Solomon's phone conversation—she knew she wouldn't understand a word anyone said anyway. Besides, the pamphlet in her hands was much more appealing.

"*Shalom*," Alon spoke as he held the phone in one hand and motioned to Solomon to come closer with the other, "I am the manager of the Karmiel Absorption Center and I am calling on behalf of a new *oleh* from Ethiopia who is looking for his brother, Kebede Rahamim. He has reason to believe that he is in the Dimona Absorption Center." Solomon pulled hard on a hangnail and watched a drop of blood trickle down his finger as Alon listened to the other end of the phone. "He's there, you say?" replied Alon as he turned to look Solomon in the eye, "Can you give me the phone number for their office?" Alon pulled a pen out of his shorts pocket and hurriedly wrote down the number that would lead Solomon to his brother, and Azmera to her real father. Solomon breathed a sigh of relief at how easy it all was with an Israeli by his side to help.

"He is in Dimona, just as you thought," said Alon with a sigh, "But it's about as far away from here as you can get in our tiny little country. They should have an Ethiopian working in the office, so you won't need my help calling them. Here's the phone number."

Alon handed Solomon a crisp, yellow piece of paper with sticky glue on its back. Solomon thanked Alon and excitedly headed over to his niece to prepare her for the next call they were to make. Her father's voice was just a phone call away.

Solomon put a token into the phone and slowly and carefully dialed the number. It was his first time using a phone by himself. Once on a visit to Gondar, he had seen a pay phone close to the university, but he had no use for it—he of course knew no one who owned a phone. Azmera stood by his side, her eyes locked on the curious gadget in front of her. When a woman answered on the other end of the line and introduced herself as Hadass, Solomon didn't hesitate to request to speak with an Amharic speaker. There would be plenty of opportunities to practice his Hebrew, he thought to himself. This should not be one of them.

When the Amharic speaker picked up the phone, Solomon asked to speak with his brother, but was promptly informed that he was currently in *ulpan* class and therefore unavailable.

"Can you tell him that Solomon and Azmera called? We are in Israel at the Karmiel Absorption Center. Please ask him to call us back at 04-912409," said Solomon. He read the center's office number off the pamphlet Azmera had collected, careful not to misread a single number. Azmera squirmed with excitement as she listened to Solomon leave a message for her father, this being the first sign of life he would have received from her since he left their family months ago. How thrilled her father will be to receive the message! He surely would call them the moment he received it. Now it was time to send word to her mother.

Azmera—April 1985

Dear Enati,

I made it! I am safe in Israel. Solomon and I arrived a few days ago and were taken to an absorption center in Karmiel, which is way up in the north of Israel. We hoped we were going to be near Abat, but it turns out that Karmiel was the only absorption center with room for us. Abat is in Dimona, in the south and far from us. We already called him—yes, we used a telephone!—and left a message with the office. I'm sure he'll call us back any day now and then we can finally reunite with him.

Since I've arrived, I've eaten more and slept more than I have in my entire life. I was so weak when we arrived that my body needed catching up. Besides, the food here is delicious! I can feel myself getting stronger with every meal I eat. The Israelis love to eat hummus, a pasty spread made of chickpeas (kind of like our shiro*), and an endless supply of fruits and vegetables. While I still dream about your* injera, *I have no complaints.*

We start our ulpan *and culture class next week, so for now there's not much to do here. The days are long and quite boring. Please don't think I'm complaining—I know how fortunate I am to be here—but somehow my arrival to Israel has been quite anti-climactic. All the other people here in the center are Beta Israel. Most of them are from villages around Gondar and Debark. All of them were on the airlift with me, and it turns out that most of them were at the camp in Country X with me.*

I share a room with a girl named Adeneko for now, but she's quiet most of the time and keeps to herself. I don't know for sure, but I think she might have lost some of her family in the camp in Country X. She's here all alone and

Solomon said she will probably be placed in a boarding school soon. I spend most of my day speaking Amharic with the others. Sometimes it's easy to forget I'm in Israel.

Since arriving, Solomon and I try to go to the moadon *(like a gathering place) in the evening to watch the news on a large color television. At first, both he and I would just stare at the screen in awe of the flashing pictures and the smart Israelis talking on and on in Hebrew, but now we've gotten used to it. Solomon listens and tries his best to understand and explain to me everything I missed, and I've even managed to learn a few more words in Hebrew.*

Nothing here is like I imagined. Somehow, it's all much less holy than I had built up in my head. There are hardly any religious sites in Karmiel and almost none of the Israelis we meet cover their heads or keep kosher.

Yesterday, they brought a doctor to the center to check us and to give us shots to prevent us from getting sick. The doctor checked me and said that I need to take iron pills every day to make me strong—I've never swallowed a pill in my entire life until now! He asked me if I had started bleeding down there. I was so ashamed! I reluctantly told him that I have not started to bleed down there yet, and he told me that I need to see a doctor for women to make sure everything is okay.

The day after we arrived, Solomon and I walked to a shopping center in Karmiel to buy some new clothes with the money the Israelis gave us. I felt like I was playing staring games with the Israelis. They couldn't stop staring at me, and I couldn't stop staring at them—at the Israeli men with black hats and black robes, at the Israeli teenager girls with short shorts and T-shirts that don't cover their bellies, and at the Israeli girls and boys wearing army uniforms and carrying guns on their shoulders . . . there was just so much to look at! One girl soldier even came over to me and welcomed me to Israel with a hug so tight you would have thought she was my sister!

Oh, and Enati—*you can't even imagine how many stores there are here. How many clothes! I had no idea what to buy, so I asked a lady working at one of the stores to help me choose. I ended up buying a few new shirts and skirts. You wouldn't recognize me; I look so different!*

I'm excited to start ulpan next week and get our life started here. I plan on being the best pupil in the class. You'll be so proud of me! By the time you make it to Israel, I'll be a real Israeli, fluent in Hebrew, and I'll be able to help you and the children get around.

Enati—please, please write back to me. I am dying to hear how you and the children are doing and to hear if I have a new baby brother or sister!

You know, I've written you countless letters since I arrived at the camp in Country X. I know you couldn't write me back, but did you at least receive them? If not, then I will summarize—do not go to Country X with the children, at least not for now. They will never survive. Wait and see if conditions improve, and only then consider going. Besides, no one knows when the next airlift to Israel will be, if at all.

I will write again soon. Hopefully in the next letter I'll be able to tell you about meeting Abat!

Yours, Meri

Solomon—April 1985

Dearest Meskie,

My love, I made it in one piece. We arrived less than a week ago, and ever since, all I've been thinking of is you. In Country X, every day was simply about survival—there was no time for reminiscing or for longing for anything but food and water. But now that I am here in the Holy Land, now that my belly is full and I have a warm place to sleep at night, I can't get you out of my mind. Your luminous eyes, like the ocean deep and mysterious. Your skin, soft and smooth. Your voice, like music to my ears. Your embrace, my one and only home.

Your love, without which I am nothing.

While everything here is new and exciting, I feel like I am simply going through the motions until you come to join me. It's as if I am preparing the foundation for our future lives together as Israelis—learning the language, exploring the land, and becoming one of them.

How are you feeling? Have you begun to regain your strength? Are your parents taking good care of you?

I don't want to write too much because I know how you struggle to read. Please ask Tigest, or one of the neighbors, or whoever is left to write a letter to me on your behalf so that I may know you are okay. For now, this letter is to let you know that you can stop worrying. Now it's my turn to worry about you and to find a way for you to come join me so we can start building our family— again.

Yours forever,
Solomon

Chapter Eighteen

Tigest—June 1985

"Daniel! Go help your sister," commanded Tigest as she held three-month-old Chaya in her arms.

Gabra was sitting outside her family's *gojo* with tears streaming down her cheeks, whining about how Desta and Amara had snatched her new baby doll, handmade by Tigest, and given to her before the new baby was born. Happy to assume the role of peacemaker, Daniel obeyed and ran outside to come to his sister's rescue. The boy tried to broker a deal between his brothers and sister where they would return her doll in exchange for her agreeing to leave their rock tower intact. In the meantime, Tigest took advantage of the rare opportunity to be alone with her newborn baby while the sun was still shining. She looked down at her baby's eyes, which were only just now beginning to focus on hers in return. Exhausted, Tigest sang her baby's name out loud over and over, *Chaya, Chaya*, as a tear rolled down her cheek. She hadn't stopped marveling at the miracle that her Chaya, named after life itself, was actually alive and thriving.

Life had changed ever since Chaya and Tigest returned home from Gondar. Tigest's parents returned to their village to salvage whatever crops they could after their long absence and neglect. And while Tigest returned home with her living and breathing baby full of joy and hope, those feelings quickly subsided when the reality of raising five children and tending to the house and the fields sank in. Tigest had no other choice but to lean heavily on her eldest son, Daniel, so much so that she almost knocked him over.

"Daniel, I need for you to go to Debark to buy kerosene from the market," instructed Tigest, "And while you're there, please check if we have received any mail."

Daniel nodded obediently and set off for another trip to Debark. It would surely be another disappointment when he returned home with his hands empty, save for the jug of kerosene. The fields desperately needed to be tilled and the goats were long neglected, but Tigest continued to send her boy to Debark, more so he could check for a sign of life from Azmera than anything else. If what the Americans, Josh and David, had told her was true, Azmera had to be either dead or in Israel by now. The latter had to be true. It just had to be true.

As Daniel walked out of the hut, Tigest felt a soreness creeping up in her throat. Sleep had become a forgotten pastime, almost a luxury, since returning home from the hospital, and with breastfeeding around the clock and running after her four older children, she couldn't deny the fact that her body was run down. Nonetheless, she couldn't afford to be sick. Not now. Not ever. But especially not now. And while she had tried her best to take the lessons learned from her fainting spell in the hospital to heart, life was bigger and fiercer than any promises she had made to herself. So, with her baby in her arms, Tigest reached for a clove of garlic picked fresh from the fields and swallowed it whole. Her throat burned like fire as she rocked back and forth to prepare Chaya for a nap. With any luck, though, the garlic was burning not only her throat but also the virus weighing her down like a sack of potatoes.

Tigest had long forgotten the sleepless nights during the first year with each of her older children, but she was certain that none of them remotely approached Chaya's propensity for night-time waking. When Kebede was still at home, and when the exhaustion was too much even for her, she would gently nudge him in the middle of the night, directing him to care for the baby so she could sleep more than a few consecutive hours at a time. But Kebede was no longer home. He didn't even know that a new baby had been born. It was all her responsibility. Five children. Breastfeeding. The hut. The fields. The animals. Cooking. Cleaning. All of it.

When Tigest woke up the following morning, her breath still smelling of garlic, she felt her neck stiffen and her legs ache as she attempted to get out of bed to tend to Chaya, wide awake and ready to start another long day. Tigest winced in pain as she crawled out of bed, but she didn't want her baby's crying to awaken the other children. She felt her head spin as her feet hit the cold dirt ground. Chaya quickly calmed down when she latched onto her mother's breast, giving Tigest a moment to assess the damage from the night before. She felt her glands sore to the touch and bulging out of her neck, a sure-tell sign that she was quickly spiraling downward. She was sick.

"*Enati, Enati*, come!" shouted Amara from outside the hut.

Tigest quickly stood up with her baby still nursing in her arms. Every muscle ached as she stepped outside to see what her son was doing out of bed so early in the morning. Tigest nearly dropped the baby when she saw her baby boy sitting in a pool of his own blood.

"What happened?" asked Tigest, her voice hoarse and weak.

Amara tried to catch his breath to speak but could not. Instead, he pointed to his foot oozing blood, sending his mother into the hut to frantically search for a suitable piece of cloth to use as a tourniquet. She placed Chaya down in her bed kicking and screaming. Ignoring her crying, she ran out to her son and picked him up in her arms as she wrapped an old sheet around his foot, pulling it tightly into a knot.

Tigest stroked Amara's head, his crying slowly fading into sweet whimpers.

"*Enati*, I just wanted to help you," he said, his words muffled by his tears, "I woke up early this morning and wanted to make you happy, so I came outside to clean the goat pen up for you. I was almost done cleaning it all when my foot got cut over there," Amara said, as he pointed to a sharp piece of metal poking out of the ground of the goat pen.

For months, Tigest had let Daniel "mother" and "father" his two younger brothers, Amara and Desta. They were all but invisible to her. All Amara wanted to do was to make his mother notice him. Tigest's heart melted as she listened to her little boy's cry for attention. She tried her best to remain calm when she saw Amara's tourniquet filling up with blood, but she could tell from her boy's worried eyes that he understood how serious his wound was.

"Desta, go tell Meskie we need her help!" ordered Tigest, propelling her second oldest son straight from his bed to the other side of the village.

Tigest had considered asking Meskie for help on multiple occasions, but she was reluctant to do so. No matter how difficult her day-to-day life was, she had six healthy children. She didn't want Meskie to feel like she was rubbing her many blessings in her face. But Amara's condition, combined with her own, left her no other choice.

Tigest felt her head pounding as she held her little boy in her arms. Her efforts to tune into Amara's moaning, while tuning out Chaya's wailing, were futile. As Amara and Chaya's cries worsened, she felt ready to explode. She desperately needed help.

Tigest barely recognized Meskie when she walked into the hut, her girlish face having aged since they last met. Tigest recalled Meskie as a young bride standing under the *chuppah* wedding canopy, her big brown eyes sparkling with life and joy. Now, she only saw bottomless pits of sadness. While neither Solomon nor Meskie had ever confided in Tigest their struggles to have a baby, she knew that a woman left empty-handed after six years of marriage had to be mourning the loss of something—of one baby, two babies, or more. She had to be mourning the loss of a dream. Tigest, therefore, treaded gently with her sister-in-law, not wanting to open any unhealed wounds even as her own son's wound continued to spill fresh blood.

"Meskie, thank you for coming," Tigest said as she kissed Meskie's cheeks, trying to conceal the concerned lines on her face. "I woke up this morning horribly sick. I think I have the flu. Amara here has injured himself and badly needs a doctor to look at his foot before it becomes infected. He can't lose his leg," Tigest explained, her breath short and shallow, "and I don't think I have the stamina to make the trip to the clinic in Debark." Meskie nodded as Tigest continued, "I sent Daniel to Debark and he is due back later on today, but in the meantime I have to stay and watch the other children."

Tigest tried her best to avoid any mention of her baby girl. She knew the mention of the baby—a new addition to the family—would sting far more than the mention of her older children, a reality Meskie had already accepted years ago.

"I'd be happy to help," announced Meskie, flattered that Tigest would trust her, of all people, to care for her children.

Solomon's young wife had barely stepped outside her parents' *gojo* since her recent stillbirth; she felt her eyes squint when she walked towards her sister-in-law's home in the early morning sun. Her heart raced with each step she took, knowing what awaited her—a house full of children. Children not her own. Children she couldn't ignore, children she couldn't pretend didn't exist. Despite her apprehensions, however, it felt nice to be needed. Even if she knew she was surely Tigest's last and only option.

Tigest's shoulders loosened the instant Meskie walked through her door. The presence of another adult instantaneously made her feel less alone, even if Meskie would be leaving any moment to take Amara to the clinic in Debark.

"Thank you so very much," whispered Tigest as she hugged Meskie tightly, feeling an immense sense of gratitude towards her forlorn sister-in-law.

With Amara weighing heavily on Meskie's back, Tigest kissed her little boy's bony cheeks goodbye and apologized to him for not being the one to accompany him to the clinic. Her heart ached with the thought of having abandoned her little boy in his time of need, but she had no other choice. Despite barely knowing Meskie, she trusted her to care for him. Amara would grow to trust her as well. Amara's cries for his mother slowly faded as Meskie carried him away, leaving Tigest and her rising fever alone with the baby, Gabra and Desta. With any hope, Daniel would return from Debark before sundown.

"Desta, I need you to take care of Gabra until Daniel comes home. I can barely get out of bed," Tigest mumbled, her voice strained and weak. Desta nodded, eager for the chance to please his mother and to play the role of big brother. "And Gabi-goo, my love," Tigest said as she stroked her daughter's cheeks, "I need you to let your *Enati* rest so I can get better. You understand, my big girl?"

Gabra nodded her head as she choked back the tears welling up in her eyes. Tigest returned to check on Chaya, who by now had cried herself to sleep, and crawled into bed to rest her eyes and body for as long as her children allowed her.

"*Enati*, wake up!" Tigest rubbed her puffy eyes as she heard Daniel's voice in the background.

He had made it home faster than expected, and despite having roused her from a deep sleep, she was beyond relieved to have him home. Tigest looked over at the baby and was surprised to see that she was still sleeping. She had blessed her mother with one of those rare naps long enough to afford Tigest the rest she so desperately needed.

"You won't believe it, *Enati*! Meri sent us a letter!" Daniel announced as he excitedly waved the letter, postmarked all the way from the Holy Land. "And the man at the post-office asked us to take this letter for Meskie as well. It must be from Uncle Solomon!"

Tigest felt her head pound as she jumped out of bed. Despite her illness, she had a spring in her step that had been missing for far too long. She was finally receiving a sign of life from her Meri.

As Tigest ripped open Azmera's letter, she noted how different it felt to be the recipient of a letter from her daughter than of one from her husband. She pored over Azmera's every word and found comfort in knowing not just that her daughter was alive and in Israel, but also that she had apparently written many letters beforehand that she simply had never received. Her two greatest fears—that Azmera had died or had forgotten her—were assuaged all in an instant. After reading the letter to herself, she read it out loud a second and then a third time for the children to hear. She watched them joyously jump up and down with excitement to be getting a letter—their first, as far as they knew—postmarked in the Holy Land! Tigest's head was still pounding and her fever still raging, but Azmera's letter had a healing power to it; if not physically, then certainly emotionally. She and the children talked on and on about Azmera, hanging on to every word as a small window into her new life in Israel, while speculating all that might have happened to her in the month since she wrote the letter.

"I bet you she's speaking Hebrew by now," rejoiced Tigest, the proud smile on her face distracting her from her aching head.

"I bet you she's been inside a car! And maybe she even has some *faranje* friends," added Daniel, his big brown eyes bright with excitement.

"I bet you she's already been to Jerusalem!" exclaimed Desta, the most spiritual of the children, who would join Kebede in synagogue every Shabbat, and any other opportunity that presented itself.

"I bet you she's met *Abat*!" shouted Gabra with delight.

Tigest paused for a moment and then pulled in her three children for a hug and shouted, "I bet we're all right!" trying to hide the fact that Gabra's endless faith in her father nearly broke her mother's heart.

That night, when all the children had gone to bed, Tigest opened her daughter's letter again for another read. She couldn't help but reread Azmera's words warning her not to go to Sudan, at least for now. The thought of being stuck in Ethiopia indefinitely was enough to make her stomach churn, but she knew she had to heed her daughter's words. Life in Ethiopia was next to impossible, but at least here she could keep her children alive with a fair amount of certainty. Going to Sudan, then, was out of the question for the time being. She would simply have to find another way to make it to Israel and to her daughter. But she was beginning to understand that doing anything all by herself with five children, one of them a newborn, was next to impossible. Whatever she did, and however she would do it, she would need someone by her side helping her along the way.

Tigest woke up in the morning to the sight of Amara limping into the hut with his hand rested firmly on Meskie's lowered shoulder. She felt a pang of guilt creep into her soul as she got out of bed to embrace her wounded boy, who was all but forgotten in the excitement of the unexpected letter delivered the day before.

"My little boy is home!" whispered Tigest with excitement as she jumped out of bed and ran to Amara and peeked down to see what had become of his foot.

"We had to wait a long time," Amara explained, his mouth struggling to keep up with his brain eager to deliver the news to his mother, "But after a while, my foot was bleeding really badly and Meskie got fed up. She demanded that a doctor see me immediately, and miraculously it worked! I got fifty-seven stitches and need to rest and take pills to make my blood strong again."

Without hesitating, Tigest approached Meskie and wrapped her arms around her, thanking her for doing whatever she had done to bring her son home in one piece.

"He needs to stay off his foot for four to six weeks and, just like little Amara said, he needs to take antibiotics and iron pills every day to help make up for all the blood he lost," clarified Meskie, with a satisfied look on her face.

Tigest held her little boy in her arms as she listened to him tell her all about his journey to Debark; about how Meskie carried him in her arms; about how they waited until late at night to finally be treated by the doctor; about the doctor's funny Italian accent; about how brave he was when the doctor sewed up his foot; and about how they slept at night on a soft patch of grass just outside Debark waiting for the sunrise to continue their journey home. Tigest listened to his every word, finally finding the opportunity to give him the attention he had deserved all along.

Tigest gave Amara a tight squeeze and a kiss on his cheek when Chaya woke up with a ferocious cry, her long nap leaving her wet and her stomach empty. Tigest knew that her baby needed her, but she didn't want to let go of Amara just yet. In fact, she wanted him to know that for once she was choosing him over Chaya, even though her crying would soon awaken the entire village. She looked over at Daniel who was fast asleep in bed. He was exhausted from his journey to Debark, but still remembered to cuddle Gabra snugly in his arms. It would be a shame to wake him, Tigest thought to herself. Besides, Daniel hadn't really figured out how to tend to the baby yet. He preferred to tend to the older children, which he did better than Tigest herself.

Tigest then looked over at Meskie standing in the corner quietly. Until now, Solomon's wife had barely acknowledged the existence of Tigest's new baby, instead focusing her attention solely on caring for Amara. Tigest hesitated for a moment while she looked at her sister-in-law, not knowing whether she should dare ask for help. She badly needed a few more moments with Amara, though, so with her voice timid and quiet, she asked Meskie to hold the baby.

Meskie nodded slowly. As she approached Chaya, Tigest quietly turned to Meskie, "Thank you for caring for Amara, I couldn't have done it without you. With all the excitement, I forgot to mention that while you were away, Daniel brought home a letter for you from Solomon!"

Meskie felt her eyes well up with tears and she breathed in a deep, long breath. Without even seeing the letter, Meskie felt changed; Solomon's sign of life meant not only that he had survived the journey but that he still loved her—giving her hope that one day she and Solomon would have a crying baby of their very own. Meskie gently picked up Chaya and held her close to her chest to calm down her crying. She breathed in the sweet newborn scent and kissed the top of her head ever so gently, and then subtly turned her back to Tigest to hide the tears streaming down her face.

Chapter Nineteen

Azmera—June 1985

"So, you're saying that in Israel, I can call the police if my husband beats me?" questioned Mazal, one of Azmera's classmates, with a perplexed expression on her face.

Azmera initially became acquainted with Mazal, her beautiful classmate with almond-colored eyes, when sitting next to her in the front row of their *ulpan* class. They were both eager to soak in the knowledge imparted to them by their teacher. Their relationship, however, never really took off—Mazal would hurry back to her husband at the end of each lesson, and oftentimes returned to class the following day with a swollen cheek or eye.

"Yes, that's right," confirmed Efrat, their young instructor with straight black hair so long it nearly reached her bottom.

Efrat, like many of the teachers at the newly reopened Karmiel Absorption Center, wore more than one hat, as both a Hebrew teacher in the *ulpan* and a counselor for what was termed the center's "integration" class. She spoke in slow, clear Hebrew for the benefit of her new Hebrew-speaking students. She couldn't tell by the perplexed look on her students' faces if they were shocked by her revelation or if they couldn't follow her Hebrew, so she repeated herself, this time even more slowly.

"Your husband should not beat you, and if he does, you don't have to accept it. In fact, he can go to jail for it," Efrat explained.

The girls and the women in the class listened intently as she explained for a second time the social norms in their new country, vastly different from the norms in their old one.

"In Israel," continued Efrat, "marriage is only for persons over the age of eighteen years old. And both the man *and* the woman must agree to get married for it to be legal."

Azmera breathed a sigh of relief when she learned that at fourteen years old, she would not be deemed "fit" for marriage any time soon. She had left Ethiopia just in time.

"But I got married back in Ethiopia when I was fourteen," questioned a young woman with soft skin and an uncomfortable-looking pregnant belly squished into her desk and chair, "Does that make my marriage illegal here?" There was something hopeful about the way she asked the question.

"No, this law is only forward-looking," explained Efrat, using body language and an outstretched arm to reinforce the message. "A woman who got married at the age of fourteen back in Ethiopia would still be considered married here in Israel—that is, if she is over the age of eighteen years old."

Azmera watched the young woman's face grow dim as she replied with an exasperated, "Oh," to acknowledge her teacher's disappointing reply.

Efrat continued to talk, her voice increasing in octaves as her students' whispers filled the room with white noise. Rather than share her thoughts with the others, though, Azmera wondered to herself how old her mother was when she married her father. A person's age did not have much significance back in Ethiopia, not nearly as much as in Israel, where eighteen was symbolic more because it marked the age for enlisting in the Israel Defense Forces than the age a person could legally marry. Azmera had always known that her mother married young, but in her mind her mother's age was always irrelevant. She was her mother, after all. For Azmera, her mother seemed to have a lifetime's worth of wisdom no matter how old she was. But as she sat and listened to Efrat, she calculated in her head the difference between her mother's age and her own, and came to the disturbing conclusion that her mother, in all her wisdom, must have married her father when she was approximately thirteen years old. If her calculation was correct, her mother was just a girl when she was forced to become a woman.

"Is anyone going to talk to the boys and the men about this as well?" questioned Azmera stubbornly.

She had rehearsed the sentence in her head four times before uttering it out loud in her new second language. Azmera's Hebrew was improving considerably, so much so that she often found herself surprised by the words that came out of her own mouth. While she was delighted with her progress, she was careful not to flaunt her accomplishments in front of the others in her class, especially the elders. No matter her successes, she felt deeply humbled by their excruciating efforts to learn how to read, write, and speak a foreign language. She often found herself moving back a row or two to sit next to one of the elder women. They were ashamed to ask for Azmera's help translating anything they missed but were always relieved when she did so.

"Yes, Azmera," answered Efrat, the smile on her face growing with satisfaction as she witnessed her prized student grasping the Hebrew language so easily, "The men and the boys are meeting with Alon this morning and are learning about the very same topics. We just thought that the nature of the conversation was sensitive, so we decided to separate you for the day."

"Now on to the last topic—a difficult one—for today," announced Efrat with a quiver in her voice that drew the class's attention, "Rape is when a man forces a woman to have sexual intercourse with him without her consent," said Efrat as she watched the women in front of her awkwardly avert their eyes from hers. "If a man—even your husband—tries to have sex with you, and you don't want to, you can say no. If you say no but he forces you to have sex anyway, it is against the law, and he can be punished and placed in prison. And like I said earlier, your husband should not beat you, even if he is angry or even if you don't obey him. If he beats you, he can go to jail."

The older women in the class stared blankly back at their teacher as they waited for Azmera and others to translate for them what was just said. Their mouths dropped to the floor when they realized the significance of Efrat's teachings—that many of their husbands were and would continue to be criminals in the eyes of Israeli law.

"Efrat, with all due respect, what you are telling us today is fine in theory, but it will never work in practice," contested Mazal as she placed her right hand on the side of her temple, hiding a black and blue mark earned the night before. "Our ways are different from the Israeli way. Our men are used to it. Our women are, too. The law won't change things."

Efrat looked at Mazal's swollen eye and paused to consider her words carefully; her students were eager to hear her response. "But you are Israeli now, and you are expected to comply with Israeli law and social norms. A culture that accepts a man beating his wife is a primitive one. A culture that accepts a man forcing a girl to marry him is a backwards one. A culture that tolerates rape is an immoral one. These cultures do not belong in the State of Israel, where women serve in the army and where a woman served as the country's Prime Minister not long ago."

Efrat stared back at her classroom, and for a moment regretted having said what she had just said, or at least the condescending way in which she had said it. Her students' heads were slightly lowered, their eyes avoiding any contact with hers. They were humiliated by their revered teacher for the ways of their people, which were far beyond their control. Efrat knew she had to soften the blow she had just delivered, so she continued her lecture.

"When the Yemenites came to Israel in the 1950s, they learned to change their ways too. They ended the practice of forced marriages. So did the Moroccans, as did many others. It didn't happen overnight, of course, but they knew they needed to change their ways in order to integrate into

Israeli society. Eventually, the law and social norms of Israel shaped their social norms; not the other way around. The same will happen with the Ethiopians. Your future is here in Israel and not back in Ethiopia, and you need to act accordingly."

Efrat looked back at her students to see some of them raising their chins ever so slightly, somewhat encouraged by her optimistic talk about the importance of changing their ways for the sake of their future in Israel. She felt satisfied with her delivery of this vital message, despite the hurt feelings along the way. Azmera looked at her teacher with envy. For Efrat, all this cultural talk was second nature, while for her students, including Azmera, it was an entirely foreign way of life. Azmera walked out the classroom door for the lunch break, but she had lost her appetite. She couldn't shake off the feeling that she was born out of a marriage that, at least in the eyes of Israelis, was illegitimate from the very outset. Her father had, as Efrat termed it, "primitively" forced her mother to marry him while she was still a girl. As she stood in line at the dining hall for a serving of *shakshuka*, a tomato stew cooked with egg, she wondered to herself, what did that make her?

Solomon sat next to his niece and began poking around on his plate loaded with *shakshuka*, and a side of hummus. While the food served in the dining hall tasted quite good, he found it difficult to get used to the new spices, flavors, and textures, let alone to eat them with a fork instead of his fingers. With a mouth full of hummus, Solomon turned to his niece to inquire about her morning class, curious as to whether the sensitive matter discussed with Alon in his all-male class was similarly raised before the women. One glance at Azmera, however, told him that she was in no mood for sharing. Her eyes averted his as if she were back in Ethiopia in front of one of the elders. Solomon, though, had learned to recognize his niece's cues—raising the issue directly wouldn't work with Azmera, but getting there by way of detour might.

"You know, I haven't gotten any letters from Meskie yet," shared Solomon, pausing for Azmera to acknowledge his admission. "I've sent her a few letters already, but I'm not so sure she'll know how to read them. Her parents only agreed to send her to school when she turned twelve, and even then, she only went during the dry season. She stopped going to school when she turned fifteen—when I married her."

Azmera's eyes popped up at the mention of her uncle's marriage to a girl her age, illegal in the eyes of Israelis, but remained quiet as she listened to him; she was curious to hear how he could possibly defend his, and by extension, her father's, actions. She separated the egg on her plate from the tomato stew. It didn't look nearly as appetizing standing on its own.

"But that's the way things work back in Ethiopia. You should know that," continued Solomon as he lowered his head to hide his eyes welling up with tears, "And just because the Israelis say it's a bad thing doesn't make it true. I love Meskie more than anything in the whole world. I have loved her, and she has loved me in return, ever since we got married—when she was fifteen years old. I am not going to let anyone here tell me that our love is illegitimate, or even worse—criminal."

Azmera lifted her gaze from her plate and looked into Solomon's eyes. He genuinely loved his wife. She could see that he did. But reconciling Efrat's lecture with her uncle's declaration was nearly impossible unless his love for Meskie at fifteen years of age was an exception. Her stomach started to ache as she understood that perhaps her parents' loveless marriage, not Solomon's loving one, was the rule in Ethiopia.

"Good morning, Hadass, it's me calling again. Can you please tell Kebede Rahamim to call Azmera Kebede at the Karmiel Absorption Center?" Azmera requested in perfect Hebrew with just a twinge of an Ethiopian accent.

"Yes, Azmera, I'll leave him another message, but . . ." hesitated Hadass, the secretary on the phone with whom by now Azmera had already become well-acquainted, "I hate to say it, but I'm pretty sure he's not going to call you back anytime soon."

Azmera's heart stung as she listened to Hadass tell her what she had already known for some time. Kebede had tuned out the world, including, apparently, his very own daughter. In recent weeks he had even stopped attending his *ulpan* classes, marking his sharp spiral downhill and leaving his teacher, Shifra, and the rest of the Dimona Absorption Center deeply concerned for his fate.

"Maybe you could try to come visit him and see him face to face?" suggested Hadass, a faceless person on the other end of the phone who nonetheless felt like a close friend to Azmera.

"Oh," replied Azmera, not certain she was ready for a face-to-face meeting with her father, nor for the day's long journey all the way to Dimona to visit him, "I'll have to check with my teacher to see if she'll let me miss class. If she approves my travel, is there anywhere for me to sleep there?" questioned Azmera, not yet at ease with anything outside the walls of the bubble she lived in.

"I'm sure we can find room for you, sweetie," replied Hadass, her voice warm and welcoming to cover up her pity for the young Ethiopian girl on the other end of the line.

Azmera hung up the phone and lowered her face to the burning asphalt ground. There was a line of men and women impatiently waiting in the hot sun for their turn to use the phone. She couldn't bear making eye contact with them. Ever since arriving in Karmiel, she had been leaving messages with Hadass on a weekly basis asking for her father to call her back. At first, it was easy to make up excuses. Maybe the message got lost; maybe *Abat* was sick; maybe the payphone wasn't working; maybe her father didn't know how to use the phone and was too ashamed to ask for help; or maybe Hadass didn't understand her accented Hebrew. Each excuse, standing on its own, was logical enough for Azmera to convince herself that it was true, until weeks passed by without a word from her father. Slowly, it became increasingly difficult to delude herself into believing that her father would call her in an instant if only he was able to.

Azmera examined the clock hanging on the concrete wall outside in the courtyard. Eight thirty in the morning, it read. She was half an hour late for class but felt in no rush to go anywhere. Her breathing was short and hurried, leaving her lungs longing for air. She wanted to be all alone, but also desperately needed to talk to someone. Her roommate, Adeneko, was like a lonely ghost casting its shadow all around her, and Azmera had long ago given up on any efforts to befriend her. The other girls her age also kept their distance—either they were with their families and preoccupied with taking care of their younger siblings, or they had arrived in Israel alone, carrying the trauma of Sudan on their backs and their many losses in their hearts.

Hard as it was to admit, Solomon was the only one there for her—her only "friend" of sorts for now—but he most certainly was in his advanced *ulpan* class studying with the other *Beta Israel* fortunate enough to have arrived in Israel already speaking some Hebrew. Azmera looked off into the distance, the vast green mountains sitting just outside Karmiel beckoning her to come and explore as an outlet for her sadness. She hastily placed her *ulpan* notebook on the table in the courtyard, confident that it would be safely waiting for her when she returned. Without thinking, she put one foot in front of the other and began running fast, her strong legs carrying her outside the absorption center's walls and beyond the city's bustling streets. She listened to the repetitive pounding of her feet, first on the pavement and then on soft dirt. Once she hit her stride, Azmera felt that she could breathe again.

Two hours later, Azmera returned to the Absorption Center, her clothes drenched heavily with sweat, but her head light and her legs loose. She hurried past her *ulpan* classroom, thankful for the closed door which she attributed to the expensive air conditioning surely blasting on the inside. While she felt no qualms about having needed an escape, she couldn't bear to see her teacher Efrat, lest her disappointment with Azmera's truancy bring her down any more than she already was. She grabbed her notebook and returned to her room, desperately wanting to write to her mother but not knowing which truth, or semi-truth, to tell her. She lay on her bed waiting for the minutes to tick by, sharing an awkward silence with her roommate who had grown accustomed to having the room all to herself while Azmera was dutifully in *ulpan*.

Azmera darted out of her room when the clock's minute and hour hand were both pointing to the ceiling. Solomon should just be getting out of class. His *ulpan* class was situated right next to hers, and they both finished at noon, just in time for lunch. If she timed it right, she could manage to catch her uncle walking out his classroom door before Efrat, who usually lingered in the classroom answering questions after class, would walk outside hers.

"Solomon!" whispered Azmera, catching his attention as he walked out his classroom's door while standing clear of hers, "I need to talk to you. Now." Azmera spoke with a sense of urgency that alarmed her uncle. She led him into an empty classroom with pictures of the Prime Minister, Shimon Peres, taped onto the wall. "It's time for us to face the truth and stop making excuses," she reasoned. "*Abat* isn't going to call us back anytime soon. We need to make the trip to Dimona if we want to hear from him."

Solomon stared back at his niece, confused by the salty remains left on her face—dried sweat from her run.

"What happened?" questioned Solomon impatiently, his growling stomach beckoning him to the dining hall.

"It just finally dawned on me that I have been lying to myself this whole time," reasoned Azmera, "*Abat* doesn't want to talk to me or see me—his daughter—and there must be a reason why. Otherwise he would have called by now. We need to go there to find out."

Solomon tried his best to listen to Azmera while she spoke, but he couldn't help being distracted by his growling stomach and his racing mind getting angrier by the second. Despite all Kebede's neglect, his daughter loved him and desperately wanted to reunite with him. Kebede didn't deserve a daughter like Azmera, thought Solomon. He, on the other hand, did.

Azmera convinced Solomon that they would leave for Dimona early Friday morning and return late Saturday evening after the Sabbath ended. That way Azmera wouldn't have to confront Efrat with a request to miss another day of *ulpan* after already feeling guilty for her recent truancy. It would be their first time traveling outside Karmiel alone without the comforts of a tour-guide and a chartered bus, and Azmera felt butterflies fluttering in her stomach in the days leading up to it. Other than being her father's place of residence, she knew nothing of Dimona. She was disappointed, however, when she discovered, with the help of Alon, that the journey would not take them through Jerusalem as she had hoped. Nor was there a direct bus from her home to her father's. Azmera couldn't help but see this as being symbolic of something, exactly what, though, she wasn't quite sure of just yet.

Azmera woke up before the sun rose early Friday morning, the summer air still cool from the night before. She grabbed her bag, packed two days earlier, and struggled to throw it over her shoulder as the contents of it—hand-me-down clothes of all sorts and sizes just in case she stayed longer than expected—bulged outwards. As Azmera readied to leave the room, she gazed over at her roommate. Despite the early hour, Adeneko was wide awake, her vacant stare plastered on the ceiling. Azmera murmured a soft goodbye; the night before Azmera had fallen asleep to Adeneko's muffled cries. Azmera had long sensed that Adeneko wanted and needed space from her roommate, and while she never shared her losses, they were as plain as day. As Azmera began her way up the stairs to wake her uncle, she paused for a moment. She should be grateful. Despite all the disappointment with her father, and despite her mother being an insurmountable distance away, her family was alive. Even more, she had her uncle by her side to soften the landing—if ever so slightly—here in Israel. Azmera closed her eyes and smiled to herself.

The Karmiel bus station was crowded with soldiers puffing their cigarettes and gulping down their coffee as they eagerly awaited their bus home for the short weekend. Azmera stared at the soldiers—muscular boys only a few years older than she—with awe. With sunglasses perched on top of their heads and boots reaching up to their knees, they hypnotized the nearly fifteen-year-old girl, attracting her attention despite wanting to ignore them. Azmera couldn't help but notice one soldier in particular, his height and good looks separating him from the others. She watched him standing at the bus stop next to her with his *uzi* machine gun wrapped around his shoulder while he swallowed down a falafel for his breakfast. As he wiped a dab of hummus from the side of his mouth, his eyes smiled at Azmera's just long enough for hers to smile back. She quickly averted her gaze to cover up the sudden reddening of her otherwise chocolate brown face. In her few excursions outside the absorption center, she had grown used to people staring at her—her brown skin combined with her striking beauty made her an instant attraction to the typical Israeli. But never had she felt a boy look at her like the soldier did then—like she was a real person and not some exotic animal in a glass menagerie. After regaining her composure, she looked up, disappointed to see that her soldier was boarding the green bus that hummed loudly next to her, its destination written in big letters on its front, "Haifa."

"Our bus should be leaving in another fifteen minutes," announced Solomon as he anxiously looked at the clock to double-check that they had not mistakenly missed their bus.

Solomon and his niece were just beginning to understand the importance that time played in Israeli culture, where the clock seemed to dictate nearly everything a person did throughout the day—when to wake, when to eat, and when to work—all in stark contrast to their ways back home in Ethiopia, where the sun and the moon served as their guide. Unlike so many others in the absorption center, Solomon was adamant about arriving to class on time, convinced that living his life by the clock was the first step towards integrating into Israeli society. Solomon's efforts at punctuality slowly rubbed off on his niece who was eager to put her new time-telling skills to use.

"Your *Abat* is going to be happy to see you," uttered Solomon, taking a break from anxiously pulling and tugging at his nails.

Azmera looked back at him skeptically, choosing to ignore Solomon's forced attempt at optimism. In truth, Solomon hesitated before agreeing to take part in Azmera's mission to visit Kebede, fearful that his young niece would be devastated when she discovered her father in less than a fatherly way. As a little boy, Solomon's parents always teased him for being Kebede's tail, following him wherever he went. And while Kebede maintained his big brother influence on Solomon throughout the years, as Solomon matured, he began to pick up on Kebede's less admirable traits. When Solomon fell for Meskie, he ran to his big brother to share in his exciting news, but Kebede simply couldn't be happy for him; instead, he advised him to force Meskie into marrying him just as he had done to Tigest. From that point on, he began to view his older brother in an entirely different light, seeing him for the first time not just as the strong leader and hard worker he admired, but also as the cold, entitled, selfish man he could all too often be.

Meskie's fertility struggles, therefore, were not the only force behind the ever-growing distance between the two brothers. The more Solomon fell in love with Meskie, the more he found the way his older brother treated Tigest to be shameful. This was even more the case after sitting in the cultural integration class weeks earlier, where the sting of learning that his marriage to Meskie would be a violation of the law in Israel was somehow mitigated by his learning that the law in his new country—the law that prevented husbands from having intercourse with their wives without their consent—would certainly mean that his brother was a criminal. Assuming that Kebede had sat through the same lecture on rape and forced marriage in Dimona as he had in Karmiel, it was of little surprise to him that Kebede refused to reciprocate Azmera's or his repeated efforts to reach out. If the cultural integration class managed to undermine Solomon's faith in his own marriage, even if ever so slightly, he could only imagine how it would have affected Kebede. Knowing this, Solomon felt the need to be protective of his young niece. If Azmera was going to visit her father, Solomom needed to be by her side just in case.

As Solomon saw a bus marked "Tel Aviv" pull into the station, he opened his hand to count his shekels one more time—he wanted to make sure he had the proper change for the bus fare. Solomon had ridden a bus once back in Ethiopia, traveling from Debark to Gondar with twenty kilograms of freshly harvested teff flour to sell at the bustling Gondar market. On that journey, the pushing in line, the bumpy drive and the overcrowded bus reeking of body odor overwhelmed his senses; but at least it didn't make him feel incompetent. Ahead of this journey, Solomon was so anxious that he tossed and turned in his sleep the night before, replaying in his head the directions to the station, the bus numbers, and schedule, all to avoid losing face before a real Israeli and thus preventing any unnecessary bruises to his ego.

Azmera boarded the bus first with Solomon trailing behind her, as he proudly paid with correct change for the bus fare. It was a transit bus, originating from Tzfat, a kabbalistic holy city in the north, and continuing its way to Tel Aviv. They had been first in line to board the bus, so Azmera was disappointed when she saw that there weren't two seats next to one another remaining. Both she and Solomon would have to sit next to a stranger, alone. Azmera began to sheepishly scan the bus for a seatmate who appeared welcoming. A young man with a black hat and *tzitzit* peeking out behind his black jacket sat in the window seat, refusing to look at Azmera. Azmera knew she needed to keep walking when he placed his black hat box on the otherwise empty aisle seat next to him. Further down the aisle was a middle-aged woman with smooth, black hair and skin nearly as dark as Azmera's. She looked friendly enough at first, but as Azmera approached her she deliberately placed her hand over her nose, leaving Azmera no option but to continue scanning for a place to sit.

Azmera could feel her palms begin to sweat as she scanned the few options remaining on the bus, wondering to herself what she would do if no one agreed to sit next to her. As she approached the back of the bus, Azmera finally cast her eyes on a female soldier dressed in an olive-green uniform, her dirty-blonde curly locks tussled into a youthful ponytail. The soldier looked at Azmera with a grin, relieving Azmera's sense of rejection and ending her hunt for a place to sit. When she was comfortably situated, she looked at the front of the bus and was pleased to see that Solomon had found his home sitting next to the religious man whose hat box now rested safely on his lap. The religious man apparently hadn't wanted to sit next to her not because of the color of her skin but rather because she was a girl. Strangely, she felt relieved.

"*Shalom*," welcomed the female soldier, her face much more striking up close than far away, "My name is Liat." Eager for the chance to practice her Hebrew, Azmera introduced herself and chuckled heartily as Liat struggled to pronounce her name. "Where are you from?" asked the soldier, initiating conversation following a moment of awkward silence.

Azmera stared back at the soldier, stumped by her question. "I'm from Karmiel," responded Azmera in carefully worded Hebrew.

Liat looked at Azmera and laughed. "That's not what I meant. I meant, where are you *really* from?"

Azmera breathed a sigh of relief now that she understood the direction Liat seemed to be leading the conversation. In her few months as an Israeli, she found that the limited number of Israelis with whom she had the opportunity to interact tended to prefer to gloss over Azmera's past, instead placing all their focus on the present by asking her questions about which absorption center she called home and how her Hebrew was progressing.

"I'm from a small village in Ethiopia, in the Simien Mountains not far from a town called Debark," Azmera explained as she felt her breathing slow down and her shoulders loosen. Azmera was surprised by the cathartic nature of the conversation. The more she told Liat of her home, the lighter she felt.

"Did you come here all by yourself?" questioned Liat, her jaw agape as she stared at the thin Ethiopian girl sitting next to her.

"Not really. I mean, I didn't come with my mother or my siblings, but I came with my uncle, who's sitting up front. We're actually on our way to visit my father who is living in Dimona."

Liat's eyes welled up with tears as she listened to Azmera tell of her family left behind in Ethiopia and her hope to reunite with them one day in Israel.

"I can't even begin to imagine what that must feel like," Liat said as she shook her head side to side, dumbstruck by Azmera's story. "My mother's side of the family came from Yemen back in the 1950s," explained Liat as Azmera struggled to understand Liat's rushed Hebrew, "and my father's side of the family, or the ones who survived, came to Israel from Hungary after the *Shoah*."

"I am the first *sabra* in my family," Liat continued with a proud smile on her face. "You know, my mother and her family suffered a lot when they first got here. People treated them like they were second-class citizens. They made fun of their accents. Made fun of their food. Called them animals. When my mother and father started dating, my father's parents even threatened to disown him if he dared marry a poor Yemenite girl like my mother. But they got married anyway, and my grandparents eventually got over it and accepted my mother into their family. Now, my parents have four children who are salt-of-the-earth Israelis." Liat paused to confirm with Azmera that she understood everything she said before she continued, "What I'm trying to say is that it's going to be hard for you, for all the Ethiopians, in Israel in the beginning. You're going to have lots of unpleasant encounters like you did earlier with that Moroccan woman sitting in the front," said Liat, surprising Azmera with her observation, "But just like my mother and her family, sooner or later other Israelis will treat you like you are one of us. Eventually, you will feel like you have no other home. I'm sure of it."

Azmera wiped away a tear gently rolling down her cheek as she listened to Liat tell her of the many hardships her mother overcame over the years, finding Liat's words to be uplifting in a way she didn't realize she needed.

Azmera looked out the window at the passing landscape, the tall buildings and zooming cars blocking her view of the sea. Liat fumbled around in her pocket and pulled out a crumpled piece of paper. She turned behind her and asked a passenger across the aisle to borrow a pen, then scribbled down a phone number and her name written in big, loopy Hebrew letters.

"You have to come to my family's home in Jerusalem for a Shabbat weekend," pleaded Liat with an eager smile on her face, "Yes, I'm from Jerusalem, not Tel Aviv. I got released from my base late and missed the direct bus to Jerusalem. But it was meant to be. I wouldn't have met you otherwise!"

Azmera smiled, as Liat continued. "My mother makes the most delicious couscous stew and after dinner we stay up late watching movies and enjoying each other's company. We would love to have you."

Azmera placed Liat's phone number in her knapsack, thrilled with the possibility of having made her first Israeli friend. While Liat's offer of hospitality caught her a bit off guard at first, Azmera remembered one of the more recent integration classes where Efrat had discussed Israeli generosity towards fellow Jews, a concept she claimed was born out of the Talmudic teaching of mutual responsibility.

"I would love to," exclaimed Azmera as she accepted Liat's offer with contained enthusiasm. "I've never even been to Jerusalem," confessed Azmera, explaining how the *ulpan* had postponed its planned trip to Jerusalem the month before, following an escalation of violence in and around the Old City.

As the bus jerked to a stop in the busy Tel Aviv streets, Liat returned her things neatly to her backpack, and explained that she was eager to see her parents after an unusually long three-week absence from home spent at her army base.

The bus pulled into the Central Bus Station, sending the passengers into a rushed frenzy to deboard as quickly as possible to catch their next bus and make the most of the remaining few hours before Shabbat began. Liat held out her arms and warmly embraced Azmera, confirming again their plans to get together soon.

As Liat walked onto the platform to catch her next bus to Jerusalem, she shouted to her new friend, "Good luck finding your father, and remember what I told you. It will get easier! *Shabbat shalom!*"

Azmera waved goodbye to her new friend and walked towards her uncle waiting anxiously for her inside the station. Azmera followed her uncle, letting him lead the way as she replayed in her head her conversation with Liat. Her new friend's nonchalant confidence in everything working out was refreshing and annoying all at once, the result of years of experience Azmera had yet to acquire. Somehow, though, Azmera felt the crumpled phone number stuffed in her knapsack was the first step towards something better.

Reuniting with her father, no matter what his condition, surely would be the next step. The bus to Dimona was scheduled to leave in twenty minutes.

Chapter Twenty

Kebede—June 1985

Kebede woke up in his bed damp with sweat from the night before. Israel's desert heat was at its peak, and even the night air no longer provided a respite from its oppressive rising temperatures. He lifted his pounding head up from the bed and glanced at the glass clock glued to the wall. "Ten-thirty in the morning," it read. He had missed *ulpan*—again. Not that he would have attended class had he woken up on time. He had spent the night before sitting on the balcony in a drunken stupor as he gulped down shots of cheap vodka and arak bought at the kiosk down the road. His roommate, Mengistu, no longer needed to drag him out to the balcony at the end of the day—he voluntarily did so himself. In fact, the past few weeks he had spent so much time on the balcony or in his room drinking that he no longer did much of anything else.

Ever since his forced "circumcision," Kebede felt nothing like himself. The ritual drawing of blood was intended to make him more of a Jew, but in reality it made him more lost than ever. It was as if Kebede was trapped inside a spinning tornado with no escape. His daily routine of attending *ulpan* and studying Hebrew after class gradually deteriorated into a way of life that had him shuddering at the sight of his own image staring back at him in the bathroom mirror.

Kebede's morning ritual began with a large cup of coffee to knock off the hangover from the night before. His senses slowly started to clear right around lunch time, the most dreaded hour of the day, for at that hour he was finally sober enough to process what had happened the night before. The strike of noon was like a small window of desperate lucidity for Kebede, when he was sober enough to pay attention to the fact that he had missed yet another day of *ulpan* and learning Hebrew. The strike of noon was when his senses would finally awaken and he would notice the unpleasant stench—a cocktail of alcohol, vomit, and urine—emanating from his body. The strike of noon was when his roommate would smuggle him a plate of food from the dining hall, oftentimes the only food he ate all day. The strike of noon was when he would push around his food, too nauseated to consider eating anything but rice or a stale piece of bread. It was then that Kebede would recall how hearty his appetite for food—and life—had once been.

The strike of noon was when he finally was able to see himself for who he had become—not the proud Israeli he had hoped to be but just another drunk Ethiopian immigrant who could barely speak the local language. And while the strike of noon should have been the wake-up call for Azmera's father to change his ways, instead it triggered a self-hatred burning deep inside from a place that he never knew existed. He hated himself so much that he spent the afternoon hours dozing in his bed just to pass the time away so he would have the stamina to go through the vicious cycle once again when the sun went down. He hated himself so much that empty threats to kick him out of the absorption center lest he start attending *ulpan* class had no deterrent effect. The sweet burning sensation of the cold vodka going down his throat was all he really needed.

Hadass, the Dimona Absorption Center's beloved secretary and Azmera's phone companion, would periodically leave messages for the troubled student: first in the *ulpan* classroom; then, when he no longer attended class, in the dining hall; and then, when he no longer ate in the dining hall, taped to his door. Kebede ignored them all. Of course, he felt tremendous relief when he first received word of his daughter's safe arrival to Israel, but he easily convinced himself that he was in no condition to speak with her.

"Soon enough," he told himself, "Soon enough, I'll get my act together and then I'll call her and invite her to come join me."

The days and nights went by, however, and "soon enough" never came. In his moments of lucidity, though, his thoughts often wandered to his eldest daughter; thoughts of how she was coping in Israel, thoughts of playing hide-and-seek with her as a little girl, thoughts of the day she was born, and thoughts of that infamous day, when he forced his seed inside his newlywed wife who was just a girl at the time. While he never doubted his love for Azmera, in these noontime moments of clarity, he slowly began to put together the pieces of the puzzle that had plagued him his entire adult life. He could never love Azmera the way a father should, so long as he hated himself for the way in which she had been conceived.

The banging on the door woke Kebede up from his deep afternoon sleep, but he chose to ignore it. He knew that he didn't want to see whoever it was outside his door. Hours earlier, he found himself curled up into a ball on the floor of the shared bathroom, purging into the toilet the debauchery from the night before. Kebede pulled his pillow over his head to muffle the persistent knocking and ease the pounding of his head; he was certain someone had heard him and told Shifra, and that she was coming to his rescue. Damn them all. But when Kebede heard the keyhole slowly turn, he snapped out of bed to see who possibly dared to disturb him and his privacy.

When Kebede saw Hadass standing in his doorway with a concerned frown plastered on her face, he assumed she was there to inform him that the absorption center was finally carrying through with their threat to throw him out. He was flabbergasted, though, when he saw that Hadass wasn't standing there alone. Behind her stood his daughter and brother in the flesh. They had hunted him down.

"*Abat*," whispered Azmera as she stood at the entrance of the room, not sure whether or how to approach her father, "I made it."

For months, Kebede's daughter had rehearsed in her head what she would say when she and her father finally reunited, but as she looked at him standing before her, with his eyes red and swollen and his frail body naked but for a pair of stained underwear, all the expressions of emotion she had rehearsed were no longer relevant. Without asking for an invitation, Azmera and Solomon slowly entered Kebede's room. Hadass closed the door behind them, leaving them alone with Kebede. The stench of alcohol mixed with vomit made Azmera gasp for air. Time stood still as the three family members stood in Kebede's filthy room, waiting for someone to say something.

In truth, Solomon was not nearly as shocked to see his brother in his current state as Azmera was. He had expected it. Azmera was still too young and naïve to have noticed what took place on a nightly basis just one floor above her in the Karmiel Absorption Center. For better or worse, Solomon was not. He saw how men like him slowly succumbed to the bottle, as well as their efforts to hide their downward spirals from their families. He saw them humiliated in front of their children as they watched their offspring speak fluent Hebrew while they still struggled with the basics. He saw how they felt threatened when they saw their wives, oftentimes much younger than them, assert themselves in ways they had never done before, and adapt to their new reality with much greater ease than they did. And he saw how they struggled to find their place in the Jewish homeland where they felt they would never be fully accepted as Jews. While Solomon did not allow himself to fall victim to these vices, he witnessed how far too many men did every single night. It was, therefore, no surprise for him to see Kebede, his older brother, once so strong and proud, a fallen man standing before him.

"Meri, why don't you wait outside in the hallway and let your *Abat* get dressed?" suggested Solomon, knowing that Azmera desperately needed him to break the tension in the air.

Azmera nodded and, without a second glance at her father, headed out to the hallway where she felt her body slowly let go of itself as it slid down the wall. She struggled to reconcile that the man standing inside that room could possibly be the same man she knew back in Ethiopia. And while she had certainly prepared herself for a difficult reunion—she wasn't so naïve as to not understand that his refusal to return her calls must have meant that something was plaguing him—she was in no way prepared for the miserable sight of her father, with his flaccid skin reeking and his vacant eyes refusing to meet hers in return. As she sat on the ground and watched the passers-by rushing to their rooms to get ready for Shabbat, images of her *Enati* flashed through her head, bringing tears to her eyes. Azmera lowered her head to not attract attention to her crying. She remembered her exhausted mother kneading *injera*, and beating clothes clean against the rocks down by the creek, and carrying a growing baby in her belly, and calling the boys to wash their hands before dinner, all the while singing a lullaby to Gabra after she fell and scraped her knee. Azmera couldn't possibly think of her father without thinking of her mother first, and how he had abandoned her to pursue his dream in the Land of Israel, a dream that he now appeared to have squandered.

When Azmera's crying calmed to gentle whimpers, she could hear shouting coming from inside her father's room. The muffled voices were difficult to make out, so she dragged her body across the floor and rested her head on the door that seemed to have sealed off her father's heart.

"What do you want from me?" shouted Kebede, his speech slow and slurred.

"What do I want from *you*?" responded Solomon, indignantly, "You need to decide what you want for yourself, big brother! You abandon your wife and your children for what? For this? Look at what you have become! You disgust me."

Azmera knew she was violating both her uncle's and her father's privacy, but she couldn't help but listen.

"You don't have any idea how hard it's been for me here," explained Kebede as he choked back tears.

"I know how hard it's been. I'm in this country too, you know, and I'm the one taking care of your daughter!" shouted Solomon, his voice slowly increasing in volume, "And no matter how hard it's been for you, it can't begin to approach how hard it's been for Tigest and the newborn baby and children you left behind."

Azmera heard the bus on the street below halt to a stop, opening its doors to send the passengers home to welcome Shabbat and savor the aromas of roasted chicken and freshly baked challah bread wafting through the air. Her uncle had known that her mother was pregnant on that fateful night when he took her from her family. She wondered why, then, he had never mentioned it.

"Tigest was pregnant when I left?" asked Kebede, his voice quivering as he spoke.

Solomon nodded his head slowly, giving his brother time to digest the news that he had brought another life into the world, while he was wasting away his own. Without hesitating, Kebede stood up from his bed and opened up Mengistu's closet. He frantically searched for the bottle of vodka awaiting him and opened it up with an aching desperation that filled his body from head to toe. As the vodka washed down his throat, he felt his body, and his heart, ease up just enough to keep him going.

"Damn you, Kebede!" screamed Solomon, his voice so loud that the passers-by down the hall turned their heads to see what all the commotion was about, "You have no idea how many blessings you've been given, and you're throwing them all away! And look at you! You don't deserve any of them. You have five—no, now six—healthy children. You have a wife who, for some reason I can't begin to fathom, still wants to love you even though you forced yourself on her when she was just thirteen years old! You are so selfish, wasting your life away like you are. Snap out of it, my brother, and get your life back on track before it's too late!"

Azmera listened to her uncle shout. She couldn't pretend not to hear any longer. She felt her legs shake underneath her as she pulled herself off the ground. She slowly opened the door to discover that the two men in her life—one her father, and one the man who had treated her like a father—were trading looks of sheer hatred at each other.

"*Abat*," whispered Azmera, her voice tired from listening, "What did you do to *Enati*?"

Kebede turned his back to Azmera and climbed into his bed. He curled himself up into a ball and began to cry uncontrollably. Her father didn't need to answer for Azmera to know the truth.

Hadass helped Azmera stretch a pair of freshly laundered sheets over the thin mattress lying on the floor in the spare room that would be hers for the night.

"You can stay here for as long as you want," offered Hadass, "The teen girls that were in this room just got sent to a boarding school, and there are no more arrivals, so for now this room is going to stay empty." Hadass's look of pity made Azmera uncomfortable, but she appreciated her generosity, nonetheless.

"Thank you very much," Azmera whispered as she tried to contain her tears, "And what about Solomon?"

Hadass explained to her that the men's floor was at full occupancy. Solomon would have to sleep on the floor in Kebede's room for the night. Besides, she explained, perhaps that would give Solomon an opportunity to knock some sense into his older brother.

When Azmera finished making up her bed, she paused and stared at Hadass for a moment, unsure of what she wanted to say.

"What, my dear?" questioned Hadass, with a look on her face of motherly concern for the broken girl standing in front of her.

Hadass had begun working as a secretary at the Dimona Absorption Center in preparation for Operation Moses, but she quickly became much more than that. Her ability to empathize and see the other as herself made the Dimona Absorption Center, despite its remote location, a reputable one. Hadass herself was a mother to three children, the oldest a teenage girl not much older than Azmera. The thought of her daughter standing in Azmera's shoes pulled heavily on her heart, and the mother inside her couldn't help but want to mother the girl standing before her as if she were her own.

"Why didn't you tell me he was in such bad shape when we spoke on the phone?" asked Azmera, frustrated with her naïveté over the past few months but careful not to cast blame on anyone else.

Hadass squeezed Azmera's hand before she began to explain how Kebede's condition, while severe, was unfortunately not all that unique for new immigrants from Ethiopia. Azmera tried her best to understand how her father, once so proud and strong, could have possibly lost control of himself as he did, but she was at a loss. She startled as Hadass held out her hand, her skin rough but her touch gentle and soft—much like Tigest's.

"You know, becoming an Israeli is like climbing up a steep mountain," Hadass explained, "The terrain is steep and challenging in the beginning, but the view is so rewarding once you get to the top. I'm afraid that Kebede gave up halfway up the mountain. The view was just too far out of sight for him." Hadass looked at the clock and, surprised by the late hour, apologized for having to hurry home to her family before Shabbat began.

Azmera sat on her bed and listened to the sound of silence outside, interrupted only by the occasional chirping of birds resting in the trees. She thought about Hadass's metaphoric reasoning for Kebede's downfall. While life had indeed been challenging for her since arriving in Israel, she felt that she was getting close to the top of the mountain. As Azmera rested her head before Shabbat dinner, she wondered to herself why her father couldn't do the same.

After Azmera had left his room, Kebede and Solomon sat in complete silence, each waiting for the other to make the next move. When the sun began to slowly sink into the ground, Solomon offered to take his brother to the dining hall. Food would do him some good. But Kebede refused. His pride was too swollen for him to step outside the room in his state; he would just eat leftovers from lunch smuggled in by Mengistu earlier in the day. While Kebede needed Solomon, he had made it perfectly clear that he didn't want his younger brother, or daughter, around; Azmera, on the other hand, did want his company, so Solomon decided to join her in the dining hall for a nice Shabbat dinner where they could digest all that had happened in the past few hours.

Kebede pretended to be sleeping when Solomon left the room, relieved to finally have his privacy restored. He popped out of bed when the door slammed shut, and without hesitation opened the bottle of arak bought earlier that morning at the kiosk down the street. While at first Kebede found it easy to bum a drink or two off his other drinking comrades sitting on the balcony, his drinking habit quickly began to drain out his already-thin wallet. In fact, he had used up nearly all his past month's government-issued entitlements and allowances on booze. As he gulped down the bottle's contents, though, he knew there was one thing left for him to do. He addressed an envelope and placed his last remaining stamp on it. This letter would be one he would actually send in the mail. He would drop it in the mailbox on the street corner below on his way out. Tigest deserved to be the last one to hear from him.

✡

Dear Tigy,

My hand is shaking as I write you this letter. Earlier today, Azmera and Solomon came to visit me. You'd be happy to know that our girl looks wonderful. She's gained some weight and is growing to look so much like you.

I, however, was so hungover from the night before that I couldn't even greet her. All I could do was reach for the bottle. It's the only thing that helps me make it through the day. It's the only thing that lets me forget, even for just a moment, how much I hate myself. So, I drink from it, and then I hate myself even more.

I hate myself for what I did to you, I hate myself for who I was to you, and I hate myself for what I've become here. I want out, but I don't know how. It's like I feel myself sinking into this abyss. Every time I drink, I feel myself climb upwards a bit, but then I sink down even lower than before.

The Israelis don't want me here, and I can understand them. I'm just another drunk Ethiopian who can barely speak Hebrew. I have nothing to offer them.

By the time you get this letter, I won't be here anymore.

Please know that, while I may not have shown it, I did love you, and still do. I love the children too, even the new baby . . . Please tell them so. Azmera is a good girl and I know Solomon will take care of her.

You, my dear, are the strongest person I know. The children are safe with you, no matter where you are, but I hope you will make it to Israel soon to join Meri. She needs her mother, and you need her. I know how much you love her.

I am sorry for everything I did to you. I am sorry for all of it.

I just can't live like this anymore. Please understand.

Yours,
Kebede

Chapter Twenty-One

Tigest—July 1985

Tigest neatly creased the piece of paper in her hand and stuffed it inside the brown envelope Daniel had purchased for her on his last trip to Debark. Her hands shook as she copied her daughter's mailing address, checking twice to make sure she had spelled the name of the town "Karmiel" accurately in English letters, her writing resembling a young child's handwriting. It was to be the first letter Tigest would proudly send to her daughter, and she wanted to do everything possible to ensure that it reached its intended destination, despite the unreliable Ethiopian postal service. She had written Azmera many letters since she had left months ago, but she was never able to send them. She couldn't send them to Sudan, of course. It would be asking for a death sentence.

With Chaya wrapped up tightly on her back, Tigest began her afternoon routine. Together with Meskie, she sewed and patched up holes in clothing brought to them by poor peasants seeking to salvage their worn items for just a bit longer. Having dutifully finished their chores, the older children played outside until the next rainstorm sent them running inside for shelter. After a long recovery, Amara's stitches and foot had fully healed, and he took great delight in being able to play soccer with his brothers again—and Tigest took great delight in watching him play. Meskie and Tigest's new business endeavor was as volatile as the sky above them, each day unpredictably different from the next. And while everyone around them celebrated what appeared to be the end of the drought, the two women relished those rare afternoon hours when the winds were calm and the sky was blue, providing them with the quiet and serenity they needed to work, and allowing their customers to step outside to seek their services.

The once estranged sisters-in-law worked in relative silence, interrupted only by the occasional request by Tigest to thread a needle or to hold Chaya while she stepped outside for a bathroom break. The silence while they worked was a welcome one, marked by a sense of tranquility rather than awkward tension. Both women knew that their sewing partner was simply too exhausted from life to waste any more energy talking. Both women also knew that they desperately needed the other—Tigest to survive raising five children on her own, and Meskie to come back to life after she herself failed in creating it. Plus, the extra money they earned from their new venture lent both women a refreshing sense of independence. Their men may have left them, each for their own different reasons, but they nonetheless were proving themselves to be surprisingly self-sufficient.

In truth, Tigest knew she would have drowned had Meskie not come to pull her out of the water. Once she, Chaya, and Amara appeared to be on the mend, she set herself the goal of saving two hundred Birrs from her sewing venture with Meskie; only then did she allow herself to purchase a proper envelope and a postage stamp to finally send word to her daughter in Israel. Two hundred Birrs in savings, Tigest calculated, would provide enough cushion for her to afford the extravagant costs of contacting the outside world. With her business thriving, Tigest sent Daniel on yet another journey to Debark to send word to Azmera that she and the rest of the family were miraculously thriving too. As she watched Daniel walk outside the hut, the large yellow jerrycan weighing heavily down his back, she hoped that with any luck Daniel would return home with another letter, or two, to replace the one she had just sent.

Most mornings, Chaya awoke to the sound of synchronized roosters crowing outside. Tigest would usually lay in bed and turn her back to her baby's cooing, trying to squeeze in just a few more minutes of rest before tending to her and the rest of the household. This morning, however, Tigest popped out of bed, remarkably eager to start the day, despite sleeping a mere few hours the night before. Daniel was scheduled to arrive home today from Debark. As she nursed Chaya, she looked into the big brown eyes staring back at her and couldn't help but see Azmera. It had been so easy for Tigest to fall in love with her youngest because the sight of her provided her with a much-needed reminder of her oldest.

Azmera had now been gone for more than six full moons, and Tigest had grown accustomed to her new reality far faster than she would like to admit. Her younger children didn't leave her much time to miss her eldest, but oftentimes in her late-night nursing sessions she would find herself reminiscing over fond memories of Azmera. Tigest would futilely try to grasp on to each memory for dear life. Her daughter, the love of her life, was slipping through her hands, and there was nothing she could do to stop it. Surely, though, seeing her daughter's loopy handwriting again and hearing her stories from Israel would summon up memories that were otherwise stubbornly tucked away in the back of her head.

Tigest didn't bother to hide her disappointment when Daniel returned home from Debark later that morning celebrating the arrival of a letter from his father, but not from his sister. Daniel shouted with joy as he approached the hut, beckoning Amara, Desta and Gabra to leave their chores behind and join him in opening the much-awaited letter, the first from their father since Tigest began sending Daniel to Debark. In fact, it had been months since Kebede had last sent word to his wife, and the few letters he had sent beforehand remained safely hidden from the children. Daniel's breath rushed with excitement as he flashed the letter before his mother, impatiently signaling for her to put down the baby and read them the contents of the letter. Tigest's face saddened as she watched her children jump for joy. She knew Kebede. And she also knew from Azmera's previous letters that he hadn't returned her phone calls. She couldn't possibly read the letter out loud to her children without reading it to herself first.

Tigest passed Chaya to Meskie, who now felt more like a sister to her than the stranger she once was. Despite their mutual envy for one another—Meskie for Tigest's womb and Tigest for Meskie's marriage—they had developed a functional symbiotic relationship while living together. Meskie was finally able to hold Chaya without crying, and from time to time even surprised herself by genuinely smiling at the newborn baby in her arms. With her hands freed, Tigest grabbed the letter out of Daniel's hands and shooed away her children. She'd rather they left her alone than inundate her with questions she couldn't answer. She watched her children, with their heads lowered to the ground, walk outside the hut, and felt herself wanting to cry. They really adore their father, she thought to herself as she gently wiped a tear away from her cheek. If only they knew what kind of man he was.

Tigest felt her stomach tie in knots as she got ready to open the letter. What she had hoped would be a joyful morning full of reading and rereading Azmera's letter had turned into what she dreaded most of all. She knew that Kebede's lull in correspondence was no coincidence. She was sure he was writing to tell her that he didn't want her anymore. Maybe he was writing to let her know that he had met another woman, an Israeli woman perhaps. She felt a scorching anger rise in her throat for caring. She knew that he didn't deserve it, but she simply couldn't control the way she felt towards the man—the man who had given her six children but who broke her heart time and time again. Despite it all, she still loved him, and it would break her heart all over again to read that he no longer loved her.

Kebede's handwriting was messy and shaky, a distant cry from the characteristic letters he used to etch meticulously in his prior correspondence. Tigest struggled to make out the first line, then the second, and then the third. She felt a refreshing lightness as she read that her daughter had finally met her father and that she seemed to be healthy and strong. Lightness quickly turned to darkness, though, as she continued to read. Her stomach flipped as she read the inconceivable—Kebede had a drinking problem? With each sentence she deciphered, more and more tears began to flood her face until she was hysterically sobbing, alarming Meskie, sitting to the side with Chaya in her arms, to come to her aid. She could not possibly digest the news, so she purged it out all over the floor.

Chapter Twenty-Two

Azmera—June 1985

Upon arriving at the dining hall, Azmera sat down to a warm bowl of vegetable soup for dinner. It provided her body with the comfort she needed after all the blows it had absorbed earlier. The uncle and niece ate in complete silence, but the normalcy surrounding them—the joyful noises from the bustling dining hall and the chattering from the family sitting at the table next to them—made what they had just witnessed even more surreal. Both Azmera and Solomon appreciated the inkling of an escape, however momentary, provided to them in the form of roasted chicken and potatoes. When Azmera cleared her plate, she got up for another serving. It wasn't so much her appetite dictating how much food she would consume, but rather her desperate attempt to delay the inevitable for just a bit longer. After all, after dinner she and Solomon would have to return to her father's room and confront him head-on.

Shabbat at the Karmiel Absorption Center was largely devoid of white faces, and the same was true in Dimona. Most of the *sabra* native Israeli managers and teachers had gone home for the weekend to rest with their families, leaving the Ethiopian immigrants to fend for themselves in what felt like a modern and air-conditioned Ethiopian village. So when Solomon and Azmera returned to Kebede's room to find him gone, they didn't know where to turn. Sure, Kebede was a grown man, but they had discovered in their short time in Israel that living in an absorption center could make even the most independent of people lose their sense of independence. Certainly, thought Solomon, his absence must be reported to an Israeli in charge.

Solomon gestured to Azmera to leave him alone with Mengistu to discuss what steps could possibly be taken on a Friday evening when Oren, an Orthodox Jew and the manager of the Dimona Absorption Center, would certainly not be answering his phone. As Azmera sat outside her father's room listening to her uncle and the stranger discuss their father's fate, she felt the blood in her veins boil with anger. Sure, her father was by no means perfect, but Solomon had no right to attack him the way he did, especially in his condition. She couldn't shake the feeling that, had she spoken to her father instead of Solomon, things would have turned out differently. She would have been gentler and less accusatory and he, in turn, would have been less defensive. Now her father had disappeared and there was no telling where he was. Without a doubt, her father had made mistakes, but Solomon was the one to blame for his disappearance. Or at least that was what she had convinced herself to believe. It was much easier to cope this way.

The door to her father's room opened and out walked Solomon and Mengistu, both with their eyes glassy and their jaws agape.

"Azmera, we are heading out to search for your father until we find him," Solomon explained, his commanding tone reminiscent of their journey to Sudan.

Azmera felt a lump in her throat growing so big that she could hardly breathe.

"Can I join you?" asked Azmera, her quivering voice giving away the fact that she wasn't certain she wanted a 'yes' in response.

Solomon paused as he considered her request. Azmera wasn't a little girl anymore, he knew; she had proven herself to him on their journey to Sudan. But, taking Azmera would only be a burden, even more so if they actually managed to find her father.

"No," responded Solomon with an apologetic look on his face, "It wouldn't be appropriate."

Solomon tried to make eye contact with his niece upon denying her request, but she refused to look in his direction, her eyes cast towards the ground.

Solomon knew his niece was upset about her father, rightfully so. He walked down the long hallway towards the staircase with Mengistu by his side.

"Wait for me here, Azmera, okay?" Solomon shouted from the end of the hallway towards his niece, her back now turned to his. Her lack of response didn't concern Solomon. Only Kebede did.

Azmera sat alone on the ground wanting to flee, but not knowing where to go. She knew she should stay at the absorption center and wait for Solomon and, with any hope, her father, to return. But the idea of staying all alone while she impatiently awaited the unknown was suffocating, even though she had been given a room all to herself. Solomon may have asked her to wait for him, but he didn't deserve her obedience, certainly not after he spoke to her father the way he did. Azmera wanted to show both her uncle and her father just how angry she was. She stood up from the cold ground and walked down the hallway towards the same staircase Solomon and her father had used before her. She walked past families readying their children for bedtime and teenage girls chatting away, but no one paid any attention to her. Here she was anonymous. Only Hadass and her father knew who she was—but Hadass was at home busy celebrating Shabbat with her family while her father was busy trying to escape his.

As Azmera walked out of the absorption center, she looked up at the sea of stars shining brightly in the sky. The sky above Karmiel had far fewer stars than the Dimona sky above her now. As she gazed up, a shooting star fell out of the sky; it reminded her of those rare restless nights back in Ethiopia where, after everyone in her family was fast asleep, she would step outside their *gojo* and stare in awe at the mountain sky. Azmera felt an ache in her heart. She missed the idea of home, but she wasn't sure she even knew where home was anymore.

Azmera began walking—to where she didn't know. The rhythmic pounding of her feet and the wind blowing on her face helped her to process what had happened earlier that day. She had tried to remain strong for so long, but she was now officially broken. Her father had forced himself on her mother, and she was the product of what would be considered rape in the State of Israel. Her father abandoned his family and didn't seem to care about their fate. But if only Solomon hadn't screamed at her father, perhaps he would have stayed and they would be sitting and drinking coffee together on the balcony while they caught up on lost time. Why did Solomon stubbornly have to push her father over the edge? Azmera stopped in the middle of the road and screamed at the sky, willing her cry for help to reach all the way back home to Ethiopia. Her voice ached when her screaming came to a halt, but her heart felt a bit lighter. She continued to walk down the road, using the sound of the cars passing by on the street down below as her guide.

A small, desert city, Dimona had one main road, Herzl Street, cutting directly through its heart. Azmera arrived at the street and saw one kiosk with its lights flashing, the other businesses having closed shop for the Shabbat weekend. Azmera approached the kiosk and saw its shelves lined with bottles of liquor. Her father must have frequented this establishment on a regular basis, she knew, possibly even earlier that evening.

"Excuse me, but did an Ethiopian man about your height come here earlier?" Azmera inquired of the shopkeeper, a tall Russian man with spiky hair that looked hard to the touch and yellowish fingernails that quickly gave away his smoking habit.

The man looked back at Azmera and chuckled to himself before he responded, "You're going to have to be a bit more specific, girl. I have a swarm of Ethiopians from the absorption center coming here daily. Just a few hours ago, around ten stopped by to buy cigarettes and alcohol."

Azmera stood still, astounded by the twenty-four-hour kiosk's popularity with men who just months ago were still living off the fields.

"Umm, well his name is Kebede. He is around thirty-five years old."

The shopkeeper took a drag from his cigarette and blew circles of smoke in the air. "You Ethiopians and your funny names. You think I remember a name like Kabab, or whatever you said?"

Azmera restrained herself from flashing the man the look of disgust he so badly deserved. She still needed to use him for one last piece of information.

"Are there any buses running this evening?" Azmera asked.

The storekeeper pointed down the road to the city's single traffic light, now flashing yellow. He explained to Azmera that there were shuttle vans that stopped at the light from time to time to take passengers all over the country, even on Shabbat.

"With any luck," he explained, "another shuttle should be arriving soon."

Azmera reluctantly thanked the man and wished him *Shabbat Shalom*. She walked in the direction of the traffic light and felt thankful for having met numerous warm and friendly Israelis thus far, so many that she was easily able to disregard as an aberration this nasty man to whom her father had apparently sold his soul in exchange for vodka and arak.

When a shuttle van approached the traffic light with a sign marking "Beer Sheva" as its destination, Azmera decided to forego yet another desert city and waited to see what other options became available. A few minutes later, another van approached, this time with "Jerusalem" marked on the front. Azmera didn't think twice. She boarded the van and handed the driver the 8,000-shekel fee, money well-saved from her monthly government allowance. Azmera twiddled her thumbs as she waited impatiently for the van to fill with passengers, all headed to the holy city on the holiest of days. As the van drove past the kiosk with the flashing lights, Azmera felt the cool desert air breeze through the open van window against her face. She would arrive in Jerusalem close to eleven in the evening. As for where she would spend the night, though, she had no idea.

Azmera rested her head against the van window and slowly felt herself fall asleep to the gentle humming of the engine. The events of the past day had been both exhausting and traumatic, so she embraced the few hours of quiet the ride to Jerusalem provided her. She woke up to the sound of honking as the van approached what the driver strangely termed the "Cats Square," prompting Azmera to ask him to repeat the name of the destination for fear she had misunderstood his Hebrew. Upon confirming that "Cats Square" was indeed the name of the journey's end, Azmera fumbled around in her knapsack to count whether the money remaining would suffice for a night's stay in one of the city's hostels. She pulled out a wad of money and was surprised to find the small piece of paper with Liat's name and phone number scribbled on it. Azmera had completely forgotten about her friendly interaction with the female soldier sitting next to her on the bus, who just happened to live in Jerusalem. It felt like a lifetime ago. She recalled Liat's friendly invitation to join her family for Shabbat and her mention of staying up late Friday night and watching movies.

Azmera climbed down from the van and saw a group of teenagers sitting next to a pack of stray cats at the appropriately named "Cats Square," drinking bottles of cheap Maccabi beer and struggling not to cough while they inhaled smoke into their lungs. They appeared to be around her age, but Azmera felt too bashful to ask them where the nearest pay phone was.

Instead, she opted to ask a pair of soldiers manning the street corner.

"There's one on Hillel Street," informed the soldier as he pointed in the correct direction, "But you know that you need a phone token to use the phone, right?"

Azmera had become aware of the need for phone tokens when she first called her father many months ago, but nonetheless had none with her. She paused for a moment to consider whether she should feign ignorance with the hope that the soldiers might have pity on the new, poor immigrant.

"Yes, I did know that, but all I have is money," Azmera replied.

A short, thin soldier with brown curly hair fumbled around in his pocket and pulled out four phone tokens and a bunch of coins.

"It's for calling my family in the north," he explained with a smile on his face, "but I'd be happy to give you one. You won't be able to buy them at this hour anywhere around here."

Azmera looked back at the generous soldier and thanked him with a smile.

He turned to her and replied, "My pleasure. You are a beautiful Ethiopian girl."

Azmera thanked him again and began walking towards the phone booth. She didn't know whether to be flattered or insulted.

Azmera approached the pay phone on Hillel Street, a dimly lit street lined with shuttered cafes and clothing stores suggesting a vibrancy during the week that seemed incongruent with the stillness in the air. Her fingers trembled as she pressed the buttons one by one. Liat could be her first true Israeli friend, she thought to herself with anxious excitement as she listened to the other end of the line ringing.

"*Halo*," answered a girl with an energy that laid to rest any doubt in Azmera's mind as to the late hour.

"May I speak with Liat, please?" asked Azmera, hopeful that the voices in the background would mask the quiver in her voice.

Liat picked up the line, thrilled to hear Azmera's voice on the other end. "Is everything okay?" Liat inquired, curious but not bothered by the late-night phone call.

"Everything's okay. I just arrived in Jerusalem," shared Azmera reluctantly.

"Woah, I thought you were going to visit your father. Do you have a place to stay for the night?" asked Liat with a sense of eagerness in her voice.

Before her new friend had a chance to respond, Liat jumped in and commanded, "*Yalla*, come on over to my house. There's plenty of room here."

Azmera breathed a sigh of relief. She didn't have to make the awkward request of inviting herself over. She hung up the phone and couldn't help but smile, despite all she had been through that day. She had a spring in her step as she walked the eight blocks to her new friend's apartment building. As she walked, she was amazed to see dozens of balconies still decorated with Israeli flags from the Independence Day celebration one month before. When she arrived at her destination, she knocked on the door to Liat's apartment and walked inside. She was warmly greeted by Liat's parents and younger brother and sister, both carbon copies of Azmera's new friend. She was going to spend the night at a stranger's home, but somehow these strangers made her feel like this was exactly where she belonged.

"*Nu*, so how was your visit with your father?" asked Liat after Azmera had settled in with a cup of lemongrass tea.

Liat shared with her new friend a bowl full of popcorn as *E.T.* played in the background. Azmera had trouble concentrating. Her eyes were fixated on the television screen sitting squarely in the center of the salon. Television no longer excited her like it did when she first arrived in Israel; she had already spent hours sitting with Solomon in the *moadon* in front of the television, her eyes affixed on the imposing news broadcasters recalling the happenings of the day. But the sight of this large-headed alien creature with a curiously lit-up finger left her hypnotized.

"What, you mean to say you haven't seen *E.T.*?" questioned Liat's younger sister, Leora, just a year younger than Azmera herself, "It came out in the theaters like three years ago!"

It was clear to Azmera that Leora, and perhaps even Liat, had no concept of the life she had left behind in Ethiopia when she came to Israel, but that did nothing to lessen the teenage girl's feelings of shame. Instead of revealing the mortifying truth that this was in fact her very first movie experience, she coolly brushed off the question and continued to enjoy it.

"*Nu* . . . How was it seeing your dad?' repeated Liat, anxious for Azmera to reply.

Azmera hadn't expected to be inundated with so many questions, nor had she expected it to be so difficult to tell the truth. She stared at the television screen for a moment to consider how to respond.

"We fought," Azmera explained plainly, leaving no room for questions. Fighting with her father was an easy explanation that seemed perfectly reasonable to the two teenage girls sitting by her side.

After the movie ended, Azmera and Liat stayed awake and continued where their conversation left off on the bus ride. Conveniently for Azmera, the topic of discussion moved to Liat and her life's story, so very different from Azmera's. She told of her enlistment into the army service "just a few short months ago"; how her boyfriend from high school was stationed in Lebanon and how they only managed to see one another every few months but how she knew he was the love of her life; and of their plans to travel to South America after they finished the army. While it felt wrong to Azmera to listen to Liat chatter away about her boyfriend when her father was missing, it also felt so very right. Not only was Azmera intrigued by Liat's life's story, but she was also relieved to have the spotlight removed from herself for the time-being. It was almost morning when the two girls finally went to bed, with Azmera falling into a deep sleep on a spare mattress in Liat's bedroom.

Azmera woke up several hours later to the sweet aroma of fried dough wafting through the air. The late morning sun's sparkling rays pierced through Liat's bedroom window.

"Good morning," Liat whispered as she wiped the sleep from her eyes, "Did you sleep okay?"

Azmera groggily nodded her head, wishing she could go back to sleep.

"You hungry?" asked Liat as she pulled on a pair of hot pink jean shorts that ended mid-thigh, "My mom makes the most amazing *jahnoon*. It's a Yemenite dish. Basically, it's rolled fried dough. We eat it every Shabbat for lunch."

Azmera again nodded her head, this time much more eagerly.

While her dreams were still inundated with images of her eating freshly baked *injera*, she knew that Israeli food did not disappoint, and she was looking forward to trying more of its eclectic cuisine.

"Here, wear this," Liat said casually, as she threw a pair of khaki shorts and a T-shirt Azmera's way.

Azmera smiled gratefully towards her new friend. Her trip to Jerusalem was unplanned, of course, so her spare change of clothes had remained back in Dimona. She would have been embarrassed to step outside into the living room wearing the same clothing she had worn the night before. Back home in Ethiopia, of course, she would wear the same robe day after day until she had no choice but to take it to the nearby stream and wash it by hand. In Israel, on the other hand, everyone changed clothes—and showered—daily, without fail. She knew that her standards had to change.

"Welcome!" shouted Liat's mother as she held out her arms and her large bosom for a warm embrace, "Azmera it is, correct? Did I pronounce it correctly?"

Azmera nodded her head and flashed Liat's mother a smile, thankful not only for her hospitality but also for her genuine effort to pronounce her name correctly. Most Israelis didn't seem to mind butchering her name.

"My name is Malka," said Liat's mother with a smile. "I made *jahnoon* and lots of salads for lunch. I wasn't sure what kind of food you like, so I went a little crazy," chuckled Malka as she pointed to the dining room table covered from one end to the other with small bowls of colorful salads and spreads.

"Wow, thank you," replied Azmera, humbled but eager to eat the plethora of food resting on the table, "But you didn't have to do that for me, really. I'm happy to eat anything."

Just then, Liat's father, a tall handsome man with a full head of graying hair walked confidently into the room, interrupting the conversation, "Malka was happy to do it. Liat hasn't stopped talking about you ever since she arrived yesterday. I'm Ilan, by the way," Liat's father said as he pulled Azmera in for two pecks on the cheek, one on each side.

Azmera felt genuinely welcomed as she helped Liat set the table. It wasn't her home, but she felt more at home than she had since she left hers months ago.

Azmera helped herself to a piece of *jahnoon* and a hard-boiled egg to go with it, following the nudging advice of Malka and the others. Her mouth watered as she loaded the rest of her plate with an assortment of salads and spreads, including tehina, roasted eggplant salad, and a diced carrot salad. She hadn't realized how hungry she was until she swallowed the first bite of the *jahnoon*. It was deliciously sweet and savory at the same time. She felt slightly irritated, then, when Malka interrupted her eating by bombarding her with questions about her life in Ethiopia and her journey to Sudan. Azmera's irritation quickly softened when Malka explained frankly, "I apologize for all the questions, but I am just so fascinated by everyone's *Aliyah* or immigration story to this country. Israel really is a *Kibbutz Galuyot*, an ingathering of the exiles. I am so proud to be an Israeli, especially now after bringing you Ethiopians home."

As her stomach filled with food, Azmera found herself having more patience for the questions and more energy to answer them. She told of her life growing up in her village, of her mother left behind with her five siblings, and of her dramatic journey to Sudan with her uncle.

"Your father must have been thrilled to see you," remarked Ilan as he listened attentively to Azmera's narrative, "Liat told us you went to visit him yesterday."

Azmera uncomfortably averted her eyes from Liat's father and began pushing around the food on her plate. His question, however well-intentioned, had crossed the line.

"Your mother must desperately miss you," interrupted Malka, sensing the need for a change of topic, "I can't even begin to imagine," as she turned her focus to her three children sitting across from her.

Azmera's eyes froze as she desperately struggled to hold back her tears. There was something about Liat's home that, without Azmera's even realizing it, made her let down her guard. There was also something about sitting together for Shabbat lunch with Liat's family, not her own, that oddly made her feel full and empty inside all at once. Her eyes started to well up with tears as she excused herself from the table. She ran into the closest bathroom; its thin, plaster walls barely muffled her hysterical sobbing.

When Azmera stepped outside the bathroom, she was surprised by how unfazed her new friend and her parents were, almost as if her meltdown were expected—it was a house full of teenagers, after all. To Azmera's great relief, her burning sense of shame quickly subsided as she watched the family resume their normal Shabbat afternoon routine, so much so that she even agreed to Liat's kind offer to show her around Jerusalem. Azmera packed up her things and the two girls walked outside to the quiet streets of Jerusalem, the gentle chirping of a bird and the occasional laughter of a child ringing softly in her ear. Liat led Azmera through the center of the city where

Azmera cringed at the sight of two men wearing long, black robes with fur hats covering their heads.

"They must be so hot!" whispered Azmera, perplexed by the unseasonable and clearly uncomfortable wardrobe in the height of summer.

"Yes, I know. We call them penguins because they always wear black and white. But penguins live in cold weather! These *Haredis* must have forgotten that they certainly do not!" chuckled Liat, as she led Azmera through Jaffa Gate into the Old City.

As they walked down the uneven and slippery stones, Liat warned her new friend to watch her step. If they wanted to have time to explore the Old City and visit the *Kotel*, the last remnant from the Second Temple, before Azmera's bus departed, they would have to hurry. Liat had ambitiously planned a full itinerary of sightseeing for the day, but their late wake-up, Azmera's meltdown and their lazy-paced Shabbat left them with far less time than she had expected.

"The New City will have to wait for your next visit," Liat explained; for now, though, "visiting the Old City was an absolute must."

"You don't have to talk about what happened with your father, you know," announced Liat as the two girls waited in line for a security check.

Azmera nodded, grateful for Liat acknowledging what had happened earlier in the bathroom, but even more grateful for her not probing. Liat held out her army ID card as the border police rummaged through her bag and waved her on through.

"Speak Hebrew?" the border policeman asked Azmera in broken English as he signaled for her to approach him.

Annoyed at his presumptuousness, Azmera replied with a confident *ken* or "yes" in Hebrew, causing his left eyebrow to lift ever so slightly. He checked her mostly empty bag and motioned for Azmera to continue past him towards the golden, proud wall behind him.

Liat smiled as she watched Azmera freeze in place at the sight in front of her. For a native Jerusalemite like herself, there was something refreshing in witnessing a person's first awestruck experience in front of the *Kotel*. Azmera's jaw dropped as she stood at the top of the stairs, the *Kotel* majestically sprawled out below her. This was the place she had heard about her entire life. This was the place she had prayed towards her entire life. But while the sight of the massive wall in front of her left her gasping for air, there was also something almost anti-climactic about it. After all, it was just a wall, albeit a large one.

"Here, write down a prayer to put into the wall," Liat instructed as she handed Azmera a piece of paper and pen she had stuffed away in her bag.

Azmera had heard of the tradition of placing written prayers into the wall, but only once her nose was pressed up against the wall did she understand the beauty of it. Every crack, no matter how thin or how shallow, contained a folded-up record of another Jew's hopes, dreams, and prayers. Jews, including the women crowded next to her, had come to the *Kotel* from all over the world so that their prayers could be heard. Now it was Azmera's turn. And while God placed no cap on the number of prayers one could write, Azmera felt it would be greedy to ask for too much. She placed the paper firmly in the palm of her left hand, with the pen in her right, as she debated what to write. The obvious prayer, of course, would be for her father's safe return. She paused to consider whether that was even something she wanted. Her father's safety, after all, would mean having to forgive him for all he had done to her mother and for who he had become. Azmera felt a gust of cool air brush by, and with it an image of her mother smiling at her flashed through her head.

She took the pen and wrote in Amharic, lest she make a mistake in Hebrew, the one prayer that meant the world to her: "May *Enati* and the children make it safely to Israel soon."

"*Nu*, what did you think?" asked Liat as they walked out Jaffa Gate towards the direction of the Central Bus Station.

Azmera paused to consider how she could possibly sum up the experience in words.

"It was so amazing," replied Azmera with a look of awe on her face, "It somehow made all my troubles seem so small, even if just for a moment. When my fingers touched the *Kotel*, I couldn't help but think of the *Beta Israel* like me and my family and all our struggles to get here to this very spot. For a moment, my father's drinking problem seemed so miniscule in comparison."

Azmera's sudden disclosure of her father's vices alerted Liat's attention, but she didn't pry.

"He became an alcoholic ever since coming to Israel, you know," Azmera added, feeling a heavy weight removed from her shoulders with the confession, however shameful it may be. Liat's relative anonymity—not knowing anyone in the Ethiopian community let alone in Azmera's family— combined with her warm openness made Azmera feel comfortable to continue. "Yesterday, my uncle revealed that my father did some horrible things to my mother many years ago when she was young. I had suspected it was true, but yesterday it was confirmed for the first time. My father disappeared afterwards, and that's when I came to Jerusalem. I have no idea where he is now, but my uncle is searching for him."

Liat paused for a moment, not knowing what to say before she held out her arms and tightly embraced her new friend. Azmera leaned into the hug, Liat's physical touch comforting her in ways she hadn't known she needed. As they let go of one another, Azmera gazed downwards at her feet hitting the stone ground beneath her, allowing Liat to lead the way. The girls passed by a family—a mother, a father, and three young children, walking hand in hand—who, with their yarmulkes and prayer shawls, seemed to be heading towards the Old City for evening prayers.

"Don't you want to call and see if they've found your father?" inquired Liat, anxious to help her new friend.

Azmera looked back at her and shrugged. She was so lost that she didn't know what she wanted.

"You're not going back to Karmiel tonight, okay? You can stay with my family again. I don't have to leave for my base until tomorrow morning. After Shabbat ends, we'll call the center in Dimona and ask them if they've found your father," announced Liat, her offer more of a decision than a suggestion.

Azmera nodded approvingly, grateful for Liat's mature and sober command of the situation.

On their walk home, the girls enjoyed the feel of the brisk Jerusalem evening air against their skin. It was a refreshing respite from the day's scorching heat. Liat stood behind Azmera as they walked into Liat's home and signaled to her parents to give Azmera the space she needed. Azmera joined Liat in her bedroom, where Liat played *Mashina* records for her Ethiopian friend.

"This band is on the radio like all the time!" said Liat with an excitement one has when introducing something beloved to another.

Azmera tried to appreciate the music, but its melody was so very different from what she was used to. Still, the music helped to pass the time before Shabbat ended, taking off the pressure to talk more—and that she could appreciate. From time to time, Liat glanced over at her digital alarm clock to check whether nine in the evening had arrived, marking half an hour after the end of Shabbat and the hour at which Oren, the Orthodox manager of the Dimona Absorption Center, would be available to answer calls. When the clock finally flashed 21:00, Liat lowered the music and gestured towards Azmera that the wait was over. She asked her parents to clear out the kitchen before bringing Azmera there to make the anticipated call.

"Do you want me to talk?" offered Liat, uncertain whether her presence was a comfort or a nuisance, but nonetheless sensing that Azmera wanted her to take command of the situation.

Azmera shook her head no. She needed to be the one to make the call—and hear the news, whatever it may be—all by herself. Her hand was trembling so slightly that it escaped Liat's notice, but not her own. She carefully dialed the center's number and willed her body to gain control of the trembling fingers that had betrayed her. Azmera's heart raced as she anxiously waited for someone on the other end of the line to answer.

"Halo, Oren?" asked Azmera, her voice quivering with anxiety, "My name is Azmera and I am Kebede Rahamim's daughter. I'm calling to see if there's any news about my father."

Liat nervously watched as Azmera listened to the other end of the line wondering how else she could help her friend.

"Azmera, honey. We've been trying to find you. We need you to come back to Dimona as soon as possible."

"What happened? I have to know!" insisted Azmera.

She couldn't bear the thought of driving all the way to Dimona conjuring up images in her head of what horrible things might have happened to her father. Oren paused on the phone, not sure what to say or how to say it.

A tear rolled down Azmera's cheek as she heard Oren whisper softly on the other end of the line, "He's been injured very badly and is in the hospital. You need to come now."

Liat caught Azmera as she collapsed to the ground, the phone receiver swinging gently back and forth. The only thing she could do, it turned out, was to be there for her new friend. Her parents would certainly agree to lend her their car. All she had to do was call her commander and request to return to the base a day late. Her friend needed a ride to Dimona.

Chapter Twenty-Three

Kebede—June 1985

Despite his inebriated state, Kebede had a meticulous plan in mind when he had stumbled his way out of his dormitory room the night before. It was something he had been contemplating for some time, but seeing the disappointment in his daughter's eyes was what really pushed him over the edge. The jagged yellow cliffs just outside Dimona had always intrigued him, so much so that when he was still sober and studious, he would venture there to study new vocabulary words and soak in the arid desert breeze. There was something about the view—its rugged vastness—that strangely reminded him of the Simien Mountains, no matter how different the two landscapes were. And so, it seemed fitting to him that the same cliffs that reminded him of his place of birth would be the place of his death.

Kebede zigzagged as he walked towards the cliffs, recklessly crossing streets with his head sunk to the ground and a bottle of vodka grasped tightly in his hand. He felt drool slowly dripping down his chin, wetting his neck and shirt below. He stopped on the side of the street and pulled down his pants to relieve himself, not paying attention to the teenagers who had congregated just a few feet away from him.

"Drunk *Kushi*!" one of the boys shouted a racial slur in Kebede's direction.

It was *Shabbat* and the boy was wearing a black yarmulke on his head, but that didn't keep him from taking a puff from the lit cigarette in his hand, nor did it keep him from shouting derogatory remarks at a perfect stranger. Kebede turned to the boy and saw he was not alone. A pack of teenagers were staring at him with a look of hate in their eyes.

"Go back to Ethiopia!" shouted another boy as he shook his hand angrily at Kebede, splattering beer in all directions, "You dirty *kushim* aren't even Jewish. My father told me so!"

Kebede was drunk but he wasn't yet incapacitated. In the past few months, he had watched himself grow so indifferent to everything around him—to his studies, to his family, to himself and to his Zionist dream. But something about these boys and their unrestrained hostility upset him and sobered him up all at once. They were not much older than his own daughter, after all. Someone must have taught them all that hatred, and someone could surely unteach them as well. Kebede approached them slowly, careful to not trip on his own two feet. Maybe if he told them how revered his father had been as the village *Kes*, maybe if he told them how he would spend every Shabbat in synagogue praying to return to Israel, maybe if he told them all that he sacrificed in the pursuit of Zionism—maybe, just maybe, they would feel differently.

But before Kebede could open his mouth, he felt a punch to his eye socket knocking him hard to the cement ground. What happened next was mostly a blur for Azmera's father, but he vaguely recalled being kicked repeatedly in the ribs and head each time he tried to stand up, until he finally surrendered and laid on the cold ground. Kebede's swollen eyes watched as the hooligans ran away, leaving him alone on the dimly lit streets of Dimona. He felt the sweet and salty taste of blood mixed with tears fill his mouth. He couldn't be too angry at those boys for trying to kill him. After all, they were just completing the job for him.

Solomon and Mengistu had scoured the streets of Dimona well past midnight, searching in open stairwells and public playgrounds while asking the occasional passer-by if they had spotted a drunk Ethiopian wandering the streets. When Mengistu suggested that they head to the cliffs outside the city, noting that it had been Kebede's stomping grounds in the past, Solomon felt a lump rise in his throat. It was frightening enough to think of his brother drinking himself to a stupor in some dark corner, but it was downright terrifying to think of him chugging shots of vodka while perched on the edge of a jagged cliff.

Mengistu led the way, taking Kebede's brother to the street which served as a buffer between the neglected immigrant town and the desolate but splendid wild desert. The two men walked down the street in silence, dreading the possible outcomes that played out in their heads. The only noises audible were the occasional cry of a baby or the sound of running water from one of the apartments above them. Solomon came to a sudden halt and paused for a moment to listen to a faint moaning in the distance, uncertain at first whether it was coming from a dying animal or a dying man. He listened more closely and confirmed with Mengistu that the moaning sounds were indeed coming from a human being. Solomon picked up the pace, running faster than he had in years, with Mengistu trailing not far behind him. The moaning, while sporadic, got louder and louder, serving as a guide for the two men running down the dark street.

Solomon felt a strange sense of relief when he found his older brother, eyes shut, lying on the sidewalk in a deep pool of blood. Without a moment's hesitation, he bent down to check his brother's pulse. He sent Mengistu to call for an ambulance.

"Knock on door after door until someone answers!" Solomon commanded, as he helplessly examined Kebede's body from head to toe for wounds in need of immediate attention.

Tears streamed down Solomon's face as he looked at his brother, so battered and bruised. He grabbed onto Kebede's hand and squeezed it firmly while he whispered into his blood-soaked ear, "I'm sorry for what I said, my brother. I'm sorry. Please don't be angry at me. Please don't leave me. Please."

Chapter Twenty-Four

Kebede and Azmera—June 1985

It was well after midnight, and a repetitive beeping woke Kebede from his deep slumber. He opened his eyes only to be blinded by the bright lights, forcing him to shut them again. He thought he felt someone touch his right hand, but he couldn't be sure. His entire body was limp and numb.

"Where am I?" whispered Kebede, his voice weak and strained and directed at no one in particular.

Azmera's voice was muffled and barely audible to Kebede, but he was nonetheless able to make out "Soroka" from amongst the other words she uttered. He was in the same hospital in Beer Sheva where all the pregnant women from the Absorption Center would go to give birth, just a short drive from Dimona. He knew that if he were in the hospital then his suicide mission went awry. He wondered what could possibly have gone wrong with his plan. Jumping off a cliff into the abyss below was foolproof. Or so he had thought. For a moment, he felt ashamed to have his daughter by his side, who by now surely must be aware of what he had tried to do to himself. He heard footsteps approaching him, followed by a slight prick on his forearm which turned his head cloudy and his eyes heavy. The beeping in the distance grew faint until he didn't hear anything at all.

✡

"My name is Dr. Ben Ami. Please let me know if you need a translator. We can always call one if you need one," explained the doctor. His eyes, while tired, were filled with compassion.

Solomon nodded, appreciative of the offer but confident that by now he could comprehend the doctor's Hebrew.

"Kebede has suffered from internal bleeding in the chest and abdomen, as well as mild traumatic brain injury," the young doctor explained slowly and deliberately to Azmera and Solomon, their ears perked up to not miss any of the diagnosis. "He has also broken four ribs and lost three teeth. It will take months before he is fully recovered, but you are lucky he is still alive."

Neither Azmera nor Solomon knew how to respond to this supposedly uplifting news. They stared at the ground for several long moments, each hoping the other would break the silence.

"Unless you have any questions, I must go see my next patient. I believe I saw the police waiting for you at the end of the hall," the doctor said as he looked up at the clock hanging on the wall.

The niece and uncle stared back at the doctor dumbfounded by the rapid fire of information they were still struggling to process. The doctor paused for another moment, waiting for the inevitable round of questions that never came, and then turned his back to Kebede's family.

Azmera motioned to Liat to join them. Until now, she had been sitting anxiously in the waiting room with headphones covering her ears to appear as if she were minding her own business. While the closeness she felt to Azmera was real, she had only known her for less than forty-eight hours. She didn't want to presume to have a role in family dynamics, as complex as they were, unless specifically requested of her.

Azmera debriefed Liat on her father's condition, failing to mention what she and Solomon already suspected—that the thugs who tried to take her father's life were ironically the ones who happened to have saved it. Liat stopped at the nearest soda machine and purchased a cold can of Coca-Cola for Azmera, Solomon and herself. Azmera felt her body's senses come alive as she gulped it down. Azmera looked down the hallway at the image of the two police officers with their guns holstered on their hips and felt relieved to have Liat by her side. The two policemen walked towards Azmera and Solomon and introduced themselves as Sergeant Yossi Cohen and Corporal Moti Entebbi. The sight of the two officers close up was less intimidating than from a distance—Yossi's wrinkled uniform and Moti's boyish face softened the formality they had projected from far away. Azmera relaxed a bit, but she couldn't help but notice the curious look the two officers shot towards Liat, as if they couldn't understand what a *sabra* like her would be doing with a poor Ethiopian girl like herself. Liat, however, held her own, introducing herself as a friend of the family while conveniently leaving out any more details.

The two officers escorted the trio down one long hallway and then down another. Azmera felt everyone's eyes—the nurses in white uniforms, the patients in wheelchairs and stretchers, and the doctors with their clipboards and their hustled pace—cast on her and her uncle. Yossi and Moti stopped abruptly at the end of the hallway, entered a dark room with no windows, and invited the trio to join before closing the door behind them. Yossi poured water into flimsy plastic cups set out on the table and courteously passed them around to all. He looked down at his watch before beginning to speak.

"The hospital was nice enough to give us a room so that we can speak in privacy, but I apologize for it being so stuffy and dark," said the Sergeant as he nodded in the direction of the Corporal. "Let's get started."

Corporal Moti proceeded to read from the police report prepared thus far, detailing all the facts presently known relating to Kebede's injuries.

"The injured—that is, Kebede—had a blood alcohol level of 0.29 at the time of the incident, which explains why he wasn't able to put up a fight," Moti explained, his attention to detail somehow reassuring, "It's amazing he was able to even stand with a blood alcohol level as high as his. He must have developed a strong tolerance for it. Regardless, whoever did this to him must have thought they were leaving him for dead," explained Moti, his eyes moving back and forth between Azmera's and Solomon's.

"The injuries he sustained seem to indicate that he was attacked by more than one person, possibly even a gang or a mob of people," Moti continued as he looked at Solomon, "If you had found him just half an hour later, he may not have survived, or so the doctors told me. His internal bleeding is really bad."

Solomon stared back at the police officer and nodded his head solemnly in acknowledgment. Azmera listened but said nothing.

Without hesitation, Liat interrupted the silence. "Do you think he was attacked because he is Ethiopian?"

Yossi stared back at the young girl and then sheepishly turned to Solomon and Azmera before he responded, "Unfortunately, it's a definite possibility we must take into consideration. But rest assured," he continued, his tone of voice now unwavering, "we will find the hooligans who did this, and justice will be served."

Azmera and Solomon exchanged glances with one another. It was 3 o'clock in the morning and their eyes were heavy and struggling to stay open. They would sleep at the hospital in case Kebede's condition deteriorated throughout the night. In the meantime, there was nothing left to do but let the doctors and the police do their job.

Azmera and Liat quickly fell into a deep sleep, their bodies unfazed by the cold plastic chairs and hard wall serving as their bed for the night. Solomon couldn't rest, the bright lights and humming of the hospital keeping his mind on high alert with questions he couldn't answer. Should he alert Tigest? Was it safe for him to walk the streets at night? What would he say to Kebede once he regained consciousness? Solomon watched the second hand on the wall clock tick away slowly but steadily—he counted the hours until morning when, if he was lucky, the troubling thoughts racing through his mind would come to an end. At seven-thirty in the morning, he felt relieved to see the hospital come alive. Visitors trickled in and doctors arrived fresh-faced and eager to start a new week. Solomon left the two girls sprawled out on their chairs and returned to Kebede's room to check on his brother's status. When he arrived, he was surprised to see two white faces sitting by his brother's side.

"You must be Kfir's brother," greeted a woman with perfectly annunciated Hebrew, "I am Shifra, Kfir's *ulpan* teacher. I heard what happened just this morning and I canceled class and went directly to the hospital."

Solomon nodded warmly towards his brother's teacher—he took great delight in understanding every word she uttered in Hebrew, a milestone he had already passed but still did not take for granted. The man sitting next to Shifra introduced himself as Oren, the manager of the Dimona Absorption Center. An awkward silence prevailed when the introductions came to an end, leaving the three no choice but to focus their attention on Kebede lying unconscious in front of them, an IV in his arm to administer pain relief and tubes down his nose to help him breathe.

"I've been teaching Hebrew for ten years," Shifra announced with a tear streaming down her cheek, "And in all my years, Kfir is my biggest failure. He had so much potential, but I failed to reach him. I knew he needed help, but I didn't know what to do, so I just pretended like his problems didn't exist for far too long."

Oren turned to Shifra and patted her shoulder warmly in an effort to assuage her guilt.

And while Solomon appreciated Shifra's words of support, he couldn't fight the temptation to respond, "His name is Kebede."

Azmera resisted waking up, refusing to open her eyes long after her mind had awoken. The longer she kept her eyes closed, the longer she could pretend that none of this was real. The aroma of fresh coffee, however, proved too enticing for Azmera, and her eyes opened to the sight of Liat holding two cups and what appeared to be a grocery bag full of supplies.

"This is to wake up," Liat announced as she shoved the Styrofoam cup of coffee at her friend. "And this is to get rid of our stinky breath," she said as she pulled out new toothbrushes and toothpaste from the bag, purchased at the hospital drug store.

Azmera smiled at Liat, not knowing how to respond to such unsolicited generosity. As the eldest girl, Azmera had always been too busy helping raise her younger siblings or tending to the household chores to have any close friends. She was continually surprised by how much Liat seemed to care for her in the short time they had known each other. In the world she had left behind, her family was everything. In the world she was now in, her family was broken, with Solomon the only pillar still standing. Liat's friendship, then, was her saving grace, even if she didn't quite understand what Liat stood to gain from it. She drank from the cup of coffee, savoring each sip as it calmed her body and soul. When she finished, Liat led Azmera down the hallway to the public restroom to put the toothbrush and toothpaste to good use.

With their breath fresh and clean, Azmera looked in the bathroom mirror at the girl staring back at her. Her bloodshot eyes and the dark circles underneath spoke for themselves. She let out a deep sigh, releasing tears she had stifled ever since arriving at the hospital the night before. Liat stood next to Azmera and stroked her shoulder to comfort her new friend.

"Are you ready to go to your father's room?" whispered Liat when Azmera's crying had subsided.

Azmera looked at Liat in the mirror and slowly shook her head from side to side.

"I don't even know what to say to him," Azmera said, her words muffled by her tears, "I mean, a part of me wishes he had died. A part of him has been dead to me ever since he abandoned our family months ago. And now, knowing what he did to my mother, I just can't imagine looking him in the eye."

Liat waited for Azmera to calm down before talking. "Listen, I can't begin to imagine how you must feel, but I can tell you this. When I was your age, the whole world was black and white to me. Alcohol and drugs were bad, period. Arabs were bad, period. Then I found out last year that my father cheated on my mother with his secretary. It was just so cliché. At first, I thought my mom should throw him out of the house for such an act of betrayal. But then I saw how sorry he was and how much he still loved my mother, and it changed my entire perspective. People are human, and our parents, no matter how much we like to deny it, are human too—they make mistakes, and we must learn how to forgive them. My mom learned how to forgive my father, and I learned that life isn't as black and white as I thought when I was fifteen years old.

"Your father did what he did years ago when he was practically a child himself. Who knows what made him do it? Maybe his parents forced him. Maybe that's just the way things were, and he didn't bother to question them. You can't hold it against him forever, and neither can he. That's just my two cents, take it or leave it. I'm more than three years older than you, you know," Liat said with her chin tilted upwards and a playful grin showing all her good intentions.

Azmera paused for a moment to consider Liat's advice. She didn't think she would ever be able to forget what her father had done to her mother so many years before. For the first time, however, forgiving him felt possible.

Kebede remained unconscious until the late afternoon, when the doctors removed his breathing tube and allowed him to wake up. By this time, his room was full of balloons and flowers extending wall to wall. Visitors ushered themselves in throughout the day. Some were fellow *ulpan* classmates from the absorption center bearing fresh *injera* they had made in the dormitory kitchen. Others were leaders from the Ministry of Absorption from all over the country who wanted to convey a clear message against racism and intolerance, particularly when directed against the new and vulnerable Ethiopian community. A small number of local Dimona residents who had heard the news decided to visit the Ethiopian immigrant in a show of solidarity, and as an opportunity to address the increase in violence in their small city in recent years. Hospital staff members—doctors, nurses, and administrative staff—stopped by during their midday break to show their support. Liat's parents, Ilan and Malka, also made the trip from Jerusalem to the hospital in Beer Sheva, not wanting their daughter to make the trip back to Jerusalem alone on just a few hours of sleep before she had to return to her army base.

Azmera and Solomon greeted the visitors warmly and took comfort in the slogans and prayers they uttered, the most repeated one being that "the people of Israel are responsible for one another." For Azmera and her uncle, the visitors' concern for a stranger made that saying much more than just a slogan. They were part of a people, Kebede included. If only he would feel that he was.

Kebede opened his eyes to the sight of his daughter and brother sitting by his bedside. His head was pounding and the bright lights shining down on him did nothing to ease the pain. He needed his vodka, but there was none to be found.

"What happened to me?" asked Kebede as he turned to Solomon, uncertain if he wanted to hear the answer.

"You were attacked, by whom we don't know. The police are investigating. But you, my brother, are very lucky. It could have been a lot worse."

Solomon's eyes penetrated Kebede's. He wanted to be certain that his brother understood what he meant without having to say it out loud.

"Who brought all of this?" asked Kebede, as his eyes danced around from one bouquet of flowers to the next.

"The People of Israel did," replied Azmera, as she gripped her father's hand tightly, just like she did when she was a little girl.

Chapter Twenty-Five

Azmera—November 1985

Dear Enati,

Yesterday I went to the Sigd *celebration in Jerusalem together with Abat, Solomon and many others from the absorption center. There, we celebrated our people's acceptance of the Torah. As I listened to the* Kessim *recite prayers in* Ge'ez, *I looked out at the majestic view of the Old City of Jerusalem and couldn't help but think of you and how badly I wish you were here with me. Yesterday wasn't just a big day because of the holiday. It also was the first time* Abat *ventured outside since being released from the hospital. He's doing much better, you should know. His memory seems to be improving every day, and now he can finally concentrate enough that he is able to resume his Hebrew studies. My teacher, Efrat, helped to arrange for* Abat *to get a spot at the Karmiel Absorption Center and arranged for him to attend a weekly meeting for alcoholics here in Karmiel. He's now so proud of being sober that he makes note of each passing month—he's nearly five months sober!* Abat *is now sharing a room with Solomon at the absorption center, and they seem to be getting along well for the time being. He's been quite humbled by everything that happened to him, but Uncle Solomon seems to be doing his best to not stomp on his older brother's ego too much.*

For now, I'm enjoying going to school in Karmiel with all the other teenagers like me at the absorption center, and I'm starting to make plans for next year. It looks like, if I'm lucky, I'll be placed in a boarding school close to Haifa called Yemin Orde. *I was against the idea at first, but it turns out that it's a privilege to be sent there. It's supposed to be an amazing school which was founded years ago to house orphans who survived the mass genocide of Jews in Europe, called the* Shoah. *I'm really looking forward to it. I just hope my Hebrew will be good enough by then. It looks like Solomon and* Abat *are going to be leaving the absorption center around the same time as me. They'll be doing a job training program in Haifa, so I'll be close to them. Ever since he was released from the hospital,* Abat *has been making a concerted effort to be there for me like he never was before—we even meet for dinner now every evening in the dining hall. And I'm doing my best to forgive him for everything. The pieces of the puzzle are slowly starting to come together here. All that's missing is you and the children.*

Please always keep your ears open for word of a new operation to Israel. Knowing that one day we will all be reunited is the only thing that gets me through the day.

Send my love to all the children.

Your loving daughter,
Meri

Kebede—December 1985

Dear Tigy,
I am sorry for everything. I love you. I do. I don't know why it took me such

a long time to be able to utter those words to you, but I guess better late than never. I am strong and healthy again and plan on beginning to work, God willing, in a few months from now and will finally start saving money for our family's future. Please come. I want us to get a fresh start here in the Land of Israel. You deserve it.

Tell the children I love them.

Yours, Kebede

Tigest—February 1986

Dear Kebede and Azmera,

I'm sorry I can't write you each your own proper letter, but the postage to Israel is just too expensive these days. Both of your letters brought smiles to my face during a period where there is little to smile about. There is not enough food to feed the children, and I am forced to pick who seems to be the strongest and the healthiest of the children. Whoever it is, usually Daniel, receives the smallest ration of food. Chaya is now nearly a year old, and she is crawling and getting into everything. Fortunately, she is a content little baby who loves to suckle my milk, so for now at least I don't have to worry about having another mouth to feed. I speak to the children about you two all the time, and they shriek with excitement whenever Daniel comes home from Debark with an envelope in his hand.

The only reason we have managed to survive up to now is Meskie—my rock. She has become like a second mother to the children, taking care of them as if they are her own. *Solomon should know that his beloved wife is healthy and strong, despite all she has been through. Most importantly, she is happy. At night, after the children go to bed, I read to her Solomon's letters, and the love they share for one another gives me chills up and down my back and gives me hope. She has become like a sister to me, and I desperately hope that one day I'll be able to mother her children the way she has mothered mine. Because of her, we manage to run one of the only businesses remaining in the entire village— sewing and repairing torn and tattered clothing. But still, the money we bring in is not enough.*

Despite our hungry bellies, I know we are fortunate—it could be much worse. But there's a real sense of desperation here in the village—so many families have been split up and don't know when they will be reunited. We all want to leave, but none of us knows how or when. The Kes *claims he is in contact with the Jewish Agency and that there are plans to bring us to Israel sometime soon, but he's been claiming this now for nearly a year and nothing seems to be progressing. In the meantime, we wait out the days and will ourselves to live knowing that one day, God willing, we'll be in the Holy Land reunited as a family.*

I love you. Both of you.

Enati *(Tigest)*

Epilogue

Azmera and Tigest—May 24, 1991

Azmera sat on her bed and grabbed a handful of Bamba peanut snacks before she passed the bag around to her fellow roommates. It was Friday evening, and she begrudgingly had to stay on the base for the weekend to perform guard duty with the rest of the soldiers who were part of her commander's course. She was disappointed to have to turn down yet another invitation from Liat to join her family for *Shabbat* in Jerusalem, but nonetheless found great consolation in the lighthearted jokes and games she and her army friends invented to help pass the time. The course had only begun three weeks ago, but Azmera already felt like she had known her roommates—Sarit, Orna and Anat—for years. Azmera leaned her head back on her pillow as she listened to Yehuda Poliker's new hit "It hurts, but less" play on the radio. The words to the song had touched her since the first time she heard it back when she was still in basic training, but today the song's lyrics struck her as particularly powerful.

For what wounded me, wounded and healed,
I hardly think about it, Learned to live with it that way,
It hurts but it hurts less . . . It didn't disappear, it's just far away,
It hurts but it hurts less

It had been more than six years since she had last hugged her mother. Six years in which she had, in many ways, become a changed person. She spoke a new language, wore different clothes, and ate different foods. She had grown up and was now on track to becoming a basic training commander in the Israel Defense Forces. And while she knew that her mother and siblings were finally in a compound in Addis Ababa awaiting the day when they, too, would become Israelis, they were still lightyears away. No matter how much she tried to deny it, the longing for her mother and what was once her home had dwindled with time. And while this initially filled Azmera with guilt, she gradually allowed herself to enjoy the new life she had created for herself in Israel.

The song came to an end and Azmera's roommates instinctively quieted when they heard the three long beeps marking the hourly news broadcast. While Azmera was long fluent in Hebrew, she nonetheless found it much easier to tune out her second language than she ever did her first; besides, it had been an exhausting day navigating in the field, and her mind didn't have the energy to focus on anything, let alone the news. Her heart skipped a beat, then, when she heard the familiar rhythmic sound of the language her mother used to whisper in her ear when she was a baby. Her roommates turned to her waiting for a translation, but Azmera signaled to them that they needed to wait for the broadcast to come to an end. When it did, Azmera's jaw had dropped so far to the ground that she had a hard time closing it.

"I can't believe it," whispered Azmera as tears ran softly down her cheek. It was almost as if she were talking to herself and not to the three curious girls staring back at her. "After all these years. She's coming. They're coming!"

Orna didn't know whether to comfort her roommate or embrace her out of joy. Azmera jumped out of bed and felt her legs buckle from underneath her. She had to go tell her father and Solomon, but she was of course stuck on base for the weekend. Besides, her father—who was studying to become a *Kes* just like his father and had grown more observant in recent years—wouldn't answer his phone until Shabbat came to an end the following day. Azmera felt desperate to leave the base and run as fast as she could until she found her mother, wherever she may be, but instead she had to settle for stepping outside the dormitory for some much-needed privacy and a breath of fresh air.

Azmera felt the cool night's breeze on her back. The moon shone bright in the sky, illuminating the path to the picnic benches outside of the canteen. The reality of the news slowly started to sink in, and Azmera found herself caught up in the logistics of finding her mother amongst the thousands of other Ethiopians reportedly arriving in Israel. She wondered whether she would recognize her mother. Of course she would, she reassured herself. She knew her mother's face, hair, body, and hands like they were her own, and unlike hers, they probably wouldn't have changed much in the six years since they had last seen one another. Would her mother recognize her? She was, after all, a far cry from the girl who had left her family so many moons ago. She wondered what they would have to talk about. Azmera's world was nearly entirely consumed by the army—target practice, the cute officer who smiled at her in the dining hall, and banal army gossip had become her new normal ever since graduating from the Yemin Orde Youth Village. The simple life of her girlhood—and the world her mother was just now leaving behind—seemed like a distant memory that faded more and more with each passing day.

Azmera walked past the parking lot overlooking the mountains of the Galilee, still green from the late winter's rains. She sat on her favorite bench, the one under the terebinth tree's canopy, and stared up at the stars twinkling in the night sky. The tree had grabbed Azmera's attention since she first arrived at the base. Its shade was not the attraction, but rather its Hebrew name, *Ella*, a name that so beautifully rolled off her tongue that she caught herself saying it repeatedly. The smell of a lit cigarette wafted slowly towards Azmera from the nearby picnic table, prompting her to get up and return to her room. No matter how much she despised the smell of cigarette smoke, her year in the army had taught her to have zero expectations that the smokers around her might accommodate her sensitivities. Azmera felt her stomach churn as she climbed the stairs back to her room. She knew her roommates' hearts were in the right place, but the idea of being bombarded with questions was too much for her to handle. They just couldn't possibly understand what she was feeling at this moment. They couldn't even imagine.

When Azmera arrived at her door at the end of the hallway, she paused for a second to try to identify an oddly familiar voice coming from inside, one she recognized but could not place. Azmera walked into her room to discover her three roommates sitting on their bunk beds as they chatted freely with Doron, the commander of the base who had welcomed them three weeks ago on their first day. Doron's curly brown hair and smooth olive skin made Azmera blush, but she obeyed his request to join him in the hallway.

"Azmera, you've heard the news, right?" inquired Doron as he tried to quell the excitement in his voice.

"Yes, I heard, Commander," replied Azmera, keeping her reply short and to the point.

"The Ministry of Absorption contacted our base and asked if we could recommend a soldier who could greet the *Beta Israel* at the airport and represent them on television. Several planes have already landed, but there are apparently many more to come in the next twenty-four hours. I couldn't think of anyone better than you to do the job," explained Doron with a smile on his face.

Azmera stared back at her commander and paused for a moment before she humbly agreed to accept his offer. She couldn't help but wonder why the

Ministry of Absorption had contacted Doron out of all the commanders in the army, but then she understood. Liat. She had finished her university studies not long ago and, inspired by Azmera's story, she joined the Ministry of Absorption's headquarters in Jerusalem. There, she quickly proved herself to be a rising star, tending to the Ethiopian community as if it were her own.

Doron instructed Azmera to change out of her everyday uniform and to change into her representative uniform, which was ironed and neatly tucked away in the back of her drawer.

"A car will be waiting for you outside the canteen when you're ready to leave," Doron explained.

Azmera slowly nodded her head, a bit stunned by the VIP treatment she was receiving and the task that awaited her. Ever since arriving in Israel, she had made watching the evening news a part of her daily routine. Now that she was in the army, she could no longer watch the eight o'clock news with any regularity, yet still knew all the reporters' names by heart. The idea of her face and voice appearing on television screens all throughout Israel made her stomach flip on its head, so much so that for a moment she forgot all about her family.

The drive to the airport in Lod, just outside of Tel Aviv, was unbearably long. The crisp night air whipped against the open car windows, conveniently providing Azmera with an excuse not to carry on a conversation with the driver. Azmera looked up at the black sky and watched the stars slowly melting away as she approached her destination. She wondered whether Liat had told her superiors at the Ministry of Absorption her family's story. She also wondered whether they would have chosen her if they knew that, instead of focusing on greeting the new arrivals, she would certainly be preoccupied with finding her own kin.

The airport buzzed with an unusual air of excitement. It was the eve of Shabbat and a day of rest otherwise observed by both Judaism and the State. Liat waited anxiously for Azmera at the entrance to the terminal and jumped with sheer exhilaration when she saw her friend get out of the car. Liat and Azmera fiercely hugged each other, neither wanting to be the first to let go. Liat adorned Azmera with a media pass over her neck, and the two soul sisters followed the sea of soldiers towards the tarmac. Reporters scribbling in their notebooks shouted at cameramen lugging bulky cameras on their shoulders to move out of their way. Another plane was about to land, and everyone was desperate to stake out the best angle to capture the winning shot.

Azmera was speechless when the heavy plane door opened, revealing hundreds of hopeful souls dressed in white from head to toe. Memories of her own arrival to Israel years ago flooded her head. Her eyes filled with tears. Mothers with babies harnessed to their backs walked slowly down the stairs, overwhelmed by the audience waiting to receive them. Israeli soldiers helped old men and women navigate each step, holding onto their frail arms as if this were the most important mission they had ever been charged with. Young boys and girls clung tightly to their mothers' hips, each one terrified to get lost in the sea of people. Azmera felt tears stream down her cheeks as she saw a young man, not much older than Daniel would now be, crouch down and kiss the ground, his lips placed firmly on the solid concrete which marked the way to the rows of registration tables.

"I know, I know," Liat said to Azmera as she draped her arm over her shoulder, "I was a mess earlier today, but enough crying. You have work to do."

With a nod of her head, Azmera pushed her way past other reporters and began to welcome the new arrivals and, as instructed, inquire about their feelings upon arriving in the Holy Land. The massive size of the camera filming her was too much for even the strongest of cameramen, forcing hers to take a break from time to time. Whenever the camera stopped filming, Azmera quickly switched roles—from a reporter on the scene to a young woman desperately searching for her mother.

"Do you know Tigest from outside Debark?" Azmera questioned

anyone who would stop for her, "She should have five children with her—three boys and two girls, and she should be traveling with another woman named Meskie."

Man after woman politely told her they did not, leaving Azmera wondering whether her mother had somehow been left behind. When the plane was emptied of its passengers and ready for a return trip to the Ethiopian capital, Azmera took advantage of the lull and approached the registration tables, staffed by Liat's co-workers as well as representatives from the Ministry of Interior.

"Can you please check to see if my mother has arrived?" questioned Azmera timidly, knowing that the registration officials would surely have little patience for special requests such as hers.

"It's all field registration, handwritten," explained one of the officials, "There's no way for us to check. Ten planes have landed already, and we already have thousands of new arrivals."

Azmera walked away with her chin to the ground, the frustration slowly building up inside. She was so close to her mother, yet so very far away at the same time. Azmera caught Liat as she was rushing to speak with the Deputy Minister and pleaded for her help in finding her family.

"Azmera, I told all the registration officials to look out for your mother and siblings. They all know your story; they've known it for years. They won't let her get by without flagging her for me—and for you," reassured Liat with a warm but weary look in her eyes.

The next plane landed, and then the next, and the next. With each arrival, Azmera felt the adrenaline rush through her body, waking her up from the lull whenever the action died down. She watched as thousands of passengers disembarked, scanning their faces one by one as they streamed down the airplane steps. Still, Tigest was nowhere to be found. At four in the morning, Azmera found herself passed out on a plastic chair as she heard the roaring sound of yet another plane—the thirtieth thus far—approaching the runway. She wearily stood up for yet another round of greetings and interviews with strangers who looked like her and talked like her.

Azmera grabbed a sandwich out of her bag and pulled off the nylon wrapping. Liat had given it to her when she first arrived at the airport but, until now, the prospect of reuniting with her mother had suppressed her appetite. Azmera scarfed the sandwich down her throat as the passengers began disembarking from the plane, the protein from the omelet and hummus providing her body the boost it needed. She choked on her last bite when she saw her mother's image stepping off the airplane, with her siblings in tow. Life had aged Tigest more than the passage of time, but it was without a doubt her mother walking down the stairs, waiting to touch the same ground that belonged to her daughter, and to her people.

Tigest stepped off the stairs and, with Chaya still tightly grasping one hand, collapsed to the ground, letting the river of tears pent up inside come flowing out. Azmera hesitated, not knowing what to do next. It was, after all, the moment she had dreamed of ever since leaving her village years ago. She hesitated as she took her first step forward, but then her pace quickened to a sprint until she was standing within an arm's reach of her mother. She gently grabbed her mother's free hand and pulled her up from the ground. Tigest's face immediately softened to the touch of something unexpectedly warm and familiar, and she bolted upright to the sight of her own face staring back at her. Both mother and daughter belted out screams of joy as they looked each other in the eyes, so much so that the soldiers nearby momentarily reached for their weapons.

Azmera tightly wrapped her arms around her mother. In between heavy panting and tears, she whispered softly into her mother's curving ear, "Thank God, you're finally home."

Acknowledgments

Writing this novel was a true labor of love, one that lasted over 12 years. During that time, I had three children, moved across the Atlantic Ocean twice, and changed careers. None of that would have been possible without the amazing support I received from friends and family. I'd like to start off by thanking my husband, Oren, who tirelessly read multiple iterations of the novel and served as my sounding board in the wee hours of the night. Thank you to my parents for always believing in me and for supporting this novel in more ways than one. Thank you to my sister, Alissa Jerud, for her editing support and words of encouragement. And a sincere thank you to my many Israeli colleagues who helped to ensure the novel's historical accuracy. Any errors I made in this undertaking are solely my responsibility.

Author Bio

Kim Salzman was born and raised in Columbus, Ohio. After receiving a law degree from the University of Michigan, Kim fulfilled a lifelong dream by immigrating to Israel, where she became fascinated by the stories of Jewish immigrants to Israel from all over the world. In Israel, Kim served in the international law department of the Israel Defense Forces. She also worked for the United Nations Refugee Agency and for an NGO advocating for the legal rights of Ethiopian-Israelis. Before writing *Straddling Black and White*, Kim traveled to Ethiopia and was deeply moved and intrigued by the heroic immigration of Ethiopian Jewry to Israel. Today, Kim lives in Northern Israel with her husband, three children and dog and works as the Israel and Overseas Director at the Jewish Federation of Greater Pittsburgh.